THE DARK LEGACY OF SHANNARA

BOOK THREE:
WITCH WRAITH

TERRY
BROOKS

www.orbitbooks.net

ORBIT

First published in Great Britain in 2013 by Orbit
This paperback edition published in 2013 by Orbit

Copyright © 2013 by Terry Brooks
Insert map copyright © 2013 by Russ Charpentier
Insert illustration copyright © 2013 by Todd Lockwood

The moral right of the author has been asserted.

A CIP catalogue record for this book
is available from the British Library.

ISBN 978-1-84149-983-3

Printed and bound in Great Britain by
Clays Ltd, St Ives plc

Papers used by Orbit are from well-managed forests
and other responsible sources.

MIX
Paper from
responsible sources
FSC® C104740

Orbit
An imprint of
Little, Brown Book Group
100 Victoria Embankment
London EC4Y 0DY

An Hachette UK Company
www.hachette.co.uk

www.orbitbooks.net

For Ben Bova

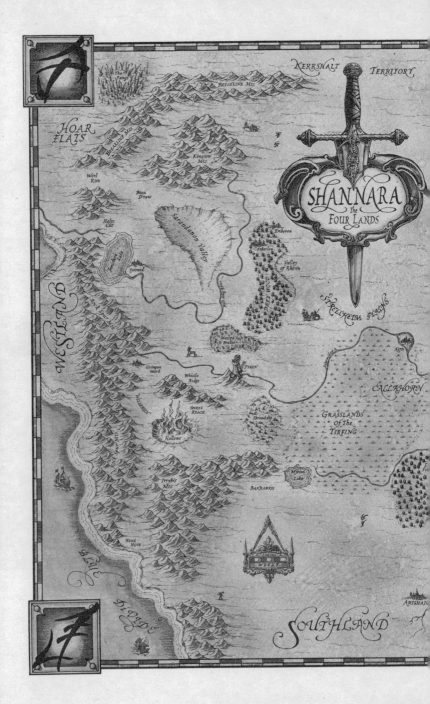

1

RAILING OHMSFORD STOOD ALONE AT THE bow of the *Quickening* and looked out at the starlit darkness. They were anchored for the night, the airship nestled in a copse of fir and hemlock, the sway of the ship in the soft breezes barely noticeable. It was well after midnight, and he should have been sleeping with the others. But sleep did not come easily these days, and when it did come it was haunted and left him wracked with a deep sense of unease. Better to stay awake where he could try to do something to control his thoughts, as dark as they were. Better to face his demons standing up, prepared to fight them off and hold them at bay.

He could not banish them, of course. He could not send them back to the empty places where they sometimes went, though increasingly less so these days.

Not that it mattered. He knew their faces. He knew their names.

Fear: that he might not be able to find Grianne Ohmsford and bring her back to face the Straken Lord because she was dead. Or because she was alive but could not be persuaded to leave the sanctuary in which she had placed herself, unwilling to risk a confrontation of the sort he was proposing. Or simply because she was Grianne and she had never been predictable.

Doubt: that he was doing the right thing in making this journey into the back of beyond because of a hope that had so little chance of succeeding. He should have been seeking his brother in the Forbidding, hunting for him there and bringing him out again in spite of the odds. Time was running out with every passing hour, and his brother was alone and had no one to help him and no way of knowing if help would ever come. Redden depended on him, and it must seem to his brother as if Railing had abandoned him.

Shame: that he was deceiving his companions on this quest, that he was keeping information from them that might dissuade them from continuing. The King of the Silver River had warned him that nothing would happen as he imagined, that there would be results he had not foreseen. The Faerie creature had told him he should turn back and travel instead into the Forbidding—the one place he knew he could never enter, so great was his terror at the prospect.

He felt himself to be a coward and a deceiver. He was consumed by his doubts and his shame, and it was growing increasingly difficult not to reveal this to the others. He tried to keep it hidden, masked by his false words and acts, but it was eating at him. Destroying him.

He left the vessel's bow and walked back toward the stern, moving quietly, trying not to disturb the sleepers. Some were on deck, wrapped in blankets; some were below, rolled into hammocks. All slept save two of the Rover crew, who kept watch fore and aft. He saw the one at the stern and turned aside before he reached the man to take up a position near the starboard railing. Small creaks sounded as ropes and lines pulled taut and released again, and snores rose out of the shadows. He liked this quiet time, this confluence of shadows and sleep. Everything was at peace.

He wished he could be so.

It had only been two days now since they had set out from the Rainbow Lake, even though it felt more like twenty. They had debated among themselves that morning, on waking, as to the best route for their journey. The Charnals were unknown country to all but Skint. Even Farshawn and his Rovers had not come this way before. Railing and Mirai had traveled the Borderlands while conveying spare parts and salvage to customers, but had not gone farther north.

Railing favored coming up from the Rainbow Lake, following the corridor that snaked between the Wolfsktaag and the Dragon's Teeth to the Upper Anar, and then continuing on through Jannisson Pass east of the Skull Kingdom and its dangers and straight along the western edge of the Charnals to the Northland city of Anatcherae—much the same route his grandfather Penderrin had taken while searching for the tanequil all those years ago. From Anatcherae, once resupplied, they could continue on to their destination.

But Skint had thought differently.

What they needed most, he declared, was a guide, someone who was familiar with the Charnals and could help them find the ruins of Stridegate, where it was said the tanequil might be found. There were few who could do that, and he was not one. In point of fact, he knew of only one man who could help them with this, one whose loyalty and knowledge they could depend upon. And even he would need persuading.

His name was Challa Nand, and he made his home in the

Eastland town of Rampling Steep. But finding him would require that the company fly *Quickening* east of the Charnals and through the Upper Anar. It would necessitate abandoning the western approach to Stridegate and finding one that came in from the east. Challa could show them, if they were able to persuade him to their cause.

Railing knew he could rely on the ring given to him by the King of the Silver River to show them the way, but using it would mean either telling them about his meeting with the Faerie creature or lying about where he had gotten the ring. The ring could always be a backup if the need arose; the better choice was to keep it a secret for now.

So he agreed to Skint's proposal, and the others went along, all of them keenly aware that they were in unfamiliar territory and needed to reduce the risks they would encounter.

Now here they were, on their way to Rampling Steep, anchored at the northern edge of Darklin Reach not far from where the Rabb River branched east into the Upper Anar. If he listened closely, Railing could hear the murmur of the river's waters as they churned their way out of the mountains on their journey west to the plains and from there to the Mermidon. It was a distance of hundreds of miles, and it made him wonder if anyone had ever followed the river all the way from end to end. He supposed Gnome or Dwarf trappers and traders might have done so at some point, but he doubted that any had ever made a record of it.

"What are you doing?"

Mirai Leah was standing next to him. He hadn't heard her come up, hadn't realized she was there. He shrugged. "Can't sleep."

"Standing out here isn't going to help. You need to get some rest. Are you all right?"

He gave her a quick glance. Her hair was rumpled, and she was yawning. "You look like the one who ought to be sleeping."

"I would be if I weren't worried about you. What's bothering you, Railing?"

He could have given her a whole raft of answers, starting with how he felt about her and what it would mean to him if he caused her harm. But all he said was, "Nothing. I just couldn't sleep."

She draped an arm over his shoulders. Her touch made him shiver. "How long have we known each other?"

"Seems like forever. Since we were pretty small, anyway. I still remember when your parents brought you for your first visit. They came to see Mother. I didn't like you then. You were kind of bossy."

"Not much has changed. I'm still kind of bossy. So when I ask you what's bothering you, it's because I know something is. So what's up?"

He brushed his red hair back and faced her. "Leaving Redden is eating at me. I can't stand it that I'm not going after him."

"Then why aren't you?"

"Because I think this is the better choice."

"Because you believe Grianne Ohmsford is alive and will come to Redden's aid?" She studied him a moment. "We've already discussed this, and I don't think that's what's troubling you at all. I think there's something else, something you are keeping to yourself. Redden's not here to confide in, so maybe you ought to try telling me."

Here was his opportunity. She had called him out on what she clearly recognized, and he could unburden himself by telling her about his meeting with the King of the Silver River. He could admit what he was doing, how he was manipulating them. But that was something he would never do. He didn't want her judging him. He wanted her to love him unconditionally and fully. He always had.

He fingered the ring, tucked deep in his pants pocket. "I need to go back to sleep. I'm sorry I woke you." He started to walk away, and then he stopped and turned around. "I want you to know that I'm doing the best I can. If anything happens to Redden because of me, I don't think I could stand it. I need you to believe that. I need you to support me and to . . ."

He trailed off. He couldn't make himself speak the words: Love *me*. "Good night."

"I will always support you, Railing," she called after him.

Without looking back, he gave her a wave and disappeared back down the hatchway into the hold of the airship.

He had thought he might sleep then, weary and heartsick. But after a short, unsettling nap he was awake again, wide-eyed and restless. Moreover, there was a tugging sensation that brought him out of his blanket and back up the ladder to the deck, where he stood peering out from the ship's railing and over the darkened countryside.

Something was out there. Something he must find.

He couldn't explain how he knew this, but the feeling was so compelling that he did not stop to question it. He needed to find out what it was. Ignoring it for even another moment was impossible.

He walked over to the sentry at the bow and told him he was going for a walk, but that he would be careful. The Rover clearly understood it would be a mistake to question the leader of their company, though he offered to accompany him. But Railing refused.

Once off the vessel and out in the night alone, Railing gave himself over to his strange compulsion, following his instincts.

He felt oddly unthreatened. It might have been because of what he had survived in the Fangs—the days of attacks by the Goblins and the constant use of his wishsong magic to throw back the hordes in the debilitating struggle to stay alive. He had proved something to himself in those terrible days when others had died all around him. He had found, through his magic, a source of strength and resilience that he had not known he possessed. He had demonstrated to himself that he could be stronger than he had believed. Before, the wishsong had never been more than a means of ramping up the excitement on each new adventure, or of pushing ever harder against the limits that common sense told him not to exceed. But what he took away from the Fangs was something different. It was a belief that his magic provided him a shield and sword he could use to protect both himself and those close to him. It was a belief that fostered confidence.

So he proceeded through the night's shadows without fear. He did not hesitate in his search for what was calling to him or consider turning back. His mind was made up. The voice reminded him of his summoning by the King of the Silver River two nights earlier, and he wanted to know why that was. While it was different—different enough that he was certain it was something else entirely—it shared a kinship that intrigued him.

Railing.

His name, spoken clearly. Spoken by a voice he could not mistake because he had known it all his life.

It was Redden who called to him.

He brushed aside his shock and pushed ahead at a quicker pace, listening for more. Everything was still again, the voice gone as quickly as it had come. Yet the pull on him persisted. He pushed through woods and soon no longer knew in which direction he was going—or even from which he had come. He was proceeding blindly, responding to the lure with a heedless disregard for his own safety, and he finally began to wonder if he was in danger and did not recognize it.

Railing.

Again, his brother's voice.

Now he slowed, no longer willing to rush ahead, worried that he had overstepped himself. He was lost at the very edge of Darklin Reach, which was not only strange but dangerous country. He was moving away from the Rabb; he knew this because he could no longer hear its rush. The silence was deep and pervasive, and only the cries of night birds broke its hush.

Ahead, just visible through the trees, a silvery glimmer caught his eye.

He wove his way through the woods and stepped out at the edge of a small lake. Fog lay eerily across its rippling surface. The waters lapped the shoreline and chopped about its windswept center in small bursts of spray. Though he tried, the boy could not make out what lay on the other side. The trees ringed the lake like a palisade, trunks dark and thick and seemingly impenetrable ten feet from where he stood. In the distance, through the gaps, he could spy the peaks of mountains.

Railing.

"I'm here, Redden," he shouted back, feeling foolish for speaking aloud to a voice that was only in his head.

Laughter greeted his response, filling the air in long raucous peals that shattered the silence and spun out around the lake in waves. Railing took a step back, unsure of what was happening, knowing only that it wasn't his brother he was hearing but something else entirely. The laughter was unsettling, inhuman. The boy would have bolted if not for the continuous tugging from inside his body, which held him rooted in place.

Then, from somewhere out in the middle of the lake, a dark

shape began to form, sliding across the surface of the water as it came toward him.

Raaaiilingg.

His brother's voice again, but it had a whining, pleading quality that it had never before possessed. He shuddered at the sound, unnerved by the neediness of its tone. But he stayed where he was, waiting on the thing that crested the lake's surface and drew ever closer. He did not feel the fear that might otherwise have driven him into the woods. What he felt instead was a deep, inexplicable revulsion.

When the dark shape reached him, it was fully formed. It stood upon the waters and looked down on him.

"Brother." Redden Ohmsford addressed him in a hollow, empty voice.

Railing was dumbstruck and could not respond.

"Did you think that if you did not come for me, I could not in my turn find a way to come to you? Did you abandon me with the expectation that I would simply vanish from your life and leave you in peace? Leave you to court Mirai alone? Did you believe that, even in death, I would not find a way to rejoin you?"

Railing fought back against a rising tide of despair. "You are not my brother. My brother isn't dead. I would know it if he were!" He swallowed hard. "What are you? A shade? A changeling?"

The creature before him shimmered and began to transform again. "Perhaps I am you."

And just like that Railing was looking at his mirror image— every detail recognizable, every line and feature in place.

"Why did you call to me? What do you want?"

"Oh, it isn't what I want. It's what you want."

"That's not true. This is all coming from you. And you are not me!"

"Well, then, descendant of Valemen and Druids, who am I?"

Railing racked his brain for an explanation, for a memory, for any hint of who or what this thing was. But he could not seem to think straight looking at a duplicate of himself.

"I have known your kin, and your ancestors great and small. I have spoken to some over the years. I spoke to Brin Ohmsford when she went in search of the Ildatch. And to Walker Boh when he went after the Black Elfstone." The laughter returned, whispery and prodding. "Does that not tell you who I am?"

It did. Abruptly, Railing found the answer—both from his memories of his family's history and from the stories told him by his father and repeated endlessly by his brother and himself.

"You are the Grimpond. You are a shade confined to this world, chained to this plane of existence."

"An immortal creature who knows secrets that no one else does. A creature that possesses the ability to see the future. A being that might be of assistance to someone like you."

Railing knew that the Grimpond was a spiteful prisoner of this world, trapped here for reasons that no one knew, hateful of all the Races, treacherous and inconstant. Whatever words it spoke—even though it did know things hidden from others—were not to be trusted.

"I thought you dwelled farther back in Darklin Reach, somewhere north of Hearthstone." It was coming back to him now, the whole of what he knew of this shade. "How do you come to be here?"

The shade rippled and changed again, and now it was his mother who confronted him, her face stern and unforgiving. "You were told not to let anything happen to your brother, and yet you did. What sort of brother does that make you, Railing? What sort of son?"

Railing ignored the insults and folded his arms defensively.

"I'm wasting my time here. If you have something to tell me, just say it. Otherwise, I am returning to my bed."

"And you think you will sleep well knowing what you have done? How you have betrayed and manipulated those who depend on you? How you hide a gift from a Faerie creature because you are afraid to reveal your possession of it? How you have become a thing much worse than what you think me to be? Oh, I seriously doubt that you will sleep well at all!"

Railing fought back against his rising anger and deliberately kept his hands at his sides and out of his pockets. "Since you seem to know me so well, you must also know that nothing you can tell me will make a difference in how I feel about myself or my brother or my friends!"

"Nothing?" A meaningful pause. "Really?"

Railing took a deep breath. "What, then?"

"You are such a disappointment to me, Railing! Such a waste of possibilities." His mother's voice, cold and scolding. Then the shade rippled once more and suddenly it was a faceless being, cloaked and hooded. "It is I who shall go to bed and leave you to your fate."

"You can know nothing of fate!" Railing's hands were clenched into fists. "Only of secrets. You are a master of trickery and deceit. My fate is in my hands."

The Grimpond went silent then, hovering like the fog from which it had emerged, the substance of it beginning to fragment and vanish. "If you are so convinced of that, go on your way. I am done with you. I would give you help, but you spurn me. You mistrust me, yet you refuse to see that I might have knowledge you lack. Knowledge you desire, Railing Ohmsford. Knowledge you crave."

Railing stepped back, shaking his head slowly. "No, you would trick me with your words and your pretenses. You seek to play games with me. You did this with others in my family. The histories tell us so. You were never less than deceitful, and I will not become your latest victim."

The Grimpond came back together again abruptly. "Why not hear my words and judge for yourself? Can mere words do so much harm that even to listen would undo you? Are you so frightened of me?"

The night closed down around the boy as he pondered a response. What should he say? Should he admit his fears and be done with it? Should he deny being afraid and demand that the other give him what he was promising? Should he walk away? The silence lengthened, and the Grimpond waited.

"I want you to do what you think you should," Railing said eventually. "If you have something to say, I will listen. If not, I will leave."

The Grimpond chuckled softly and shimmered once more. But this time it did not change form and did not give a quick retort. Instead, it seemed to consider.

"Hear me, then," it said finally. "I summoned you to see what you were made of, that much is true. Had you been weaker, I might have tried to teach you a lesson. But now I will simply tell you what it is I know that you do not. You have come in search of Grianne Ohmsford. You would know her fate, and if there is a chance that she might be brought back to face the Straken Lord."

He paused, and the boy waited patiently.

"She lives, Railing Ohmsford. She lives, and she can be what you need. She can do what you expect. If you wish that of her, you should continue on with the knowledge that what you seek is possible. Yet you should be careful what you ask for—an old phrase, but a good one to remember, because all is not as it seems. There are threads that might cause the whole to unravel, like the threads of the ring you carry in your pocket."

Railing felt a surge of excitement. His efforts would not be wasted. His chances of finding Grianne and bringing her back to face the Straken Lord—and save his brother and possibly the Four Lands—were real. He understood what the Grimpond was telling him about things not working out as he hoped, but he had known that from the first. And any chance at all was the best he could hope for.

"Is this the truth?" he asked the shade. "Are you lying in any way?"

"Not a word of what you've heard is a lie, but your expectations may turn my words to falsehood. This is not my doing. Remember that. Keep the memory of what I have told you clear in your mind."

"I will."

The Grimpond shimmered and began to recede. "Enough of this. I came to say those words and I have said them. What happens now is up to you. I will watch your progress and record your reactions to everything that happens. It will be most entertaining for me."

The boy watched the shade trail away like a shadow lost with the light's passing—there one moment and gone the next. It was still visible as it reached the fog and passed through.

Then it melted away in a scattering of tiny particles and was gone.

2

THE COMPANY SET OUT AGAIN AT DAWN, RISING to greet a sun hung low and red against the horizon, its rays like tendrils of blood stretched out across the waking land. The intensity of the crimson light against the fading night was unsettling, and the passengers and crew of *Quickening* ate their breakfast in silence, with uneasy looks toward the east. The haze that caused the light to take on that color was unfamiliar even to the Rovers, and superstition hovered in all their minds.

They set sail nevertheless, and by midmorning the last of the sunrise and its aftermath had vanished into a pale silvery mist, clouds screening all but streaks of the blue sky beyond. The threat of rain loomed north and west in a massing of thunderheads. *Storm coming*, one or two muttered to the others, just to say the words aloud. *Bad one, from the looks of it.*

To Railing, sitting with his back to the pilot box—distancing himself from the others—the gathering storm felt emblematic. Once again, he was keeping everything to himself, choosing not to speak of his meeting with the Grimpond, hiding away what had transpired. Now he was keeping two secrets of great import rather than one, both of which he knew he should have shared with the other members of the company. But he still could not bring himself to reveal anything that might spell the end to their journey. Because no matter what else happened, he could not allow them to turn back.

It was a terrible place to be. He knew the decision was not his alone to make. He knew, as well, that his actions were both selfish and dangerous. He even knew that he was probably not the best one to decide what should happen in light of his brother's plight. But nothing he had been told by either the King of the Silver River or the Grimpond had changed his commitment or eroded his determination. He was set on finding Grianne Ohmsford and using her to save his brother. The very fact that the Grimpond had told him she lived and he would reach her was enough to cement whatever cracks might have surfaced in the wall of his resolve. It did not matter that there had been equivocation in the creature's words, or that they were, perhaps, meant to taunt and tease. It did not matter that he had been warned twice—once by each of his unearthly visitors—that things might not turn out as he expected.

What mattered—the only thing that mattered—was that he would be given a chance at saving Redden.

He understood the risk he was taking. He knew Grianne might turn him away, might even dismiss him out of hand. But he believed he was strong enough that he could overcome such obstacles. He believed he could find a way to achieve what he had long ago decided must happen—even in the face of resistance.

His was a faith that was deep and burning. He had come this far riding its dark wings, and he would fly on its slippery back and steer it on its uncertain course until this business was over and he had gotten Redden back, safe and well once more.

That it might cost him his life did not matter. It was not even a possibility he dwelled on. That it might cost the lives of his companions troubled him more, but not enough to give him pause. They had come with him because they believed in what they were doing. He saw it as his mission to keep them believing.

They flew west and north into the Upper Anar, following the twisting line of the Rabb River where it wound its angular way through the forests and mountains below—a course that would take them close to where they would sheer off north in search of the town of Rampling Steep. Farshaun told him this at one point, coming over to sit beside him, worried perhaps that he was keeping himself too isolated from the rest of the company. They sat together in silence save for when the old man made the effort to engage him in conversation. But Railing had already distanced himself from discussions of this sort, finding it the easiest way to deal with the emotional fallout of his choice. Better to say nothing than to break down and spill it all.

"You do not seem yourself, boy," Farshaun said at one point. "As if maybe you've left us and gone somewhere else. Is that so? What's happening with you?"

"Nothing," Railing answered at once. He tried a smile that didn't work. "I just can't stop thinking about Redden and what he's going through. It's very hard."

"We know this. But you shouldn't shut us out."

There was nothing to say to that, and after a while the Rover got up and walked away.

Mirai didn't come by at all that day, although she waved to him in passing once or twice. Mostly, she spent her time with Austrum—an irritation that Railing couldn't do anything about without starting an argument. And he was determined to avoid fighting with the one true north in his life. He watched her in silence, remembering what she had told him earlier about the big Rover: that there was nothing between them.

But then Austrum reached for her hand and took it in his own and she did not pull away.

By midafternoon they were well into the Upper Anar, the *Quickening* benefiting from a following wind as they tacked north toward the Charnals. They had made good time all day, and their luck continued with their new heading. The approaching storm seemed to have cleared the Dragon's Teeth and rumbled on to the western edge of the Wolfsktaag Mountains, but there it had stalled out. Farshaun had stopped long enough to let him know that they would reach Rampling Steep that day, shortly after sunset.

Railing spent the remaining hours working the rigging with the crew, suddenly in need of something to do. He tried not to look about for Mirai, unwilling to find her in the company of Austrum, but when he finally did see her she was standing not six feet away, working the lines with him. She grinned knowingly, as if able to read his thoughts and divine his intentions. Blushing, he grinned back, feeling good for no other reason than an unmistakable relief in finding her close and alone.

Darkness had set in when they spied the lights of their destination, torches and lamps in large numbers burning through the inky black, the clouds massing over the mountaintops to shadow the land about them. The first few drops of rain were beginning to fall as they descended, heralding the approach of the storm and warning of a need to secure the airship with haste.

They descended smoothly, Mirai at the helm and Farshaun and Skint acting as navigators, aiming for a small airfield that sat just outside the town. There was a handful of aircraft moored on the field—none of them ships-of-the-line or even vessels the size of *Quickening*. Most were dilapidated and poorly tended, and had the look of ships that hadn't flown recently and might never fly again. No one moved about on the field as they settled down; no one appeared to greet them or aid them in their mooring.

None of this mattered to the Rovers, who were used to handling everything on their own. They scurried about the decking, hauling down the light sheaths, securing the radian draws and lowering anchors and ropes for moorage. Railing watched for the first few moments, then his gaze shifted to Rampling Steep. It was too dark to see very far, but if the number of lamps and torches were any indication, this wasn't much of a town. For one thing, it was situated far up in the foothills that shadowed the mountains, and the only reason for its existence seemed to be its location—all of the passes leading into the Charnals from the west began here. Farshaun had told him that the town's only value was as a way station for trappers, hunters, and travelers seeking guides. No one would come this way otherwise.

Looking at it now, catching glimpses of the closest buildings at the edge of the airfield, he could tell that upkeep and repairs were not a high priority for the town's residents. Sideboards were cracked and splintered, roofs were sagging or collapsed, windows were broken out, and every other building appeared to have given up the fight years before. A few had been maintained so that they seemed able to weather a storm and keep their inhabitants warm and dry, but even those lacked pretense at being anything more than basic shelter.

Farther on, the lights were thicker and brighter, suggesting that the town center might be slightly less decrepit. When he listened closely, the boy could hear the sounds of singing and laughter.

"Morgan Leah came this way a long time ago," Mirai said. She was standing at his elbow, looking out at the town with him. Her hair was tied back, and strands caught the distant lights in golden glints. "He was traveling with Walker Boh and the girl Quickening, among others. The company had come in search of the city of Eldwist and the Stone King, Uhl Belk, seeking the Black Elfstone."

"I remember the story." Railing tried not to look at her, afraid of what she would see in his eyes. "We heard it from our father when he was telling us the family history. That was in the time of Par and Coll Ohmsford. The Shadowen were abroad and hunting them."

She said nothing for a moment, her eyes focused on the town. "You be careful when you go in there."

He glanced over then, catching a hint of something like regret in her words. "You won't be coming?"

She shook her head. "Skint doesn't think it's a good idea. He thinks I'll attract too much attention. Farshaun agrees. Women in towns like these serve only one purpose."

Railing nodded. "They're probably right. It's too risky."

But he was still surprised. Somehow he had believed she would be going simply because they always stayed close whenever they were together. It felt odd knowing she wouldn't be with him.

"Maybe you should go anyway," he said, wanting her to agree. "A cloak and hood would hide . . ."

She gave him a quick look and walked away, not waiting to hear more. He stood looking after her, the rest of what he was going to say forgotten, the unspoken words a bitter taste in his mouth.

Moments later the company gathered on the main deck, summoned by Farshaun, who seemed to have assumed command in the absence of any involvement on Railing's part.

"Everyone stays aboard but Skint, Railing, and myself. The three of us will go into the town and try to find the man we need. It might take us awhile, so you will have to be patient. But no one," he continued, looking specifically at Austrum and the other Rovers, "leaves the airship while we are away."

"Not much of anywhere to go," Austrum allowed with a grin. "I don't think you need worry, Old Man."

He said it affectionately, and Farshaun took it that way, giving him a grin in reply before adding, "You'll find out just how old I am if you disobey me."

So while the others set about finding something to do in the interim, Skint, Railing, and Farshaun descended the rope ladder and set off.

They crossed the airfield through the darkness, heading for the lights of the town, picking their way over humps and ruts and clusters of rocks as they went. They reached the first of the lights—a lamp attached to what appeared to be an equipment shed but looked like little more than another ruin. They found a path there and followed it through a scattering of buildings— some of them homes, some sheds, some barns—moving steadily toward the laughter and singing. Debris was scattered everywhere, and no one was about. A few of the better-maintained houses were dark, the shutters barred and the curtains drawn. No one else moved on the path, not until it turned into a weather-eroded roadway. Even then, the men they passed walked with their heads down and their eyes averted. Some stumbled drunkenly. Some turned aside to slip from view between the buildings. No one spoke to them. No one evinced the least interest in who they were or what they were doing.

By the time they were finally approaching the town center, the storm had caught up to them and it had begun to rain. The rain increased in intensity while they plodded up the roadway, the ground beneath their boots turning soft with mud and standing water. Ahead, the lamps burned dimly through the gloom, and the torches sizzled and sputtered.

At the first inn they reached, Skint paused. "Wait here."

He disappeared inside and came out only moments later, beckoning them on. Railing was hungry by now, along with being cold and wet, and was impatient to reach their destination. But they slogged on past several other taverns without slowing and had almost reached the far side of the town when the Gnome Tracker motioned them through the door of a dilapidated building whose sign read PAINTED LADY. Smoky air and dim lighting greeted them; the haze was nearly as bad inside as out. The room in which they stood was big by any standard. The floor space was filled with tables and benches, and most of them were occupied. A bar against which a clutch of men leaned, drinking and joking, took up one long wall. A few heads turned, but most of the tavern's customers ignored them. Skint stopped just inside the doorway, glanced around, then directed them to a table near the far wall. They threaded their way through the tables and bodies and arrived at their destination unchallenged. They were close to a huge fireplace with a fire blazing in the open hearth. They removed their cloaks and felt the heat begin to chase off the chill that had settled into their bones.

"Better now, eh?" Farshaun said to Railing, who nodded absently.

Skint left them without a word, moving over to the bar. A few minutes later, he was back with tankards of ale. "Get a little of this inside you. Our man will be over in a moment."

They sat drinking the ale, waiting. Railing wanted to ask something more about the man they were supposed to be meeting—Challa Nand—so that he would have some idea of what he was like. But Skint had said nothing about the prospective guide earlier and he offered nothing now. So at this point, it seemed better to hold his tongue and let matters unfold.

Suddenly Skint straightened in his seat. "Here he comes. Let me do the talking," he said, the words so soft that Railing almost didn't hear.

A huge Troll was coming toward them, winding his way through the closely bunched tables as if unconcerned whether he avoided them or knocked them over. The occupants of the tables he passed were quick to move aside, either out of courtesy or to avoid being crushed; it was hard to tell which. Challa Nand wasn't just big. At three hundred pounds or more, and topping out at just under seven feet, he was huge. The bark-like skin and blunted features were a familiar sight, but it was the man's build that was more impressive. Railing was willing to bet that there wasn't an ounce of fat amid all that muscle. Challa Nand looked as if he could pick up any table in the room—occupants and all—and fling it out the door.

He reached them and sat down at the end of the bench next to Skint, who quickly made room for him. His dark gaze passed over all three men before settling on the Gnome Tracker. "What do you need of me?"

He spoke the Southland dialect that had become commonplace during the last century, his voice a deep rumble, harsh and jagged about the edges. Railing tried to stop staring at him and failed.

"We need a guide into the Charnals," Skint replied. He seemed calm enough sitting next to the Troll, who looked to be three times his size. "Into country not many know or dare to go."

"Where, exactly?"

"The ruins of Stridegate."

A rough chuckle. "Urda country. Why would you go there?

Never mind, don't tell me that. I don't need to know. Stridegate. That's inside the Inkrim." He glanced at Railing and Farshaun. "Just the three of you?"

"We have a ship. A crew of Rovers. Two other passengers."

"A warship?"

"No, but it's well protected."

"It'll need to be. That's dangerous country even for men who know it, which I'm guessing you don't. Deep inside the Klu, which are deep inside the Charnals." He shook his massive head. "An old man, a skinny Gnome, and a boy. Are the rest any better suited to this than you?"

Without waiting for a response, he took Skint's tankard of ale and drained it. "You should get us another round, don't you think?"

Skint glared at him but complied. The Troll watched him go, then turned to Railing. "There's something about you—I sensed it right away—and it troubles me. I can't put my finger on it, though. You don't look very impressive, but there's something there, right enough. Where do you come from, boy? What's your name?"

Railing flushed at the assessment, his irritation at being addressed so bluntly almost getting the better of him. "Railing Ohmsford. From the village of Patch Run on the Rainbow Lake."

The Troll studied him. "Never heard of Patch Run, but your name is familiar. Why do I know it?"

Railing met his dark gaze without flinching but said nothing. Why should he tell this creature anything?

Skint returned with the tankards of ale. Challa Nand took all four from him, pushed one at Farshaun, one at the Gnome, and kept the other two for himself. Railing's face darkened further.

"You think me bold?" Challa Nand shrugged. "Let me tell you something, Railing Ohmsford. I am a big, strong man. You can see as much. I get what I want most of the time because of my size and strength. There's not much reason for me to worry. But every now and then, something or someone comes along who, for one reason or another, is my match. Early on, I didn't sense it the way I do now. I've learned to look for it, though. I've learned not to rely too strongly on size and strength, not to take it for granted that my physical gifts will see me through. Knowing your limitations is important in this world."

He drank from his tankard of ale. Then he pushed the second tankard toward Railing. "I sense those limitations now, with you. You have magic, don't you? Magic strong enough that you don't see any real need to be afraid of me. What form does it take?"

Railing hesitated, then reached out and accepted the tankard. "It's called a wishsong. I can use my voice to reshape and manipulate physical things. It runs in my family."

The Troll glanced at Skint for confirmation and got a nod in reply. "Ohmsford," he repeated, and suddenly his face changed. "Grianne Ohmsford?"

"My great-aunt."

He nodded slowly. "The Ilse Witch. What's going on here? Why are you making this journey?"

"You said you didn't need to know," Railing shot back.

"I didn't need to then. I do now. Your name changes everything. If you want my services, you'd better tell me the truth."

Railing and Skint exchanged glances. "Up to you," the Tracker said to him.

Railing thought about it a moment. If Skint thought they needed this man as their guide, there wasn't much choice. Certainly, the Troll looked able enough. Besides, if he were in the other's shoes, he would want to know, too.

But that didn't mean he needed to know everything.

So he told Challa Nand that they were searching for Grianne Ohmsford's remains—that when she left the Druid order she went into the Charnals, carrying with her a powerful talisman the Druids would pay well for if it were recovered and brought to them. He told it all with a straight face, trying to avoid embellishments, knowing that reticence would serve him better in persuading the Troll to their cause. He said nothing of the collapse of the Forbidding or the threat to the Four Lands from the creatures imprisoned within. He said nothing of his brother's imprisonment. He knew that if he did there would be no stopping, no place where he could cut it off without telling it all. A story based on the promise of money for services rendered would fly better with a man like this.

Except that when he was finished, Challa Nand just laughed, his booming voice causing heads everywhere to turn in surprise. "If even half of that is the truth, I'm a Spider Gnome's twin!" He shook his head. "But maybe in your place I wouldn't want to be too open about things, either. Not even to your guide—even though your guide could choose to abandon you somewhere you could never find your way out of if he became displeased." He paused meaningfully. "So where does that leave us, huh?" He looked at Skint. "What's my pay for this fool's errand?"

"A hundred gold pieces and anything you find along the way that catches your fancy save what we are looking for." The Tracker eyed him. "You get the gold now."

"A carrot on a stick? I like you, Skint, but I know you too well to trust you. Still, the offer is a good one, even not knowing what I am letting myself in for. So. We can fly in—get through the Charnals, the Klu, the Inkrim, and right up to Stridegate. It won't be easy and won't be safe, but you must know that already. There are Urdas and Gnome raiders. There are worse things, too—and if they bring down your ship, that's probably the end of us. Well, not necessarily for me, but almost certainly for you."

"You would abandon us if that happened?" Railing demanded.

The big Troll leaned forward. "I might if you fail to tell me the truth somewhere along the way. I'll risk myself up to a certain point, but not for people who don't trust me. Are we clear about this?"

Railing took a deep breath and nodded. "If I tell you the truth at some point, will you stick with us to the end?"

"If I decide the truth merits it? Yes. If not, I will ask you to set down and let me off and you will be on your own. Of course, you can ride the back of that particular current as long as you choose. You are master of your own fate in this business, Railing Ohmsford, scion of the Ilse Witch. Just know that I am big and strong but not stupid."

He brought his tankard to his lips and drained it. "We're done for now. Come back for me in the morning. Right here. Bring the gold. As soon as I've seen to its safety, we'll set out."

He set down the tankard and got to his feet. "I hope you know what you're getting yourselves into, but I doubt it." He gave Railing a look. "You'd better be good at using that magic of yours." He stretched. "I'm off to bed."

He lumbered across the room and out the door. Railing, still feeling combative from the confrontation, was surprised to find that, in spite of everything, he rather liked Challa Nand.

Though it was hard to explain exactly why.

They were on their way back to the *Quickening* when the boy remembered the offer Skint had made. "Where did you get a hundred gold pieces?"

Skint's wizened face tightened further. "From him."

He pointed at Farshaun, who shrugged. "It's only coin, and

coin can always be replaced. We can't replace Redden, though."
He put a hand on Railing's shoulder. "He's worth it, isn't he?
Your brother? He's worth more than that to me. You're family,
after all, and we Rovers look out for one another."

Railing was momentarily speechless. A hundred pieces of gold
was a lot of coin. "Thank you, Farshaun. I never even thought
about having to pay."

The old man nodded. "Good thing I'm here, then." He
glanced over at Skint. "That Troll had better be worth it,
though."

The Gnome hunched his shoulders against the rain. "More
than worth it. You'll see."

Railing kept silent. He was back to thinking about the secrets
he was keeping and the deceptions and manipulations he had
employed as a result. He felt ashamed of himself, that he could
not make himself trust his closest friends. But not ashamed
enough that he was persuaded to change his mind and tell them
the truth.

Not when it might mean turning back.

They walked the rest of the way with their heads lowered and
the rain sheeting down.

3

THAT NIGHT, RAILING DREAMED OF MIRAI.

He wondered afterward why he didn't dream of Redden. Virtually every waking thought he had was of his brother and what was needed to get him back, so it made little sense that his dreams should be of Mirai. He was troubled by her renewed interest in Austrum, but not as troubled as he was about his twin.

Yet she was the one he dreamed of that night.

They were walking across a field, holding hands and talking. They were deeply in love, and the look in their eyes reflected their commitment to each other. Ahead, a stretch of woods loomed in dark relief against a bright, sunshine-splashed sky. Railing was aware of the forest, but not afraid of it. They would go around it when they got too close. Mirai would know not to go there, and she would steer him away.

But the closer they got, the less certain he became of her intentions. She seemed oblivious to the danger that awaited, her gaze directed solely toward Railing.

Turn back, Railing tried to tell her, but the words would not come. They passed his lips, at first softly and then more insistently, but they made no sound.

As they drew steadily closer to the trees, he began pulling on her arm, trying to turn her aside, but his efforts were futile. He was not strong enough to change her course, and she would not allow herself to be guided. She kept gazing at him with love and adoration, but she would not respond to his entreaties.

They were almost to the trees. Ahead, within layers of shadows, hands were reaching out to seize her. He could just make them out in the gloom, writhing like tentacles. They were going to take her from him and he would never get her back again. He was frantic with fear, riddled with despair. He was shouting at her to turn back, to veer off, to do something to get clear before it was too late.

He screamed her name.

Then hands were shaking him hard and abruptly he was awake, tangled in his blanket, lying in a hammock belowdecks, hot and twisted about, the images of his dream still fresh enough to seem real.

"Quiet down, boy!" Skint hissed in his ear. "You'll wake the whole ship with your shouting."

Railing nodded quickly, able to see just enough of the Gnome's face to recognize the concern mirrored there. "I had a dream," he whispered.

"I know," Skint said. "Likely everyone on the ship knows. But it's over and done. Get back to sleep."

He moved away, but Railing remained in the hammock, trying to banish the last of the dream. Yet even though he lay there for long minutes waiting for it to happen, his memories of the dream refused to fade. At last he rose and made his way over to the ladder leading up and emerged into a night gone still and deep. The storm had passed and the skies had cleared. Stars filled the dark firmament—thousands upon thousands in a wondrous sweep. He walked to the deck railing and stared, dazzled by the display.

Then, abruptly, he was crying. Tears fell from his eyes unbidden, running down his cheeks, and he couldn't seem to make them stop. The weight of what he was trying to accomplish bore down on him, and it was immense. What made him believe— even for a moment—that his efforts were going to make any difference? His brother's fate would, in all likelihood, be decided by forces over which he had no control, and this foolish, reckless effort to bring back a woman lost to all of them since before they were born was stupid beyond words.

He gave in to his misery for a few minutes more, only barely managing to keep the sounds of his weeping silent. Then, very slowly, he began to recover until he had stopped his tears and regained his composure. But the weeping had emptied him out, and he was left bereft of strength of will and sense of direction. It was all he could do to stand there and stare out at the star-swept sky and the sharp-edged darkness.

He wasn't sure how long he remained at the deck rail before he heard her voice and felt her presence.

"Isn't it beautiful?" Mirai said. She had once again come up on him so quietly that he hadn't heard her. "It's as if the storm swept the sky clean of everything but the stars. Look at them shine."

"I know," he said.

He felt her hand cover his where it rested on the rail. "Are you all right? You seem lost."

"I'm fine. Just tired."

"Not sleeping?"

"Sleeping with bad dreams for company."

"Railing, what is it?"

He didn't reply, couldn't make himself give voice to the lie he intended to offer.

She moved around until she was facing him, placing herself between the deck rail and himself, standing so close he could feel the heat of her breath on his face. He tried to move away, but she seized his arms and held him fast.

"I want you to stop this." She waited for his response, tightening her grip. "Don't say something you'll regret. Don't pretend you don't know what I'm talking about. I've seen the way you watch me—especially when I'm with Austrum. You have to stop it. You and Redden are my best friends, but you don't own me, either of you. You can't tell me what to do."

"I know that," he answered, sounding defensive even to himself.

"You don't act like you do."

"I don't like seeing you with him."

"That's more honest, but that doesn't change things. You need to remember what I just said and stop being jealous. Some things you can't change. What happens with you and me, or Redden and me—or me and someone else—isn't set in stone. What happens just happens, on its own."

She paused, searching his eyes. "But that's not the worst of it, is it? Something else is bothering you. I've sensed it since we started after Grianne Ohmsford. You can't hide that sort of thing from me; I know you too well. You're being eaten up inside, and it's going to destroy you if you keep hiding it. You know something no one else does, don't you? No, don't pretend you don't understand what I'm talking about. You do."

He tried to say something in response and failed. Suddenly he wanted to tell her everything, to confide it all, to share the burden he was carrying. But confiding in her meant risking everything, and he would not do that.

"I'm just afraid for Redden," he said instead.

She gave him a look, then released his arms and stepped back. "When you're ready to tell me the truth, I'll be there to listen. But don't wait too long, Railing. I can feel you slipping away from me—in every sense of the word—and I would hate for that to happen."

He watched her walk away, aching for her, wanting her to turn back, hating that she was right and he could do nothing to change things, knowing that in the end he was going to lose her. The revelation shattered him, and for a moment he sagged back against the deck rail, his strength depleted.

I'm going to lose her.

It was barely an hour after dawn broke that Skint returned with Challa Nand in tow, and the *Quickening* lifted off and turned north. The big Troll spoke a few words to Farshaun and the other Rovers, discussing the route they would be taking and the dangers that would obstruct their passage. Railing listened to a little of it, but then Mirai called him over to join her in the pilot box where she was manning the helm and working the ship's controls, and he left off listening for the pleasure of her company. The pleasure wasn't much, however. As soon as he was standing next to her, she handed off her position at the helm and walked away.

Moments later she was standing amid the Rovers, listening to their conversation with Challa Nand.

The morning passed slowly but uneventfully. They flew northeast along the central corridor that partially bisected the Charnals from north to south and would eventually lead to the Tiderace many days farther on. Railing remained at the helm for the greater part of the time, although both Farshaun and Skint dropped by to chat with him. Mirai pointedly stayed away. Mostly, when he saw her, she was working the lines with the Rovers, joking and laughing and seemingly at ease. He found himself looking for Austrum, but only once did he see the two in close proximity and that was only for a few moments.

The sun was just reaching its zenith when Challa Nand found him sitting forward of the mainmast, his back against the heavy wooden pillar, and sat down next to him. Surprised, the boy glanced over at the giant Troll, but his newly arrived companion simply stared ahead toward the bow and said nothing.

Then, after a few endless minutes of silence, Challa Nand said, "Thinking of your brother, Railing?"

The boy stared at him. "How do you know about Redden?"

The other shrugged. "Men talk. Everyone talks. On a ship this size, there aren't many secrets. I found out about your brother this morning. I found out a few other things, too."

Railing reached up and tightened the headband that held back his red hair, which he hadn't cut in weeks. It had grown long and unruly.

"It seems you haven't been in the least forthcoming with me," the Troll added. "Shame on you."

Railing almost laughed. "What is it that you think you know?"

"That your brother is missing and you want to find him. That he might be someone's prisoner and you want to free him. That you are twins. That we are going in search of your great-aunt the witch because, for some reason, you think she might be alive after more than a hundred years. And that if she is, she might be able to help your brother." He paused. "All of which suggests that we might be on a fool's errand, just as I feared, and therefore I have every right to abandon you at the first sign of trouble."

No mention of the Forbidding. None of the Ellcrys or the

Straken Lord or the danger to the Four Lands. His informants were being selective in their disclosures, it seemed. Railing supposed it was inevitable that some of what he was keeping from Challa Nand would leak out. He was only surprised it wasn't more.

What he wondered, all at once, was how much of it was *worth* hiding from this man—especially when he was hiding so much more from the rest of them. He had believed it a good idea to be discreet, to reveal as little as possible, but now he was questioning himself. Was he exercising good judgment or just being stubborn in his refusal to trust the only man aboard who could get them where they were going?

"You don't know the half of it," he said finally.

The Troll nodded. "I don't expect I do. Why don't you just tell me the rest? You're going to have to sooner or later."

So Railing did. Just like that, he made the decision and he told the Troll everything. About the collapse of the Forbidding, about his brother's capture and imprisonment by the Straken Lord, about the destruction of the Druids and their companions, about the failing of the Ellcrys—all of it. Except for what he was hiding from the others aboard—about his meetings with the King of the Silver River and the Grimpond and what they had told him. That, he continued to keep to himself.

He felt surprisingly better when he had finished. Perhaps it helped relieve him of the stress he was under to give up a few of his secrets. Or perhaps it was just the right thing to do.

"I would say you were lying, except no one could make up such a story." Challa Nand growled, a deep rumbling in his throat. "It might be better if you were lying, given what this all means. At least I see the point in agreeing to guide you to Stridegate. Not that I am persuaded for a second that what you are trying to do is even remotely possible."

"No one really thinks it is possible—no matter what they claim—except me." Though he wondered about Mirai.

Challa Nand went quiet for a few long minutes. "The witch might still be alive and might be persuaded to come back with you to face the Straken Lord. You believe this to be true?" The big man shook his head slowly. "Either you are deeply delusional or you know something that the others don't. Which is it?"

"I'm just trying not to give up in the face of what seem impossible odds." Railing kept his eyes lowered. "I don't want to lose Redden."

He felt the Troll's eyes watching him. "I think you are a complicated boy," the other said finally. "And I think you are good at keeping secrets. But be careful. Kept secrets have a way of coming back to bite you. Remember where you are—on a ship with your companions and all of you in this together. It's hard to separate yourself out when you know that if things go wrong you won't be the only one who gets hurt."

They sat together in silence after that, neither looking at the other. Railing found himself drawn to Challa Nand once again, admiring the other's steadiness and perseverance, and still wondering why he had revealed so much to him. But there was something trustworthy and reliable about the Troll, and even after so short a time he believed the other would stand by him— by all of them—when it was needed.

A while later, without so much as a word, Challa Nand rose and moved off. Railing watched him go—part of him wanting to call the Troll back so they could speak further, part of him relieved the conversation was over. His conflicted feelings on the matter troubled him, but not enough that he was moved to do anything about them.

Fifteen minutes later, while he was still leaning against the mainmast, staring out at nothing, the *Quickening* was attacked.

Austrum saw the enemy first, working the lines on the port side. "Raiders!" he shouted.

There were more than a dozen of them, Gnomes in stripped-down flits fitted with swivel crossbows. The flits were fast and maneuverable, but highly vulnerable, as well. A single shot from a rail sling could knock any one of them out of the sky and send its rider tumbling to his death. The flits relied on speed and skill and superior numbers to overwhelm the larger and better-equipped airships they preyed upon.

"Get below!" Railing heard Farshaun yell at Woostra, and then Railing was on his feet, racing back toward the pilot box. As he fled, he caught sight of Mirai at the stern rail, crouched behind a rail sling with another of the Rovers.

Challa Nand charged past, all size and speed, shouting at Farshaun to take them higher. But the old man, a veteran of countless air battles, had already thought of that, and the *Quickening* had begun a steep climb that would enable it to find stronger air currents, causing problems for the lighter, less stable flits.

Even so, the Gnome raiders gave chase, pursuing the larger ship like troublesome gnats, swivel crossbows firing on its passengers and crew. But the Rovers were prepared for an attack; Challa Nand had warned them in advance that it might come. As a consequence, the rail slings and both fire launchers were mounted and ready when the raiders struck, and in only minutes the Rovers had them aimed and firing. Two of the flits were brought down in the span of thirty seconds, and another was damaged and had to turn back. The rest zigged and zagged in reckless patterns, their riders trying to damage the *Quickening*'s light sheaths or disable its crew so that the ship would be forced to descend. The raiders would have other attackers waiting in reserve, and if the airship were crippled, they would join the fight. Then the weight of numbers would bring the Rover vessel all the way down.

For a few furious moments, the fighting was intense, but the outcome was clear. The flits were making no progress against the better-defended *Quickening*, and five of the raiders were destroyed or damaged. Challa Nand's efforts at preparing the crew for the attack had prevented the raiders from catching them by surprise, and the weapons on the larger airship were far superior to the crossbows and javelins the attackers were using to try to shred the sails.

Then a fresh cluster of Gnome flits emerged from a cut in the mountains ahead, trying to cut off the *Quickening*'s advance. There were more than twenty of them, swarming out of the rocks and coming in at full speed. The Rovers shifted their weapons toward this new threat, but there were too many to even think of stopping them all. Arrows from the crossbows began to make sizable rips in the light sheaths. Two of the Rovers were down, and one of the rail slings was out of service, its mechanism jammed. Challa Nand, standing at the starboard fire launcher, was sweeping his weapon's barrel across the rows of flits. But the launchers were big and cumbersome and difficult to aim accurately. A couple more of the flits went down, but it made little difference in the fury of the attack.

In the pilot box, arrows protruded from the protective walls like porcupine quills, bristling in bunches about the control shields. Farshaun had been wounded twice, seriously enough the second time that he had relinquished the controls to Railing. The boy was working hard at keeping the airship steady so that the defenders could use the slings and launchers effectively, but the flits were everywhere, and when they were this close the Rovers couldn't use the deck weapons for fear of hitting their own vessel.

"Farshaun!" Railing shouted over his shoulder at where the other was crouched down in a corner of the box. "Take the controls from me!"

But the old man had collapsed, his arms gone limp, his head sagging. It looked as if he had lost consciousness.

"Farshaun!" the boy screamed.

Abruptly, Mirai appeared, leaping into the box and taking the controls. She exchanged a quick look with Railing as she did so, and he could see at once that she knew what he intended.

Then he was over the protective walls and racing across the decking toward the bow, already singing, the wishsong summoned and responding. Arrows flew at him, but the wall of his magic shielded him and the missiles bounced away harmlessly. As he ran, he heard Challa Nand call his name, and he watched in disbelief as the big Troll charged toward him protectively.

"Get back!" he screamed at the other, his warning quick and hard-edged in the tumult of the attack. But Challa Nand either didn't hear him or refused to pay attention, and even though Railing tried to shift the wishsong's magic away from him, the big Troll ran straight into its wall and went down in a crumpled heap.

But Railing had no time to worry about Challa Nand. His concentration now was entirely on manipulating the wishsong to strike out at the attacking Gnome raiders. He sent it spiraling outward, the sound as dense and impenetrable as stone. All the while he kept moving toward the deck rail, forming and re-forming, molding the magic, pulling together elements in the air and wind to create a protective shield, angling it so that the *Quickening* would not be harmed.

The flits were not so fortunate. Unable to see what blocked their way, they flew into the wall of sound heedlessly, shattering against its hard surface and tumbling away. A dozen went down before the rest broke off in terror and went flying back into the cover of the mountains, their riders hunkered down, thrusters shoved forward to attain maximum speed.

In seconds the skies were clear and the *Quickening* and its crew were flying alone once more.

Railing quit singing, allowing the magic of the wishsong to die into silence. He stood watching the fleeing Gnome raiders a few seconds longer before turning back to the others. Several, Austrum among them, were staring at him in disbelief. Challa Nand was awake again, sitting on the decking, rubbing his head. He had a look of confusion on his face until he caught sight of Railing coming over; then the look abruptly changed to one of rage. He staggered to his feet to face the boy.

"What else are you keeping from me that I ought to know about?" he snarled. "Because I have had just about enough of you!"

"I tried to warn you," Railing shouted back, aware of how angry the Troll was. He slowed his approach, but Challa Nand was right on top of him, his huge body towering over the boy as if intending to crush him. "You just kept coming! What was I supposed to do?"

The Troll glared at him for a moment, then turned away dismissively. "You used your magic to save the airship. That's good enough for me. But a word or two in advance to the rest of us wouldn't hurt!"

Then he stomped away, beginning the task of clearing pieces of wreckage and debris from the decking. The Rovers joined him in this effort, leaving Railing free to continue on to where Mirai was kneeling beside Farshaun in the pilot box.

"How bad is he?" the boy asked.

She shook her head. "I can't be sure. He's bleeding internally, and he's very weak. He's old, Railing. He doesn't recover from injuries like he once did. Help me carry him below. I'll do what I can for him down there."

They picked up Farshaun and hauled him out of the pilot box and down the ladder to the interior of the airship. Austrum came over to give them a hand, then disappeared topside again.

"That was quick thinking," Mirai said as she worked to cut away Farshaun's clothing from his wounds; Railing was standing by in case there was something he could do to help. "You saved us."

"I waited too long to act." He was feeling anything but happy about how things had gone. "I should have used the wishsong right away. I was too slow."

"You can't think of everything in situations like that one. We were fighting for our lives." She stayed bent over Farshaun, studying the crossbow wound, looking for a way to stanch the bleeding. "Everyone does the best they can."

"Maybe."

She kept working, and finally she was satisfied with her efforts. The crossbow bolt was removed, the bleeding slowed, and the wound washed and stitched up sufficiently that infection might be prevented. All through this, the old man slept, unconscious and unaware.

"Have you thought about what I told you earlier? About sharing whatever it is you're hiding?"

Railing pushed back his long red hair and retied the band that held it in place. "You have to stop asking me. I don't want to talk about it."

She shrugged. "I think you probably do. You just don't want to talk about it with me."

"It isn't that . . . "

"What is it, then?"

"I can't tell you. I just can't. I have to work my way through it on my own. There's more at stake than you know." He looked away. "I'm in love with you, you know. There, I've said it out loud. I love you. I always have."

She nodded, standing up and moving next to him. "I'm not sure you know what that means."

"What? It's difficult to understand that because of how I feel about you I can't just open up and tell you certain things? Well, I can't! Not yet, at least. Maybe when we reach Stridegate. Maybe then."

She stared at him a moment. "You should listen to yourself. You should hear yourself the way I do. Railing, if you were really in love with me, you could always open up to me. You wouldn't have to hide things."

He shook his head. "It doesn't work like that."

"I think it does." She stepped away again. "Don't let the clock tick all the way down. Don't wait so long that by the time you decide to confide in the rest of us it's too late to matter. Because that can happen. Do you understand?"

"I think so."

She gave him a wan smile. "I wonder if you do."

Then she turned and walked away.

4

THEY FLEW *QUICKENING* ON THROUGH THE sun's setting and into twilight, reaching the place where the Charnals began to broaden into a split range with multiple layers before setting down for the night. Here, the mountains were visible for miles in all directions, vast and immutable, great silent sentinels of the Northland east. The attack by the Gnome raiders was far behind them by then, and the town of Rampling Steep farther still. There were no settlements this far north, only hundreds of miles of empty space and broken rock. Staring out at it, Railing could only think of how bleak his life had become.

They slept aboard the ship that night with a close watch at both the bow and stern. Too many dangerous creatures prowled this region of the world, Challa Nand had warned. Gnome raiders were one thing; Gnawls and the like were another. Railing didn't bother asking what a Gnawl was. He didn't want to know.

He wasn't asked to stand watch on either shift, however, and when Mirai showed no interest in speaking with him further, he rolled into his blanket and quickly fell asleep.

When he woke, after what felt like only a few hours, it was raining again.

The sound of it brought him awake. He heard the thrumming against the decking overhead and rose, wrapping himself in his weather cloak, and went topside to find himself caught in a torrential downpour. It was raining so hard, it was coming down in sheets that obscured everything more than a few feet away. He peered about for the other members of the crew but could see no one. Ducking his head and pulling the cloak and hood tight against his face and body, he fought his way through the deluge to the pilot box, thinking to find someone there.

But the box was empty.

He left and went to the stern railing. Nothing.

Suddenly he was panicked. Was the entire ship deserted? No, he had seen Farshaun wrapped in his bandages and blankets, asleep below. One of the injured Rovers was resting close by the old man—the only one hurt badly enough in yesterday's attack to be so confined. He also seemed to remember catching sight of someone moving through the gloom, a shadow passing along the walls of the vessel in the faint light of the smokeless torches the Rover airships relied on. But that might have been a dream.

He went back down the ladder and inside the ship. Farshaun was still sleeping, as was the injured Rover. Over in another corner, he found Woostra asleep as well. He hesitated, then knelt and shook the Druid scribe awake.

Woostra peered up at him. "What's wrong?"

Railing hesitated. "I can't find anyone aboard but you and Farshaun and that injured Rover. Can't think of his name."

"His name is Aleppo." The scribe rubbed his beard, then his eyes and yawned. "I've been asleep. Are you sure about all this?"

"Aleppo. I knew that. I just forgot. And yes, I'm sure."

In fact, he was embarrassed at his lapse of memory. He rose. "I'm going back out on deck. Please watch out for Farshaun." He started away and then turned back again, a premonition tugging at him. "Don't try to come after me. Wait until I come back for you."

He left the bewildered scribe staring after him. And tightening his weather cloak once more, he went up the ladder and out on deck. The rain hadn't lessened; if anything, it was more severe than before, pummeling the wooden decks and hull with deafening force.

He stood amid the tumult and the chilling, invasive downpour for a moment to get his bearings, then started toward the bow. He hadn't checked there yet. In his haste to find someone, he had skipped the bow in favor of a more thorough search of the hold.

So, maybe . . .

He was almost all the way forward when a figure detached itself from the gloom ahead. Railing started in spite of himself, thinking for just a moment that he had encountered a wraith rather than a man. But it was only one of the Rovers cloaked and hooded against the weather.

In fact, he realized, watching the figure draw closer, it wasn't even a Rover. It was Mirai.

She came up to him and stood close so that they could see each other in the downpour. "Where is everyone?" Railing demanded.

Mirai looked worried. "Gone off ship. They left about an hour ago. A search party. Both members of the second watch disappeared shortly after their shift began. Not a sound, not a trace. Challa Nand wanted to wait to see if they would show up on their own. The implication was that if they didn't, they were dead and therefore a search was pointless and a danger to everyone else. But Austrum insisted he would not leave his men behind without making sure they couldn't be found."

"I suppose he felt he had to."

"It was stupid of him," she muttered, shaking her head.

"So there's no one left aboard? They're all gone?" Railing felt a sudden rush of fear. "Skint went with them, too?"

"Challa Nand didn't think the Rovers could find their way back without help, and Skint agreed. So they both went. Leaving you, me, Woostra, and the injured." She turned away. "I've got to get back on watch. I can't see anything, but it makes me feel useful. Want to help? I let you sleep until now, but since you're up I could use the company."

Railing nodded and went with her. Together they moved to the front of the airship and took up stations port and starboard of the bowsprit. The wind had changed, coming out of the north now rather than the west, howling down the canyons between the peaks with a wailing that chilled the boy to his bones. He tried to shut it out by tightening the laces on his hood, but nothing helped. Because he was facing directly into the storm, rain blew through gaps in his gear and quickly left him drenched. He imagined Mirai was no better off, but that didn't make him feel any less miserable.

He bent his head against a gust of rain. He liked it that Mirai had called Austrum foolish. It was petty to feel like that, but satisfying, too.

More rain found its way under his cloak. He wished that he had brought an aleskin on deck. He wished he hadn't come on deck at all. He wished a dozen other things because there wasn't anything else to do to pass the time. Peering into the rain seemed pointless. He couldn't see a thing. A pack of Kodens could come crawling out of rocks and onto the ship, and he wouldn't see them until they were right on top . . .

He quit searching the gloom. He quit breathing.

Something was out there.

He felt its presence all at once—a sort of tingle on the surface of his skin that quickly turned to a cold shiver. He couldn't see it, couldn't know what it was, but it was there and it was coming toward the ship. Without stopping to consider what he was doing, he rushed around the blocking on the bowsprit and dragged Mirai away from the rail, a finger to his lips as he did so, motioning her to silence as he pointed into the rain and gloom.

Together they dropped into a crouch by the forward bins in which the spare light sheaths were stored, the two of them hunching down, forming dark, wet lumps against the wooden sides.

"Don't make a sound!" Railing whispered.

Whatever tone of voice he used, whatever inflection he employed, it froze Mirai in place. Maybe she sensed it, too. Maybe she realized something was out there in the haze. Whatever the case, they hunkered down in the shadow of the bins, two barely recognizable shadows in the shifting layers of rain and gloom, waiting.

Then they heard a small sound from behind and, turning, found Woostra creeping across the deck. Railing quickly put a finger to his lips in warning and beckoned hurriedly.

As the scribe knelt beside him, Railing pulled him close. "What are you doing?" he hissed. "I told you to wait!"

Woostra scowled. "I got tired of waiting," he whispered. He glanced worriedly into the gloom. "What is it? What's out there?"

Railing shook his head, refusing to answer. "Just don't move!" he said. "Don't say anything!"

He was already summoning the wishsong, convinced that

whatever was coming was too dangerous for them to risk waiting. A low hum, barely more than a whisper, it rode the ensuing silence like a ghost in search of a haunt, building on itself, forming into an amorphous and malleable presence that could be shaped and dispatched in the blink of an eye.

Out in the haze, something moved. Something very big.

Railing exhaled soundlessly. He could just make it out through the gap in the bins where he crouched between Woostra and Mirai. The latter must have seen it, as well, for she gave a small gasp and pressed more tightly against him. She was so close he could feel her breath against his face, warm and feathery. Woostra had adopted a hedgehog defense, collapsed into a tight ball, head buried in his arms. Together they waited, so afraid it was all they could do not to bolt and run. But flight from whatever this was would be pointless. Doing anything that caught its attention would be the end of them.

The rain strengthened suddenly, gusts blowing across the decking and into their eyes. A second later a clawed hand reached for the rail and fastened in place, close to where the bowsprit jutted into the darkness. A sleek shape rose into view— what looked to be an immense lizard—towering over the airship bow, dozens of feet in length. It was hard to determine more than the general size and shape, but it appeared thick-bodied and sinuous as it hauled itself halfway onto the foredeck.

Railing was singing full-out now, using every last vestige of his magic to gather and shape the elements around him, forming a cloaking for Mirai, Woostra, and himself. He made their smell vanish and their shapes dilute. He masked their presence with a combination of darkness and damp, drawing in and thickening the rain and gloom. He watched the creature sway slowly from side to side, an unwelcome invader looming over the bins, the foredeck, and themselves. A silent shudder ran through him but he held fast to the wishsong, keeping the cloaking in place.

Then, abruptly, the creature lowered its head until it was almost touching the coverings of the bins, its bulk directly atop them. Its jaws split wide, filled with rows of jagged teeth that were monstrous and threatening. Railing could feel Mirai shaking. He had his arm about her, and he tightened his grip on her shoulders.

Make no sound, he willed her. *No movement. All will be well. I will protect you. I will give my life for you.*

For several endless seconds he believed they had been discovered and that—with the swiftness for which lizards the world over were known—it would snap them up like helpless insects. But then the creature withdrew, slithering away again, retreating over the rail and off the airship. Railing watched it go, still singing, still holding fast to what he had begun, taking no chances. The lizard's head swung back briefly, as if making sure; then it skittered off into the rain and gloom.

For a long time afterward, Railing didn't move. With Mirai still pressing close against him and Woostra huddled near, he stayed where he was behind the bins, crouched down beneath the sheltering magic of the wishsong. He kept it in place, his voice soft and steady, until the danger was clearly past.

Finally, as the rains began to abate and the gloom to clear, he let it die away into silence.

Mirai looked at him questioningly, then lifted her head to look about. Woostra, sensing her movement, did the same. Together they rose and stood peering through the lessening gloom, trying to decide if all was indeed safe again, if the creature was truly gone.

"The next time this happens," Woostra said finally, "I can promise you I will be staying below."

When the searchers appeared abruptly from the west, trudging sodden and discouraged out of the damp and dark, all three hurried out to greet them.

Challa Nand lounged against the aft rail next to the boy as Austrum and his Rover companions ran up the sails on the *Quickening* and prepared to get under way. With the storm beginning to slow and the heavy weather to move on, the Troll had advised that there was no reason for further delay and every reason to get the airship aloft, regardless of the fact that it was still deep into the night.

"That creature was some sort of mountain lizard," he advised, looking out into the new day's persistent gloom as if he might still catch sight of it. "A Wynendot or a Spurken, one of those sorts. There's not all that many of them left, but this far north you have to be wary. I thought we were still south of their range, but apparently not."

The search party had returned embittered, frustrated, and empty-handed, just as the Troll had anticipated they would. They had found no trace of the missing men, although at least they hadn't lost any more. Skint and Challa Nand had managed to keep the rest of them safe while they floundered around looking for their fellows.

"The lizard took them during the storm," the Troll advised. "It has a long tongue—very adept at snagging food—so it probably happened pretty quickly. The storm must have hidden their screams. There wasn't much anyone could have done. It was just bad luck it found the ship in the first place."

Then he looked over at Railing. "It was good luck, though, that you kept your wits about you when it came back for a second helping. Those lizards are very aggressive. If you'd tried to defend yourself, it would have come at you, and you would have had to kill it—if you could have managed it, and that's far from certain. Better that you didn't try at all. Using the magic to hide yourself, the scribe, and the girl was the right choice. That was quick thinking." Then he paused. "But how did you know it was there? You couldn't see a hand span in front of your face."

"I sensed it." Railing gave him a look. "I just did."

"Hmmm." The Troll considered and then shrugged. "You are a constant source of fresh surprises."

"I'm just getting by the best I can."

"As are we all." The Troll pushed back from the rail. "We're down two men. More, if you count the old Rover. I don't like how he looks, by the way. So you have a choice. Do we continue on or turn back? Let's hear you say it out loud."

Railing never hesitated. "Continue on."

"As I suspected." Challa Nand began walking away. "Don't forget to let me know when you're ready to tell me the rest of what you're hiding."

Railing scowled. The Troll was as persistent as Mirai.

They released the lines and lifted off shortly after, turning into the heart of the Charnals and setting a course northwest through the maze of peaks. Standing at the bow a short time later, Railing stared out across a dark sea of mountains that reached to the horizon and, for all he knew, to the end of the world. Mist capped the peaks; overhead the skies remained black and clouded, although small windows of starlight could be glimpsed here and there along the horizon. The mountains glistened with snow at their higher elevations and with the damp of the storm farther down. All of it had an eerie, shadowed look, but also seemed hard-edged and immutable.

With Farshaun still lying below, injured and incapable of taking the helm, Mirai and Austrum shared that duty throughout the dark of the night. Railing offered to help, but Challa

Nand suggested he might be more useful keeping watch from the bow. He could sense things the rest of them could not; that was clear enough from tonight's events. If any other dangers awaited them, he might be able to warn them.

So the boy spent the rest of the night standing against the forward rail, casting surreptitious glances back at the pilot box to see if Mirai and Austrum were spending time together. No one seemed able to sleep, too keyed up from the night's events, and he could not seem to help himself; his jealousy was undiminished. Even though she had called the Rover stupid for insisting on searching for his missing men, Railing could not shake the feeling that she continued to be attracted to Austrum and that her infatuation was undermining their own relationship. In spite of the fact she had told him, bluntly, that friendship was as much as he had the right to expect, he still harbored hopes for something more. How could he not? He had loved her for as long as he could remember—he dismissed the fact that Redden had loved her, too, because it didn't seem to him that his brother had loved her quite so much—and it had always seemed to him that she was responding to his feelings, reciprocating in her own way.

But not since Austrum had appeared. Not since his dramatic rescue of the company in the Fangs and the way he had brazenly kissed Mirai. That had changed everything.

He stayed at his post as the damp returned in a fine mist that soon morphed into a steady drizzle. Challa Nand had already determined they would keep flying through the night, weather permitting; setting down in these mountains had proved entirely too dangerous given the nature of the creatures that lived here and the terrain they inhabited. Better to stay above it all, the big Troll admonished when Railing had suggested it might be safer not to fly through mountains in the pitch-black. Better to take your chances with things that never moved than with things that never stopped moving.

Railing stepped away from his post at last, unable to stand it another minute, relinquishing the helm to Mirai. Then he went down into the hold to see if Farshaun Req was awake.

After stopping to speak with Aleppo first, Railing moved over to the old man and knelt by his side. He was, indeed, awake. Those still-sharp eyes found him in the gloom, and a brief smile crossed his lips. "I thought you had forgotten about me."

"No one could ever forget about you." Railing bent close. "You look a little worse for wear."

"I don't feel all that good, either. Where are we?"

"Somewhere inside the Charnals, flying northwest toward the Klu. I hope."

Farshaun nodded. "Mirai says you saved her life tonight. Again. Maybe you saved us all. You're becoming good at that. You saved me back there in the Fangs, remember?"

Railing shook his head in denial. "We saved each other, you and me. We were warriors, weren't we?"

"I'm not much of a warrior anymore. I'm just tired."

The boy didn't like the sound of the old man's breathing, harsh and uneven, as if he was struggling to use his lungs. Railing wished he had taken time to learn how to use the wishsong's magic to heal, as others in his family had done. But he had not, and trying anything with Farshaun now was too dangerous. "Can I get you something to eat or drink? Are you taking the medicine Mirai's been giving you?"

Farshaun grunted. "Oh, that girl thinks a potion or an ointment is the answer to everything, but she's just making it up as she goes. It's age and nothing else."

"It's arrows in your chest and arm and loss of blood. You really are a stubborn old man."

Farshaun laughed weakly. "Always was. Just kept it hidden until I got old enough to admit it." He coughed, and there was blood on his lips. "You listen to me. That girl, she's worth a dozen of you or me. She's got grit and determination that hasn't even been scratched in other people. She's got heart. And she loves you."

Railing stared. "No, she doesn't. She doesn't even like me much."

Farshaun reached out and took hold of his wrist. "You don't see things the way I do, Railing. Not about this, or about Redden, either. You've got no distance from these matters. You're too close to them. Just step back and take another look."

"She likes Austrum just now." He was uncomfortable with this whole discussion. "He's the one she wants."

Farshaun released his wrist. "You think that way if you want. No one can tell you anything, can they? Go on and get back to your post. I need to sleep. I'm too tired to think now. We'll talk again in the morning."

Railing took the old man's hand and squeezed gently. Then he lay the hand back on the other's pallet, rose to his feet, and stood looking down at the already sleeping man.

Come back in the morning? He would be back in an hour. Maybe less. Farshaun was failing.

He climbed the ladder to find Mirai and tell her so.

5

SOMETIME JUST BEFORE DAWN, FARSHAUN REQ died.

He did so quietly, making no fuss or sounds of distress or efforts to save himself. His passing did not awaken Mirai, who was sleeping right next to him. When she opened her eyes the following morning and looked over at him, his face was calm and peaceful. He seemed, she told Railing, as if he had just decided it was time. As if he had fallen asleep in mute acceptance of the inevitable and drifted away.

All of which did little to assuage her grief. She was inconsolable all that morning, distancing herself from everyone. She took her turn at the helm and worked the lines with the Rovers, but kept herself apart as she did so. She cried constantly and didn't bother to hide it. Railing saw her in tears more times than he cared to think about, but when he tried to approach her, she quickly turned away.

Later on he saw her with Austrum, standing together near the pilot box, her head buried against his chest while he held her, his arms wrapped tightly about her. Railing felt so helpless and ruined in that moment that he could barely breathe. He turned away at once, but the damage was done. He'd seen enough to know what was happening. He guessed he had always known.

But he was sensible enough not to ask her about it. People handled grief in their own way, and it was mostly a private matter. As it was, he had his own grief to deal with, and it was a complicated and debilitating process. He was riddled with guilt by what he now perceived as his failure to save the old Rover. Farshaun Req had been like a father to him, had mentored him as an airman, and had stood by him through everything that had happened since they had set out from Bakrabru all those weeks ago.

It was his fault, no matter how you looked at it, that Farshaun was dead. It was his insistence on making this journey that was responsible.

He stewed on it for the rest of the morning while going through the motions of whatever his tasks required of him, speaking a few words here and there when necessary, accepting condolences, listening to tributes, all of it a jumble of words that felt more like accusations.

The Rovers had wrapped Farshaun in a section of sailcloth and placed him belowdecks in the cold locker at the stern of the airship. Because they wanted to bury him and mark his grave, they had to fly on for a time to find a spot where this was possible. It might take them until evening, Challa Nand advised. But the body would keep well enough in the cold locker until then.

"You should say something when we lay the old man to rest," Skint said to Railing at one point. "You were close to him; you meant something to him. He would want you to speak for him. More so, I think, than any of the Rovers."

Or he would prefer Mirai, Railing had thought at the time. She loved the old man, too—maybe more than Railing did. It seemed to him that she might do the better job of it. At least she wouldn't be burdened with the guilt he carried. At least she wouldn't have to speak the words and know she could have done something to prevent the need for them.

But now, having seen her with Austrum, he wasn't sure he could ask her anything. He wasn't sure he could even speak to her without finding a way to turn it into an attack. All he could think about—when not dwelling on his guilt for Farshaun's death—was how much he wished that Austrum had never come into their lives and how badly he wanted Mirai back again, whatever the nature of the accommodation they might be able to find, so long as it didn't include the big Rover.

But he might as well have wished for time to move backward for all the good it was going to do him. All he had the right to hope for now was a reasonable end to his efforts to save Redden. If he could manage that much, he would have gotten all he was entitled to.

So when the *Quickening* set down toward sunset, descending to a broad meadow of tall grasses and wildflowers cupped in the valley of a series of massive peaks, high above sea level and well hidden from everything that couldn't fly, he turned his attention to doing what he had promised both Skint and himself he would do. With the entire company in tow, he left the airship and walked with the big Troll down into the meadow and laid Farshaun Req in his final resting place. The air was sweet and unexpectedly warm; the meadow seemed to be encapsulated in its own climate zone. Birds wheeled overhead and butterflies and bees zipped about through the wildflowers and grasses, oblivious to what those gathered were doing. Farshaun was lowered into the earth still wrapped in the sheeting, a stone marker was set in place at the head of his grave, and Railing stepped forward.

"I've never known a better man," he said, his voice resonating loud and clear in the stillness of the moment. It echoed off the peaks, sounding eerily distant and disconnected. "He was admired by everyone who knew him. He was my friend, and he understood my dream of flying airships and taught me most of what I know. He taught Mirai and my brother, Redden, too. We all loved him, and we will miss him terribly. I wish we had been able to keep him with us a little longer. I wish I had never agreed to let him come on this journey."

He paused, steadying himself. "But Farshaun was never someone who let others dictate his choices, and I don't expect I could have done so here. I take comfort in knowing he died in the place he loved most—in the air, aboard an airship, with airmen he admired and the world at his feet. I imagine he is flying somewhere now, off in the blue, off on another journey. I can't imagine him doing anything else. I will always think of him this way."

He stepped back, shaking his head, fighting the tears, drained of words and emotional strength. He stood with his head bowed as the Rovers sang a short, traditional song that was meant to speed the dead on their way to a place of safety and peace and to help the living let them go. Challa Nand closed the proceedings with a pronouncement calling on the forces of nature that inhabited and protected the mountains to take notice of their loss, and include their friend.

Then it was back to the airship, the light failing quickly now, though the air remained warm. Night was coming on, darkness speeding its way out of the east in lengthening shadows and a dimming of the skies, the winged herald of day's end. Railing trudged back to the airship with the others, walking close to Skint. He was vaguely aware of Mirai walking with Austrum, but he refused to look at her, not wanting to be troubled by their body language or wonder at the nature of their words. He was suddenly exhausted, and felt like he could sleep for a week.

"That was well said back there," Skint observed, dropping back to walk beside him. "I was right about you and the old Rover; you and he did have a strong connection."

Railing gave a desultory nod. "Well, it's gone now."

The Gnome Tracker snorted. "Oh, I don't think so. Such things survive death. They live on in the hearts of the living. They help keep the dead from being forgotten. Didn't you know that?"

He moved away. Railing walked on for another few moments, and then he stopped where he was. He watched the others move ahead of him, so despairing that he no longer wanted to keep their company. Instead, he turned around and started back toward the grave site.

"What are you doing?" Woostra asked as he passed him.

"Just spending a little more time with Farshaun," he answered, not bothering to slow. "I want to be alone with him. I'll be along."

Woostra grunted something, but by then Railing was too far away to hear it. He breathed in the unexpectedly warm air and smelled the meadow flowers and wished for things he couldn't have. He glanced at the darkening sky, but didn't mind that the light was going. He preferred it dark. He wanted to disappear.

Moments later, he was standing over Farshaun's grave. The Rovers had covered it with heavy rocks after the old man was interred, intent on protecting his remains from scavengers. Railing knelt next to it, undid the band that held his red hair off his face, readjusted it, and began to speak.

"I let you down, Farshaun," he said softly. "I failed you. I've failed everyone on this journey, and you and Mirai most of all. I should have told you about the King of the Silver River and the Grimpond. I should have been honest and up front about what I know. At least then a vote could have been taken and, if you had wanted to go back, you could have. But I didn't do that. I let you think that nothing had changed, but everything had. Everything was different."

He took a deep breath to steady himself, and now his voice was shaking. "The King of the Silver River told me that it was wrong for me to seek out Grianne Ohmsford. He told me not to try to bring her back from wherever she was, that it wouldn't happen as I hoped, even if I could manage it. The Grimpond told me she was alive and well, and I could do what I wanted, but there was something in the way he said it that warned me against it. Both creatures gave me the same message, but I ignored them. I didn't care what they said. I cared about getting Redden back again. I was afraid you and the others wouldn't go any farther if you knew ..."

"What are you doing out here?"

Mirai was standing next to him, staring down questioningly. He felt his stomach lurch. "Nothing. Just talking to Farshaun."

"It sounded like you were confessing. I heard some of it." She looked angry. "Does it make you feel better when you tell your secrets to a dead man rather than to me?"

He shook his head. "I couldn't talk to you. I wanted to, but I couldn't."

She snorted. "You couldn't? You didn't even try!"

"I started to say something, but you just turned away." He was suddenly feeling threatened. "I didn't think you wanted me to—"

"If you wanted to talk to me, you should have done so!" she snapped, interrupting him. "The problem with you is you've lost all your confidence. You don't know who you are anymore. You think too much. You talk everything to death. *What's happened to you?*"

She put enough emphasis on this last part to let him know that she was fed up with him.

"You were always the confident one, the reckless one. So much more so than Redden. He might think things over, but not you. You simply charged ahead. You dared anything. It defined who you were, but that's all been lost. I don't know who you are, but it certainly isn't anyone I know!"

"I'm still who I was," he insisted.

"Then show it!" She dropped to her knees beside him, her face right up against his. "Stop being so pathetic. Go back to acting like you have a spine."

He glared at her. "Oh, I see. You want me to be more like Austrum, is that it? I saw how he was holding you."

She shook her head and rocked back on her heels. "Austrum again. You just can't let that go, can you?" Her brow furrowed. "If you're so worried about Austrum, why don't you do something about it?"

He stared. "What do you mean?"

"You're jealous of him. You can't stand it when I pay attention to him. You hated it when he kissed me, and you suffer every time he comes near me. You think all sorts of things are happening between us. If you care about this so much, do something to change it."

"You want me to fight him?"

She gave him an exasperated look. "Try to think about this in other terms. This isn't about you and Austrum, it's about you and me. Understand, Railing? You and me! Tell me—do you love me or not? Which is it?"

"You know I love you." He brushed strands of red hair from his eyes. "I told you I did."

"Well, then, it's pretty simple, isn't it? If you love me, why don't you show it? Stop telling me you love me and do something to show it. You look capable enough."

"Do something? Do what?"

She glared. "Do I have to tell you everything?" She punched him hard on the shoulder, and then exhaled sharply. "When you want something badly enough, sometimes you just have to take it. So why don't you do that, *Railing*?"

The emphasis again, this time on his name. Bitter and demanding and something else he couldn't quite define. Urgent, perhaps?

"I don't ..."

"Are you listening to me? Why don't you just take me?"

"What?"

She leaned close enough that he could see the wildness of the emotions roiling in her green eyes. She seized the front of his tunic and yanked hard. "You heard what I said. If you love me, take me!"

"But ..."

"Take me, Railing. Your brother did!"

Had he heard her right? A wash of bright anger and shock flooded through him. He skidded from one emotion to another, all in a matter of seconds. He felt all the air go out of him, the weight of her words huge and crushing. He felt everything inside turn suddenly tense and dangerous.

She was right in front of him, waiting for him. He reached for her, pulled her into him, and kissed her hard—none of it gentle or sweet, just demanding. He kissed her repeatedly and found suddenly that she was kissing him back.

He forced her down then, onto the ground amid the tall grasses. Except for the sky overhead—now almost completely dark, with the first stars beginning to reveal themselves—the world had disappeared.

She pulled him over her. "Don't stop," she said.

And he didn't.

*

Afterward, they lay together in the shelter of the meadow grasses, night fully descended, the world silent in the aftermath of what had just happened. They weren't speaking yet. Railing was still too caught up in his feelings, still lost in a lingering sense of wonder and contentment. He dozed for a time. When he woke, Mirai was pressed back up against him, and he found himself wanting her forever, determined that he would never let her go again, not for a single moment—but wondering at the same time if such a thing were possible.

Then he remembered what she had said about Redden, and some of the joy left him. He knew he should leave the matter alone, but he couldn't make himself do that.

His hand covered hers. "I always wondered about you and Redden."

He felt her shrug. "Maybe you should have asked him about it."

"We never talk about you. Not in that way."

"You sound like you think I might be shattered if you did. I wouldn't, you know. I'm pretty strong."

"I know." He was silent a moment. "What you said about Redden and you . . ."

"It never happened."

He was caught off guard. "But you said . . ."

"Forget what I said. You needed a little nudge, so I provided it." She looked back at him over her shoulder. "Sometimes, you just have to know. You have to find out."

"So you made it up?"

"Have you ever wondered how I can tell the two of you apart so easily?" she asked. "It's because of the way you act around me. It's not the same. You probably don't realize it, but you're always eager and he's always restrained. One or two sentences, a few words even, and I know which is which. Sometimes a look is enough. Or the way you move."

She turned over to face him. Her hand reached up to stroke his face. "You haven't been right since Redden went into the Forbidding. You lost yourself for a while, lost everything that makes you who you are. The way you fussed about Austrum? We talked; that was all. He's interesting because he isn't afraid of me. He lets me know right away what he's thinking. Kissing me was bold. I liked that. But he's not for me."

Railing couldn't help himself. "And I am?"

She looked away. "I don't know. I'm not sure about you. You're still out there somewhere, hiding out, keeping apart. You haven't come all the way back, even now."

"But this . . . what we just . . . "

"That isn't enough. Don't you see? It's just something that happened. Yes, I wanted it to happen. I did. But it was just what I said before—a finding out."

He locked down everything he was tempted to say and put it all in a safe place. He breathed in the scent of the grasses and the night air and looked up at the stars.

"I want more of you than you've given me," he said. "I want a lot more. Maybe I want everything. I'm saying this to you straight out because I don't want you to think I would ever take what just happened lightly. I understand what you're telling me about myself. I know you're right. I've gone way off into the woods, and I can't seem to find my way back. But I will."

She was silent a minute, then she got to her feet. "We shouldn't be out here like this. We might not be safe. Besides, I'm getting cold."

He rose with her. He tried not to look at her, but failed miserably and was filled with an aching that worked its way from his exposed skin right down to the deepest part of his heart. He desperately wanted to hold on to her, but he didn't know if he could.

When they were ready to set out for the airship, Mirai suddenly turned back and faced the grave. "Just a minute." She clasped her hands in front of her. "Good-bye, Farshaun. Thanks for teaching us so much. Thanks for believing in us and always being there. You had a good heart. Railing and Redden and I will miss you every day."

She paused. "And don't be offended by what happened between Railing and me. I think it helped us both to cope with your loss. I think if you could tell us, you would say that you approve."

She turned away again, not bothering to look at Railing. "Come on, let's go."

As they walked back toward the *Quickening*, Railing decided to do what he should have done days earlier—what he knew instinctively she expected him to do if he loved her as much as he claimed. He told her about his meetings with the King of the Silver River and the Grimpond. He told her everything he had been keeping secret from her and held nothing back. He opened himself up and let it all come out. He did it in a clean, straightforward way, being as honest as he could about what he thought it all meant and how it made him feel.

"I knew what I was doing by hiding all this," he said when he had finished. "I knew it was wrong, that I was being selfish and arrogant. I just couldn't accept having to turn back because no one else felt as strongly about finding Redden as I did. But I couldn't face the prospect of going into the Forbidding after him, either. I can admit that now. The idea terrified me. Finding Grianne Ohmsford seemed the better choice. I convinced myself of it. If I had it to do over, I might make the same choice again. I can't say I wouldn't. Redden means everything to me."

"And you thought I didn't feel as strongly about him as you do?"

He shook his head. "I didn't know. Well, I guess I did. I didn't think you would turn back. Not really. But if it was just you and me, how could we manage? We need the airship to carry us and the others to help sail it. I was afraid that, if you knew, you might think you had to tell them. I just couldn't risk it."

"But now you've changed your mind? Why?"

"You know," he said.

They reached the ship and climbed the rope ladder, which apparently had been left down for them. One of the Rovers on watch grunted an acknowledgment and pulled the ladder up after they were aboard. They said good night to him, and together they walked to the empty pilot box and sat down in front of it, shoulder-to-shoulder, staring out at the night.

"I don't much like you for being so self-centered," she said after a few minutes, "but I understand why you did it. And at least you're telling me now. I appreciate that."

He looked into her eyes, forcing himself to meet her steady gaze. "In the morning, I'll tell the others."

She shook her head. "No, I don't think that you should. It doesn't matter now. We've come too far. No one's turning back at this point."

"But they should know. I have to tell them. It's bad enough I didn't do so before."

"It's bad you didn't. No argument there. But you won't accomplish anything by telling them now. Farshaun gave his life for this quest. Everyone believes in it, and it would be wrong to take that away from them. Besides, you don't know for sure what the warnings mean. Or even if they're real. You don't know what's going to happen."

She reached across and gripped his arm hard. "You've committed us to this thing, and you can't back out of it now. We have to keep going."

They stared out at the stars for a few moments. Railing tried to think what he should say, but it was Mirai who spoke first.

"You're looking at our task in the wrong way. You're thinking only of Redden. Find Grianne, bring her back from wherever she is, and maybe she can save him from the Forbidding—that's your plan. But there's more at stake now than there was in the beginning. The Ellcrys is failing; the demons are breaking out of the Forbidding. Everyone in the Four Lands is at risk. Bringing Grianne back to face the Straken Lord is about more than helping Redden. It's about helping everyone. Maybe Grianne can do something to stop the Straken Lord; maybe she can prevent him from invading the Four Lands."

"If she even exists," he said.

"Don't talk like that. You're the one who thinks she does. That's why we all came with you. You better not stop believing now."

He drew back defensively. "Don't worry. I won't."

She shook her head, as if uncertain of his answer. "She was a powerful witch before she left Paranor and disappeared. Everyone knows the stories about her. But that was a long time ago. We just have to find out if she still is. We have to hope she can help."

She paused. "We need you to return to the way you once were. We need you to be strong for the rest of us. We've lost all but two of the Druids, and neither one of those is here to lead us. We've lost Farshaun. There's no one else. You're the leader. You're the one we all look to."

She went silent again, this time for much longer. The Rovers on watch traded positions fore and aft, walking past like ghosts in the darkness. Railing tried to imagine what would happen if his efforts failed and he had to go into the Forbidding and find Redden by himself. He would do it, of course. He would do anything for his brother.

Except give up the girl sitting beside him, he thought suddenly.

Or would he even do that for Redden?

He glanced over and away again, quickly. "I won't say anything to the others. We'll just go on like nothing's different, like everything will work out."

She gave him a look. "Nothing is different. Not where this quest is concerned. And everything *will* work out, one way or the other."

He felt scolded and turned away. "I guess it will."

He felt her eyes on him, cool and appraising. "I'll say it one more time. We all need you to be who you were when you left Bakrabru. The man Farshaun knew. You got back to that a little while ago, in a small way. Don't forget what it took."

He almost smiled at the implication, but managed with some effort to remain expressionless.

She stood. "I'm going to bed."

He scrambled up. "Can I . . . uh, maybe . . . ?"

She gave him a hard look. "What do you think?"

He twisted his mouth into a grimace. "I just wanted you to know that I still . . . " He couldn't finish.

She stepped close and kissed him on the cheek. "See you in the morning."

He watched her walk over to the hatchway and climb down the ladder. He waited for her to come back out again, even knowing she wouldn't. He spent a long time in the dark, looking at nothing, thinking about her.

None of his thoughts were particularly constructive, but he enjoyed examining them nevertheless.

6

A PHENGLOW ELESSEDIL WAS RUNNING HARD. She had given up on Cymrian, leaving him to follow as best he could. He was too badly wounded to keep up, but she had thrown caution to the winds.

The Federation had taken Arling!

She couldn't make the words sound real. That Arling had been given over to their enemies so willingly was inconceivable, however well intentioned Sora and Aquinel's decision. Why had they been so ready to act without knowing more about who Arling was? They had barely bothered to make an inquiry before handing her over and ridding themselves of the burden of caring for her.

Aphen ran faster, propelled by shock and rage. The sodden earth squished muddily beneath her pounding boots, hindering her efforts. She could see east across the fields ahead to where the forest encroached, forming a dark wall. The Federation airmen were in there somewhere. They would have landed their vessel where it could not be readily discovered. That assassin would have wanted it concealed while he took his creatures and came hunting for her. She saw his face in front of her, twisted with hate as he died. She remembered how hard he had tried to kill Cymrian. Could the people who had come with him—the Federation airmen and their captain, still aboard the ship with Arling as their prisoner—be any better?

She was closing on the forest when she saw the Federation warship rise above the treetops into the rain-clouded skies.

She screamed out Arling's name, not caring that she might be heard, but knowing it did nothing to help. She summoned the Druid magic at once, bringing it raging and furious to her finger-tips, gathering up its threads and weaving them into a cohesive whole. She would burn that airship out of the sky! She would incinerate those who had taken her sister, just turn them all to ash, make them sorry they had ever been born!

Gasping, shaking in fury, she raised her arms and extended them, fingers pointed at the warship. Then slowly she lowered them and began crying silently. It was no good. Her magic wouldn't cause enough damage to matter. The vessel was too far away.

And even if it could, would she really destroy it in midair with Arling aboard? Would she risk her sister's life like that?

She knew she wouldn't. She stood helplessly, watching the airship disappear into the horizon, headed east across the Tirfing.

Seconds later Cymrian was beside her, his eyes on the ship as it slipped farther away in the grayness. "Did you see any flags or pennants?" he asked.

She shook her head. "I was too busy dredging up a magic that wouldn't serve any purpose to be bothered with something that might." Her words were edged with bitterness. "I'm sorry."

She didn't know why she was apologizing except that she

should have done better when she'd had the chance, and this was just one more example. She wiped at her eyes, feeling empty and lost inside. "We have to go after her, Cymrian," she said. "We can't give up."

He put his arms around her and held her against him. "We are going after her, and we're not giving up. We'll get her back."

She was not sure if she believed there was any real chance. Arling was on her way to an unknown destination. Even if they discovered what it was, they would still have to find her. The Southland cities of the Federation were unfamiliar to them; they wouldn't know where to begin to look.

No matter the risk of discovery, she knew she would have to use the Elfstones, or Arling would be lost to her.

Cymrian had stepped away and was searching the countryside. "We'll need a skiff or horses, whichever we can find first. Come on, we've got to hurry!"

They set off again, with Cymrian leading the way, heading east in the direction of the Federation vessel, which by now was out of sight. Aphen followed obediently, not knowing what else to do, having no better idea of where to go and hoping that her protector did. They crossed the fields parallel to the woods ahead and soon encountered a river. Cymrian stopped once more, cast about for a moment, then turned upstream. In a short while they came to a narrowing in the river and a wooden foot-bridge.

"Did you know this was here?" Aphen asked in surprise as they started across. "You did, didn't you?"

He shrugged. "I know the Westland pretty well."

"Where are we going, then?"

"A town called Marchand, just a few miles ahead. We should be able to find what we need there."

They continued on, and although she was drained to the

point of exhaustion, Aphen kept going. It couldn't be any better for Cymrian, who had fought a fierce battle that would have killed most men only hours earlier. And if he wasn't complaining, then she certainly wouldn't.

It took them less than an hour to reach Marchand—a bedraggled little village of huts and cottages occupied mostly by farmers and herdsmen, situated at the edge of the Tirfing astride a tributary of the Mermidon. Cymrian took her through the village and down to a stable at the north end, where he made a bargain with the owner to purchase two horses. He looked them over first, inspecting hooves, mouths, and withers, and added in saddles and bridles before paying. Where he had gotten the coin, or even why he had it on him, was something Aphen didn't need to ask. It didn't matter so long as it was there and served the purpose.

They were about to leave when Aphen pointed to Cymrian. There was blood all over his clothes, and they were badly torn. Cymrian hadn't even noticed. And Aphen wasn't looking much better, as the Elven Hunter pointed out. He talked the stableman out of two cloaks hanging on a rack. The man handed them over without a word.

It was late in the day by now, but Aphen did not want to stop to sleep. She wanted to leave at once. And after a bit of an argument and a little foot dragging, Cymrian agreed.

So they rode through the night, traveling east across the plains in the general direction of the big Southland cities and Arishaig, in particular. Because of what the assassin had said before he died, they expected that Arling would be taken to Edinja Orle. Likely, that meant the Federation vessel would fly to Arishaig, where the Orle family kept its residences and the new Prime Minister would have been installed.

They lasted until after midnight; then it became apparent that neither could go any farther. A combination of exhaustion and accumulated damage had rendered them incapable of continuing without serious risk of further injury. They found a grove of trees where they could shelter themselves and the horses, rolled into the blankets they had added to the tack before leaving Marchand, and fell deeply asleep with barely a word to each other.

Even so, they were awake at sunrise, rested enough to be able to continue and anxious to be off.

"We have to determine where they've taken her," Aphen said as they ate a little of the provisions Cymrian had bought along with the blankets. "I don't think we can assume anything."

"You want to use the Elfstones?" he asked.

"I think I have to."

"It's a big risk."

"It's a necessary risk."

He didn't argue the point. He had always been good about that. She brought out the pouch that contained the Stones and dumped them into her palm. They glittered brightly, even in the dim morning light. She studied the talismans for a moment, remembering how she had managed to use them to seek out the missing Elfstones, and then began thinking of Arling. She took her time, picturing her sister's face until the image burned in front of her, and then she brought the magic into her hands in a roiling blue light and sent it flying away.

It was a reassuringly familiar experience. The light exploded into the hazy morning, spearing through shadows and gloom, covering miles in seconds, all across the width of the Tirfing to the walls of a giant city—one much bigger than Arborlon. The light vaulted the city walls and arrowed down wide boulevards, angling off into smaller streets and narrow alleyways, all the while burrowing deeper and deeper into the city's core.

Finally, the light reached a black tower that soared above the buildings around it, intimidating in both size and appearance. Stark walls of blackened stone were buttressed with parapets and iron railings and gargoyles looking down on those bold enough to pass beneath, their expressions hungry, as if searching for victims.

The light entered the building and wormed its way to a bed-chamber where Arling Elessedil lay sleeping in white sheets and warm blankets, to all appearances safe and secure.

Then the light flashed once and died away.

Aphen and Cymrian stared at each other. "She looks to be all right," Aphen ventured, "but where is she?"

"She's in Arishaig." Cymrian shook his head doubtfully. "I think maybe Edinja has her tucked away in that tower. You're right; she doesn't appear to have been harmed. But that doesn't mean she's safe."

"Do you think something might happen to her before we reach her?"

"I think no Elf is particularly safe in that city. Especially a young girl in the hands of Edinja Orle."

Aphen didn't care to speculate further. "Then let's go find her."

They packed and saddled their horses and set out once more. They rode all day, and two more days beyond that, in the direction the magic had indicated, keeping a steady pace save for when they stopped to rest and water the horses and eat and drink something themselves. Aphen was driven by a fresh sense of urgency. Knowing Arling was being cared for helped assuage her worries, but still she felt a desperate need to reach her sister before anything happened to change all that. If she was in the hands of Edinja Orle and the Federation, nothing could be taken for granted.

It was the night of the fourth day since the crash when the walls of Arishaig finally appeared in front of them, the rough stone surfaces lit by hundreds of torches burning down from the ramparts and up from the outer edges of the moat that surrounded the city. A roadway wound through rugged terrain and past freestanding watchtowers and lines of burning torches that directed travelers up to the city gates—a clear indication of which way those coming into the city were supposed to go.

Cymrian reined in his weary mount and peered ahead. "The gates are open. They'll let travelers come inside, even at night, because they're not at war."

Aphen settled back in her saddle. "What do we do once we're inside?"

Cymrian shrugged. "Find a tavern, have a few glasses of ale, and make a plan."

He spurred ahead, and Aphen couldn't tell if he was joking or serious. They rode onto the approach road and past the guard towers. No one challenged them, even though both could pick out the tower guards keeping watch over the countryside. They weren't stopped until they reached the city walls, where the portcullis was lowered even though the big iron gates stood open.

A pair of sentries walked up to them. "Names and the nature of your business," one said in a bored voice, barely looking at them as he readied a record log.

"Deris and Rodah Merring," Cymrian answered at once, not even glancing at Aphen. He had pulled his recently acquired cloak tight around his shoulders to hide his bloodied clothes. "My wife comes to help her sister give birth to her first child. We'll visit with her family for several days and then go home after the baby comes."

The sentry glanced at Aphen and then looked down again, writing. "Your wife's family's surname?"

"Caliphan." Cymrian looked at the other sentry. "Quiet tonight, is it?"

The man shrugged. "Tonight and every night."

"Quiet on the road, too."

The man ignored him.

The first sentry had finished writing and nodded to the second, who called to someone inside the towers bracketing the entry to raise the portcullis.

When the opening was clear, Cymrian clucked and his horse moved through. Aphen dutifully followed. "Your wife, is it?" she said quietly, once they were out of hearing.

Cymrian looked flustered. "They're less likely to be suspicious of a married couple. No reason to give them any cause to ask more questions than they need to."

They rode into the city proper, traversing streets of all sizes and configurations, most lined by a mix of businesses and residences set side by side. There were people about, even though it was after dark, the city buzzing with the steady drone of voices punctuated by bursts of laughter and occasional shouts. There were carriages and other single riders, but most walked at the edges of the roadways along narrow paths. The torches that shone from the building entries and lighted rooms beyond were smokeless. Everything looked clean and new and sterile. Aphen searched for trees and found only a few.

"I don't like this place," she said at one point.

Cymrian nodded. "They see things differently here. Not in the Elven way."

Eventually they reached a different section of the city, one less pristine—rougher and with everything jammed together. Cymrian took them to a stabling service where they quartered the horses. Shouldering their packs and blankets and tightening their cloaks anew about their tattered clothes, they set out on foot into a district thick with taverns, gambling halls, and pleasure houses.

"What are we doing here?" she asked him after they had walked for some distance.

"Looking for someone."

"An Elf?"

"A Rover who works for Elves."

The crowds were growing thicker and more rowdy, with prospective patrons pushing and shoving one another, trying to get into the establishments that offered whatever entertainment they were seeking that night. Their talk was raucous and their laughter wild, and Aphen found herself in such close quarters she didn't even want to breathe the air.

They stopped finally before a heavy wooden door with a small sign that read LOCKSMITH in florid black, the writing shadowed by a red stripe. Cymrian knocked once, very loudly, paused, then knocked twice more softly.

No one answered.

Cymrian repeated the knock sequence, but still no one appeared. "He must be out working," the Elven Hunter announced, stepping away from the door and looking up at the front of the building to the darkened windows above. "Probably until very late."

"Who is it we're looking for?" she asked him.

"His name is Rushlin." He looked around expectantly. "We'll have to find somewhere to spend the night."

"Can't we just do this ourselves?"

"Go after Arling? No, we can't."

She glared at him. "I don't like the idea of waiting. Anything could happen to her while we're sitting around."

"I realize that. But both locks and wards likely protect the place where she's being held. We need someone who either knows or can find out what we're up against."

She took a deep breath. "Rushlin?"

He nodded. "It's what he does. We'll come back in the morning and put him to work. He'll know better than you or I what's needed to reach Arling and bring her out safely. Come along."

Taking her arm in the way a husband might his wife's, he maneuvered them back out into the crowds milling about the streets, but in a more forceful and direct manner so that others were quick to step aside.

"What are you doing?" she snapped, trying to free herself.

"Appearances matter down here," he replied, eyes darting left and right as he chose their path. "Our behavior determines the nature of our relationship. So stop struggling and laugh a bit. Just pretend."

They worked their way up the street they were on, down one alleyway that connected to another and then on for several more blocks to an inn called Port Arms Redoubt, its sign decorated with a military crest that Aphen did not recognize.

"We stay here," he told her, opening the door for them.

"We can do better," she pointed out, looking around doubtfully.

"Much. But remember who we are supposed to be and how we should look to those around us. We are not people who can afford to do better or even care about where we stay. We just want to get into bed with each other."

He squired her up to the innkeeper's desk, requested a room in a decidedly salacious manner, patting her rump possessively as he did so. He signed the register with a flourish, gave the innkeeper a knowing wink, then wheeled Aphen away from the desk and practically dragged her up the stairs to the second floor.

When they were in their squalid little room with its single bed, its worn chest of drawers, and its rickety wooden chair, she gave him a look. "You enjoyed that."

He sat down on the edge of the bed and looked at her.

"Maybe just a little. Look, I did what I felt I had to do in order to prevent the innkeeper from thinking we were anything other than a man and a woman out for a good time. There are dozens just like us passing through this fine establishment, so we fit right in. He will already have forgotten about us. We don't want him talking about us while we're here, and we don't want him remembering us after we're gone."

She stared at him a moment. "You've done this before, haven't you? You know all about it."

He shrugged. "I know how to blend in. I know how to pretend to be something I'm not. I learned that when I was spying for the Home Guard. I was sent to the Southland cities to find things out, and I had to disguise who and what I really was from everyone around me. Sometimes for months." He paused. "And, no, I haven't done this before. Not this *exactly*. I was always on my own."

She nodded quickly, chagrined by her outburst. What was wrong with her? He brushed at his white-blond hair and watched her closely. "Are you hungry? Do you want to get something to eat?"

She stood where she was, studying him some more. "I know barely anything about you. We've been together for weeks, and I know next to nothing."

He looked away. "You know what matters. You know why I'm here. Arling told you, didn't she?"

"Yes."

"Do you want something to eat?" he repeated.

"No. I'm too tired to eat. I just want to sleep."

He got up from the bed immediately. "Lie down. I'll sleep on the floor."

She shook her head. "No, I don't want you to do that. Stay in the bed with me. It's cold in here."

He lay back down and she scooted against him, arranging their cloaks to cover them both. She could feel his warmth through her clothing.

"That's better," she said. "Put your arms around me."

He did so, saying nothing, but she could feel the tension in him. He didn't seem to know what to do with his hands, so she put them where she wanted them. "Just hold me. I want to feel good about something. I'm tired of feeling wrung out and lost."

They lay there for a long time without talking, allowing the warmth they generated to infuse and wrap them about. Aphen listened to his breathing, to the rustling he made with little changes in his position. She felt him pressed up against her from behind, and it gave her a sense of peace and well-being.

"I'm sorry I've been so difficult," she whispered into the darkness.

"Would you mind if I kissed you?" he asked.

"No."

So he kissed her on the back of her head and then on the side of her face and then on the mouth before pulling back. "I would like it if you really were my wife," he said.

She was on the verge of saying she didn't think she would mind it either, when she found herself remembering Bombax. She felt a sharp pang of guilt, or perhaps only sadness. Her promised, her partner, her lover—dead such a short time ago. It gave her pause. It suddenly felt strange to be thinking of Cymrian when she had just lost Bombax. Yet the Borderman was gone, and he was not coming back. And she had come to love her protector, perhaps as much as he loved her. She had kissed him fiercely when he had gone off to face Stoon and his mutants. She had been so afraid she would lose him, too.

Was there good reason to mourn Bombax any longer than she already had? How long was long enough?

"We could pretend to be husband and wife," she said quietly. "Why don't you kiss me some more?"

So he did as she asked. His kisses were slow and sweet and welcome, and she let them continue without pulling away.

Then she began kissing him back, and suddenly neither one could stop.

When she woke, he was turned away from her and she felt the cold that the separation had left between them. She took a moment to study him in the pale dawn light—the lines of his face and the strength in his features—before rising. She found herself captivated by what she saw, drawn to him with fresh need, warmed by memories of what they had shared. But last night was gone, and Arling needed them.

There was a basin on the chest of drawers, and she splashed some of the water it contained on her face to help wash away the sleep. She went to the dingy window and looked out and wondered when her life would ever become something she valued again.

They ate breakfast on the street from a food cart and walked back to the shop they had visited the night before. It was still early, but neither gave a thought to waiting just because Rushlin had been out late the night before. Finding Arling was far too important for delays, and they had already lost the better part of four days.

Cymrian knocked in the same sequence he had the previous night, and this time the door opened almost immediately.

"I knew it was you," the man standing there announced. "I could smell you."

He was young and smooth-shaven with dark hair and quick, anxious eyes that kept looking around as he waited for them to enter. He had a fox face, sharp-featured and narrow, all planes and angles. For someone who had been out and about for most of the night, he was surprisingly alert and rested looking.

"We came looking for you last night," Cymrian admitted.

"I was working," the other replied. "Come in and sit. I've made some tea."

They went into a small sitting room with a work desk and some chairs and sat. Rushlin brought out a worn tea service and filled the cups. For a few moments they said nothing, enjoying the aroma and taste of the tea.

"A green tea," Aphen ventured.

"Good guess. What is it you think I can do for you?"

Cymrian told him, giving a full and careful description of the building they were looking for. "We need to get inside. But we can't be caught going in or coming out."

Rushlin whistled. "That's Edinja Orle's residence. Why don't you just find a cliff and jump off and be done with it? Word is, no one who goes into that building uninvited ever comes out again."

Aphen gave him a look. "My sister is in there."

He shrugged and smiled. "Then you can be the exception that disproves the rule, I guess." He glanced over at Cymrian. "Are you sure about this?"

"If you can point out the building and tell us a way to get inside. Or even if you can't."

Rushlin nodded, his features crinkling. "Like that, is it?" He gave them a conspiratorial grin. "Hope it doesn't lead to tragedy. I'll need today to find out what I can about possible ways to get you in. Getting out will be up to you."

He stood, and they did the same. "Come back a few hours before nightfall. You won't want to try entering that place until dark anyway. Find something to do. Take a carriage ride in Federation Square. Visit the museum of culture; that's always good for a laugh. Go be a tourist. See the sights."

He led them to the door and ushered them out. "But stay away from all things Edinja until you come back here. What you're trying to do will require that you stay in one piece. At least going in."

He closed the door with a small wave, leaving Aphen and Cymrian staring at each other.

7

ARLING ELESSEDIL WAS WRAPPED IN A WARM cocoon of sheets and blankets and near darkness, and it took her a long time to decide that she needed to open her eyes and look around—and that was only after what felt to be an endless sleep. She experimented first with moving her fingers and toes, arms and legs, and finally her head from right to left before taking the plunge. She could feel small twinges in her body—especially her back—from injuries she knew she had suffered when the *Wend-A-Way* had exploded into flames and fallen into Drey Wood. But she could also tell that her wounds had been treated and were healing beneath the bandages wrapped about her body.

When her eyes overcame gravity and drowsiness sufficiently for her to open them, she found herself in a beautifully furnished bedroom with drapes pulled tightly across the windows to keep out the light. The stone-block walls were whitewashed and layered with colorful tapestries and large paintings. Everything was very quiet—so quiet she could hear the sound of her own breathing. She lay motionless and expectant, cautious in this strange place, using her senses to see if she could detect another's presence while taking everything in with slow, methodical care.

But she was alone.

She thought back to the crash that led to this moment, remembering the explosion, the flames, the feeling of the ship tumbling earthward, and the terrible certainty that she was going to die. She remembered seeing Aphen clinging to the back railing where she had fallen after using her magic against the Federation warship. She remembered Cymrian close to her.

After that, it was all a collection of snippets and glimpses. She remembered nothing of the actual crash. What she recalled next was the sound of Aphen's voice and the feeling of sharp pain as objects were removed from her body and wounds were closed. She was weak and disoriented, and she couldn't tell if she was dying or not. She went in and out of deep slumber and a dark interior seclusion, where she hid and waited for a reason to emerge. Two pairs of boots came and went, worn by people whose voices she heard but whose faces she did not see. Hands lifted her and she was placed in a wagon that bore her away, wheels creaking and traces jingling.

Then she was in darkness aboard an airship; she remembered the rocking motion and the sounds and smells of the wood and iron. People came and went, but no one spoke to her or touched her. She was alone then for what seemed on reflection to have been a very long time.

Now she was here, in this bedroom, and she had no recollection at all of how she had gotten here, how much time had passed, or even where she was.

She wondered what had become of Aphen and Cymrian. Why weren't they there with her? Or were they, and she simply hadn't realized it? But that didn't feel right. Too many other things had happened where they were not present. She had become separated from them, and she needed to find out why.

Abruptly, she remembered the silver seed the Ellcrys had given her to carry to the Bloodfire. She had concealed it in a leather pouch and strapped the pouch under her cloak. She moved her hands over her damaged body. She was no longer wearing the clothes she had been traveling in when the *Wend-A-Way* had crashed. She was wearing a nightgown of soft linen.

And the pouch with the precious seed was gone.

She couldn't believe it. Even though she knew it made perfect sense that it would have been taken with her clothes, she couldn't accept that it was gone. She searched herself frantically, hands feeling all through the bedcovers and over her body, desperate to find the missing seed.

She went still the instant the door latch released and the door swung open to admit a dark-cloaked figure backlit by the daylight that until now had been shut out of the room.

"Awake at last," a woman said softly. "I've been worried about you. You've been asleep for five days."

She let the door close behind her—as if perhaps she felt more comfortable in the dark—her slight form returning to the shadows. "How are you feeling?"

"Fine," Arling answered, forcing her hands to move slowly back to her sides. "A little sore."

The woman stopped at the Elven girl's bedside, looking down from inside the hood. "You suffered dozens of wounds, but they seem to have been treated by someone who knew what they were doing and are healing nicely. Do you know who treated you?"

Arling almost told her, but something stopped her. "No. I was unconscious. Where am I?"

"You are in my home." The woman's voice was warm and welcoming. She pulled back the hood of her cloak to reveal a beautiful, fine-featured face with startling eyes and silver hair. "You were found in Drey Wood by the captain and crew of one of our vessels and brought here. What happened?"

Arling hesitated. "I was in an airship crash. I don't remember much after that. But there were people with me. What happened to them?"

"I don't know. A man and woman brought you to where my airship was anchored and asked the captain if he would take you somewhere safe."

A man and a woman. The shoes. She felt a chill go through her. "These people didn't say if there was anyone else?"

The woman shook her head. "I don't think they had much interest in anything but getting you off their hands. Peasants, from the sound of things. Would you like a drink of water?"

Without waiting for an answer, she moved over to a table set off to one side, poured water from a pitcher into a cup, and brought it back to the bed. Reaching behind Arling with one arm to brace her, she helped the girl into a sitting position and let her sip the water, careful not to give her too much or cause a spill.

Arling, for her part, was grateful for the water and for the time it took the woman to bring it over while she fought to get her shock under control. Was it possible that everyone else was dead? But wouldn't this man and woman have discovered any bodies? Wouldn't they have said something? Or would they have kept quiet because the less said the better?

"Who were you traveling with?" the woman asked, setting aside the water and seating herself next to Arling on the side of the bed. "Were they family or friends?"

Arling couldn't help herself. "My sister."

The woman shook her head in a gesture of regret. "Well, we must hope for the best. I will do what I can to find out what happened to her." She rose abruptly. "It's best if you sleep some more. Let me come back a little later and bring you some food. For now, just rest."

"Wait!" Arling called out. "Did you take my clothes?"

The woman gave her a sharp look. "Yes. I still have them."

"Was there anything with them? My pack?"

"No. Just your clothes, and they are ruined. I've already thrown them out."

She wheeled away and was at the door before Arling could say anything more, her dark form silhouetted against the light as she opened the door. "You should rest now."

Arling gritted her teeth. Her sister and Cymrian were missing and maybe dead. The Ellcrys seed was gone. She was injured and miles from anyone she knew. It was then, for the first time, that it occurred to her she might not have been rescued, but captured by the very people the *Wend-A-Way* had been fleeing. She might not be a patient, but a prisoner.

"Who are you?" she called out to the woman.

"A friend," the other replied, pausing in the open door. "Just go back to sleep."

Arling started to get out of the bed. She needed to have a look outside her room; perhaps that would tell her something. Or maybe if she could have just a peek through one of the windows . . .

But almost immediately the woman was back at her bedside, gently pushing her down. Too weak to resist, Arling fell back again. She was surprised to find herself so listless. She seemed to have no strength at all. She looked up at the figure bending over her, and suddenly she was afraid. Something in the other's eyes, in the sharp edges of her face, in the set of her mouth, warned her.

"Go to sleep," the woman whispered.

Arling's eyes were already beginning to close, and she could feel herself slipping away. The last thing she remembered thinking before she dropped off entirely—so quickly she seemed to fall asleep mid-thought—was that this woman was not to be trusted.

Edinja Orle walked out of the bedroom and down the hall a short distance before stopping to consider her impressions of Arling Elessedil. The girl was young, but she wasn't stupid. Already she suspected things were not as they seemed; Edinja had seen it there at the end in her eyes, heard it in her voice. The gentle approach she had planned to use to unmask her secrets was not going to work. Time's demands did not allow for it.

There was no question that Arling was hiding something. But Edinja wasn't sure what. She'd admitted to having a sister and had been straightforward enough about what had happened to them in Drey Wood, but there was something else going on, something Edinja didn't yet understand.

She took a moment to recall what the captain of her warship had reported on arriving back from Drey Wood. They had engaged the Elven ship in combat after tracking it, losing it and finding it again, and then they had brought it down. Stoon and the mutants had left the ship to track down the survivors, but none of them had returned. Finally, not wanting to go himself—Edinja's interpretation of things from the way the captain squirmed while telling this part of his story—he had dispatched two members of his crew. When they returned, they told him that Stoon and all three mutants were dead, and their uneasy looks and whispers made it clear that they were done with this business.

But then, just as they were preparing to lift off, a husband and wife had appeared with a wounded Elven girl lying in the bed of a cart. The couple, clearly farmers or foragers, had asked if the captain knew the girl or could take her to people who did. The man, in particular, seemed anxious to have her out of the way. The captain, not entirely a fool, realized what he had—one of the two Elessedil sisters whom they had been hunting. He might have gone back to look for the other or their protector, but he would have had to go himself at this point because his crew had already made it plain that they were having none of it.

Deciding, therefore, that a bird in the hand was worth more than the two still in the bush, he had carried the girl aboard and headed for home.

But Edinja had warned the captain personally before he had set out that she wanted both women alive and under her control. He had been charged with making certain this happened, even if Stoon did not. So his assumption that she would settle for half a loaf was a big mistake.

Still, there was nothing to be done about it now. While she had expected to have both sisters brought to her—she didn't care one way or the other about their protector—she would have to settle for the one. Because of her age, she knew the one she had must be the younger, the one that was a Chosen in service to the Ellcrys.

Arlingfant.

That meant she wasn't the one carrying the Elfstones. The older one—Aphenglow, the Druid—would be doing that. So why was this one so concerned about her clothes and her pack? The clothing had been searched and discarded. But the pack was missing, lost or left behind. Had there been something of value in it?

She would have to wait to find out. For now, the girl would sleep, and the drug Edinja had added to her water would do its work.

She thought momentarily about Stoon. She would miss him in some ways, but none that truly mattered. He had his uses and his strengths, but didn't they all? She would have had to rid herself of him sooner or later, and she always felt bad about having to do it herself. This time it had been someone else's doing, and even though she had always known it would end like this, she could take some comfort in the fact that she hadn't been the one to wield the weapon.

What she wondered now was whether or not the older sister and her protector were dead, too. That would prove more troublesome because it meant the Elfstones were likely lost, as well. And she would have to send someone back into Drey Wood to the wreckage of the Elven vessel to search for the bodies of the Druid and the Elven Hunter and the talismans, as well. She was already thinking of whom she might choose to do this.

Once, the choice would have been easy. It would have been Stoon.

"Poor Stoon," she murmured.

She went off to prepare for the girl's awakening—if she had calculated her dosages right, it would be about an hour from now—knowing that her approach must change. But first she would feed Cinla her favorite treats.

Arlingfant didn't know how long she slept after the nameless woman who was caring for her had left, but when she woke again the woman was sitting on the bed beside her. "There you are," she said. She smiled, but there was no warmth in the expression. "Tell me your name."

"Arlingfant Elessedil," Arling replied at once, even though she hadn't intended to.

"And your sister's name?"

"Aphenglow Elessedil."

"And your protector's name? The Elven Hunter who accompanied you on your journey?"

"Cymrian."

She couldn't seem to help herself. Whatever the woman wanted to know she was willing to tell her. No, it was more than that. She *needed* to tell her. She was *compelled* to answer, and answer truthfully. She was horrified. Why was she doing this?

"It's the drink I gave you," the woman said, noticing her change of expression. "It puts you to sleep, and when you wake you find yourself unable to do anything but speak the truth. It's a combination of drugs and magic I concocted some time ago. Rather useful."

She leaned forward, the smile gone. "So we can dispense with games and get on with being truthful with each other. You know who I am, don't you? You must have suspected, and now there can be no doubt. Say my name."

"Edinja Orle."

"There, that wasn't so hard. Now all the introductions and identities are out in the open. Are you thirsty?"

"Yes," Arling replied, cringing. She said it because it was the truth, but she didn't want any more of what Edinja had already given her.

The sorceress rose, walked back to the table, and poured a fresh cup of water. She glanced over her shoulder at Arling. "This isn't what you drank earlier. This is pure. Untreated. You've had enough of the other to serve my purposes. Do you still want it?"

"Yes."

Arling took the water and drank it down, suddenly desperate to cool her throat. She hated what was happening, what this woman was doing to her, but she couldn't make herself stop responding.

Edinja sat down again on the side of the bed. "Now tell me what was in your pack that you don't have with you anymore."

Arling fought to keep from giving the answer. "I don't have a pack."

"Yes, I know. You lost it or left it behind or whatever. What was in it?"

"Nothing."

Edinja was momentarily confused, but only momentarily. "Never mind the pack. What were you carrying that matters so much to you?"

Now Arling had no choice. The words came unbidden. "A seed from the Ellcrys tree."

Edinja stared. "How did you come by such a seed? Why would you have something like that in your possession?"

"The seed was given to me by the tree."

"For what purpose?" Suspicion reflected in Edinja's eyes now. "Why would the tree give you its seed?"

Arling hiccuped when she tried to change the answer she was compelled to give. She was suddenly having trouble completing her sentences, the result, she assumed, of her efforts not to say anything. "The Forbidding is failing and the demons imprisoned ... are breaking free. The Ellcrys ... must be renewed by the magic of the Bloodfire. I have been chosen ... to make this happen."

A long silence followed. Edinja looked away and then back again. "How did this happen?"

Arling didn't know what to say, the words catching in her throat. Edinja reached out and slapped her hard across the face. Arling jerked away. "The tree is dying! She must ... renew."

The sorceress rose and stalked about the room for a time, stopping once to pull back the curtains and peer out the window. "What happens if the seed does not reach this Bloodfire you speak about? What happens if the tree dies?"

Arling had lowered her head in shock from the slap, her eyes filled with tears. "Then the creatures of Faerie ... imprisoned there ... come back out into the Four Lands."

"They would kill us all if that happened, wouldn't they?" Edinja murmured, mostly to herself. "Can the Druids stop this from happening?"

"No."

"Only this seed you carry can stop it?"

"Yes."

"Except you're not carrying the seed anymore, are you? Where is it?"

Arling shook her head. "I don't know. I had it ... before the crash. Now it's gone. I thought ... you took it."

Edinja turned away. "Someone took it. That much is true." She walked away again, then turned around slowly. "Let's consider your sister's situation. If she's alive, what will she do once she finds you missing?"

Arling squeezed her eyes shut as she gave her answer. "She will come looking ... for me."

"Exactly what I thought. She will come looking for you. A smart young woman with Druid skills and magic. She will figure out where you are and come to Arishaig to rescue you. From me." She laughed. "Won't that be convenient?"

Arling lurched up on one elbow, fighting to hold on to the words she wanted to speak. "Don't hurt ... her. Don't."

Edinja walked over and pushed her back down again. "You should be worried about yourself instead of your sister. You should be worried about what might happen to you."

"If anything happens ... to me, the Ellcrys ... dies."

Edinja made a dismissive gesture but said nothing. Arling swallowed hard. "Doesn't the captain ... or any of those ... who brought me here know what happened ... to the seed? Or to my sister?"

"Perhaps." The sorceress pursed her lips as if considering. "They said nothing of it to me, but they might be hiding something. Frightened men often do that. Should we go and find out? At least you could be doing something useful while we wait for your sister to appear. I think you can handle doing this much to help move things along, don't you?"

She hauled Arling out of bed by sheer force, bundled her into a robe, and put slippers on her feet. She was strong for someone so slight and managed the task easily. With her arms locked about the girl, she guided her from the room and down the hallway to where a panel in the wall concealed a massive iron door that opened into the interior of the building. A stone stairway spiraled downward into darkness and disappeared into a pool of impenetrable gloom.

Edinja gave Arling a friendly squeeze, as if they were close friends off on an adventure. "I don't think you're ready to attempt such a dangerous descent without help, let alone make the long climb up again after we're done. I'll have you carried."

She reached into a niche beside the doorway and produced a small bell. Holding it out over the stairwell, she rang it three times. Then she returned the bell to the niche. Together the sorceress and the girl stood waiting.

A flaring of torchlight within the darkness accompanied a slow tromping of footfalls.

When the creature appeared, Arling very nearly bolted. It was vaguely human, but mostly something less—a huge semi-human with blunted features and listless movements. It climbed into view with slow, measured steps, as if repeating from clouded memory a process it had gone through many times but did not entirely understand. It did not glance up at them or seem to look anywhere at all. It carried its torch held out before it, but stared straight ahead as if light were unnecessary. There was an emptiness to its gaze that was frightening.

Edinja said something to the creature in a language that Arling had never heard. Then, after passing the torch to the sorceress, it abruptly picked up Arling without even looking at her. Cradling her in its huge arms, it began to descend the stairs once more. Arling, too frightened to struggle, let herself be borne into the depths of the building.

Edinja walked in front of them, holding up the torch so that the gloom was at least partially dispelled. "Stay calm," she said to the girl. "He won't hurt you."

Arling didn't believe this for a moment, but she was still too weak to do anything to help herself, and certainly nothing that would allow her to escape. So she steeled herself and kept her eyes averted from her bearer's blank expression and empty eyes.

The descent seemed to take forever, each step measured by another footfall. At the bottom of the stairs they passed down a corridor that ended at a huge iron door. Arling could hear sounds from behind the door—grunts and squeals and guttural mutterings that suggested things more animal than human.

Edinja touched a series of studs on the door, and it swung open with a ponderous groan.

Arling gave a small gasp.

The room was cavernous and gloom-filled, but there was no mistaking its purpose. Chains hung from racks, and cages lined the walls. Metal tables were scattered across the room, many with sharp blades and tools of extraction resting on their bloodied surfaces. Fluids ran down funnels into drains and buckets. More creatures resembling the one that bore her were shambling about the room, moving slow-footed and witless. In the back of the room, men in cages screamed and begged, gripping the bars or sagging in postures of hopeless dejection.

Edinja directed the creature carrying Arling to the back of the room where the cages holding the screaming, moaning men were bolted to the floor. They saw her approach and began calling out to her: *Lady, Mistress, please help me! Release me and I will never return. Please, I beg you, let me go. What wrong have I committed? Why am I here?*

They seemed to be addressing Arling, their attentions turned to her rather than to Edinja, their hands reaching through the bars as if to grasp at the chance they thought she offered.

"Here are the members of the ship's crew, the ones who brought you to me, eager to be of service." Edinja motioned for the creature to put Arling down. "Ask them what you wish. If they have an answer, they will be most willing to give it to you."

Arling was so horror-stricken she could barely get the words out. "Why are they here? What have they done?"

"They disobeyed me. This is what happens to those who don't do as I ask." Edinja seemed impatient. "Now, don't waste my time. I brought you here so you could find out something about your sister. This is your chance. Ask your questions."

Arling turned to the men. "Do any of you know what happened to my sister? Or to the other Elves?"

The muttering was pronounced. *Nothing, Lady. They are fine and well! No, they weren't even there! We never saw them! They must be safe by now! They killed those creatures we brought aboard—they looked like this one. And the man Stoon. We saw them dead, my mate and I. No one else! Please! Believe me!*

So it went, words spoken in desperation, answers tinged with fantasy and lies, all of it useless. Arling turned away. "Can they be set free?" she asked Edinja without looking at her.

The sorceress shrugged. "I will give it some thought."

But she wouldn't. Arling could tell from the way she said it. "Can I speak with the captain of the ship?"

Edinja Orle gave her a sympathetic look. "That might be rather difficult."

She took the girl by her arm and steered her across the room to a table. Another of the creatures was fastened to it, bound by leather straps, limbs splayed across its metal surface, head pulled back, mouth open. A funnel had been forced down its throat, and it was gagging on the metal end lodged in its windpipe and quaking as if with a fever.

Beneath the table, a huge ginger moor cat, its colorings starkly beautiful, was gnawing on a piece of meat.

Edinja reached out and extracted the funnel. The creature did not look at her, its eyes fixed on a point somewhere between the table and the ceiling of the room. It had the look of a dead thing, as if any spark of what had made it human had been leached away.

Arling cringed, suddenly realizing who it was.

"Captain," the sorceress said, "have you remembered yet what happened to this girl's sister?" She waited a moment. "No? What's wrong? Cat got your tongue?"

Then she looked over at Arling and began to laugh.

8

ORIANTHA SAT WITH TESLA DART ATOP A ridgeline perhaps a mile distant from the sprawling camp of the Straken Lord's army. Sunset was approaching, the surrounding landscape stretching out its shadowy fingers from the east as the skies slowly darkened and the lighter gray of daytime changed to twilight. She was weary and footsore, and she would have liked a bath. But there was no water for bathing and no respite for sore feet save rest and sleep. She wasn't tired from the journey's length so much as its circuity. Unwilling to trust to a straight line of travel that would have had them trailing along like obedient dogs, she had opted instead for brief forays around the army's flanks and all the way forward to where Tael Riverine flew a dragon at its head, trying to discover where in the Forbidding they were going. Admittedly, she'd had help from Tesla, who scurried left and right with unbridled energy and seemingly endless fascination with the whole of the countryside and those passing through it. But even so, she refused to let the Ulk Bog bear the entire weight of this effort and so had inserted herself into the equation to shoulder an equal share of the burden.

Now, many hours later, she was ready to sit right where she was for as long as the light remained and then hopefully get some sleep. But it wasn't a given that sleep would be permitted her—or, at least, any sort of useful sleep. Tesla Dart had dispatched the Chzyks—including the Ulk Bog's favorite, Lada—a few minutes ago, sending a handful of the little creatures down into the enemy camp to see if they could pinpoint the location of the cage imprisoning Redden Ohmsford. If they were successful and if the conditions allowed for it, she would leave after midnight to attempt a rescue.

She was momentarily distracted as Tesla Dart leapt up and dashed off into the distance, weaving her way through clusters of rocks and clumps of thorny brush, a small wiry shadow in the disappearing light. Oriantha watched her until she was out of sight, wondering what had attracted Tesla's attention this time and how she could manage to muster the effort to go look. The shape-shifter had spent some of that day asking Tesla about the Ulk Bog people, thinking to learn something about her in the process. But what information Tesla Dart was willing to share was dispensed in sudden, brief bursts that ended almost before they began and did little to provide any useful insights.

Mostly, it appeared, Ulk Bogs were like gophers or moles, living in burrows and eking out a living through foraging and thievery. Tesla's uncle, Weka Dart, who had befriended and aided Grianne Ohmsford when she had been trapped within the Forbidding decades earlier, had been the Straken Lord's Catcher once, but it was unclear what his niece had been doing beyond waiting for Grianne to come back into the land of the Jarka Ruus.

Although why Tesla would do this or even expect it to happen was baffling.

Not that it mattered. Weka Dart's history was incidental to what was occurring, and Oriantha was nothing if not pragmatic. She had remained behind in the Forbidding when she had been given the chance to escape because she could not abide leaving Redden Ohmsford behind when there might be a chance to help him. She had lost her mother and thereby her reason for coming on this expedition. Going back now offered no resolution to her rootless life. If anything, it felt like a betrayal. Her mother wouldn't have gone back; she would have kept going. Just as she had with Khyber Elessedil—right up until the very end. Could Oriantha do any less and still live with herself?

Of course, there was more to it. She wanted to free Redden Ohmsford—even though they had only just met and she had no real attachment to him—because she was fond of him and did honestly want to help.

But what she wanted most was revenge on Tael Riverine.

For her mother.

For the other members of the ill-fated company.

For the inhabitants of the Forbidding.

This creature—this so-called Straken Lord—had ruled the Jarka Ruus, the denizens of his world, for decades and perhaps centuries and had done nothing to help them. Tael Riverine's sole achievement was to gain domination, and his sole objective was to procreate so that his line could continue to rule. She found it repugnant in both demonkind and humankind. There was no suggestion of advancement or enlightenment or useful purpose. There was only the promise of raw power exercised by one ruler so that it could be bequeathed to others.

A good part of her outrage was derived from her connection with the creatures imprisoned here. She was more of an outsider in her own world than she was in this one, and her sense of kinship with the Jarka Ruus was strong. Like her, they were different, and their differences set them apart. But in this world she was just one of many, and all of them very much in the same situation. In her world, she belonged to a tiny group of mutant creatures who were mistrusted and disliked and set apart from the much larger populations of Men, Elves, Dwarves, Trolls, and Gnomes. There, she lived a life in the shadows, disguising the truth about herself.

It didn't escape her that the creatures of the Forbidding lived the same sort of life here—the same sort of persecuted existence—that she lived in the outside world.

She might not be able to do anything about an entire world in which her fate was subject to the prejudices of the general population, but perhaps she could make a difference in a world in which a single individual's removal could change everything.

She was toying with these thoughts as Tesla Dart reappeared from out of the increasing gloom, chattering away.

"Furies, dozens of them. Roaming the boulders and brush like vermin. Hate those Furies, I do. Mindless killers." She gave a look over her shoulder as if to make sure the Furies weren't following her. "Want to make sure. They could see us, come for us."

"They won't bother," Oriantha told her. "They serve the Straken Lord for now."

The Ulk Bog made a rude noise. "Serve themselves is what they do. All teeth and claws and no brains." She gave a noticeable shiver. "Keep them far away, shape-shifter. You listen."

Oriantha was listening, but she was not particularly worried. She could manage Furies if they found her. Shape-shifters were clever and resourceful. When you could become anything—even the air you breathed if it was dark and hazy enough—there wasn't much that could harm you unless it got very close or caught you unawares.

Suddenly Tesla Dart squealed and leapt up excitedly. "Lada returns! Come, Lada! Come, Chzyk! Tell me all! Here to me, Lada!"

The lizard raced across the open ground and leapt into the Ulk Bog's arms, where the latter proceeded to pet and rub the little creature in fond welcome. Lada turned around and around, raising and lowering his scaly head and tail, and generally doing everything he could to make himself available for the other's welcome attentions.

Then he began to chirp, and Tesla Dart chirped right back, the two engaging in a conversation that had all the elements of a comedic parody. But apparently each understood the other, for when they had finished Tesla put the Chzyk down again and turned to Oriantha.

"This is no good, shape-shifter girl," she said solemnly, shaking her head for emphasis. "Tael Riverine has put boy in cage at camp's center, next to tent where he sleeps. Boy is watched closely. Guards right by him. You go in, even at night, they catch you quick."

"How many guards around the cage?" Oriantha asked. "Exactly."

The Ulk Bog chattered at the Chzyk once more, and the little creature responded in kind. "Four, one on each side. Goblins. But demon-wolves loose in camp near cage, too."

Oriantha nodded, considering. "No worse than what I thought."

"You don't do this," the other pleaded. "Let this be. You wait. A better chance comes later. Do this now is foolish!"

"This whole business is foolish if you stop to look at it too closely." Oriantha sat back and regarded the Ulk Bog solemnly. "Let's wait until it gets dark and take another look at it then."

In fact, she stayed where she was until after midnight,

sleeping several hours in between, eating a little something and staring out across the wilderness to the fires of the Straken Lord. She watched the shadows in the firelight, tracking their movements, immersing herself in the flow of the camp. She breathed in the night air and centered herself for what lay ahead. She had already decided she was going after Redden, in spite of Tesla Dart's warnings. Her chances were far better in a crowded open place than if she were forced to enter a confined space with only one way in and out.

She looked at the sky and waited for moonrise. When the orb appeared in an overcast sky, slipping out from behind clouds and mist, it was only a small crescent and the light it shed was pale and weak.

She stood up and looked down at Tesla Dart, who was staring up at her with wide eyes and a look of disbelief.

"I'll need Lada to show me the way. Will you allow him to do that? Just to take me as far as the cage?"

Tesla nodded mutely, her face stricken.

"Wait for me until you see the army begin to move out again. If I am not back by then, go your own way. Leave all this behind and have no regrets. This is my choice. Any consequences that attach are mine to bear."

"This is a mistake!"

"It is my mistake to make," Oriantha said.

The Ulk Bog gave her a desperate look. "Wait, then. I have something." She fumbled in her pocket and finally produced a small key. "Take this. If you find boy, you will need it. Tael Riverine fits him with conjure collar to keep him from using magic. Key will open lock and release collar."

"How do you happen to have this key?" Oriantha asked, suddenly suspicious.

"Weka gave it to me. He kept it after he was dismissed as

Catcher. If he was imprisoned, he knew he would be fitted with collar, too. He would not allow such. Use it to free boy."

Oriantha took it and tucked it into her tunic. "You are a constant source of amazement, Ulk Bog."

"You are a fool!" the other snapped. "Please, don't go! You will end up like the others. You will not come back!"

Oriantha bent over and kissed the little creature on the cheek. Then she was gone into the night.

Redden Ohmsford lay huddled in his cage, rolled into a ball in an effort to escape the creatures that took every opportunity to shake the iron bars of his prison or reach inside to torment him. They came in all shapes and sizes, all types and forms—things he had not only never seen but also never imagined. They screamed at him—howls and shrieks that caused his skin to prickle and his stomach to clench. He was made physically ill from the harassment, his insides roiling, bile rising to his throat, but there was little he could do about any of it. By staying in the center of the cage with his body tightly balled up, he could just avoid their grasping fingers and claws. By closing his eyes, he could almost pretend they weren't there. But nothing really helped.

There were guards on each side to keep his tormentors at bay, but they showed little interest in doing so. The Straken Lord had come by to look at him only once since the day ended. He had not spoken a word. He had watched his minions torment the boy, then moved on.

Now, with darkness fully descended and the world around him gone fiery with torchlight, the smoke from the burning brands acrid and thick in the air, and the sounds of the camp an undiminished cacophony, Redden Ohmsford, already beyond despair, was just waiting to die. He no longer had any hope of escape or rescue or intervention on even the most basic level.

His death was assured, and he had reached the point where he would welcome it.

Somehow he kept from crying out, even though the urge was so strong it threatened to break free in spite of his efforts to hold it in. But it was the one aspect of his life he could still control, and he was afraid if he gave in to it, he would be lost entirely. So he went deep into his mind and dredged up tiny scraps of memories that he had all but forgotten and tried to re-create them fully. If he worked at it hard enough, it took him away from his immediate surroundings and placed him in a softer world of better days.

It didn't save him entirely, but it allowed him to stay reasonably sane. It gave him respite from his misery. It allowed him small moments of time in which to regroup.

But it wasn't enough and he knew it.

The smells and sounds of the camp invaded his cage. The stink of the Straken Lord's creatures and their animals—especially the monstrous wolves that prowled the perimeters of his cage with their rangy muscular bodies, bristling hides, and glowing eyes—as well as the stench of the raw, bloodied foods that fed the army permeated the air. Chains rattled and traces creaked; wagon wheels rumbled through the camp—great iron-rimmed wooden disks that could crush anything unfortunate enough to fall in front of them. Breath steamed in the cooling air. Raucous laughter, screams, and shouts rose and fell with the power of an ocean crashing over rocky shores.

Redden's thoughts were of Railing and home, but they were disjointed and confused, and one memory bled into another. He could feel them re-forming—an amalgam of separate and distinctively different shards forming a larger, more cohesive creature that was false in most respects. But even realizing what was happening, he refused to let go. If he could not manage to separate out the bits and pieces that were real, he would settle for the imagined whole that wasn't. Building on it in the darkness of his mind, with the horror all around him closing in, he could feel himself disappearing a little at a time, becoming steadily more removed from the reality of his life. In his musings, in his re-created memories, he found relief and sanctuary of a sort that demanded only that he let go of the real and embrace the imagined.

He found it to be a small trade-off.

Yet he was strangely detached from the process. He could feel his mind going, could sense the erosion of his sanity, but was too weary and too beaten down to stop it from happening.

Just let this end, he begged into the dark.

Just let it be over.

Oriantha left the shelter of the rocks running in a low crouch, not wanting to be caught silhouetted against the horizon even though the sky provided little more than a dim skein of starlight from scattered breaks in a heavy blanket of clouds and mist. She moved swiftly, keeping on a direct course as she went. She was not yet close enough to the Straken Lord's camp to be worried that she might stumble on any of its members, but Tesla Dart had warned of prowling Furies and she sniffed the air as she went, trusting her shape-shifter instincts to warn her of the vicious little beasts.

Because if they found her, she was finished.

But she did not believe this would happen. Her confidence was high and her determination strong. She would find Redden Ohmsford and she would bring him out of his prison to safety before the night was over. For she had her own Furies buried deep inside, and they were every bit as dangerous as the real thing.

She was still some distance from the perimeter of the camp when something small and dark flashed by her boot. A second later Lada was in front of her, standing on his hind legs, chirping softly. He watched her for a moment, then dropped down on all fours and scurried away. Quickly he was back again, peering up at her.

She understood. He wanted her to follow.

She smiled. In spite of all her predictions of doom and gloom, Tesla Dart had sent Lada to lead Oriantha into the camp and to the cage of Redden Ohmsford.

She changed then, discarding her human form, turning into a phantasm composed of shadows and smoke. She was transparent and amorphous as she moved down through the darkness toward the camp, a shapeless gathering of detritus from fire and dust. Lada scurried on ahead of her, zipping first one way, then another, always careful to make certain no one was looking and to choose a path cloaked in shadow.

It was a long journey to their destination, and more than once Oriantha thought she had been discovered by one of the enemy. A head that was lifted and swiveled, searching. A voice that paused in mid-sentence and went still as eyes shifted warily. A near collision that was avoided only by her quickness. A shriek or a snarl that signaled a suspicion all was not right.

On each occasion, she was in danger of discovery. Her shape-shifting abilities had their limitations. So long as she remained untouched by a living creature, she could remain hidden from view. But if she were bumped or grabbed or just brushed against even for an instant, her disguise would fail and she would be revealed. If that happened, she would have no chance. She was stronger and quicker than most, but she was surrounded by enemies who would overwhelm her by sheer numbers long before she could get clear of them.

She pressed ahead nevertheless, wafting through the Jarka Ruus as if she were just a part of the campfire smoke. She followed Lada, but tried to choose paths that were less crowded and more easily navigated. She had gone into a mind-set where she was exactly the thing she was pretending to be, all the way down to lacking real substance or cohesion. It was extremely taxing, requiring intense concentration. She had carried off this particular effort before, but not when the risk of discovery was so great or when the time required for maintaining the disguise was so protracted.

The minutes dragged. Lada kept going, darting here and there, a quick bit of movement beneath boots and clawed feet and iron-rimmed wheels. Oriantha expected the Chzyk to be crushed at any moment, but he always managed to avoid the worst. At one point, he darted so far ahead that Oriantha lost sight of him completely, and was then cut off by a clutch of Goblins that crossed her path while hauling weapons and supplies. She was forced to wait until she could get clear of the crowd before trying to continue, advancing blindly through the masses, trying to maintain the same direction, searching for something that would tell her where to go.

But then Lada reappeared, coming back for her in a series of short rushes that took him through scores of creatures, stopping long enough to let her see him before turning back again and darting off.

The hunt continued for almost an hour. The Straken Lord's camp was huge and his army massive. Stopping and starting again was frequently necessary. Detours and changes of direction were mandated by a continual shifting of the positions of the creatures all about them. But they pressed on, Oriantha managing her disguise and keeping her eye on Lada until time lost meaning and her thoughts were of nothing but continuing her advance.

When it finally reached a point where it seemed her ordeal would never end, Oriantha stumbled into a cluster of tents that included one so large she was certain she had found Tael Riverine's quarters. Seconds later she rounded a tent wall—and there was the cage, with the crumpled form of Redden Ohmsford inside it.

She stopped where she was, pressed close against the canvas as she watched Lada rush toward the cage then veer off sharply as one of the prowling wolves wandered too close. Oriantha could see the danger of trying to do more. Even if the Chzyk managed to leap into the cage to allow the boy to see him, he would be completely visible to anyone looking in. A quick snatch of a hand or snap of jaws and it would be over. Oriantha held her breath as the Chzyk tried to approach the cage a second time. This time one of the wolves turned its head toward the little creature and sniffed the air, growling deep in its broad chest.

Lada had endured enough. He darted back to where Oriantha hovered in her smoke-and-dust form and looked about for her. Then, having done what he had been sent to do and having no way to reach the cage that held the boy, he scurried back the way he had come and was gone.

Oriantha held her position by the tent wall, studying the movements of the wolves and the Goblin guards. The guards remained stationary when they weren't chasing away the curious and the troublesome, but the wolves roamed aimlessly through the entire area surrounding the cage and what she was assuming to be the Straken Lord's tent. She could find no pattern to their movements, and it was impossible to know from one moment to the next what they were going to do. If she attempted to reach the cage, she would have to react to their wanderings and sudden changes of direction spontaneously.

It was an incredibly dangerous situation. One mistake and the game would be up. One small bump against one of those wolves and she would be revealed.

But she had known the risks before she set out and had come too far to turn back now. And looking at the slumped figure of Redden Ohmsford, she thought she was probably too late in any case. She hadn't seen him move since she had found him. She hadn't seen any sign of life at all.

Still, they had him caged, and that meant they were keeping him a prisoner. So he must be alive.

She knew she was thinking too hard about what she needed to do and should just get on with it. Tightening her disguise and dropping farther into her shape-shifter mind-set, she eased away from the canvas wall of the tent and moved toward the cage.

Right away one of the wolves stopped where it was and began to sniff the air. Nervously, Oriantha slowed but did not cease her forward movement. She kept easing ahead through the smoky light, all darkness and wafting gray haze, indistinguishable from the air. The wolf sniffed about a few more times before losing interest and resuming its wanderings. None of the other wolves seemed to have detected anything. But they growled and snarled at one another and anything else that came too close, enough so that even the Goblin guards shifted uneasily at their positions in front of the cage.

But just as it seemed she might reach the cage safely, she sensed that something was out of place. She slowed further, her instincts sparking inside her shape-shifter form in tiny bursts, too strong for her to ignore. There was magic at work—a strong magic—and close at hand. She reached out for it, seeking its source. Not the wolves or the Goblin guards, she decided. Nor was it attached to anything moving; it was stationary, but very close. Her attention returned to the cage, and she moved right up to one corner, staying between the guards on either side as she peered in, able to see Redden Ohmsford clearly and note the tiny movements of his body as he breathed.

He *was* still alive.

Her gaze shifted to the door of the cage, situated right behind the Goblin on her right. It was fastened in place by a simple hook lock and chain. Much too easy to break apart if someone strong enough attempted a rescue.

Then she scanned the cage again. The magic she had sensed was recognizable now. It encased Redden Ohmsford's prison from floor to ceiling and wrapped the iron bars front-to-back. She couldn't be completely certain what it might do if disturbed, but she could take a reasonable guess. Try to force your way past it, and a reaction of some sort would follow.

She backed away. Her choices were simple. She could ignore the magic, force her way inside the cage anyway, and take her chances. She could give up her disguise long enough to pull the boy out of his imprisonment, then attempt to reapply it so that it covered both of them and steal him away before the guards and the wolves overwhelmed her.

Or she could back off and wait for another, better chance, hoping that at some point in time she would find one. She could leave Redden Ohmsford to his fate and hope he would survive it.

She held herself perfectly still while she considered. Her strength was already depleted by the long struggle to get this far. She believed she could get out again, even carrying Redden, but not if she had to break him free and fight her way out.

Slowly, reluctantly, she backed away from the cage, realizing she must do the one thing she had told herself she would not do.

But how could she leave him?

*

Inside the cage, Redden was deep inside his mind, neither asleep nor awake, but in a state that took something from each. He was remembering a time when he was very little and had become separated from Railing while playing in the yard. He had gone off to look for him. Had he found him? Or had he become lost himself and subsequently found by his brother?

Still searching for the elusive fragments of his memory, he was awaked by a violent commotion just outside his cage. He snapped back into the present, the memory gone in a heartbeat. He lifted himself on one elbow and peered out to see a tremendous fight between two of the wolves and one of the Goblin guards. The guard was down and his body was already ripped open in several places; his blood was everywhere. No one was trying to do anything about it, but then who would be bold enough to get between the dying Goblin and the wolves?

He closed his eyes and lay down again. What did any of it matter?

Then he heard a voice speaking to him in a whisper so soft he almost missed it.

Redden. Don't give up. I am close.

He took a quick, startled breath.

The voice belonged to Oriantha.

9

EDINJA ORLE HAD ARLINGFANT CARRIED FROM the cellars to the upper levels of her home and deposited in her former room. The girl was nearly hysterical, shaking and sobbing uncontrollably, barely able to keep from falling apart completely. Shocked by what she had witnessed in the building's cellars, horrified that men could be altered in the ways Edinja had mastered long ago, she was clearly terrified that the same thing might happen to her. That was the point, of course. Edinja wanted the girl frightened enough that she would prove compliant when it was necessary.

She locked the door to the bedroom as she left and beckoned to the serving woman who was standing just outside on watch.

"Give her fresh water in two or three hours. Make sure it comes from there." She pointed to the ceramic pitcher on the table across the way. "Otherwise, keep her locked in."

She walked the hall to the main staircase and started down. She had given as much time to this matter as she could spare. As Prime Minister, she had duties and obligations to fulfill. A general meeting of the Coalition Council was scheduled for midday, and she would be expected to give an address. What she would say was problematic, but she was beginning to get an idea of what might best serve to further her current undertaking. In any case, it would be hours before she could return here.

As she descended the staircase, she was thinking ahead—well beyond this day or even this week. Ahead to when she had Aphenglow Elessedil in her power and the Elfstones in her grasp. Ahead to when she had located and dispatched whoever had stolen the Ellcrys seed and claimed the seed for herself. Ahead to when she could begin to see all her planning and scheming and manipulating result in the goal she had set herself many years ago.

Domination over not only the Federation but the remainder of the Four Lands, as well.

It was an end toward which she had been working long before she became Prime Minister of the Federation, or even before she knew for certain how she would achieve what she was trying to accomplish. Like most members of the Orle family—or at least those who practiced magic—a certain mysticism governed her decisions and actions. It was in the nature of magic users to rely on the unseen and the unknown. It was a sort of trust in the belief that if you wanted magic to perform in a certain way badly enough and you were willing to put aside what was said to be impossible, you could always find a way.

She supposed, in that respect, she was not so different from Drust—save for the all-important fact that she had the means and the skills to achieve what she wanted, and he didn't.

On the next level of her descent, she turned down the hallway and went to her personal quarters. Her bedroom was lavishly decorated with fine furniture, carpets, silk throws, tapestries, and paintings. Racks of clothing filled a series of deep alcoves that lined one wall, and a bureau made of teak and black maple displayed bottles of exotic liquids. Cinla was sprawled on her sleeping pad at the foot of her bed, but she lifted her head as Edinja entered.

"Beautiful Cinla," she cooed as she reached down to stroke the cat's silky neck and ears. She spent some time giving her special attention, speaking soft nothings to the big moor cat, listening to the sounds of pleasure she made at her touch.

When she was finished caressing Cinla, she moved over to her clothing racks to choose a garment for her appearance before the Coalition Council. She was vain and prideful and not in the least reluctant to admit it. She knew how to sway men and women to her cause and how to keep troublemakers at bay. And how she looked was a part of the process.

She dressed slowly, thinking about all she had accomplished over the past ten years and reveling in the sense of satisfaction it gave her.

It started with her experiments at changing humans into creatures that could better serve her purposes. Such efforts had been a part of the Orle canon of magic through the centuries, but she had managed to advance the study to heights previously unattained. Not only did she discover a combination of chemicals and magic that would create obedient servants, but she also found a way to turn them into thinking creatures capable of making decisions within the framework of a set of commands she provided in advance.

It took years to achieve this. It took countless experiments— all of which ended in failure but nevertheless brought her ever closer to her goal. She was a skilled and powerful sorceress, and her ambitions were buttressed by her firm belief that the ends justified the means. Expendable lives were plentiful and cheap in Arishaig, especially among the poor, and she was never at a loss for human subjects on which to experiment. She was willful and determined, and the lives of others had never meant much to her. If you weren't a member of the Orle family, you were a lesser life-form. Other people were there to be used in whatever ways she saw fit. Other people didn't really matter.

The real breakthrough in her efforts had happened by accident. She had mixed magic and chemicals as usual, but at some point in the effort both got away from her and produced an entirely unexpected result. She ended up with a creature that could change shapes at will. It could be anything it wanted. Even better, it was incredibly smart. Unlike almost all of the others, it was capable of independent thought and action. It knew how to weigh choices and make decisions. It could reason and act on that reasoning.

Best of all, it was loyal to her—totally devoted and obedient to her commands.

She knew at once what she wanted of it, exactly how it would be used. For a long time she had been looking for a way to get a spy into the Elven hierarchy. A well-placed spy in Arborlon would give her access to secrets of state and magic that would help advance her own interests. There was no way a Southlander could accomplish this, but her changeling creature could.

So she sent it to take the place of someone who would have access to information she might want. She had familiarized herself with the Elven royal family long before and chose her victim carefully. She had no idea at that point in time exactly what sort of information she was looking for, so she gave her creature a set of parameters on which to rely, a sort of checklist of possibilities. She taught it to communicate using the arrow swifts, and to distinguish between those dispatched by her and those from a handful of others she trusted to act as go-betweens. She sent it there to live out its life, to serve as her eyes and ears, to become her surrogate in her incessant search for ways to acquire power.

For two years she waited in vain for the one important discovery that would change everything. She learned much about the royal family and the members of the Elven High Council. Now and then, something would happen that gave her fresh hope. But none of it ever came to anything.

And all the while, she sought to re-create the mixture of magic and chemicals that had produced her greatest success, but she could not. She tried everything, heedless of the number of failures, the lives sacrificed. Some of those victims found death quickly, and some found it through enduring unspeakable perversions, lingering pain, and eventual madness. It was all the same to Edinja. Nothing she did produced the results she wanted, and the detritus of her failed efforts was washed down the drains and out into the sewers.

But now, out of the blue, a miracle had occurred. The miracle had really begun weeks earlier when her creature discovered, quite by accident, that Aphenglow Elessedil had found something important enough during her search of the Druid Histories for her to hide it in her clothing and take it from the archives. An attempt to steal it from her while she sat reading it later that same night failed, as did several later attempts. But whatever it was had taken Aphen to her grandfather, the King, in an attempt to gain possession of the Elfstones, and it had brought a Druid expedition into the deep Westland which had resulted in most of the order being exterminated.

Now there was this business of the Ellcrys failing and its seed being presented to Aphenglow's sister and then having been stolen—possibly by the couple that had found her and brought her to the unfortunate captain and crew of the Federation warship that had carried Stoon and her three mutants in search of the sisters. The crumbling of the Forbidding, the dying-off of the Ellcrys, and a desperate effort by the Elves to put the wall back and keep the Faerie creatures imprisoned from breaking free—it was all connected in some way, and she was going to find out how.

She finished dressing and studied herself in the mirror. Severe, proud, and beautiful in a cold sort of way; she was looking at a woman who was very much in control of her own fate.

She smiled. Of one thing, she felt certain. Good things were coming her way.

After Edinja Orle departed the bedroom, Arling Elessedil waited several minutes before she quit pretending. She waited for the snick of the lock on the door, counted to one hundred, and then quit crying. Not that she wasn't distraught and frightened; she was. She just wasn't quite as hysterical and out of control as she wanted Edinja to think she was—not after all she had been through in the past few weeks. She had never been the sort to give in to her fears; never the kind to panic and lose control. But letting the other woman believe she was completely terrified might cause her to let down her guard.

Arling sat up on the bed and took a deep breath. All that screaming and crying had hurt her throat, but she wasn't about to drink any more of the water—or any other liquid, for that matter—until she was out of this house. She knew whatever she was given to drink would likely contain more of the same stuff she had already been fed—a drug that would make her tell Edinja anything she wanted to know. As of right now—she had decided this on her way up from the cellar and its horrors—she was done doing what Edinja Orle wanted. Before the day was over, she was going to find a way out of there.

But a slow, careful inspection of the bedroom was not

reassuring. There was only the one door. There were windows, but they were locked, and iron bars were affixed to the stone of the walls on the other side of the glass. There appeared to be no secret doors or hidden panels. The ceiling was too high for her to reach it without a ladder, and there didn't appear to be any openings in any case.

Momentarily defeated, she sat back down on the bed and tried to think it through. There had to be a way.

But she was in an impossible situation. She was trapped in this room with no way out. She could do nothing but wait for the return of the woman who was keeping her prisoner and would do the same with Aphenglow if she got the chance. Arling was frightened her sister would use the Elfstones to come looking for her and, in the process, end up in the same situation. She couldn't let that happen. She had to escape and find Aphen first. But she had no idea where Aphen was or how to go about finding her.

She had to find the missing Ellcrys seed, too, and she had no idea how to do that, either. She didn't even know for certain what had happened to it.

She could eliminate several possibilities, however. Aphen wouldn't have taken it and then left her; she would have stayed with Arling no matter what. It was a good guess the captain of the warship and his crew hadn't taken it, either—not without Edinja finding out. Not after what had been done to them. So that meant it had been left behind in the wreckage after she had been thrown clear, or stolen by the couple who had carried her away and left her with the Federation warship.

One of them, she remembered suddenly, had been called Sora.

She shook her head as if doing so might clear away all the confusion. Time was running out. She tried not to think about it, tried to shut it out of her mind and just concentrate on the problem closest at hand. She needed to get free before she could find her sister, find the missing Ellcrys seed, find the Bloodfire, and do whatever she could to put the Forbidding back in place.

She sagged back on the bed, fingers knotted against her mouth, realizing suddenly what she had just done. Without meaning to—but without any hesitation at all—she had just embraced the fate the Ellcrys had ordained for her. Even in spite of her determination not to, she had let her thoughts take her down that road.

All the way down.

She began to cry again, and this time it was real.

Three hours later, as the daylight darkened with a fresh onslaught of storm clouds that had moved in from the north, roiling and churning across the expanse of the Prekkendorran, the bedroom door opened. The servant woman carrying the pitcher of treated water stood in the opening for long moments, her free hand on the door, clearly ready to slam it shut again if the need arose. She saw the figure lying on the bed, wrapped in blankets with her head on the pillow, unmoving. Even then, she hesitated, obviously not wanting to take any chances.

Finally, seeing no movement at all, she entered the room, and Arling leapt out from behind the open door to strike her a heavy blow and knock her unconscious.

Arling then lowered the section of the bedpost she had managed to remove and set it aside. She dragged the unfortunate servant around to the other side of the bed where she could not be seen, took a moment to look around the room to see if anything seemed out of place, and then moved quickly to the door. She peered out cautiously and found the hallway empty.

Without further hesitation, she burst through the door and ran for the stairway.

*

In another place entirely, a disgusted but determined Oriantha trekked along the rocky flatlands of the Forbidding in the wake of the Straken Lord's advancing army, watching the indefatigable Tesla Dart scurry ahead of her like a water bug, with Lada and one or two other Chzyks as company. She had managed only a few hours' sleep the night before after returning from her failed effort to free Redden Ohmsford, and she was tired and irritable. Both were due as much to her dissatisfaction with herself as from physical exhaustion.

She gazed off into the distance, where the dust raised by the passing of the enemy army filled the air. Her body ached, warning her to slow down (or, better yet, to stop) before she collapsed from the effort of keeping up with the Ulk Bog. But she knew she wouldn't do that; she was determined to push ahead. She had a streak of stubbornness a mile wide, and once she set her mind to something, it took more than aches and pains to stop her. It took more than a cage ringed with magic, as well.

In any case, she wasn't about to stop, turn back, or even slow down while that annoying Ulk Bog was capering about as if completely immune to the weariness that was affecting her. She wasn't going to prove less able and willing, and then have to listen to the little creature's pointed comments all the way back to whatever doorway would release her from this prison and put her back into her own world.

She spit some dust from her mouth and slogged ahead. She wasn't giving up. Not until she got Redden out of that cage.

Although once she did so, she fervently hoped that Tesla Dart's boast about being able to put them back in the Four Lands was more than just talk.

She returned to thinking about how she would deal with Redden's magic-warded cage. There had to be a way to get past the Straken Lord's magic. Or a way to negate it. Or to strip it away.

She wished she knew more about that sort of thing, but in spite of her hopes of being allowed to join the Druid order, she possessed limited knowledge of magic. It was one thing to be a creature of magic; it was another entirely to have knowledge of its use.

The truth was that she didn't have much experience at all; she only had the talent with which she had been born. That might seem to be enough, given that she could turn herself into smoke. But passing through iron bars laced with magic was impossible, even with a shape-change that left her as insubstantial as air. She would, out of necessity, have to brush against the bars or touch some part of the cage in order to gain entry, and that would be all it took to engage whatever magic was in place. Even reaching through the bars might be enough to give warning. If the Straken Lord was going to this much trouble to haul the boy along with him on this march, he must have an important reason for doing so. That meant every precaution against his escape or rescue would have been taken.

She considered the number of Goblin guards and demon-wolves assigned to stand watch on Redden: many more than were necessary, unless their real purpose was not so much to keep him in as to keep others out.

Tesla Dart reappeared in a rush from the wilderness ahead, a flurry of waving arms and churning legs. Oriantha held out her hands to slow the Ulk Bog down before she knocked her over.

"Lada returns!" Tesla announced in an excited voice. "There is an opening close! Different one, not familiar. We are going out!"

The young woman stared. "What do you mean? We are going out where?"

The Ulk Bog grinned, showing all of her considerable teeth. "Into your world, shape-shifter! Back to your home!"

She turned and darted away again, running hard, apparently afraid she might miss something if she lingered even a moment longer. Oriantha gave chase, suddenly frantic. What was Tesla Dart talking about? Why would they be going out into the Four Lands? But she knew the answers almost as soon as she asked the questions. This was the invasion the Ulk Bog had warned about, the invasion Tael Riverine had warned he would mount if he were not given Grianne Ohmsford. Somehow Oriantha had thought they would have more time before the Straken Lord acted on his threat. Apparently she had been wrong.

"Tesla, wait for me!" she called.

The chase went on for perhaps fifteen minutes, and it would have gone on much longer had the Ulk Bog not decided to turn around and rush back to offer fresh insight.

"Tael Riverine does this to show strength," she announced, coming to a ragged halt in front of Oriantha. "He demonstrates his power to your people. Will wait to see what they do. Maybe he attacks. Maybe not. He is unpredictable. Very much dangerous."

"Wait!" Oriantha snapped as she sensed the other was about to sprint off again. "Are you sure of where we're going? How can Lada know?"

"Ha!" Tesla Dart was convulsed with laughter. "Lada so fast. Lada runs circles around army. Goes way, way ahead to see what he can find. Finds the opening. Can sense what it is. Opening must be to one place. Your world."

True enough, Oriantha thought. Where else would Tael Riverine be taking his hordes? She glanced skyward, catching sight of the Straken Lord aboard his huge dragon, circling overhead, just visible through the clouds of dust and dirt.

"Maybe he's not going through the opening just yet," she said suddenly. "Maybe he's just taking the army up to the opening and then will have it wait there to see what happens. Maybe he will send someone through to speak with the Elves and ask about Grianne."

Tesla cocked her bristly head as if studying a very strange insect. "Tael Riverine will ask? No, shape-shifter. He demands, and then he takes!"

They continued on, the Ulk Bog and the Chzyks scouting ahead, Oriantha trudging along behind, no longer bothering to hurry, knowing it didn't matter. She was not fast enough either to keep up with her companions or to get ahead of the army traveling in front of her. The army wasn't quicker than she was, but it was much, much wider. It sprawled across several miles of wilderness, and any effort to go around it would require a sizable detour. Without knowing where it was going—because there was no way to know where this new opening would take them—she might as well wait and see where they ended up before making any decisions about what to do. Whatever she did, she needed the invading army to stay in one place long enough for her to leave it and return with whatever help she could find.

She realized she could not go back into the enemy camp when night came to try to free Redden. Doing so would risk death or capture, and she could afford neither because she was the only one who knew what was about to happen and could give warning. With the Druid order decimated, she would have to get word to both the Elves and the Federation's Coalition Council. She would have to warn the Dwarves and the Border Cities. A united Four Lands would be needed if the Straken Lord's army were to be stopped and turned back.

Even then . . .

She didn't want to speculate further. Getting that far would be difficult enough.

She thought about the reason behind the appearance of the openings. It was obvious the Forbidding was collapsing and the creatures trapped inside were breaking loose. For that to be so, didn't the Ellcrys have to be failing? When had this happened and why hadn't the Druids known about it—especially the three who were Elves, and who should have been aware of the problem long ago?

She picked up her pace, worried now that she would be too slow in doing what was needed. The day was fading, and with it the gray light that washed the barren landscape. Here in this prison of ancient Faerie creatures labeled demonkind, it was never brighter than the twilight of her own world, but she could still feel the approach of a deeper darkness.

Yet it was still light when she saw the wash of brightness ahead—a long swath that cut across the landscape's horizon, pulsing softly, promising that something new and different was waiting. She hurried faster, catching up to the Ulk Bog and the Chzyks, which had slowed for her. By then, the front ranks of the demon army were already passing into the light and disappearing beyond. Atop his dragon, Tael Riverine was urging them on, sweeping across the sky in great arcs.

"Hurry!" Tesla Dart hissed at her.

In minutes they were positioned at the rear of the army's left flank and could follow it through the opening in the Forbidding with a minimal chance of being recognized. There was so much dust and dirt in the air that it was impossible for anyone to see clearly for more than a few feet. All they had to do was pretend to belong. Oriantha began encountering Jarka Ruus almost immediately, but they were advancing through the roiling haze with heads down and eyes averted. She moved swiftly in their midst, a shadowy figure intent on avoiding physical contact. One of many, she angled in fits and starts among the trudging figures, making the same sounds they did, snapping and growling, animalistic and predatory. She tried to keep Tesla Dart and the Chzyks in sight, but they had disappeared somewhere ahead.

She was left on her own, much the way she preferred it—a reflection of how she had lived most of her life.

But after a long period of groping through clouds of dust, she passed through the wash of light flattened against the horizon and found herself outside the Forbidding and back in her own world. Haze changed to brilliant light that blinded her, and then to familiar sunlight. She recognized the Four Lands immediately; the changes in color and taste and smell were unmistakable. One minute she was inside the Forbidding and the next she was clear.

Yet she was still in proximity to creatures that would kill her in a second if they realized who she was.

She turned aside quickly, angling away from the ragged minions of the Straken Lord, beasts hacking and coughing from the dust in their throats, eyes gone red and narrow. She faded into nothing—just for a moment, just long enough to find conceal-ment—before crouching down in heavy brush to get her bearings. She looked about and knew instantly she was nowhere near the Breakline or even in the deep Westland. This country was lush and green. A river shimmered in the distance, winding its way through hills and grasslands. There was farmland all around, plowed and seeded. The sun was bright and the skies clear.

Tesla Dart appeared from behind her, crouching close. "This is your world?"

"It is," she acknowledged, still looking around.

"You know this place?"

Then she saw it, just visible through a screen of woods and tucked down between low rolling hills to her right. Sunlight glinted off metal surfaces in bright flashes and burned the black-ened stones of massive walls and towers.

It was a city fortress, huge and forbidding.

She caught her breath. She knew the city instantly.

It was Arishaig.

10

THE SPEECH BEFORE THE FEDERATION'S Coalition Council had gone well. Edinja Orle was pleased. She was a formidable presence in any case, no matter the occasion or circumstance, but never more so than when she commanded an audience and could address them directly. The members of the council were already sufficiently intimidated by her that she could expect a certain deference. But when she struck the right chord, they would roll over and bare their bellies in an effort to demonstrate their submission.

She had spoken this day of the future, knowing that the uncertainties of the past year must be laid to rest. Three Prime Ministers in the span of twelve months were entirely too many for comfort—especially when the circumstances surrounding the deaths of the first two were infused with elements of violence and mystery. But she was the survivor who had escaped their fate by dint of cleverness and determination. She was the victim who had refused to yield to the fate her predecessor had assigned her, the strong-willed daughter of a family that had endured for centuries as a pillar of the community and an example of resilience.

It didn't hurt that she infused her words with magic, giving her an aura that transcended expectations and instilled in the gathered a mix of unabashed hope and old-fashioned pride in their city and its people. For the delegates to the council, Edinja was exactly what they needed and had been hoping for. All concerns for her alliance with magic wielders and conjurers were set aside in tacit acceptance that everyone possessed a few flaws. All worries about the rumors that she engaged in dangerous practices and vile experiments were dismissed. Here was a woman who was not afraid to show her masculine side. Here was a woman who understood what a leader should be and who would advance the interests of the city in a way that would allow them all to share in a bright and shining future.

She wasn't even sure what she said. When she spoke, she tended to go into a sort of trance and allow the words to flow unstructured and unedited. This was not to say she spoke without a purpose for what she was saying. But the tone and feel of her words were more important than the words themselves. If she could gain control of the emotions and the hearts of those listening, she could win them to her side on that alone. She knew how to do this, and she took advantage of it.

Now she walked the council chamber halls, the speech finished, her day's work on that front complete. She had given them cause to believe and had set them on a course of action. Over the next few weeks, they would be reworking the taxation system to pay for her new undertakings, both of public works and military construction. She had asked for a stronger presence throughout the Southland and beyond. She wanted embassies in all of the major cities of the other lands—an outreach that would allow her to connect more directly to both the Elves and the Dwarves and even to the Federation's longtime nemesis, the Borderlands of Callahorn.

It was her intention, in fact, to travel to the latter within the next month to meet with the body of representatives of those cities at the Rotunda in the city of Tyrsis, there to propose a fresh alliance—one that she intended would benefit them more than her. At least, it would do so in the short run and on the surface. Lay the groundwork for what you really wanted to accomplish by instigating a plan of misdirection, then wait for the right time to reveal your true intentions.

It was an approach she had learned from various members of her family through hard lessons witnessed and suffered. They were a rapacious, dangerous brood, the Orles—and none more so than those who were closest to her. Her father had murdered his first two wives and a brother. Her stepmother was an accomplished poisoner who was every inch a match for her father and who had helped him to dispatch the wife before her. Their lives thereafter were spent in large part keeping close watch on each other, although their union somehow endured.

Her brother was a monster.

She and her brother were the children of the previous wife and kept alive mostly because their father insisted on heirs and his present wife did not care to bear them. But instead of growing closer, as one might have expected, they were set apart and eventually against each other by the circumstances. Edinja had never liked or trusted her brother, even when she was very young, but she had never been given cause for this beyond what her instincts told her. Her brother was five years older than she, and had pursuits of his own to occupy his time. So, mostly, he ignored her.

But when she grew old enough to draw his attention—somewhere around the age of eleven or twelve—he began a systematic campaign of brutality. At first it was defined by small acts of cruelty practiced when no one was looking and later denied. An older and much better liar than she, he was able to refute her claims when she dared to make them. At that point, she was still small and unskilled and could not hold her own. But as the acts grew more frequent and more devastating—pets killed or made to disappear, special treasures ruined, sweets soiled in vile ways, and pain inflicted when they were alone and there was no one to intervene—she began to see that no one would save her if she did not save herself. Complaints to her father and stepmother were pointless. In the Orle family, you swam or sank on your own.

When her brother began to visit her bed at night, shortly after she turned thirteen, compelling her to perform unspeakable acts, she knew she could tolerate him no longer.

Her one advantage lay in his belief that she could not hurt him back, that she was too small and intimidated even to attempt it. But she had been growing up in other ways, especially in her innate understanding and gradual mastery of magic. There were writings and books on it tucked away in her father's office that she discovered while he was away. Careful readings and experiments led to the happy discovery that she had a natural aptitude for magic—a practice that had been a part of the history of her family for many centuries. Trapped in a desperate situation with no allies to stand up for her, she found that magic gave her a new confidence and a sense of empowerment. Her parents and her brother did not have use of this skill, so she kept her own powers a closely guarded secret. What mattered was that, for the first time, she felt she could do what was needed to protect herself.

What she decided to do was to remove her brother from the picture entirely; otherwise he would keep tormenting her until he killed her. To prevent that from happening, she must find a way to eliminate him first. But she couldn't let her father and stepmother know she was responsible. Her father doted on her brother and would never forgive her, no matter the reason.

Since misdirection followed by swift action had always been the solution to the problems of the Orle family, so it would be here.

She waited until they were vacationing in the countryside near the borders of the Eastland. They had a home there, one shared by various members of the Orle clan. There was another family visiting at the same time, bringing the number of visitors to nine. She took note of who was there, and she chose a cousin from the other family who was close in age to her brother and whom she liked no better to be her unwitting accomplice. She went to his sleeping chamber on the first night they arrived and seduced him. She would not have been able to do so before her brother's unwanted advances, but she found it easy enough now. When they coupled and were close and intertwined, she used a magic she had been experimenting with for some time to subvert his mind and bend him to her will.

When they were finished, she dispatched him to her brother's room carrying a knife sharp enough to do the job. And while her brother lay sleeping, her cousin gutted him from neck to groin. Her brother's death cries aroused the family. Her father rushed to his son's room, found the other boy standing over him with the knife, and killed him on the spot.

After that, things improved in Edinja's life. Her father, never having had much interest in her anyway, found her presence a cause for irritation. Evidently, he had never been keen on her as heir to his fortune. Her stepmother, who openly disliked her, sent her to live with an aunt, but what neither knew was that the aunt, who had no children of her own, was a far more accomplished magic user than her niece. Thus, she quickly developed a friendship with the secretive thirteen-year-old and began teaching her the secrets behind her own formidable skills. Edinja arranged for a permanent change of residence when both had agreed it would be better if they lived together so Edinja could spend more time developing her skills. The planting of a subtle suggestion in her stepmother's treacherous mind—one that seemed to provide a simple solution to the problem of what to do with her now that her father no longer wanted her around—was all it took.

All that was a long time ago, but it had set her on the path she followed now.

She left the building and walked back to her residence. A few of those passing nodded or spoke a word of greeting, but most simply crossed the street as if their business lay on the other side. She barely noticed. With the speech to the Coalition Council behind her, she had turned her attention to more immediate concerns.

When she reached her black tower, her fortress home and sanctuary, she took a moment to try the door without releasing the locks. When the latch gave easily, she smiled. All well and good. Everything was going as planned. She went inside, removed her cloak, and climbed the broad winding stairs to the second floor. She stopped there to look around, to glance down the hallway, to test the air, to smell and taste it. Then she continued on to the third and finally the fourth story and down the hall to the girl's bedroom.

The door was closed, but when she turned the handle it gave easily. No locks in place. She entered and found the makeshift dummy in the bed and the serving woman still unconscious on the floor on the other side of the bed. She brought the woman awake and helped her to her feet. When the woman went into hysterics and started screaming, clearly believing her failure would result in a terrible retribution, Edinja was quick to calm her, reassuring her that she had done nothing wrong.

Then the woman explained through continued sobs and shudders how she had been fooled by the dummy in the bed and had been struck from behind when she entered with the pitcher of treated water.

All of it exactly as Edinja had planned.

She patted the serving woman gently on her flushed and tear-streaked cheeks and sent her off to get some rest. Then she took one more look around and left the room, satisfied that things were proceeding as they should.

Arlingfant Elessedil was clever, but she was not nearly so clever or experienced as her captor when it came to deception. Edinja had known all along that she was not the weak and frightened girl she pretended to be. She was the sister of a Druid and one of the Chosen, and no one with that background would give way to her fears so easily. More to the point, she would not lie around waiting for the worst to happen. She would want to get word to her sister—or better yet find a way to reach her.

She would try to escape.

So Edinja had let her.

But not before she had planted a marker under the skin behind her neck and beneath her hair where it wouldn't be noticed. Not before assuring herself that the girl could be found quickly when it was time to do so.

She had done the same thing with Stoon before sending him off in search of Aphenglow—a necessary precaution against the assassin deciding not to follow through as she had instructed. A tiny sliver of glass, a crystal imbued with magic, slipped under his skin, a marker that would have let her track him, as well, if he hadn't gotten himself killed.

It was always better to expect the worst when dealing with unpredictable people.

In a dingier part of the city, not too far from where the Federation Prime Minister was congratulating herself on her ability to anticipate the actions of others, Aphenglow and Cymrian were sitting in the back of the locksmith shop with the Rover thief Rushlin, listening to his explanation about the difficulties of breaking into Edinja Orle's home. Impatient, they had arrived somewhat earlier than instructed, but still Rushlin had answers—albeit not encouraging ones.

"The locks are manageable, but then I knew they would be. The problem is with the wards she's set to back them up. Dozens on every floor, all of them dangerous, even to a skilled magic user like yourself."

"How do you know about these wards?" Aphen asked.

He shrugged. "I've learned to sense them. There are ways. I can tell when they're in place. But you can test them out for yourself if you like."

Aphen leaned forward, irritated by his smug certainty. "Why don't you tell me something useful?"

"Why don't I learn to fly, while I'm at it?" The dark brow furrowed. "If there was good news to give you, I would do so. Since there isn't, I am giving you what news I can. Nothing very helpful, but you may see it differently than I do."

"Just finish telling us what you know," Cymrian snapped, beginning to grow irritated himself.

"If you could get to the roof, you might find a way in from there. But word has it others have tried and their heads were found separated from their bodies. You might try coming in from underground. There are drain tunnels that run the length and breadth of the city to deal with sewage and flooding. Most have access to the buildings they service. But the tunnels to Edinja's house are closed off with iron grates, and the catch basins inside are stocked with creatures that eat flesh."

Aphen leaned back. "We're looking at this the wrong way. Edinja's home is well protected because she has enemies. But she would not leave herself only one way in or out. She would have a bolt-hole, and she would have a secret exit."

"Which could give us a secret entrance, if we could find it." Cymrian pursed his lips. "What of that, Rushlin?"

The Rover shook his head. "I've never heard anything about it, but I think you're right. She would never leave escape to chance. She would have provided for a quick way out years back so that she could be certain she would never be trapped."

"Which is not to say it isn't warded. In fact, it almost certainly is." Aphen shook her head. "But this seems like our best chance."

They sat silently for a moment, staring at one another.

"No," Cymrian said finally, "this isn't our best chance. Our best chance is to walk up to the front door and see if someone won't open it. If they do, we save all the trouble of having to break in uninvited."

Aphen stared at him. "Then all we would have to do is figure out how to get back out again."

Another silence. Rushlin shook his head and rose. "I need to spend a few hours away from here. Wait for me to come back. By then, one or the other of us will have thought of something. Maybe I can find out who goes in and still comes back out again. Mostly, it's been a one-way street."

He arched an eyebrow and went out the door, locking it behind him, the CLOSED sign turned out.

Aphen turned to Cymrian. "I don't think we can wait. I don't think we can afford to leave Arling in that woman's hands for one more minute."

Cymrian nodded. "I know. I don't think so, either."

"Then we have to do something. Right now."

"Why don't you use the Elfstones? Let's see how things stand."

She hesitated, aware of the danger of using magic this close to so many other magic users. Edinja Orle was the real danger, but there would be others, as well, in a city the size of Arishaig. Then again, with so many people crowded so close together, it would be difficult to identify a single user. Magic always left a residue that could be tracked, but not if it was done quickly. Such residues tended to dissipate.

In any case, she didn't see that she had a choice.

She rose from the table and took the Elfstones from their pouch, dumping them into her open palm. Closing her fingers about them, she faced toward the doorway, set her mind on Arling, and willed the magic to show her what had become of her sister. A certain fear accompanied the act—an unwillingness to be shown something bad—but she tamped it down. At some point, she would have to learn her sister's fate no matter what. Better that she do so while there was still a decent chance Arling could be saved.

A surge of magic rose from the Elfstones, going into her body and then back out again through her fingers, shooting away into the shop's gloom and out the door. It was gone in an instant, streaking down streets and across rooftops, into alleyways and narrow lanes, whipping left and right but always onward. No one but she could see it, the vision invisible to all not standing at the source, so she had no fear that it might be noticed by others.

For a few quick seconds the blue Elfstone light was a zigzag blaze cutting through the city, and then in a sharp burst it found Arling Elessedil.

But not where they had thought she would be.

*

Arling was working her way through the city streets, trying to blend in with the crowds while at the same time avoiding encounters with Federation soldiers. She had left Edinja's house through the front door; the lock had released without resistance, and no one had appeared to stop her. She could hardly believe her good fortune. But even though she mistrusted it, she was out and free and on her way to safety. She moved quickly down the steps and away from the building, taking more deserted streets until she reached busier ones. She was still wearing the night clothes Edinja had provided while she lay unconscious, but she had wrapped herself in a travel cloak she'd found hanging by the entry on her way out. Wearing slippers and keeping the hood to the cloak raised, she looked like many of the other young women she passed.

Her plan was to reach the closest of the gates leading out of the city and pass through it before anyone found out she was gone. Once free of the city, she could then begin her search for Aphenglow and Cymrian. Somehow, she would find them. And together they would return to the Westland and determine what to do next.

It was a rudimentary plan and didn't begin to address the bulk of her problems—like finding out who had taken the missing Ellcrys seed and recovering it, or searching out the Bloodfire and immersing the seed so that the Ellcrys could be quickened, then returning to Arborlon to discover what was needed to make that happen ...

But she left off thinking about it, knowing she could not look too closely at what it would require. It was all she could do just to get free of Arishaig and away from Edinja Orle.

Especially knowing that her captor would likely come after her.

Still, she had gotten this far, hadn't she? She had tricked the

serving woman and escaped the house. She had freed herself
from the sorceress and her dreadful creatures. Remembering
what she had been shown in the cellars of Edinja Orle's home
made her shudder. Whatever else happened she would not allow
herself to end up like that. She would kill herself first.

It was a bold, reckless threat—one that she probably could
not carry out—but it strengthened her determination to keep
going until she was safely away.

She caught sight of a pair of Elven traders standing with their
cart of handwoven scarves and head coverings, and she hurried
over to them.

"I'm new to this city, and I've gotten lost," she told them. "Can
you point me toward the city's west gate? I'm supposed to meet
my mother there."

The men looked at each other. "Why don't I accompany you,"
said one, "so you won't get lost again. It's easy to do that here."

"Thank you, but no. Just show me the right direction."

Shrugging, he did so, and she was off again, moving quickly.
She had rejected help she could have used without thinking,
instinctively wanting to keep everyone at bay. She pressed ahead
through crowds that were gradually growing larger, intent on
reaching her goal. The buildings surrounding her were much
bigger, making her feel ever more claustrophobic. The smells in
the air were rank and fetid. She tried to breathe through her
mouth, covering her face with her sleeve. Bodies jostled her,
almost knocking her off her feet.

Ahead, she could see Arishaig's west wall, its massive gates
standing open to the plains beyond, and she felt a surge of
excitement. She was almost clear.

But then shouts rose from atop the battlements—only a scattering at first, but then dozens more. People on the streets took
up the shouts—a few dozen turning into hundreds and then

thousands. The shouts blossomed into screams, and everyone began running, crowds rushing in every direction at once, people fighting to get away, swarming back through the streets. One huge surge was coming directly toward her, and she pushed and shoved her way frantically to reach the protection of a doorway, letting the mass of people fight their way past. She couldn't understand what they were saying, and her attempts to stop anyone were unsuccessful. The fleeing people looked wild-eyed and frightened.

Ahead, in the direction in which she had been going, she saw the massive gates begin to move, swinging on their iron hinges, the sounds of iron rubbing against iron adding a raucous shriek to the screams.

She felt her heart freeze.

The gates were closing.

Aphenglow and Cymrian were following the map provided by the Elfstones' vision, working their way through Arishaig's streets. Neither could imagine how Arling had managed to escape Edinja Orle. If the sorceress's home was as carefully pro-tected as Rushlin had led them to believe, it seemed impossible that she could have gotten free. Yet somehow she had, and that meant sooner or later Edinja would come looking for her. Given the sorceress's reputation, it seemed unlikely that Arling could evade her for long. They had to reach her quickly.

Cymrian drew up short. "We're wasting time. You have to use the Elfstones again."

Aphenglow looked around. "Out here? In the street?"

"No, not here. It's too crowded." He pointed toward the roof of a long, square building nearby. The roof was flat and open to the sky. "Up there."

There were huge roll-up doors that opened into the building, but they were locked and barred, so Cymrian chose to break through a smaller door off a side street. No one was inside once they entered. The building was a warehouse filled with large crates carefully stacked in bays. A metal stairway led up to a doorway in the ceiling and out onto the roof.

Once they were on the roof, Aphen didn't waste any time. She brought out the Elfstones, settled into her by-now-familiar trance, and summoned the magic. It flared to life almost immediately, gathering power in the palm of her hand and then flashing away into the distance. From high up on the roof, they could see the walls of the city and two of the gates. The magic went straight toward the west gate, speeding almost to its massive portals before dropping down to a street leading in that direction and to an image of Arling wrapped in a cloak and hood as she made her way to freedom. Then the magic flared and died.

"I know where she is," Cymrian declared, already racing back toward the stairs.

They went back through the empty warehouse and out the door into the street beyond. Cymrian led, with Aphen a step behind. The crowds were thin at first, but quickly began to grow in size until moving through them became all but impossible. Aphen grew frustrated and, throwing caution to the winds, she invoked a magic that moved people out of their path. But even this didn't solve the problem entirely because she could only impact those closest, and the larger mass continued to press toward them.

Then all at once shouts and screams rose from the direction in which they were heading, growing quickly from a scattered few to hundreds. Heads turned and people stopped where they were, milling about and trying to decide what was happening. Aphen and Cymrian attempted to move forward, but the street was entirely blocked now as the crowd clustered before them became a solid mass of bodies.

"What's happening?" Aphen shouted over the din.

Seconds later the screams and cries reached the head of the crowd and people began to surge back toward the Elves. Aphen and Cymrian were forced against the walls of the flanking buildings, unable to do anything more than get out of the way. The cries were spreading throughout the city, rising all around them, filling the air until nothing else could be heard.

In frustration, Cymrian began grabbing passers-by, demanding to know what was happening. At first, he got no coherent answer. Those running were just following everyone else. Something terrible was happening, but it wasn't clear what. All anyone knew to do was to get away.

Until they stopped a young man who shouted, "The city's under attack! Thousands of them, out on the flats!"

"Thousands of what?" Cymrian snapped.

The young man pulled free. "They say it's demons!" he answered, and raced away.

11

KEETON WAS SLEEPING WHEN THE HANDS began shaking him. "Commander, wake up!"

The urgency of the plea got through the layers of sleep that clogged his brain and brought him instantly awake. No small task, because he had been working all through the night and had only gotten to bed a little before midday.

He rubbed his eyes and peered up at his second. "What is it, Wint?"

"The city is under attack."

It was such an outrageous statement that, for a moment, Keeton thought he must have heard wrong. Then he sat up quickly. "Under attack from whom?"

"Don't know yet for sure." His second hesitated. "The reports say it's demons, but I don't see how that can be. Whatever they are, though, there's a lot of them."

Keeton rose, splashed water from the basin on his face, and began dressing. "You haven't been to the wall yourself? You haven't seen any of this firsthand?"

"No. I just now got word from those who were there and managed to get back here. The city's a mess. People crowding the streets, running everywhere, screaming like it's the end of the world. Even if I could get to the wall, I'd have real trouble getting back. Besides, you wouldn't be there with me, and I think you need to be."

"I always value your assessment, Wint. Thanks for waking me."

"You don't mean it, but I appreciate your willingness to say it. You barely got to sleep. I didn't want to wake you, but I think this is something bad."

Keeton finished buttoning his uniform, then ran his hand through his shock of prematurely gray hair and set his shoulders. "Let's go find out. We'll take a flit, get an overview. No crowds up there to get in the way."

They went out of his private quarters and into the barracks hallway. Immediately he was in a different world. Soldiers were rushing everywhere, and shouts were echoing up and down the halls. Some stopped long enough to salute and then hurried on once more. Some didn't even stop for that. He wondered where they were charging off to since no one seemed to know exactly what was going on. Someone must have given an order to mobilize. If the city was under attack, the high command would want the entire army on the walls and at the gates right away.

"Where's Commander March?" he asked. Tinnen March was senior commander of the Federation army; his involvement in any decision making was unavoidable.

"At the west gates, where the enemy's massed. Assessing the situation." Wint didn't sound happy. "I believe he's considering his options."

Keeton shook his head. "Which he will continue to do until the Prime Minister gives him his marching orders, but you didn't hear me say that."

"Things were better under Commander Arodian," the other offered quietly. "At least he knew what he was doing."

"Right up until he fell overboard during that ill-considered attack on Paranor. Another political decision resulting in another disaster. At least we got rid of Drust Chazhul, too."

"Good point. Things are so much better now with Edinja Orle."

Keeton glanced over and caught his second's sly smile. They shared the same opinion when it came to their new Prime Minister. More competent than the old, but more dangerous and unpredictable, too. Keeton was fifth-generation military, Wint seventh. They neither liked nor trusted politicians—especially ones who interfered with army matters. Both Drust Chazhul and Edinja Orle were guilty of that sort of infringement; apparently it was a troublesome characteristic of career politicians.

Keeton continued on through the barracks and out into the yard that led to the stacked hangars and the flits. First Response, the shock unit of the City Watch—of which he was commander—had its own designated squadron of flits, all heavily armed and armored, all two-man machines built for combat. One hundred men and women, all highly trained, the best of the best, hand-picked by Wint and himself to serve in an elite corps fashioned specifically to act as protectors of the city proper. The regular army answered to Tinnen March, and the warships to Sefita Rayne. They, in turn, answered to the Prime Minister of the Federation Coalition Council.

But he answered to no one but himself and those soldiers he commanded whenever there was a threat to the city.

He assumed the order remained undisturbed, enemy at the gates or not. Which meant Commander March would wait for him to appear with an assessment before he took action. Even if Edinja Orle tried to interfere, he would stall.

Keeton was a big, strong man with a full set of combat skills and a family history of military service so deeply infused in him that he had never even considered doing anything else with his life. He had applied early to the academy, been quickly accepted, and gone straight through school and training to the top of the Federation army command to assume this position. It had taken him less than a dozen years to demonstrate his competency and his commitment. The old Prime Minister had asked for him personally, had insisted he be given command of City Watch and First Response. If the city was attacked, he had said rather famously, he would prefer that the last person standing between him and death be Keeton.

High praise, but a testing of the old man's judgment hadn't been necessary until now. After the end of the war on the Prekkendorran, things had quieted down considerably in the Southland. Aside from skirmishes and small brush fires here and there, no threats had arisen until this past year when Drust Chazhul had been chosen Prime Minister and launched his personal crusade against the Druids and Paranor.

And now this new threat, whatever it was.

Wint had moved ahead, making his way toward their flit, giving it a quick inspection before climbing aboard and settling himself into the weapons compartment. While Keeton was big, Wint was huge, and he had trouble fitting himself into the tiny space. It was always something of a mystery to others that he managed to do so. But Wint had been his second for almost the whole of his time as City Watch commander, and the two knew each other well enough by now that they had no secrets. Keeton wondered sometimes where he would be if not for Wint keeping watch at his elbow, ready to talk him through every situation, willing to do what was needed to make sure no mistakes were made.

"Do we have a First Response team ready to go?"

"We do." Wint was cranking back the straps on the rail slings. "Two, as a matter of fact. We can have them airborne in minutes."

"Then let's have a look, see if we need them."

He opened the parse tubes on the two-man and moved the thrusters forward. The flit lifted away, power flowing down the sleek radian draws from the narrow light sheaths to the diapson crystals and out the exhaust of the parse tube. Keeton took the flit up several hundred feet and wheeled west. He glanced down at the city, saw the streets filled with mobs of people, and noted the damage already done to carts and wagons and storefronts. Soldiers from the Federation's regular army had begun blocking off the streets, containing the masses so that they could be dispersed. Barricades shut off the government buildings and the avenues leading back to the west gates. Better if the citizenry were somewhere else, out of the way.

Nearing the west wall, he made a rough count of the number of soldiers gathered on the ramparts and directly inside the gates. Companies were forming up in the square fronting the gates, unit by unit coming together. Sentries on watch had not only closed the gates and thrown the heavy locks but also placed the huge crossbar in its twin seatings so that there could be no chance of a breach. It was as chaotic here as everywhere else, but with at least a semblance of military order as men rushed to join their units. Keeton guessed they had been rousted from all over the city, homes and barracks alike, and from the size of the companies few had been excused.

He took the two-man over the walls and out onto the flats, rising into the air lane just above the approach road and the watchtowers bordering it. Passing over the towers, he was surprised to discover that they were all still manned. Normally, the men and women stationed in those towers would have been brought in right away if an invading army threatened.

Which made him wonder why that hadn't been done here and who exactly was attacking Arishaig.

Once past the last of the towers and out over the grasslands, he found the answer to the second question quickly enough. A huge army was massed all along the ridgeline that formed the extreme south end of the Prekkendorran Heights. But this wasn't an army of the sort he or anyone else he knew had ever encountered, and he sensed immediately that it did not consist of either Elves or soldiers from Callahorn's Border Cities. It was massive beyond anything he had ever seen—beyond anything he had even imagined possible, for that matter. It measured hundreds deep and was stretched three or four miles wide. There was no order to it, no recognizable formation, and there was no obvious indication of how it was being commanded. It was simply a huge collection of bodies of all shapes and sizes, all looks and behavior, pushed to the edge of the ridgeline and somehow held in place so that it advanced no farther.

"What army is that?" he heard Wint exclaim in shock.

He might have answered if he'd been given more time, but he was distracted by a flurry of winged forms rising from the masses directly toward his flit. Reacting instantly, he spun the craft away and raced down the edge of the invading army, escaping this fresh assault while still trying to make out something recognizable in the faces and bodies of its members.

"Those creatures aren't anything we know," Wint shouted from the weapons hold behind him. "Maybe they really are demons!"

Keeton didn't believe that for a second, no matter what they looked like. There weren't any demons in the Four Lands.

Hadn't been any in centuries, and even those were mostly rumors. This was something else, but he didn't know what.

And he didn't have time to speculate on it now or even to try to sort through the different creatures he was looking at. The winged things were coming for them, closing the distance separating them more rapidly than should have been possible. A flit was fast and agile, and Keeton didn't know of anything living that could keep up with it in the air.

He glanced back at them as he pushed the flit's thrusters forward to gain speed. *Were those women's faces on those giant birds?*

Then Wint used the rail slings, and several of the birds went down in a tangle of nets and metal weights.

Seconds later they were in the clear, heading back toward the watchtowers and the approach road. The winged creatures had broken off their attack, apparently satisfied simply with driving the flit away. On the ridgeline, the invaders howled and screamed, and Keeton felt a chill go down his spine in spite of himself.

"Have those sentries in the watchtowers evacuated as soon as we get back, Wint," he shouted to his second.

The other made a gesture of acquiescence, his eyes watching for fresh attackers, not persuaded that some sort of reprisal for their decision to come so close to the invaders wasn't still possible.

Keeton sped toward Arishaig's walls. He did not like how what he had just witnessed made him feel.

Edinja Orle had broken off her vigil on hearing of the approaching army and made her way to the walls above the west gate, where she had found and confronted Tinnen March.

Her words were laced with iron. "I want the army assembled and I want it ready to counterattack if the city is further threatened," she snapped at him.

March nodded. "I have already ordered all soldiers to form up right here. We have placed units at all of the city gates and sent everyone not in the military to their homes to wait this out. If we are attacked, we will be ready."

"Have you sent scouts to find out what these creatures are and where they come from?"

She had been seeking an answer to that question from everyone she encountered since arriving at the wall, but no one seemed to know. Not that it mattered. She knew. She had pretty much known from the moment she heard mention of the word *demons*. What Arling Elessedil and her Druid sister had been trying to prevent was already happening. It was inconceivable, but at the same time inescapable. The demons inside the Forbidding were breaking out, and for some unknown reason they had come to Arishaig.

Tinnen March was speaking. "We are waiting on Commander Keeton who is doing a flyover. Protocol dictates that First Response makes the initial determination in situations such as these. It won't take long. He will be back soon."

Situations such as these. What would you know about it? Edinja cocked her beautiful face as if studying an odd insect and smiled with pure malice. "Then we'll wait, won't we?"

She didn't like Keeton. She had tried to win him over early, had invited him up to her rooms in an effort to show him the benefits of becoming an ally, and had worked hard at persuading him of her interest in him. But Keeton was cut from a different cloth than most. Military through and through, he was suspicious of politicians and their motives. He wasn't stupid, but he was troublesome.

She turned and walked away from Tinnen March, unwilling to spend another moment with such an idiot. She doubted he could lace his own boots without help. How had such a man ever risen to his present rank? Drust Chazhul had made him commander of the army after dispensing with Lehan Arodian, and that was proof enough that he was a servile dupe. Of course, she had left him in command for the same reasons; no effort was needed to get him to comply with her wishes. Now with the city under attack, she regretted not appointing someone stronger. But it was too late. Changing horses at this point would only frighten people and irritate the members of the Coalition Council.

Her thoughts drifted momentarily to Arling Elessedil, wandering about somewhere in the city streets. Cinla might still be tracking her, but she doubted it. Given the size of the crowds, the big moor cat would have had to turn back. Cinla could make herself invisible in situations where she had space and time to move, but she didn't have either today. Edinja experienced a fresh twinge of rage. This whole business was ruining her plans for tracking the girl and finding her sister. At least she could take some comfort from knowing she had placed her marker on Arling and could always find her at some point. Nor did she have to worry about the girl getting out of the city. All exits were shut down, and an attempt to flee at this point would be foolhardy.

Demons! She said the word in the cool silence of her mind, but the venom it aroused burned like fire.

The sound of a returning flit drew her attention, and she watched the two-man slide into view and settle onto the landing platform at the corner of the battlement. Tinnen March was already striding over, accompanied by his adjutants. She waited until she saw Keeton climb from the cockpit and then walked over to join them.

" . . . can't be sure of the number," Keeton was saying. He glanced over at her approach, but only for a second. "They're stretched out along the ridgeline for miles."

"But what are they, Commander?" she interrupted, moving close to him. "Can you tell us that?"

He shook his head. "I don't know what they are. They're not human. They're nothing of what we know in the Four Lands."

"They are demons," she said simply. "The Forbidding has broken down, and now those imprisoned are coming out. What are you going to do about it?"

He stared at her. "How do you know this?"

She gave him a sly smile. "I just do. Answer my question."

"Commander March is senior officer."

"I'm asking you. You *are* still commander of First Response, aren't you?"

Keeton somehow managed to keep his face expressionless. "Right now, I am taking a squad of flits back out to bring in those soldiers still in the watchtowers." He turned to March. "With your permission, of course, Commander?"

He didn't need that permission, and they all knew it. He was simply making Tinnen March complicit in his plans. The commander was still staring at him speechlessly when he turned and hurried off.

Edinja watched him go without comment, her mind already working through the choices she would have when he returned. Without glancing at Tinnen March, she said, "Hadn't you better get working on a plan for defense of the city, now that you know what we are up against?"

March and his adjutants moved quickly away.

Keeton caught up with Wint as he was speaking with another two-man pilot from First Response. "What have you found out about those soldiers in the watchtowers?" he asked his second.

The other shrugged. "March gave no order for their return, so they're still out there. I have a transport and five flits standing by to go get them. Unless you want to let them try it on their own. They might have time for that. That army doesn't seem in any hurry to do anything."

"Maybe. But they were quick enough to send someone after us when we left the protection of the city walls. I don't like the idea of those people trying to get back here on an open road. It's two miles front to back, and that's too far."

"A transport then?"

Keeton shook his head. "Too cumbersome. Speed and maneuverability are important. Let's use sleds. Hook them to the flits, fly them out, load them up, and make a run for it."

Wint grinned. "Sleds, huh? Can I drive?"

The sleds were wooden platforms with rings and loops for tying down ropes and chains. The platforms rested on steel rails filed and sanded down until their surfaces were so hard and smooth, they could skim over rocks and hardpan and not shatter. Mostly, the sleds were used for quick supply transport rather than for conveying soldiers, but they would serve the latter purpose here just as well.

Wint was already ordering a team of First Response soldiers to the storage lockers to haul out four of the sleds to hook up to the flits. Keeton went to help, deciding to switch the rail slings in favor of fire launchers. Rail slings might not be enough against whatever was out there. The effort took less than twenty minutes, and when everything was ready he called pilots and weapons officers together.

"This is the plan. We have four flits with sleds to rescue the men and women in the twelve towers bracketing the approach road. We'll start with the ones that are farthest away and work our way back. Fly out, swing around so we're facing toward the city, land on the road, load everyone aboard, then pull for the city. When the soldiers in the towers closest to the city see what we're about, they'll come down to ground level right away and we'll load them, too. They might even start out on their own."

He paused. "The second and I will be in the last flit, flying interference against anything that gets too close."

"It won't be easy getting everyone aboard the sleds," Wint said. "There are a lot of people in those towers."

Keeton gave him a look and then directed it toward the others. "Everyone comes back. No one gets left behind."

He beckoned them close. "No heroics. No unnecessary risks. We don't know exactly what we are up against, and that's part of what we're going out there to discover. But let's not make that discovery the hard way."

They murmured their acquiescence. Eight soldiers—five men and three women. He knew them all. None of them had combat experience of the sort they were about to encounter. Nor had he. It was a definitive moment for all of them. Training and character would be tested. The Prime Minister and the military high command would be watching.

But he didn't tell them that. They didn't need to know any of it to do their jobs. They just needed to remember who they were and what they were about.

"Wint, assign the towers for each two-man and let's fly."

He broke the circle, and the eight members of the First Response team caught the second's quick orders and raced to board their vessels.

Atop the walls above the west gates, Edinja Orle was watching them. She saw Keeton speaking to his team, watched as he dispatched them to their flits and then boarded his own with his second. Quick and efficient, no hesitation, no delay. The flits powered up, then one by one they rose into the golden light of late afternoon. She squinted at the sky for a moment. It was a clear, cloudless day, but the sun was sinking fast over the western horizon, its rays lancing into the eyes of the fliers as they raced toward their targets. What must that be like, flying half blind at an unknown enemy?

She kept watching as the flits crossed above the wall and sped toward the watchtowers, towing the sleds behind them. Clever of Keeton to think of using sleds instead of transports. She didn't like the man, but she admired his intelligence. His manners could be improved but she couldn't find fault with his military skills.

She glanced down the wall to where Tinnen March was conferring with his officers in a heated discussion. She saw them all gesturing at him, saw him shake his head and walk away.

She had an uncomfortable feeling about the man.

And she might have to do something about it.

12

AT FIRST, EVERYTHING WENT SMOOTHLY.

With Wint and Keeton in the lead flit, the squad flew out from the walls of Arishaig, shadowing the line of the road toward the grasslands beyond. The light might have been against them, but they were experienced fliers, on their home turf. They were formed up two abreast behind the commander's aircraft, with the sleds tethered behind them and a safe distance between each pair. On the ground, nothing moved. The men and women in the towers—who must have seen them approaching—stayed where they were.

On the ridgeline farther out, the invading army bunched close to the precipice, howling and screaming with such fury that Keeton could hear it even over the rush of the wind in his ears.

"Such beautiful music," Wint said over his shoulder.

Keeton was readying the fire launcher, using his trigger finger to press the lever that would charge the diapson crystals embedded in the weapon's stock, drawing energy from a line connected through the flit's walls to the light sheath that powered it. A strong pull on the trigger would send the launcher's deadly beam toward whatever target it was centered on. Keeton could narrow or widen the beam using a slide on the launcher's barrel. He had fired the weapon many times, and he was very good with it.

He thought he would probably need to be better than good today.

The formation reached the outermost towers, passed out over the grasslands, and swung back around, following Keeton and Wint's flit as it swooped down toward the approach road. One by one, pairs of flits broke away from the formation to drop onto the road between the towers. In some instances, the doors opened immediately and the men and women within came rushing out to board the sleds. In some instances, it took longer—an unfortunate delay caused by a failure to anticipate what the flits were trying to do. But within minutes of the landings, all of the towers were emptying out and the sleds were filling up.

Wint brought the flit in which he and Keeton were riding back around again to face whatever response the rescue effort might have triggered in the invading army. The commander and his second didn't need more than a moment to discover the answer. Even before the flit had cleared the middle towers on its return run, they saw a swarm of cat creatures pour over the edge of the ridgeline and bound after the escaping soldiers. They split into packs, dozens of them, strange feline faces twisted with something that Keeton could only describe as hunger as the gap between them narrowed.

"Hold steady!" he shouted to Wint.

He brought the barrel of the fire launcher around, sighted down its length, and pulled the trigger all the way back. The light beam shot out of the barrel's end in an explosion that caused the weapon to recoil sharply. The charge arced into the forefront of the attacking pack and incinerated the leaders. Keeton moved the weapon's barrel from one pack to the next, trying to stay calm, to keep his aim steady and accurate.

But the motion of the flit made it difficult for him to be as effective as he would have liked against the very swift and elusive wildcats. They veered left and right after the first strikes, zigzagging across the grasslands toward the towers, spreading out to widen the distances among themselves. Now there were hundreds of targets, and even if Keeton had been more effective with the launcher than he was, he couldn't have stopped all of them.

Wint, seeing the problem and knowing that the flits and their sleds were too slow to escape the pursuit, acted swiftly. Yelling at the commander to cease fire, he brought the nose of their two-man around sharply, flew directly at the foremost attackers, dropped down as if to land atop them, and then spun around so that the exhaust was exploding into their front ranks as·he guided it down the front wave of the attackers in a long slow expulsion of fire. It took a pilot with Wint's skills to perform this maneuver, but it turned aside a sizable portion of the attack and left the savage cats further scattered and in some disarray.

Still, they kept coming. They leapt onto the flit, trying to find a grip to climb aboard. Two did so, and one raked Wint from neck to hip with its claws before being dislodged. The second got to Keeton, but he thrust it away quickly and sent it tumbling off the craft.

Below, all of the towers were emptied out and all of the rescue flits and sleds were racing for the safety of the city. But a handful of the wildcats had reached the rearmost of the sleds and leapt aboard, shrieking and clawing at the soldiers clinging to the grips. Keeton could see clearly the struggle taking place, the soldiers kicking and punching at their attackers, trying to use their weapons without killing or maiming their own people. But a handful of each tumbled off. Sprawled on the approach road like rag dolls, the soldiers were quickly torn apart. Chaos ensued as the trailing sleds tried to go faster, to get away from their pursuers, until at last one of them lost its balance and went over completely. The flit pulling it was dragged down with the sled, and then it flipped, crushing the First Response members who manned it.

There was nothing Keeton or Wint could do to save any of them. By the time their flit was winging toward the gates, its fire launcher scattering the savage felines that had gotten close enough to provide a further threat, all those toppled with the sled or pulled down as stragglers were beyond help.

Still, the rescue effort was a success. Most of those in the watchtowers had been saved. Only one of the sleds had been lost; the other three were now nearing the gates and safety.

Keeton glanced back at the army on the ridge, and his blood turned to ice.

A huge wave of creatures was coming down off the heights and swarming across the grasslands toward the walls of Arishaig. These attackers were different—larger in number by far, encompassing all sizes and shapes, and all manner of appearances and movements. Some had the agility of jackrabbits and deer; some lumbered like great Kodens. There were flying things and crawling things. He could make out huge jaws with teeth each the size of his hand. Coats of thick hide rippled next to those of coarse hair. Eyes flared scarlet and emerald out of heads that were triangular and bony. Claws ripped at the earth and hooves tore at the grasses.

Above them all, a huge mottled red-and-brown dragon swept across the sky.

Wint saw something else, too. "We're in trouble," he shouted.

He was pointing ahead, and now Keeton saw what he meant. The flits and their loaded sleds were nearing the west gates, ready to enter the city.

But the gates were still closed.

Atop the city walls, Edinja Orle watched the chase unfold, saw one of the four sleds and its flit brought down, and saw the others continue unimpeded as Keeton's flit fought back against the attackers and burned away those close enough to cause trouble. She watched as a mass of attackers—too many for most armies to stop, let alone the handful of men and women seeking the sanctuary of the city—streamed down off the bluff. She felt the desperation in the hearts of the pursued, knowing that only moments separated them from either safety or death.

She waited for the gates to open.

Cinla stood beside her. The moor cat had returned from tracking Arling Elessedil, discouraged by the crush of citizens swarming the streets. Cinla had sought to resume the hunt twice once the crowds had been broken up and disbanded, blending in with her surroundings, becoming a part of the buildings and streets as she hunted. But the scent of her quarry had been buried by hundreds of others, and she could not pick it out.

She had conveyed all this to Edinja, for they could share a single mind when necessary. Now she sat beside her mistress, calm and steadfast.

Down the wall's walkway perhaps a hundred feet away, Tinnen March was dispatching runners to all four quarters of the city, summoning reinforcements to the west wall, shoring up his defenses—realizing, perhaps, that the danger he was facing was much greater than he had first supposed. He shouted and gestured, and men raced everywhere at his command.

But the gates did not open to those outside the wall.

Edinja had seen enough. She stormed down the walkway in fury, the white-hot heat of her displeasure clearly visible as she neared the Federation army commander. She could feel Cinla following a step behind, her great head swaying from side to side.

"What are you doing?" she screamed at March, unable to help herself. "Open the gates!"

He gave her one swift glance. "It is too late for them. The enemy is too close. I cannot risk it."

"I order you to open those gates, Commander!" Her small body shook with rage. "Now!"

He gave her a scathing look. "I command the military in this city, not you." He turned, beckoning to a handful of guards. "See that the Prime Minister is placed safely away until she calms herself . . ."

He never finished. Edinja made a sweeping motion with one arm, and the guards tumbled away. Then she snatched Tinnen March by the front of his military jacket and marched him to the edge of the wall.

"You command at my pleasure," she hissed.

Then she lifted him off his feet with what witnesses later would describe as superhuman strength and threw him over the wall.

He was still screaming when she turned to the soldiers who had watched it all happen and shouted, "Now get those gates open!"

Outside the walls, the rescued soldiers were gathered in a knot before the gates, having abandoned the sleds after the flits had been forced to cut them loose. Daylight was fading quickly. First Response still flew overhead, offering what protection it could, making wild sorties into the teeth of the attacking army as it swarmed over the grasslands and approach road, watching in horror as the enemy overran watchtower after watchtower on its way to the walls of the city.

Keeton was searching the walls for some sign of activity near the gates—anything that would indicate they were about to be opened—when a body came flying over the wall. It was a man in Federation military uniform, but that was all he could tell. He watched in shock as the man tumbled earthward and struck with such ferocious impact that there was no question about whether he still lived.

"Who was that?" Wint whispered.

Seconds later the gates opened, and the soldiers trapped outside poured through.

Wint took the two-man out onto the approach road for one more run at the attackers as they surged across the grasslands and past the watchtowers on their way to the wall, giving the rest of the team an opportunity to cross the walls and manage a landing inside. Then he swung the craft about and raced after them.

Back on the ground, below the west wall, hundreds of soldiers were flooding through the open grounds fronting the gates, heading for the battlements. Weapons were being unhooded and swung into place. Huge fire launchers were charged and rail slings loaded. The gates were sealed anew, the locks set, and the crossbar dropped back into place. Dust and shouts rose into the air—a wild cacophony of sound that smothered Keeton's attempts to tell Wint what he wanted next from First Response. All around him, the soldiers of the Federation army were preparing to defend Arishaig.

He was barely out of the two-man when one of Tinnen March's adjutants rushed up to him. "The Prime Minister requests your presence on the wall immediately!" he blurted, forgetting to salute until he had finished delivering his message. "Sir."

Keeton glanced up, then nodded. "Who fell off the wall?"

The adjutant couldn't seem to get any more words out. He saluted again, a quick sharp act, and rushed away.

Keeton managed to tell Wint what he wanted from First Response and then set off for the top of the wall. When he got there, he found Edinja Orle waiting for him.

"Commander Keeton," she greeted him. Her words were sharp-edged, but her voice steady. The big moor cat Cinla was sitting next to her, watching him. "Commander March has been relieved of his command. You are his replacement. The defense of the city is in your hands."

Keeton stared. "I don't want the job," he said finally.

"Well, you don't have a choice." She stepped close, lowering her voice so that only he could hear. "Tinnen March panicked. He was not going to open the gates. He was going to leave you and the others out there to die. I saved your life."

He raised an eyebrow. "That's who went over the wall?"

"He deserved what he got. I can't have cowards and fools leading the army at a time like this. You and I don't much like each other and we've not gotten along well, but I respect your abilities and your courage. I hope you respect that my responsibility as Prime Minister and leader of the people of Arishaig requires that I make the best choices possible when I am required to do so. This is one of those times."

"I just don't—"

She stopped him with a sharp hiss. "This isn't up for debate. We don't have time to argue about it. You are being given command of the army. You are being charged with the safety of the city and its people. Would you refuse to do your duty when so many lives are at stake, Commander?"

Then she pivoted and walked off without a backward glance, the moor cat trailing after her with long, loping strides.

The demons did not attack immediately, as it had appeared they would. Instead, they stopped just short of the closest pair of watchtowers, perhaps five hundred yards from the west gates, and stood howling and screaming at the walls of the city. The sound was deafening, and it continued uninterrupted, the creatures of the demon army massing as if held back by an invisible barrier and giving vent to their frustration and rage.

Shortly after sunset, a second wave came down from the heights to join the first, doubling the size of the attacking force and creating an ocean of bodies that churned and thrashed amid the tumult of shrieks and roars, with an occasional ongoing surge threatening a breakout that would take them to the walls, sending shudders down the spines of the Federation soldiers watching from the battlements.

Keeton used this time to meet with his divisional commanders and prepare a coordinated defense. Saddled with a responsibility he could not morally or emotionally refuse, he had resolved to do the best he could in the way the soldiers in his family had always done. Whatever he might think of Edinja Orle, he could not ignore her charge to defend the city of Arishaig and its people. He was a soldier first and always. If he was called upon to serve where the cause was right and the need obvious, he must accept it.

So he set about building a defensive plan that would allow the city to weather the onslaught that was about to descend.

Survival was not assured. A rough count put the number of the enemy at ten times that of the defenders. More troubling, while the demons lacked sophisticated weapons, they made up for it with an unmatchable savagery and predatory instincts

honed and tested within the crucible of the Forbidding. Keeton
was aware that there were dozens of species of demonkind, and
each would have its own set of skills and abilities, about which
almost nothing was known.

Keeton brought the bulk of the Federation army to the west
wall to defend against the hordes gathered there. But he was
careful to leave reserves at each of the other walls, knowing
better than to strip any defensive position of enough men to
withstand an unexpected attack. Rail slings and fire launchers
were mounted on the permanent swivels built into all of the
walls surrounding the city and readied for use.

As a further defensive move, he summoned Sefita Rayne, commander of the Federation Airship Fleet, to discuss her role in
protecting the city. She had heard of Tinnen March's fate,
although not the details surrounding it, and he was quick to fill
her in. While no fan of the dead commander, she understood well
enough the danger that Edinja Orle posed to the army's remaining commanders if they somehow managed to displease her.

"You don't want this command, do you?" she said quietly,
steering him away from those gathered close. The blue highlights
of her streaked hair glittered in the pale moonlight. "Admit it."

"Not a bit of it," he acknowledged. "But here I am anyway."

She nodded. "Better you than March." She was tall and rangy,
and she had that airman's gait that made it look as if she were
always braced against the roll of a vessel. "What do you wish of
me?"

"A few of your warships to begin with. They have creatures
that can fly, but only the dragon is big enough to pose problems
for a ship-of-the-line. Most of the attackers are earthbound and
can't reach an airship. If we put a few of the big boys aloft, we can
attack them from above and break apart their attempts to force
the gates. We'll just have to keep a close watch for the dragon."

"I'll have lookouts aloft with specific instructions," she agreed. "This is new territory. We really don't know yet what that dragon is capable of. But the fire launchers should be able to keep it at bay. The ships are mostly outfitted and ready to fly. I'll have a pair of them brought up right away, one for the pads on each end of the wall. When the attack comes, I'll have them come in from the flanks. If you signal that the gates are in trouble, we'll counterattack."

"That sounds exactly right. But don't discount the possibility that they might break off here and come at us from another direction."

She looked out over the walls to the masses below, wincing at the fury of the shrieks and screams. "Quite the animals, aren't they? Don't worry; the rest of the fleet will be ready to fly. If these things choose a different avenue of attack, we'll be on top of them immediately." She paused. "Have you thought about going after them right away?"

He nodded. "A preemptive strike? I thought of it, but that changes the dynamic. We're set up to defend and counterattack, not to be the initial aggressors. I decided we would be better off using the natural protection of the walls. Let these creatures come to us. Let them break their strength against the stone and iron before we get involved."

Sefita shrugged. "Your command. Have we sent word to the other cities?"

"We sent word, but told the military there to stay behind their walls. If they try to come to our aid, they provide the demons with an inviting target. They could be caught out in the open and massacred."

She looked out over the walls again. "Other than what we can see in front of us, how many are there?"

"I don't know. I sent flits out three separate times to fly

beyond that ridge." He pointed. "None of them returned. Who knows what's back there hidden out of sight?"

She exhaled sharply. "Maybe you could send someone out through the underground tunnels?"

He gave her a smile. "Are you volunteering, Sefita? Because so far no one else has."

"I take your point."

"Don't misunderstand. I might have to send somebody. But what I was thinking of doing was sending another flit out after it gets dark. Harder to see it then."

He paused, giving a quick glance down at the hordes gathered below the wall. "Be careful, Sefita. Tell your airmen to do the same. These creatures aren't like anything we've fought before. I don't know what they can do, but we don't want to take anything for granted. So watch yourself."

After she left to return to her command, Keeton found Wint down below, inside the First Response hangar, and pulled him aside. "I want to hold the First Response team in reserve. All of them. If the walls are breached, I want us there to plug the hole."

Wint nodded but didn't answer. Keeton looked around, out the hangar doors to where the west gates stood locked and barred. "Have them build a redoubt fifty feet back. Right about there." He pointed. "Two levels, places for fifty men. Install four fire launchers. The big ones. Two on each level, evenly spaced. If the gates go, I don't want anything to get past the redoubt."

There was nothing more to do after that. Not until the attack began. He went back up on the wall and stood looking down at the invading army. He had convinced himself some time back that it was demons he was facing. He had no idea how Edinja knew this, or how she knew they had broken through the Forbidding, but the moment she had said it he knew it was so. These things weren't indigenous to the Four Lands; there hadn't been creatures of this sort seen in centuries. Why they were here now was a mystery, but the fact of it was enough.

He thought momentarily of the Prime Minister, wondering what she was doing. He hadn't seen her since she had ordered him to take command of the army. He had assumed she would be back to find out how he was managing things, to watch over him as she had watched over Tinnen March and make a similar judgment on his efforts, but there had been no sign of her. He couldn't decide if this was good or bad.

As twilight deepened, Keeton became increasingly convinced that the attack was going to come after dark. Perhaps these creatures saw better at night and wanted to take advantage of it. Perhaps this was their natural hunting time. Whatever the case, he set about trying to remove whatever advantage they perceived.

He started by ordering torches lit all around the city walls. While light this high off the ground wouldn't penetrate down to where the attackers were clustered, it would illuminate them clearly if they attempted to scale the walls. In addition, he had flammable oil released into the shallow trough that encircled the city some ten feet from the walls and spiked outward in trenches dug at regular intervals perpendicular to the main ring for distances of from five to ten yards. Their oil reserves would hold for up to ten days if they were frugal. But Keeton didn't care about ten days. He was worried about three or four. So he released oil until the ditch was filled.

Finally, he had pitch barrels brought up to the archers on the battlements so they could dip the tips of their arrows and add further light to any defensive effort.

Then he sat back to wait.

Time passed. The darkness deepened as the daylight faded and disappeared. Stars and a crescent moon appeared in a hazy night sky. Then unexpectedly the weather changed. The temperature warmed, storm clouds rolled in from the north, the haze deepened, and the stars and moon disappeared. Keeton abandoned his plans to send out a fourth flit. He couldn't convince himself it was worth risking another airman's life to confirm what he already suspected.

The hordes in the darkness continued to howl and threaten, but stayed put. Keeton thought to light the oil in the ditch but held off. *Not until they attack*, he thought. *Not until it begins*.

All around him, the men and women of the army stood waiting, eyes fixed on the darkness and the sounds of the demons.

Anytime, Keeton thought.

But no attack came.

13

ON THE MORNING FOLLOWING FARSHAUN
Req's burial, the *Quickening* and its passengers
resumed their journey into the Charnals. They
departed at sunrise on a day that started out badly and steadily
got worse. Dawn showed as a band of crimson and pale silver
that lasted less than twenty minutes and then dissolved into
gloom. Massive banks of clouds obscured the skies for as far as
the eye could see and turned the whole of the mountain range
sullen and threatening.

The members of the company went about their tasks pur-
posefully, but no one could shake their sense of unease. That a
storm was coming was a given; all that remained to be determined was how severe it would become and how long it would
last. It was a commonly held belief among airmen that a red sky
at dawn was a clear sign of an impending storm, and the more
intense the color, the harder the blow to follow.

Because Farshaun was no longer with them, Austrum
assumed command of the helm. An argument might have been

made that either Railing or Mirai was the more capable pilot, but neither felt inclined to suggest this. Mirai barely glanced at Austrum when he climbed into the box and took over the controls, moving instead to the bow to begin helping the other Rovers work the lines. She didn't spare a glance for Railing, either, which irked him, but nevertheless felt consistent with the way he expected she would behave from here on out. Last night was last night; it was over and done with, and he would get no special attention because of it. Not in the midst of their journey and not with any of the others around to take note. She had told him how it would be. She would wait to see how he conducted himself. If he found the means to toughen himself against his doubts and to set an example for the others, then things might change.

So he tamped down the twinges of regret and doubt about her seeming disinterest in him and concentrated on taking his first steps toward getting back to the person he had once been—Redden's twin, yes, but the one who wasn't afraid to risk anything, the one who was never in doubt. He plunged into the work of helping to fly the airship into the teeth of what everyone knew would be a very bad storm and set everything else aside.

He found himself beside Challa Nand at one point. "Doesn't look good, does it?"

The Troll glanced at him. "Nothing gets by you, does it, Railing Ohmsford? Got any magic to get us through this?"

The boy shrugged. "Maybe. If it comes to it. And I do have some flying skills that might be useful when Austrum gets tired."

"You'll be needing them." Challa Nand paused to look out at the darkness approaching. "We'll miss the old Rover this day, I think."

"He was the best of us when it came to flying an airship.

There wasn't anything he couldn't do." The memories came flooding back, and he shook his head. "What I said about him at the burial site was true. Everything I know, I learned from him."

Challa Nand glanced over. "Then try not to forget any of it," he said, and moved away.

The morning slogged on, with everyone's attention on the darkening skies. To the north, lightning flashed in jagged streaks—bursts of brightness followed by deep rolls of thunder and then long periods of silence. The wind came up an hour past sunrise, hard and quick, given to sudden bursts strong enough to knock you off your feet if you weren't paying attention. It howled down the canyons and through the peaks, ripping at lone stands of blasted trees and jagged rock. It slammed against the hull of the *Quickening* with such force that it repeatedly knocked them off course and forced them to stay well clear of cliffs against which they otherwise might have been smashed.

Before long, Austrum relinquished the helm to Railing, moving out of the pilot box and back down onto the deck. As he handed over control of the ship, he gave Railing a look and a quick nod. How much did he know? Did it matter? Railing nodded back, but kept his expression neutral.

Railing found that his arms were aching after only an hour of holding the airship steady. The concentration necessary to withstand the force of the blow required forgetting about everything else, and he was grateful to do so. Skint was forward, monitoring their progress from the bow. Challa Nand stood next to him in the pilot box, listening to the Gnome Tracker's warnings before suggesting adjustments. His huge presence was a comfort as he pointed out favorable avenues of passage, gaps that might better serve them, heights and depths they might more easily travel. He seemed to know a great deal about flying airships, particularly in these mountains, and Railing paid attention to his advice. They would make it through this patch of bad weather, he kept telling himself. They would find a way.

Shortly after, the storm struck—a curtain of black rain that left them all but blind. Railing could no longer either see or hear Skint from where he crouched at the bow. *Steady, steady*, Challa Nand would say every few minutes. And Railing would respond.

Austrum relieved him not long after, telling him to rest. Railing didn't argue. It was barely three hours after sunrise, and yet it felt like they had been flying all day. Worse, the sun hadn't showed itself since dawn, and the light was so bad you could only see a few yards ahead. Challa Nand seemed to see farther than the rest of them, his eyes sharp enough to pick out the cliffs that hemmed them in. They might have tried taking the airship higher, but once above the peaks the winds were blowing fiercely, threatening to shred the sails and bring the ship down completely.

Woostra had long since gone below, so airsick he could barely stand. He was forced to occupy the space alone since by now everyone else was well enough to stay topside, including the previously injured sailor, Aleppo. The Rovers and Mirai were working the lines and monitoring the power of the diapson crystals, ready to change them out if needed. Railing watched them through the rain and gloom for a few minutes, then worked his way forward to the bow and dropped down beside Skint.

"Do you have any idea at all where we are?" he asked.

The Gnome shrugged. "Somewhere in the Charnals? Of course, I'm just guessing."

"How are we going to get through this? I can't see anything beyond the end of my arm."

"Challa Nand knows where we are and how to get to where we are going. He told me this morning we're about two hours out from the Klu. We just have to ride out the worst of this storm and hope there isn't another one waiting up ahead." He glanced over at Railing and grinned. "Admit it—this is sort of fun, isn't it?"

Railing stared at him, and then realized he was right. In a reckless, bone-jarring sort of way, it was fun. He grinned back. "As long as you're an airman or a crazy Gnome Tracker, maybe so."

Skint laughed, then took Railing down into the hold for a drink of ale. Sitting near the keg that held the amber liquid, they sipped from cups, sodden and bedraggled in the near dark.

"You look a wreck," Skint offered, raising his cup and clinking it with Railing's.

"Your health," the boy responded.

They drank and leaned back against the bulkhead. "Sorry about Farshaun," the Gnome said after a minute. His wizened face was solemn. "He was a good man. I liked him. He had iron in him."

"That he had." Railing looked off into the gloom, thinking of what Farshaun had said to him about Mirai on his deathbed.

That girl, she's worth a dozen of you or me. She's got grit and determination that haven't even been scratched. She's got heart. And she loves you.

He believed it all except for the last, even though it was the last he most wanted to believe. He didn't feel like she loved him, not really. Not even after last night. But he loved her; there was no disputing that. Now, more than ever. But in a different, more complex way. He loved her intensely and completely enough that he wanted her to love him back in the same way.

"You seem a little less distant today," Skint said suddenly. "You were keeping pretty much to yourself after we left Arborlon. Something was bothering you. Did you get past that?"

Railing nodded. "I think maybe I did."

He meant it. He could tell that he was different—his attitude, his temperament—ever since he had opened up to Mirai and confessed the secrets he had been keeping. It hadn't changed the reality of how things might play out when they reached their destination. It hadn't changed the wrongness of what he had done to the others. But it had allowed him to breathe again. Keeping his meetings with the King of the Silver River and the Grimpond to himself had suffocated him. Sharing it with Mirai had been the right thing to do, and he felt stronger for having done so.

He sipped at his ale, working hard not to spill it as the airship lurched side-to-side and bucked against the force of the winds.

"If I get through this in one piece," Skint said suddenly, "I'm going back into the Eastland mountains and I'm never coming out again."

"We'll get through," Railing answered at once, and he meant it.

Skint got to his feet, put down his cup, and started for the ladder. "You'll be the one to make it happen, if anyone can," he called back.

Railing stayed where he was just long enough to finish his ale and then followed him up.

On deck, he joined Mirai and the Rovers in working the lines, taking his place among them. He said nothing to the Highland girl, although they exchanged a brief glance. He was thinking—even in the teeth of this monster storm with winds lashing them and rains drenching them and the whole world around them gone as black as night—that they were going to get through. *He* was going to get through. And he would find a way to make certain the others got through with him. He would find Grianne Ohmsford, and he would persuade her to come back to help them, no matter what it took. He was strong enough for this. He was the one with the wishsong magic; even Challa Nand, that huge, seemingly indestructible Troll, had said they would need his magic before this was done. They all knew what he was capable of, and he didn't have the right to doubt himself when they depended on him like that. There wasn't room for doubt. There was only room for belief in himself and determination to make what was needed happen.

But reality has a way of demonstrating the limits of self-belief and determination, and shortly thereafter, one of the Rovers was caught by a sudden gust of wind that blew him sideways and right over the railing. His safety line jerked taut, keeping him from dropping into the void, and Austrum and Railing, who were working on either side of him, rushed to pull him back aboard.

But before they could do so, his safety line snapped—the wind too strong, the rope too worn. With a wrenching wail, he pinwheeled away into the void and disappeared, leaving the Rover and the boy holding the broken line and staring at each other helplessly.

By midmorning, to everyone's relief, the storm had moved on. The winds had gone still and the downpour turned to a steady drizzle. Ahead, the clouds began to clear and they at last caught a glimpse of the bright sun as it peeked through the clouds. No one was saying much of anything at this point, the entire company made silent by the loss of yet another of their members and by the exhaustion that had gripped them all, in spite of the fact that it was not even midday. Railing was back at the helm, with Mirai standing next to him in place of Challa Nand and Skint, who had gone forward to study the lay of the land ahead. Neither was saying much, and nothing of consequence when they did speak, confining their conversation to remarks about navigation or the weather.

Unexpectedly, Austrum appeared behind them, coming up

the steps and into the cockpit. "I think it would be best if both of you stayed in the pilot box until we reach our destination," he said.

Railing and Mirai exchanged a startled glance.

"I'm suggesting this for a reason," the Rover said. Pointing to Railing, "Everything we are doing depends on you. If we lose you over the side the way we did Ekstrin, this entire trip will have been for nothing." He pointed to Mirai. "And he'll need someone to spell him when he tires."

"But you could spell . . ." Mirai began.

He shook his head quickly. "How will it look if I let my men risk their lives while I stay safe and sound inside the pilot box? No, you share the helm duties, and I'll work the lines with my men. The matter is settled."

And with that, he vaulted out of the pilot box and did not look back.

"He knows," Railing said after a moment.

Mirai nodded and said nothing.

They flew on through calmer skies for another quarter hour, at which point Challa Nand came into the pilot box and told Railing and Mirai that their destination was just ahead. Leaving Mirai at the controls, the boy walked out on deck with him and up to the bow, where Skint was looking out over the Klu. The mountains they were sailing toward were more heavily forested than those they had passed through earlier. The light caught the thickness and sweep of the trees—a deep green carpet that spread away through the tangle of peaks like an emerald stream.

"That's the Inkrim," the Troll advised, pointing farther north to where the Klu opened up to form a wide valley.

The Inkrim clearly took its name from its color. It was virtually black, with shadows and rock formations and the huge dark trunks of the trees, which grew in heavy clusters, and odd formations that seemed to have been caused by a massive upheaval in ancient times. Railing tried to imagine his grandfather, Penderrin Ohmsford, navigating this country on foot when he had come in search of the tanequil. It looked impossible. But his grandfather had not been given a choice. He and the others with him were being hunted by Druids who wanted them dead. Their airship had been destroyed, and travel afoot was the only option that had been left them.

At least this time, the boy thought, *we have the means to fly over this mess.*

He returned to the cockpit so that Mirai could go forward for a look of her own, and Skint came into the box to join him. The sun was almost fully out by now, and the world again had a peaceful look to it, even if the land below was dark and forbidding. "Challa Nand says we can fly right up to Stridegate's ruins and set *Quickening* down. The natives—the Urdas—would tear us to pieces, if they could, for doing so; the ruins are sacred ground for them. But they have a strict taboo about entering; it applies even to them. Still, if they can find a way to reach us, they will. So we have to be careful."

The boy understood. He knew a little of the history of his grandfather's search for the tanequil, and the Urdas had featured prominently. Because they were afoot, Penderrin and company had been attacked and nearly overrun by the natives, and had barely managed to gain the sanctuary of Stridegate.

With any luck, they should be able to avoid repeating that—although luck hadn't been particularly kind to them so far.

They sailed on for another half hour, Challa Nand setting them a roundabout course to reach the Inkrim and Stridegate's ruins. His purpose, he explained, was to avoid being seen by the Urdas. So they were flying outside the perimeter of the valley with a screen of peaks to shield them from view. When they emerged again, they would be directly in front of Stridegate and perhaps be able to land the *Quickening* swiftly enough that they would not be noticed.

"It will all have to happen quickly, so be ready when I tell you," he said to Railing. "Take it down to just above ground level. We'll moor it from there and descend using ladders. I don't want it on the ground if we have to make a quick escape. I want it ready to lift away."

"I am to stay at the helm?" the boy asked.

The Troll shrugged. "It's your quest."

They swung north and then sharply west again—a swift change of direction that Railing executed perfectly, keeping the *Quickening* low in the shelter of the peaks, trying to move it through shadows cast by the mountains so it would be less visible. Ahead, the Inkrim was a huge bowl of darkness, its interior filled with jagged rocks and trees, ravines and ridges, and layered shadows.

Challa Nand was back beside him, gesturing. "Down there. That's Stridegate."

Railing could just barely pick out the tangle of broken walls that had once formed buildings. The remains of the city spread out over several miles amid clumps of trees, tall grasses, scrub, and wildflowers. If it hadn't been pointed out to him, he probably would have missed it entirely.

"Fly there, the closest end. Where the darkness is heaviest."

Railing did so, taking the airship down to just above the tree-tops, then into the ruins at the near end, clear of the darkness, which he now realized was a combination of shadows and heavy mist. There seemed to be a microclimate of some sort at work— a reordering of the weather that darkened and deepened everything. There was no evidence of it anywhere else.

He found an open space among the jagged sections of walls

and towers and eased the airship into position, holding it in place just off the ground. The Rovers scurried about, dropping mooring lines and then descending the rope ladders port and starboard to secure them. Everyone moved as quickly and as silently as they could manage, and within less than ten minutes they were anchored in place.

Leaving the Rovers and Woostra aboard ship, Challa Nand took Railing, Mirai, and Skint with him to begin the search.

Descending from the airship, they gathered in what amounted to the aftermath of thousands of years of abandonment and decay, staring into the ruins. "Where do we go from here?" Challa Nand asked.

Railing hesitated. He had no idea at all. What he did know was that this was as far as they were going to get unless he did something to help them determine where the tanequil could be found—and that meant using the ring the King of the Silver River had given him. He glanced around a bit longer, stalling while he tried to come up with something else, but there wasn't anything. He would have to use the ring.

He moved away from them, looking out into the rumpled carpet of crumbled walls and ruined buildings that stretched away into the mist and shadows, and his hand dipped into his pocket and brought out the ring. He glanced at it momentarily before slipping it on his finger. He couldn't hide what he was going to do next, so he turned his back to them as he pulled one of the golden strands free of the woven band and held it up. Instantly the thread disappeared in a blinding light that caused him to close his eyes protectively. When he opened them again, the thread was gone and he knew where to go.

"What was that?" Skint asked him, as the others came over. "Where did you get that ring?"

"It was a gift from Aphenglow," he answered quickly, trying

not to look at Mirai. "It helps find things that are hidden or ways in and out of places when you don't know them. She said I might need it."

The Gnome and the Troll exchanged a quick look that suggested they had doubts, but then the latter shrugged it off and said, "Lead the way."

They set off into the ruins with Railing in front. The thread was there inside his head now, an instinct that tugged him along in a strange but not unpleasant way. He set a brisk pace, moving through the rubble, picking his way over broken rock and around half-formed walls. He could tell already they were headed into the heaviest of the mist shrouding the ruins, the darkness before them steadily deepening.

When the mist was sufficiently thick that they could barely see a few yards ahead, Challa Nand said, "You're sure about this, are you?"

"He's sure," Mirai answered for him, then moved up to his shoulder. "You are, aren't you?" she whispered.

He gave her a quick glance and a smile, and she nodded and dropped back again.

A short while later the mist and shadows fell away, and they found themselves standing before a fully formed and undamaged wall draped with flowering vines and deep green ivy. It was such an astonishing transition that everyone just stopped and stared for a few minutes. Railing felt the tug of the thread within his mind, urging him on.

And then, abruptly, there was something else—a sort of presence. It wasn't inside his mind; it was in the air he was breathing. It was close enough that he felt it brush against him. He took a step back in surprise, trying to decide what it was.

–Enter–

The voice came out of nowhere, but he knew at once it was

the presence that had just touched him. He looked again at the wall. There was an arched entry that opened about twenty feet to his right. He started toward it at once, and the other three followed.

Once they passed through the arch, they were inside magnificent gardens. Iron trellises of flowering vines backed up against the stone walls, and rows of flowering bushes grew everywhere in neat, orderly rows. Beds of brilliant color spread away through statuary, fountains, ponds, and huge old hardwoods thick with leaves. The sun shone out of cloudless skies, bright and warm and unimpeded by mist or shadows. There had been no sign of such a place when they were in the air; nothing of what they were seeing had been visible from overhead. It was as if they had entered another country—as if by stepping through the arch, they had come into a place completely apart from the ruins they had passed through only moments before.

Railing looked about in disbelief, aware the others were doing the same. He had heard that the Meade Gardens in the Dwarf city of Culhaven were wondrous, but he couldn't imagine they were more incredible than these.

Mirai was back beside him. "Who do you think tends these gardens?" she asked quietly.

He hadn't thought of that. Someone must. The grounds were immaculate. Everything was pristine, with no sign of wilt or decay—and nothing growing that didn't belong. He felt the presence brush him again. More than one, he realized suddenly. Surely they had something to do with how these gardens came to be protected when everything else had been destroyed.

–Come–

"Who are you?" he whispered into the air.

–She waits–

They were urging him on, but they would not answer his

question. He looked around doubtfully, seeking reassurance from the ring's thread, but it had quit prodding him. It was gone, he realized.

"What are you doing?" Mirai was standing close to him, her voice deliberately low.

He shook his head. "Something is calling to me. I can't see what it is, but it's there."

"The aeriads?"

"I can't tell. But I think so."

They stood together, looking ahead into the gardens, listening. A few paces behind them, Challa Nand and Skint waited, watching them. A hush had settled over everything.

–Come–

The voices. An entire chorus now. "They're calling again," he said to Mirai.

He reached for her hand, took hold, and started away once more. They continued walking in the same direction, through the hedgerows and bushes and flower beds, through the statuary and fountains, bright sunlight splashing everywhere as they walked. The minutes passed, but the voices did not return. The gardens continued to stretch out ahead of them with no discernible end in sight. Railing began to wonder if they had made a mistake of some sort. But if they had, wouldn't the voices say something?

"Railing," Mirai said suddenly, her hand tightening on his.

As they slowed, he followed her gaze to something off to the left. It was a formation of some sort, and at first he couldn't decide what it was. But as they drew a little closer, he saw it was a bridge—an arch constructed of ancient stone blocks reaching across a broad ravine to a stand of huge old-growth trees and jagged rock formations. The trees rose hundreds of feet toward the sky, the branches meeting overhead to cast dark shadows on the earthen floor. It was impossible to see much beyond the perimeter, even though the trees were widely spaced and passage through looked unimpeded.

When they got closer still, he saw that the ravine was so deep and shadowed he could not find its bottom. It seemed to encircle the stand of old growth as the sea surrounds an island.

–Cross–

He shook his head. Instinctively, he knew that was a mistake. Crossing over that bridge would change everything. Something dark and dangerous waited there. Maybe it was the tanequil and maybe it was something else. But it wasn't anything he wanted to face.

–Cross–

Yet the voices demanded it, and if he wanted to discover the truth about what had become of Grianne Ohmsford, he would have to do as they asked. The answer was there. Both the King of the Silver River and the Grimpond had said so. He had come all this way believing he would find what he sought. He had come to help his brother, and any thought of turning back now was out of the question. Whatever the risk, he would have to take it.

He reached down and pulled a second thread from the ring, its slender strand sliding free, flashing swiftly and disappearing. He asked this time where Grianne Ohmsford could be found. It was the only way of reaffirming that she was in the same direction he was being led. Sure enough, he knew at once that he would find her on the forested island on the other side of the ravine.

He knew as well he would find the tanequil there.

He looked at Mirai. "I have to cross that bridge."

"I know," she said. "I guessed as much. I'm coming with you."

"You can't do that."

She was suddenly angry. "I can do what I want, Railing."

"No, I don't mean it that way." He glanced back at Skint and Challa Nand. They were watching them, but keeping their distance. "I can't take you any closer because I don't want the tanequil to think I might agree to trade you for Grianne. She's there, somewhere in that forest, but so is the tanequil. I can't take anything for granted. Remember what happened to Penderrin and Cinnaminson? The tree took her in exchange for the staff. That sort of exchange isn't going to happen. Either I find Grianne and bring her out or I don't. But no one stays behind like Cinnaminson did."

"Maybe you won't have a choice. What if the tree demands that *you* stay?"

He shook his head. "I'll find a way. Grianne will do the right thing; she will come because I will make her understand it is the right thing to do."

"If you won't take me, then at least take Skint or Challa Nand. You need someone with you."

"But it would be the same, Mirai. I would simply be risking their lives instead of yours. I've done that for the last time. I won't do it again. I have to go alone."

Mirai studied his face, then slowly nodded. "You're set on this, and I know I don't have the right to stop you. I was the one who insisted you find yourself again, and you have. You're the Railing I remember, and that's who I want you to be. Who you need to be. But I don't like letting you leave me behind."

His smile was wan and brief. "I don't like it much, either."

"Your mother will never forgive me if something happens to you, too."

"She probably won't forgive any of us for anything that's happened, if she ever finds out."

Mirai smiled in spite of the tears in her eyes. "I'll explain it to the other two. I'll make them understand." Then she put her arms around him and kissed him hard. "I'll be waiting for you," she said.

Wordlessly, he turned away and started for the bridge.

14

RAILING FELT THE IMMENSITY OF WHAT HE WAS about to do pressing down on him as he approached the steps leading up to the bridge and hesitated one final time.

The voices would have none of it.

–Cross–

He resisted the urge to look back at Mirai and her companions—to seek reassurance where no reassurance could be found—and instead obeyed the voices and began to climb. The world around him receded, the colors and smells and sense of peace all fading away. At the top of the steps, he felt the pull of the gloom and shadows that lay ahead. All around him, the voices wrapped him in their invisible whispers and soft caresses.

–Cross–

He made his way onto the bridge, allowing himself to take his time, working hard at staying calm enough to think everything through. The bridge arch provided a wide span for crossing, but there were no guard-rails or walls. As he moved onto the walkway, he could see down into a ravine that fell steeply away below. It was an endless drop into blackness, and, after twenty feet of walls grown thick with vegetation and gnarled roots, it became a void.

He took a single glance to either side and did not take another. He forced himself instead to focus his attention on the stone pathway before him. He kept to the exact middle of the span so that he would not be tempted to go closer to the edge. The lure to do so was present; he could feel it. But because he was always taking risks, always tempting the fates—just as Mirai had said—he knew better than to put himself within reach.

As he neared the far side of the bridge and began looking up into the huge old trees that grew there, he heard singing. It was in the air around him, swirling about, drawing him in. The voices were soft and sweet, and while the words were indistinct, the music was soothing. He could feel his fears and doubts diminishing and his confidence growing. It was an unwarranted response to what was happening, but the voices were compelling.

He came down off the bridge and stood looking into the forest. The trees towered over him, their huge trunks more than a dozen feet across, their great limbs canopied overhead to blot out the sky, leaving the forest dark and layered in shadows. Nothing moved within the trees; no sounds came from the gloom.

Where was he supposed to go now?

–Come–

As if they had read his mind, the voices beckoned. Their music shifted and took him forward and slightly left of where he stood. The bridge disappeared behind him. His companions vanished. He was alone on his quest, and he was faced with discovering at last if his journey had been in vain or if it might provide some hope for finding Redden and putting an end to the threat from the Straken Lord. Even as he considered what he was trying to achieve, he was confronted anew with the foolishness of it. To think that he would be able to find a woman who had disappeared more than a hundred years ago alive and well and then persuade her to come back with him to face a monster that wanted things of her she could not possibly provide was the height of arrogance. He wondered at what had made him think he could do this.

And yet, right from the beginning, it had seemed to him that he could succeed. He had told himself that this was the path he must travel. Even knowing how impossible it seemed, he was drawn toward it. He wondered now, remembering how he had disdained the advice of the King of the Silver River, how he had ignored what his instincts told him about the Grimpond's duplicity, how he had refused to allow common sense to intercede and the possibility of failure to color his hopes. The warnings had been given, the odds against him made clear, and still he had persisted.

He continued ahead, knowing only that he was moving toward something and whatever he found would bring about some sort of resolution. He told himself—insisted to himself—that it would be enough.

Questions crowded his mind as he listened to the music of the creatures leading him. Would he find Grianne Ohmsford here, somewhere in the ruins of Stridegate, as the ring suggested he would? Was she still alive? He felt from the tugging of the thread that she was, but he couldn't be certain. The tugging might just as easily lead him to her grave.

"Who are you?" he again asked the voices leading him.

This time, they answered.

–Aeriads–

Aeriads. Spirits of the air. The creatures that served the tanequil. "Where are you taking me?"

–She waits. She knows–

"Who?"

–Come–

He felt them moving away, and so he followed. The thread seemed to be following them as well, prodding him in the same direction. He was deep in the forest now, surrounded by the great old trees, a part of the shadows, a tiny transient life-form among ancients. He glanced about for movement, but found none. There was no sign of anything present save for the voices.

As he advanced, he rehearsed in his mind what he would say to Grianne. What words would he need to persuade her to his cause? He had come so far and risked so much, and yet he had no firm idea of what it would take. Even now, after all this time, he was uncertain.

He felt a chill run through him. He wasn't equal to this; he didn't have what was needed. He was going to fail.

–Come–

But to turn back now was unthinkable, an act of cowardice and an admission of defeat. He must do what he came to do and find a way to succeed.

–Here–

He was in a clearing, dappled with sunlight and permeated with a warmth he had not felt before. The voices were singing loudly now, their music filling up his senses. He looked around for something he would recognize, for a sign of Grianne, for the "she" the aeriads had told him was waiting, but there was nothing to see. The clearing was empty.

Then, abruptly, everything went silent, and in that same instant he felt the tugging inside his head disappear.

–Railing. I am here–

A voice in the air, disembodied. "Grianne?" he whispered.

–I am what Grianne has become–

He hesitated, a sinking feeling in the pit of his stomach. *What she has become?* "Are you one of them? An aeriad?"

–I am–

"You exchanged yourself for Cinnaminson?"

–I did. When I left Paranor, I came here to offer myself for the girl who would later become your grandmother. She had given herself for me, so that Penderrin could come into the Forbidding and free me. I chose to do the same for her and let her return to Pen–

He felt a rippling in the air and heard the soft voices of the other aeriads calling.

–My time to speak with you is short. Tell me why have you come, my brother's great-grandson, child of my blood. Tell me what you seek–

So he did. Quickly and efficiently. He told her how he and Redden had accepted Khyber Elessedil's request that they come with her to the Westland in search of the missing Elfstones of Faerie, of how their efforts had gone so badly awry and how Redden had become a prisoner of the Straken Lord and was trapped inside the Forbidding. He told her how Tael Riverine had demanded that Grianne be brought to him so she could become his Queen and bear his children. Finally, he revealed that the Ellcrys was failing and the wall of the Forbidding was coming down. The Straken Lord intended to bring his demon hordes into the Four Lands and take what he wanted, Grianne included, if she did not come back to him on her own. All of this had persuaded him to seek her out and ask if she would return to help them in their struggle—if she might not be able to show them a way that Tael Riverine could be destroyed. He had discovered her fate in the diary written by Khyber and had followed it here.

"I thought you might return with me because Redden is your blood descendant and you loved Penderrin and would want to help his grandson." He exhaled sharply. "I came to find you, really, because I didn't know what else to do to save my brother."

–Railing, I cannot help you–

The words were tinged with regret, but were no less bitter for being so. Oddly, they were the words he had been expecting to hear all along, but had convinced himself she would not say.

"Is there nothing you can do?" he pressed. "Even if you came back long enough to face him and tell him what you have become, perhaps that would be enough. If he saw what you were, maybe he would no longer have interest in you and be persuaded to abandon ..." He trailed off helplessly, aware of how foolish that sounded. "Or maybe you could just persuade him to let Redden go because his imprisonment serves no purpose."

–The Straken Lord will be persuaded of nothing. He will be enraged. He is not human. He is a demon. He craves power, and when he cannot have me, he will turn his anger on others–

Railing felt the first twinges of desperation. "If you are an aeriad, you are beholden to the tanequil. But Cinnaminson was an aeriad, and you found a way to replace her and set her free. Can't you do that now for yourself? Can't you get free of the tanequil, at least long enough to come back with me?"

–I have been an aeriad for a lifetime, not for mere weeks. I am nothing of what I was and cannot impact the world of humans and Elves as once I did. I cannot come back with you–

"But you must!"

He blurted out the words in a paroxysm of frustration and dismay. The air around him went still in the aftermath, and for a second he thought she had left him, unwilling to listen to more.

"What about the Druid order? It is destroyed because of Tael Riverine! Would you let that happen? Would you do nothing to help preserve it?" He paused, waiting for an answer that did not come. "Grianne! Are you there?"

–I cannot help you, Railing. You must leave–

He took a deep steadying breath. He stood at the edge of a cliff, and she was pushing him from behind so that he would fall and all would be lost. He was devastated, but he was angry, too.

"I will go to the tanequil and speak to it! I will insist you be freed from your service and come back with me! My brother's life is at risk, but so are the lives of everyone in the Four Lands!"

There was a rush of movement as the other aeriads whipped about him—or perhaps it was only Grianne, suddenly become aggressive and swiping at him repeatedly.

–Do not do this–

"What else can I do? Give up? Go back without you? Go back with no way to save my brother?" He gathered himself. "I won't leave until I am sure there is no other way. Not until I've spoken with the tanequil. Will you help me or not? Will you persuade it to speak with me, just for a minute, just to hear what I have to say?"

–The tanequil already knows–

"Then take me to it!"

–Beware, Railing Ohmsford–

Her voice was soft, but there was iron behind the silk. For an instant, he was certain he had gone too far.

"Just . . . let me try," he said finally.

–You risk more than you realize–

"I would risk everything for my brother!"

–So you do. So you will. Good-bye, Railing–

And she was gone. He could feel her leave-taking. He could sense the emptiness she had left behind and hear the silence that filled it.

"Grianne?" he called out anyway.

Nothing. And then . . .

–Come–

The voices of the other aeriads, calling him away. Where would they take him now? To the tanequil or back to the bridge? If the latter, he would refuse to cross. If they would not take him to the tree so that he would have a chance to say what was needed, he would not follow them.

He began a lengthy trek through the forest, weaving in and out of the great black trunks, shadows draping his way and shards of sunlight providing fragments of illumination to guide his footsteps. The aeriads sang to him so that he knew where to go, but there was no further communication with Grianne Ohmsford. If she was there with her sisters, she was keeping quiet. If she was monitoring his journey, she was doing so in secret. He hardened his heart against her, still disappointed and angry at her refusal to help, still frightened that he was going to fail in his efforts.

But if he found the tanequil and spoke with it, there was still a chance that something could be salvaged. The aeriads served the tree; if the tree agreed that Grianne should be set free to come back with him, that the Four Lands needed her to stand against the Straken Lord, wouldn't she have to change her mind and do what Railing asked? Wouldn't she then be bound to aid him in his efforts?

He held on to that hope like a lifeline, knowing it was all he had left.

It became clear after a short while that he was not being taken back the way he had come. The trees were getting larger and the way darker. The forest canopy was closing out even the little light that had filtered down previously, and the whole of the forest through which he walked was gloom-filled and hazy. The aeriads had stopped singing, but every so often they would speak that single word—*come*—to let him know where he was to go. The hugeness of the trees diminished him further, and he experienced a withering of hope and confidence. The audacity of his efforts to persuade Grianne resurfaced, and he saw again how foolish he had been.

As he navigated the maze of the forest, the warnings of the King of the Silver River whispered anew from his memory. He was doing something that was forbidden. He was asking for what he could not have. If he persevered, he would not get what he was hoping for; he would get something else entirely. Grianne Ohmsford was lost to his world and belonged to another. He could not bring her back again. He should forget this quest and simply go after Redden on his own. But was that even possible? Was there any way he could go back into the Forbidding and free his brother from the Straken Lord?

His trek wore on, and the gloom deepened. It must be late in the afternoon by now. The stresses of both the morning and the trek caught up to him, and he grew sleepy. The aeriads had resumed singing, and their music was weaving about him in a soothing blanket that left him heavy-eyed and slow-footed. He took a moment to stop, and when the aeriads did not object he sat down to rest.

Just for a moment.

But in seconds he was asleep.

His sleep was deep and dreamless, and when he woke again the sun was lower in the sky. He blinked a few times and waited for his lingering lethargy to disappear, wondering how he had managed to sleep at all with the mix of emotions roiling inside.

And yet he had. He had slept, and slept deeply.

–Railing–

He sat up quickly and looked around. A voice, calling his name, but it wasn't the aeriads. This voice was deep and resonated with distant thunder and the roll of the earth in a quake. It took him only a moment to find the source. A monstrous tree loomed over him, all gnarled and studded with boles, its limbs so broad they seemed to have forced the surrounding trees to fall back in deference. There was a surreal aspect to this tree, as if it had come from another world or another plane of existence, a creature alien and unknowable. Its trunk was black, but streaked with tinges of orange, and the green of its leaves ranged from bright emerald to the darkest jade. Even in the windless silence of the morning, its canopy shivered softly.

It was the tanequil. The aeriads had brought him to it, and Grianne, for all her protestations and warnings, had not denied him his chance.

He sat up slowly, discovering as he did so that there were tiny roots clutching at him, slender tendrils attached to his body and limbs. He looked down at them in wonder. Had they sprouted while he slept? How could they have managed to do that in so short a time?

In his mind, he heard his name spoken once more.

–Railing–

But the voice was more distant now, less clear—as if the communication had frayed or the distance between them increased.

"Tanequil?" he replied.

Nothing. He waited, but there was no response. What was he doing wrong? The aeriads had responded quickly enough; there had been no problem communicating with them. Why was the tree not answering him?

He lowered his hands to the ground for leverage as he prepared to stand. But the minute he did so, the tiny roots began wrapping about him anew, entwining his fingers and wrists, their feathery touch strangely compelling.

–Railing–

The voice was strong again, clear and precise in his mind. It was speaking to him through the roots, he realized. He kept his hands where they were and remained kneeling so that the roots could continue to make contact with him.

Then, on an inspired whim, he spoke the tree's name in the silence of his mind.

–Tanequil–

The answer was instantaneous.

–Railing. What do you require of me–

The boy could hardly contain his excitement.

–Grianne Ohmsford's freedom. She must come back with me into the Four Lands. It is a chance to save my brother. A chance to save everyone–

Quickly he blurted it out in chaotic, disorderly fashion, facts mingling with emotions, details interwoven with pleas. He revealed the whole of what he was seeking, sparing nothing of himself and his doubts and fears, opening up in a way he had not done before, not even with Mirai. His thoughts passed through his mind in a rush; he could not seem to help himself. Everything burst forth from where it crowded together and found its way to the tanequil in a stream of raw emotion.

When he had finished, he was exhausted from the effort. The tree was silent for a long time. Railing, waiting impatiently, wondered if he had done enough or too much. He couldn't be certain; his perspective was skewed and his nerves rubbed raw.

–Mother Tanequil commands the aeriads. They belong to her and answer only to her–

Mother Tanequil? What is the tree talking about?

–But you're the tanequil, aren't you? Are you female? I thought you were male–

–I am both. My trunk, my branches, my leaves are male. I am Father Tanequil. My roots, grown deep into the earth are female. I am also Mother Tanequil–

Railing struggled with the concept.

–But aren't they one and the same? Aren't the two joined together? Do you not think and act as one–

–We are one, but we are separate, too. The aeriads serve Mother Tanequil. She must decide if one of them is to be released. Have you brought an offering in exchange for your request–

The boy took a deep, uncertain breath. He had been dreading this moment.

–No–

–Nothing–

–Nothing should be required. If my request is denied, the whole of the Four Lands will be overrun with the demons released from the Forbidding and everything and everyone will perish. You would be at risk, too–

The tree seemed to consider. Its roots stopped their caressing, and its leaves ceased their shivering.

–I am never at risk. Things that are mortal cannot destroy the Faerie–

–But you would be left in a world filled with evil beings seeking ways to destroy you or possess you or dominate you. This can't be something you want–

–Evil has tried to dominate us before. Evil has tried to destroy your kind before. You always survive–

Railing was furious.

–But it doesn't have to happen! It can be prevented if Grianne Ohmsford comes with me–

–Mother Tanequil will decide–

Railing sat back on his heels and tried to think of another argument he could make. But he had talked himself out, and he sensed that the tree did not want to hear more.

–Do I need to go to her? Do I need to speak with her–

–She hears what I hear. She knows what you want and is deciding. She chooses to help you or not. You must wait–

–I will not give up, even if she chooses not to help me–

It was a bold statement, born of frustration and a need to make clear that he would accept only one answer. He spoke with a creature thousands of years old, a creature of Faerie and of the world's beginning, but he could not let that frighten him.

The tanequil's deep rumble was restrained and even. –You are reckless and foolish. You act without thinking. What you need is not what you seek–

What does that mean? Haven't I made my needs clear?

–If she chooses to help, Mother Tanequil will give you what you need, though perhaps not what you want–

Railing stared at the tree, confused. How could there be a difference? He started to say something, to ask for an explanation that would dispel his confusion and a rising sense of doubt. But the tendrils that caressed his hands and limbs were withdrawing.

–Return to the bridge–

The touching ceased, and the links of communication were broken. Railing remained where he was, arms at his sides, hands against the earth, staring up at the tanequil. *Speak to me*, he willed it. *Don't leave me.*

But the tree had finished with him. There would be no more talking. After long minutes, he got to his feet again, trying to decide what he should do. Should he return to the bridge as the tree had ordered, or should he remain where he was in case it chose to speak to him further?

–Come–

The aeriads were making the choice for him. He hesitated a moment, and then he turned in the direction of their voices and reluctantly walked away.

*

Once, when Redden and he were small, they had walked into the Duln from Patch Run without telling their mother. They had been forbidden to do this, but they were wild and reckless even then, and such admonitions seldom deterred them once they had decided on a course of action. They were looking for a were-cot—a small and very rare animal that had been seen in the forests surrounding their home perhaps twice in the last hundred years. This did not trouble them. If someone else had seen a werecot, they would see it, too.

So off they went on an adventure, but they managed to go much deeper into the Duln than they had intended and soon were lost. This might have frightened other boys, but it was of no particular concern to them. After all, they had the use of the wishsong, and they knew that if they were really in trouble, the magic would come to their aid. What they had failed to consider, however, was that magic doesn't necessarily solve all your problems. In this instance, they could not figure out how to use it to find a way out of the forest. So they wandered for most of the day, trying to rescue themselves and failing, and it was nearing nightfall when they finally stumbled clear of the woods, miles from where they had started out.

Remembering this, it occurred to him that what was happening here was very like what had happened in the Duln when he and Redden were boys. He was discovering all over again that there were limits to what magic could do. Not just the wishsong, but other magic, as well. These limits were defined by the nature of the magic, but also by the character of the user. The tanequil, though it had the power to help him by using its magic to free Grianne, might not have the inclination to use that magic.

It also occurred to him that this was the longest period of time he and Redden had ever been separated.

When he arrived back at the bridge just after sunset, he slowed to a stop and stood staring out across the ravine to where he had left the others. There was no sign of them, not from where he was standing. He was certain they were there, however. What he was less certain about was whether he was ready to face them. A part of him wanted to remain where he was, waiting to see what would happen with Grianne, hoping against hope that the tanequil would grant his request and set her free, at least long enough to come back and help his brother. Another part of him felt he should cross over and tell the others what had transpired and face up to the strong possibility he had failed and this entire expedition had been for nothing.

–Cross–

Once again, the decision was made for him. The aeriads whispered the word in the still evening air, and without even pausing to think about doing otherwise, Railing Ohmsford walked to the stone arch and began to climb the steps leading to its broad span. He had gotten halfway across when he saw Mirai jump up from the bench on which she had been sitting to give him an encouraging wave. He saw Skint and Challa Nand, too, all of them on their feet and moving toward him.

He made himself return the Highland girl's greeting, trying to look encouraging and feeling anything but.

"What happened?" Mirai asked as soon as he was standing in front of her once more. "Did you find her?"

He was grateful for her restraint. She hadn't tried to hug or kiss him in front of the other two. She was keeping her voice level and direct. If she was excited or anxious, she wasn't showing it.

"I found her. She's alive. But she won't come back." He paused. "She's an aeriad. She serves the tanequil, so really it's the tree who makes the decision about what's going to happen next."

Mirai stared. "The tree is deciding what she will do?"

Close enough, Railing thought. "I spoke to it. I made all the arguments. I gave all the reasons. But I don't know. It didn't seem persuaded. If anything, it seemed reluctant. It kept telling me that even if it decided to grant my request, I wasn't going to get what I wanted. I don't know what that means."

But he was thinking that it was surprisingly close to what the King of the Silver River had told him, and he wondered if that might be a harbinger.

"But she's still alive? She could actually return with us?" Skint shook his head. "I would never have believed it. Not really. Even though I came on this journey with you, Railing Ohmsford. Even though."

"She isn't here yet," Challa Nand mumbled.

Mirai took hold of Railing by his shoulders and turned him so they were facing each other. "You did what you could. You couldn't have done more."

He smiled bitterly. "I could have tried harder."

They sat down together on the stone benches and talked about it for a while longer. Railing filled in the details, even the ones that were so painful he could barely speak of them—the tanequil's seeming indifference to the fate of the Four Lands, Grianne's deep commitment to her life as a spirit of the air that precluded disobedience to the tree—because it seemed to lessen the hurt he was feeling when he did so.

They were quiet for a time after that. Skint wandered off to study the walls of the gardens. Challa Nand stretched out on one of the benches and fell asleep.

Mirai moved over to sit close to him. "I am proud of you, Railing," she said. "Proud of you for trying. Proud of you for risking so much to see if there was something that could be done. If it doesn't work out the way you want it to, I want you to know that I will still stay with you until we find Redden and bring him home. No matter what."

It was exactly what he needed to hear, and his relief was so strong that he couldn't manage a reply. He only barely managed to keep from crying.

So they sat in the gardens of Stridegate and waited for something to happen. Dusk deepened into night, and more than once Railing thought just to go and be done with it. Grianne wasn't coming, they were wasting their time hoping she would, and the matter was decided. He kept waiting for one of the others to suggest they leave, but none of them did. They simply waited with him, staying silent, their thoughts kept to themselves.

The stars were twinkling brightly overhead when Mirai, standing a few yards off, said softly, "Railing?"

He glanced over and saw that she was staring at the bridge. He leapt up at once.

A figure was crossing the high span, moving slowly and deliberately toward them. Hooded and cloaked, its features were concealed in the dark, but Railing felt a surge of excitement. It could only be one person. Grianne Ohmsford.

They watched her come, all four of them clustered together by now, measuring her progress as she made her way toward them, her footsteps painfully slow, her efforts extreme. Her garments were old and frayed, the ends ragged and the fabric tattered. In the moonlight, she had a spectral look to her—as if she were one of night's shadows, a wraith come out of the darkness. For just an instant, Railing wondered if she might be no more than a shade and that this was what the tanequil had been trying to tell him, but he dismissed the idea as absurd. Why would she return to him as a shade? She was still alive, wasn't she?

But as the figure drew closer, he saw that something was

seriously wrong. In the look and the walk and the posture—
everything was just slightly skewed from what it should have
been. He exchanged an uneasy glance with Mirai. She saw it, too.

The figure came to a stop in front of them.

"She released me, Railing. I am here for you."

Grianne Ohmsford pulled back the hood, and the four
standing in front of her recoiled in shock. Her face was ravaged
by age and time so that she seemed more a haggard crone than
simply an older woman, more skeleton than flesh and blood. Her
features were twisted and hard, her hair white and stringy, and
her skin devoid of color, washed of all but a faint gray cast. Her
hands and arms, where they were revealed, were withered and
spotted. She was—it was apparent, even within the cloaking—
no more than a shadow of the woman she had been, and that
shadow only a single step from the grave that must already be
reaching out to claim her.

But it was the eyes that told Railing everything he needed to
know about who she was and of what the tanequil had been
trying to warn him. Her eyes were filled with a hatred and rage
that ran so deep, it had no bottom. They glittered with the intensity of it, and in that glitter there was the promise of pain and
suffering. There was inexorable purpose.

What you need is not what you seek.

"You have me back," she hissed at him. "What do you intend
to do with me?"

It wasn't Grianne Ohmsford that Mother Tanequil had
returned to him.

It was the Ilse Witch.

15

THE DEMON ATTACK, WHEN IT FINALLY CAME, caught everyone defending the city of Arishaig—and Keeton especially—by surprise.

All night he had waited for it, his soldiers stationed on the west wall, listening to the howling and shrieking of the creatures massed in the darkness just beyond the glow cast by the torches on the battlements. Midnight came and went. The night rolled on toward early morning and the approach of dawn.

But just before the first brightening of the east sky, while it was still too dark to make out anything clearly, the demon hordes attacked.

Not at the west wall, but at the south.

Somehow during the night, under cover of darkness, the attackers had managed to maneuver a second attack force into the lowland hills that rippled below the city. While the defenders' attention was focused on the creatures massed at the west wall, thousands of their fellows had circled silently around from where they had been hiding earlier behind the ridgeline until they were in position.

When they attacked, no one inside the city was ready for it. There were soldiers on the south wall stationed at regular intervals with orders to keep watch and be ready, but larger numbers occupied the west battlements because all the enemy activity of the previous day had been centered there.

To Keeton's credit, he did not panic. The fact that the initial attack had come from the south did not mean that those creatures gathered below the west wall were no longer a threat. The first attack could be a ruse to draw his soldiers away; the west wall could still be the main point of attack. So he took every third soldier out of the defensive line and sent them to reinforce the south wall and followed them over to see for himself how bad it was.

It was much worse than he had imagined. The army below the south wall mirrored the one threatening the west in size and ferocity. The attackers were already swarming the gates, surging up against them and hammering on the ironbound timbers with clubs. Dozens of creatures were climbing the walls, finding grips in the rough surface of the stone that would never have served ordinary men and women.

The defenders seemed stunned. A few were reacting to the assault, manning the fire launchers, training them on their attackers, but too many were just standing in place, waiting for the attack to come to them.

Keeton snatched the closest torch from its rack and dropped it into the oil trough, igniting the flammable liquid and instantly setting fire to dozens of attackers. Racing down the wall behind his soldiers, he slapped them on the shoulders and screamed at them to fight back, snapping them out of their shock, propelling them into action. New soldiers from the west wall appeared in droves and suddenly everyone was responding to the threat. Spears were used to dislodge the creatures climbing the walls when they got within range. Pitch was poured out of barrels onto the assailants massed at the gates and torches dropped to ignite it. Archers rushed to fire their arrows down into the hordes trying to scale the walls.

It was chaos, but the effort of defending against the surprise attack was working. The assault might have reached the south wall, but it had failed to force the gates, and fire launchers had cleared away most of those attempting to climb the walls.

Then the first of the warships was aloft, circling over the massed attackers through a wash of hazy light, everything misty and surreal but clear enough for rail slings and fire launchers to find targets. Keeton watched as the vessel roamed back and forth through the gloom, bursts of fire erupting from the launchers, the deep hum of the rail slings reverberating in the brume.

Then, abruptly, everything changed.

The dragon they had seen circling overhead the previous day materialized out of the concealment of the mist, swooping into view above the warship. The airmen were concentrating their efforts on the creatures on the ground and never looked up. Even the lookouts failed to spy the danger in time, caught up in the excitement of the moment, their eyes directed out and down rather than up. Although Keeton and dozens of others on the wall screamed in warning, their efforts were to no avail. The dragon attacked, its maw opening wide as it did so, raking the vessel end-to-end with fire, which burst in a steady stream from its great throat. In seconds ship and crew alike were aflame and falling earthward.

When it crashed, the diapson crystals that powered the ship and launchers erupted in a series of massive explosions that consumed the wreckage in seconds.

The attackers on the ground who had fallen back in the face of the fires from the trough oil and the fire launchers returned, carrying makeshift ladders that they threw up against the walls. Then they began to climb. Again the defenders used poles and spears to try to push the ladders off, but attackers still on the ground held the scaling equipment in place while those clinging to the rungs grappled with the implements being shoved at them and wrenched them away. Fire launchers and rail slings were brought into play, and archers sent arrows raining down on the climbers. Many were stricken and dropped away, but some got through and, once on the wall, became almost unstoppable. Heedless of their own safety—or their very lives—they tore at the defenders like animals, leaving them shredded.

The battle seesawed back and forth as dawn broke and the sun rose into the morning sky from behind the eastern mountains. The gloom faded, but the haze remained, thick and swirling in the rising heat and the slow approach of a storm coming down out of the north. Screams and shouts reverberated across the city, and men and women died with the passing of every minute as the struggle intensified.

An hour after sunrise, the army massed at the west wall attacked.

Keeton, still rallying his soldiers on the southern battlements, left for the west instantly. By then Sefita Rayne had four warships in the air, two flying into each battle. It made all the difference. Fighting as a pair so that one vessel warded the other and both had sentries aloft in the crow's nests watching for the dragon's return, they hammered the attackers on the ground with onslaughts of rail sling missiles and fire launcher flames alike.

It became a war of attrition on both walls, but the deciding factor was the presence of the warships. The dragon returned briefly, but was sighted quickly in the improving light and met with intense weapons fire from each pair of vessels when it tried to approach. Only once did it get close enough to set fire to one of the light sheaths, but the sheath was cut loose quickly and dropped away before the fire could spread.

On the ground, the defenders kept control of both the south and west walls, and the gates held firm against any number of efforts to force them open. As noon approached, the demon army began to withdraw, leaving their dead and wounded where they had fallen. They turned away with studied indifference to the arrows still tracking them, their rage undiminished. Keeton was appalled that his soldiers had killed so many of them and still the creatures seemed as numerous as ever. He called for a ceasefire from his defenders, not wanting to waste resources that would be needed later.

Below the west wall and on the approach road winding between the now abandoned watchtowers, scavenging beasts from the demon army caught hold of the bodies of fallen defenders and dragged them far enough away that they could feast on them, still within view of those soldiers manning the city walls.

Standing with Wint, peering through the smoke and ash rising from the last of the oil burning in the trough, Keeton watched the remnants of the demonkind slowly disappear into the distance.

"They'll be back, Commander," his second said quietly.

Keeton nodded in agreement. "They'll be back."

Seersha was exercising on the Home Guard practice field, using various members of the elite corps as sparring partners, when the messenger arrived. He stood to one side looking flushed and impatient until there was a pause in the fighting, then he rushed over.

"The King wishes to see you immediately," he said.

No matter its portent, this was welcome news. The Druid was eager for anything that would break the monotony of her current life, of endless hours spent waiting for the King to mount an Elven advance into the deep Westland to monitor the prospect of an anticipated demon breakout. She had thought it would happen long before this. She had been certain, after Aphenglow and Arling departed with the Ellcrys seedling, that their grandfather would move quickly to advise the High Council of the danger and then act on it.

She had been wrong.

The old King had waited two more days before telling the High Council of the collapse of the Forbidding, of the fate that had befallen the Druids and their companions, of the warnings given by the Ellcrys of its failing, and of the need to prepare for war.

But the members of the High Council had split into two groups, and the one led by the King's son Phaedon had urged restraint, arguing that no one really knew anything, as yet. A breakout could be weeks away; the words of a young girl who might or might not have fully understood what the Ellcrys had told her were no reason to dispatch an entire army into the wilderness of the Westland. Better that flits be sent to skim the countryside and search for signs of a breakout. Better that the army be properly mustered and prepared. Better that everyone know more than they did at the moment about what was happening.

In spite of support from both Emperowen and his brother Ellich, the younger Elessedil carried the majority of the Council. Heads in the sand, the lot of them, Seersha had thought at the time. It was especially disappointing when the old King went along with this nonsense. Seersha had been enraged, but resigned to waiting them out. What else could she do? She could take Crace Coram and fly back into the Westland, just the two of them, searching for a way back into the Forbidding. But what she needed was a strong military force so they could withstand an encounter with the Straken Lord and his demonkind.

Admittedly, she kept thinking the King would change his mind, that he would grow impatient and realize that delay in this matter could prove fatal and he must act, High Council support or no. But days went by and nothing happened, and she lacked a way to force the issue. She was a Dwarf, not an Elf—an outsider and a visitor of limited status in Elven country—and all her allies had gone elsewhere save for Crace Coram. More to the point, she was a Druid, and the prevailing view on Druids was that they could not be trusted.

No one was going to listen to her.

But now, at last, after more than a week of waiting, it seemed things might change and the waiting come to an end. She couldn't imagine another reason the King would summon her. Her impatience to confirm that she was right was matched only by her exhilaration at the prospect of doing something besides sitting around.

Nevertheless, she took time to strip off her protective gear and weapons, gather them up and put them aside, and then straighten her clothes and hair. She would see the King looking somewhat better than a tavern brawler—whatever the news he was about to impart.

A part of her was anxious to make her escape from Arborlon and the Elves because of how uncomfortable she was with both. *A fish out of water* didn't begin to describe it. She was a rough-featured Dwarf woman with an eye patch, multiple tattoos, and a body ridged with scars acquired in countless battles both while serving as a Druid and before. She was not openly shunned by the Elves, but she was clearly avoided. Except for a handful of the Home Guards who respected her skills as a fighter and cared nothing for the prejudices harbored by so many others against all things and people Druid, she was pretty much alone. Only Sian Aresh had shown more than a passing interest in spending time with her, talking at length about military tactics and training. But while the Captain of the Home Guard visited with her as often as he could, he was limited by the extent and demands of his duties.

At least she had Crace Coram for regular company, and they had whiled away long hours reminiscing about growing up in the Eastland and the Dwarf communities that had been home to them at various times in their lives. Coram was as impatient with their inactivity as she was, and in the last two days he had begun coming to the practice field to spar with her, as well. The two shared the common bonds of Race, homeland, warrior background, and the events of the Druids' ill-fated journey into the Westland to find the missing Elfstones.

But it was the absence of Aphenglow that really left Seersha feeling isolated and alone. The two had been friends from the beginning of their time together at Paranor. Whatever secrets or private thoughts they chose to reveal, they revealed them to each other first, even after Aphenglow fell in love with Bombax. This sense of closeness had only increased since the rest of the Druid order had been decimated. And now, with Aphen gone in search of the Bloodfire, Seersha felt increasingly isolated.

She finished cleaning up, stowed her fighting gear, and signaled the messenger that she was ready. As she departed the practice field, a few of her sparring partners called out, making tart, rough-hewn comments and wishing her well, bringing a smile to her face. She waved back to them, cheered by the sense of camaraderie.

Things really weren't so bad, she decided.

With the messenger a few steps ahead, keeping silent and apart as they walked back through the city toward the palace grounds, Seersha found herself studying the young man's lithe, slender frame and comparing it with her own thick, stocky build. Here was another contrast that served to point up the obvious differences between Elves and Dwarves. She was enormously powerful and could probably crush the messenger's head between her bare hands. But while she was inordinately strong, she was slow afoot and not particularly agile. She envied him his ability to move so smoothly and with such little effort. She envied all Elves, for that matter. She could never expect to move like that.

Normally, she wouldn't have given that jealousy more than a moment's thought. But it was an uncomfortable reminder of why she felt so out of place in Arborlon, where there were so many Elves and almost no Dwarves.

She let that feeling persist for a few minutes longer before dismissing it as self-indulgent. There was no place or reason for that sort of thinking. She was better than this, in any case, and letting such feelings trouble her was irritating.

She had forgotten the matter and improved her attitude by the time she reached the palace grounds and walked up to the front doorway of the ancestral homes of the Elven Kings and Queens. Home Guards shadowed their progress coming in, and two were there to meet them at the door. After determining that they were expected, the guards admitted them, and the messenger took her down a hallway to a reception room and departed.

She waited no more than a few minutes before the King and his brother, Ellich Elessedil, appeared in the doorway.

"Thank you for coming," the former greeted her, taking her

hands in his own. He made it sound as if it mattered a great deal that she was there, and she was immediately suspicious. "We need your services badly, I am afraid."

"Whatever I can do, High Lord," she said.

Ellich closed the door behind them, and the three moved over to a gathering of chairs in a windowless corner of the room. The King seated Seersha across from him while Ellich moved over to the window as if intent on keeping watch. Outside, the gardens were flowering, and the air was thick with scents that wafted through cracks in the window sash.

"The demons have broken out of the Forbidding," the King announced without preamble. "Sometime yesterday, they started massing around Arishaig."

"Arishaig?" Seersha repeated, unable to keep the surprise from her voice.

"I thought the same," Ellich interjected, looking over at her. "Why there? Why not here? The Elves are the obvious enemy of the creatures in the Forbidding. But we still don't know the answer."

"There is every reason to think the city will be taken." Emperowen was leaning forward now, his voice lowered. "If that should happen—something we think likely because of the size of the invading army—Ellich and I believe we will be next. We can't sit around waiting for that to happen."

"Like you have been doing up until now," Seersha pointed out.

The King was taken aback by her bluntness, but he nodded in agreement nevertheless. "We will follow the steps taken by Eventine Elessedil when he was King and the Forbidding failed all those hundreds of years ago. We will unite the Races and make a stand against our common enemy."

"The Dwarves will fight," Seersha said at once.

"I thought you would say as much. But we will need more than that. We will need the men and women of the Borderland Cities, as well. And the Trolls from the deep Northland. Word will be sent at once, asking for their help." He paused, glancing at his brother. "Ellich and I believe we need to make an immediate effort to save Arishaig. There are hundreds of thousands of people trapped in that city, and if a way to stop the attack of the demonkind isn't found, they will be overrun and killed. Do you agree?"

"The Federation army is the strongest in the Four Lands," Seersha pointed out, looking from one to the other. "Their largest garrison is housed in Arishaig. The city won't be easily taken."

"Nevertheless," Ellich said.

She looked at him. "Yes, the city will be taken sooner or later. The creatures of the Straken Lord will keep attacking until it has fallen. Which is why we shouldn't be sitting around discussing the matter. We have lost time to make up for. If you can assemble an army, I will travel with them to Arishaig at once. Crace Coram will return to the Eastland to inform the Dwarf tribes and rally their fighters to our—"

Emperowen held up one hand to stop her in mid-sentence. "Our course of action is clear, but not yet approved. There is a problem."

She nodded slowly, a sinking feeling in the pit of her stomach. "The Elven High Council?"

"I require their permission before I can declare war and dispatch an army of the size required. It is by no means certain that the Council members will grant this."

"There are some among them who will never even consider allying the Elves with the Federation," Ellich interjected. "Our history is a bitter one, and some among our people have long memories. There will be no problem with allying ourselves with the Bordermen or Dwarves or even the Trolls, but those alliances have traditionally been formed against the Federation."

Seersha sat down slowly. "So the High Council may choose to leave the Federation to its fate rather than swallow their pride? They will abandon our strongest potential ally because of a history that is now more than a hundred years in the past?"

"Sadly, yes." Ellich left the window and walked over to a sideboard, where he poured three glasses of ale and passed them out. "There are prejudices and resentments that will be difficult to overcome."

Seersha had heard enough. "What I know of Elven history suggests that Eventine Elessedil did not have this problem. Nor would he have stood still for an entire week of delay while his land and people were threatened with invasion. Where is your conviction in what is right and necessary, High Lord? Where is your courage?"

"Do not speak to my brother like that!" Ellich snapped at her. "Remember your place, Druid!"

"My place?" she snapped back. "My place is to advise you! How am I to do that if I hesitate to be honest in my appraisal of things? An entire week of preparation has been lost! And whose fault is that? How much more time do you intend to waste on a Council that will not act?"

Emperowen Elessedil held up his hands in a placating gesture. "Please! Enough from both of you." He stood, facing Seersha. "We go before that recalcitrant Council to make a plea for their support. We would like you to accompany us to this meeting and give the members of the High Council a clear picture of what it is we are facing. Word of the massing on Arishaig is already spreading, but you are the only eyewitness available who can speak to what happened in the Westland and therefore pass judgment on what's likely to happen here. We need your help. Will you give it?"

She took a deep breath. "Of course I will. But whatever happens with the High Council in this meeting, High Lord, I am all done sitting around and waiting on others. I intend to act as I see fit afterward."

The old King gave her a slow smile. "I would expect nothing less from you, Seersha."

"That's enough!"

Phaedon was on his feet, his face red with anger and frustration, his posture combative as he faced Seersha across the table where the Elven High Council was gathered.

"More than enough," the Druid agreed, meeting his furious gaze squarely.

"Elves don't need a Dwarf Druid to tell them how to conduct themselves!" he hissed. "We were here long before you, and we have mastered knowledge and skills far beyond anything you ever even thought of. Don't presume to tell us how we should conduct ourselves toward those who have done so much to destroy us!"

Seersha stayed calm. "Is it presumptuous to suggest that common sense should guide your decision making, Elven Prince? Is it wrong to weigh the consequences of selflessness over selfishness? Does it really need to be explained that a preemptive strike against those who would annihilate you is a better course of action than waiting for annihilation to come knocking on your door?"

The two had been arguing for the better part of the past hour as the discussion of what to do about the demon invasion had gone back and forth between advocates of two points of view— one that favored immediate intervention in the assault on

Arishaig and one that favored sticking with known friends and allies to meet the threat when it moved on from the Southland and came north.

Emperowen had made his presentation to the Council and argued that immediate action was essential. With Ellich's support, he had pointed out the advantages of including the Federation in the alliance—an alliance against an enemy that hated all of the Races equally and would do its very best to see them ground into dust. Deliberately choosing to exclude the ally with the strongest army and most advanced weaponry seemed a dangerous choice. Perhaps in this instance, if no other, sending Elves in support of the Federation was the proper course of action.

But Phaedon was quick to slide past that argument with reminders of the Federation's history of treachery and unpredictability. These were cities that, for centuries, had sought to subjugate not only the Elves but the other Races, as well. Less than two months ago, a Federation fleet had attempted to seize Paranor and destroy the Druid order. How could they even think of forming an alliance with creatures capable of such behavior?

At that point, without being asked, Seersha had entered the discussion. Taking her cue from Ellich, who glanced her way, she caught the attention of the King and asked permission to speak to the members of the High Council about what had happened to the Druid expedition when they had encountered a break in the Forbidding just a few weeks earlier. Granted that permission in spite of a disapproving look from Phaedon, she had launched into a graphic rendition of the events surrounding the struggle within the Fangs and the Forbidding by those who had gone with her. She described in detail the nature of the creatures they were up against and the savagery these creatures would display if allowed to gain a foothold in the Four Lands. She described the deaths of her friends and companions, and the terrible emotional toll taken on those few who had survived.

She closed with a warning. Aphenglow and Arling Elessedil were in search of the legendary Bloodfire that would quicken the Ellcrys seed and restore the failing wall of the Forbidding, but there was no guarantee how long that quest would take. There was no guarantee that it would succeed. The only sensible approach was to assume the worst and expect that it would fail utterly. Taking control of your own fate was the better choice. Fight now and fight hard, and your chances of survival were immediately improved.

Thus the two, Elven Prince and Dwarf Druid, had become locked in a combative argument.

"You make it sound as if the end of Arishaig is a foregone conclusion," Phaedon resumed, sitting down again and giving her an irritated look. "You suggest there is only one choice, and you are the one to make it. Where is the reason and judgment in that course of action? Would you have us appoint you as our leader, as well? Should we dispense with our own military commanders and simply accept you as the better man? Or woman?"

She shook her head in reproach. "I do not propose to lead. I propose to stand with you. All I am saying is that time slips away."

"Oh, yes. Time slips away. In point of fact, it slipped away entirely from your order, didn't it? Taking with it most of its members. So now you need a new situation and a new cause. Because you did so well with the last, no doubt."

"Phaedon!" his father called out in warning.

The Prince was baiting her, but Seersha did not bite. "I did poorly in my last situation, as did we all. But we learned valuable lessons, Prince Phaedon, and lessons that are paid for with blood and lives should not be ignored. So I say to you again: Do not mistake the extent of the danger that faces you. Act now to prevent it from getting closer. Put aside the past and embrace a future that can be different for all concerned. Assemble your army, convey it by airship to the walls of Arishaig, and end the demon invasion."

"Let's put it to a vote!" Ellich Elessedil insisted.

There was a general murmur of approval, and sensing the favorable mood of the Council the King was quick to act on his brother's suggestion. Only Phaedon and two others voted to withhold support for the Federation and besieged Arishaig. Seven others, the King included, voted in favor.

When the Council was adjourned, Phaedon rose and departed without a word or a glance at anyone.

"Well done, Seersha," the King whispered, his face expressionless as he escorted her from the chamber.

Deepest night.

Edinja Orle's creature slid through the darkness like the passing of a great cat, all swift movement with only a suggestion of substance, carrying its limp burden easily. It had come from its place of hiding among the Elves, changing into its true form, discarding its disguise until it finished what it had come to do. No one had seen it, and no one would. It would do what it had been given to do before this night was out and then return to its hiding place and resume its other identity with no one the wiser. This night's mission would remove one more obstacle to its mistress's plans, and it would accomplish that mission and leave again with no sign of its passing.

Its instructions had been delivered earlier in the day by an arrow shrike, the favored messenger of its mistress. The creature had found the bird at the usual place, away from the city and the prying eyes of its citizens. The message had been plain and direct. There was no chance of a misinterpretation or a misunderstanding.

The instructions were to be carried out this night, and they were to be followed to the letter.

The creature understood and obeyed. This was Edinja Orle, after all. Refusals were not allowed.

It made its way through the city, keeping to the back paths and staying in the shadows. When it reached its destination, it took to the trees that grew thick and plentiful throughout the sprawling grounds, their branches closely intertwined, providing a perfect avenue to avoid being seen. Moving smoothly from branch to branch and tree to tree in spite of the weight of its burden, it passed above the heads of the guards keeping watch below, some hidden and some in view but none suspecting for a moment it was there.

It could not allow itself to be seen. It could not be detected. It must be as if it were never there at all.

From the trees, it passed above the roof of the building and dropped onto a section no one slept beneath so that the sound of its landing was not heard. Carrying its limp burden, it made its way across the tiles to where an enclosed courtyard sheltered interior gardens, and dropped down onto its stone walkway. From there, it entered the house through a pair of windowed doors and moved deeper inside, passing through living quarters and down a hallway to the bedrooms.

Security was light. Strong outside, where it was intended that any threats would be met and quickly dealt with, but absent altogether once inside the residence.

Even though it was the royal palace and the ancestral home of Kings and Queens, and the Elves should have known better.

It knew the layout of the home; it had been here many times before, always in its other form, always as a welcomed guest. It had been given many opportunities to study the home's rooms and passageways, and it could find its way about easily.

It knew exactly where the old King slept.

When it entered his room, it found him slumbering in his bed, unaware of the danger. Edinja's creature wasted no time. It set aside its burden, moved to the bedside, slid the knife from its belt sheath, pinned the old man to the bed with one hand covering his mouth, and drove the knife into his chest.

Emperowen Elessedil shuddered once as the knife reached his heart and then went still.

The creature withdrew the knife in a rough, jerking motion, spraying blood and creating the impression that the attack had been violent and heated. It threw bedclothes on the floor, overturned a chair, and arranged the King's body to suggest that a terrible struggle had taken place and he had been all but dragged from his bed. Then it turned to the unconscious man on the floor, smeared the King's blood on his clothes, and placed the knife in his hand.

Satisfied, it took a final look around, and then picked up a vase and threw it through the glass of the bedroom window, the sound reverberating in the night's stillness.

Seconds later, it was back in the courtyard as the Home Guards rushed inside to discover what was happening, climbing the walls to the roof before leaping into the cover of the trees and disappearing.

16

SEERSHA DID NOT VISIT THE PRACTICE FIELD THE next day, although she was awake before sunrise. She had intended on going, but her body was aching from more than the pains of combat and she was feeling sick. When she laid a hand on her forehead, it was hot and clammy. Somehow she had picked up a fever. She wasn't so unwell she couldn't manage on her own, just uncomfortable enough not to want any strenuous movements in her life for at least the next twenty-four hours.

She rose while it was still dark to wet a cloth in cold well water and mop her forehead and cheeks. After doing so, she drank a glass of ale, then re-wet the cloth and, carrying it with her, returned to her bed. Her way of dealing with sickness usually consisted of drinking liquids and getting rest, and she wasn't inclined to vary what had always been a successful treatment.

Nevertheless, she had barely gotten back to sleep when she heard a knock at her cottage door. Because Mirai and the others were gone and she was living alone, no one else was going to answer the door. Fine with her, she told herself, intent on ignoring the summons.

But the knocking continued, steady and insistent, and it occurred to her it might be Crace Coram or a messenger from the King or something that involved plans for the Elven army's travel south to Arishaig, so she reluctantly roused herself, threw on some clothes, and shuffled her way to the front door.

When she opened it, she found Sian Aresh standing in front of her looking decidedly agitated.

"May I come in?" he asked. Without waiting for her response, he pushed past her and closed the door quickly behind them.

"Is someone after you?" Seersha asked jokingly, cocking one eyebrow at him.

He shook his head. "No, someone is after you."

She took a closer look and saw that his lean face was fatigued and his clothes rumpled. More troubling was the haunted look in his eyes.

"What is it?" she asked. "Who's after me?"

"I am. I'm here to arrest you."

She started to grin and then realized he was serious. "Why would you do that?"

"I wouldn't, as a matter of fact. But that's why I am here." He glanced around the darkness of the room. The moon was down, but dawn was not far away. "Can we move away from the door and the windows to a place where someone looking in won't see us talking?" he asked.

She took him into her bedroom where the curtains were still drawn. "I woke up feeling sick, so I've been trying to rest." She gestured at the rumpled bedclothes and the cluttered floor. "Excuse the mess."

He shook his head. "I have a bigger mess than this one to deal with, Seersha," he said. "Emperowen was murdered last night. Stabbed to death. His brother Ellich was found on the floor of his bedroom next to him, blood on his clothes and a knife in his hand. He's been charged with murder and locked up."

Seersha stared. "That makes no sense at all! Why would Ellich kill his brother?"

The Captain of the Home Guard moved over to the bed and sat down, rubbing his face wearily with his hands. "He wouldn't. He didn't. But someone made it look like he did, and Ellich can't explain what he was doing there. He claims he was asleep one moment, and on the floor of his brother's bedroom the next. He denies everything, but that's not going to save him."

Seersha started to ask why, and then realized who was behind this. "Phaedon," she said.

The Elf nodded. "With his father dead, he declared himself King. His father had already designated him as his successor, so crowning him is a formality. No one has a better claim, and the Elves don't deviate from tradition without a very good reason. It's unfortunate, but it won't be the first time something like this has happened. In any event, he was quick to make the decision to lock up his uncle. A few objected, myself included, but he paid no attention to us."

"Doesn't he have to answer to the High Council? He isn't King yet, after all."

Sian Aresh shook his head. "Not in a situation like this. This is an emergency, a crisis. No one is going to object. People are frightened. First the demon breakout and the attack on Arishaig, and now the King is dead. Phaedon has taken advantage of this to claim the throne and to demonstrate his ability to lead by example. Unfortunately for Ellich, his example is not well considered."

"Should you be talking to me about this?" she asked him.

"I shouldn't be talking to you at all. I should be hauling you off to join Ellich. Phaedon has decided this is a Federation plot to subjugate the Elves and that you are a part of it. Your insistence on marching the Elven army to Arishaig's aid is evidence of your complicity."

"But first I decide to murder the King?" She almost laughed. "That makes no sense at all."

"Not much of anything makes sense at the moment, which is why I am here. I am supposed to arrest you and bring you before the Prince to answer the charges, and afterward I am to lock you up until he decides what to do with you." He paused. "That could be a very long time."

"Maybe until it is too late to do anything about it?"

He nodded. "Of course, in order for me to do this, I have to find you, and so far I haven't been able to do so. If you were to leave right now, I imagine I would have a great deal of difficulty tracking you down."

"But that would suggest I am guilty of something," she snapped. "I should stay and defend myself."

Aresh shook his head. "I don't think the rules of fair play are going to apply in this situation. Phaedon has waited a long time to be King; he is intent on elevating his stature in the eyes of the Elves. Bringing those involved in the death of his father to justice would be a good start."

"And few would be troubled if one of those judged guilty was a Druid," she finished. "But his own brother? Why would anyone believe Ellich would do such a thing?"

"Phaedon will come up with a reason and find a way to make others believe it. He is good at that sort of thing. I've watched him at work in the High Council for years. He is an accomplished manipulator."

He stood up abruptly. "We've already talked for too long. You have to go now. Find Crace Coram, get down to the airfield before the search for you begins in earnest, and steal one of the smaller airships. Do it quickly."

Seersha rose, shaking her head. "I don't like this. It feels wrong."

Aresh walked from the bedroom to the living quarters and peered out the window. Already, dawn had begun to lighten the eastern sky in a wash of silver and rose.

"Away from here, maybe you can do something useful. If nothing else, maybe you can warn Aphenglow of what's happened. Phaedon has no use for her, either."

Seersha was appalled. "He wouldn't do anything to her. Arling wouldn't stand for it, and she carries the Ellcrys seed! Without that, we are all as good as dead. Even Phaedon must know that."

"Is there a back door?" he asked.

She turned away abruptly and strode through the house to the rear entry. "I'll find her and warn her," she said.

"Do so quickly." He peered through the window and then opened the door. "Don't assume anything about Phaedon and what he might or might not do. That is still unexplored country."

She started outside and then turned back. "What will you do, Sian?"

He smiled sadly. "Whatever I can. Good-bye, Seersha."

Then he slipped past her and was gone.

Seersha dressed at once, did what she could to tamp down her fever, shook off her lethargy, and slipped from her cottage into the new day. She went quickly from there to where Crace Coram was staying in a block of old barracks at the edge of the airfield. By his own request, he had kept himself out of the city proper, preferring woodland surroundings to clustered buildings. He was more mountain man than city dweller in spite of his designation as Chieftain of his village, and he could not come to terms with being settled in the midst of so many people—even Elves, whom he held in high regard.

But she did not find him in the quarters assigned to him. Nor were any of his belongings there. Everything seemed to have been cleared out, as if he had already moved on. She was immediately worried that something had happened to him, and that she was already too late to save him from Phaedon. Even though Sian Aresh hadn't said anything about him being in danger, she couldn't assume he wasn't.

She hurried from there to the practice field, aware that by now they might be looking for her and that she was risking her freedom by showing herself so boldly. But when she got to the field, she found Crace Coram sparring with one of the Home Guards while the rest stood watching and waiting for their turns. She took a quick look around to see if there was any indication of a trap, but found nothing.

Taking a deep breath, she walked right up to the Dwarf Chieftain, calling his name. "Crace! Leave off. We have to go."

He backed away from his opponent, his bluff features nonplussed. "Go where?"

"I'll tell you on the way, but you have to come right now."

He didn't seem inclined to do that, so she made a hand gesture familiar to Dwarves everywhere, one that warned him he was being stupid or worse. He gave her a surprised look, read the expression on her face, and finally realized something was wrong. He put down his weapons, stripped off his protective gear, and came over.

"I'll be back soon, so be ready!" he shouted over his shoulder at the Home Guards, who returned his challenge with hoots and jeers.

When they were far enough away, Seersha, leading him

toward the airfield, said quietly, "Where are your clothes? They weren't in your room."

"I threw them out. They were in tatters. I'm wearing what's left. Now what's going on?"

Quickly, she summarized what Sian Aresh had told her, ending by saying they had to assume both of them were already being hunted, so they needed to get clear of Arborlon.

"On an airship?" he asked, cocking an eyebrow at her. "I don't know anything about flying airships. Can't we just ride horses?"

She shook her head. "Too slow. We have to get away quickly. I think you need to return to the Dwarves and warn them about what's coming. They might already know, but we should make certain. The tribes need to form an army that can stand with the Elves if the demons come north from Arishaig."

"Stand with the Elves? What chance is there of that happening with that madman as King?" Corum Crace snorted in disgust. "The Dwarves will go their own way."

She gave him a hard look. "Let's see how things play out. Whatever the choices given us, we'd better be ready to pick one." She paused. "You know what we'll be up against."

"All too well." He pointed ahead. "Which vessel do you intend to steal?"

She peered across the field, which had just come into view, searching for a likely candidate. At first, she didn't see anything that looked manageable. The big warships were out of the question, and even skiffs the size of the *Wend-A-Way* were easier to handle when there was more than one person to fly them.

Then she caught sight of something that made her smile. A worn but serviceable two-man flit set off to one side was marked with signs that said it was available for private hire. She gave a quick glance around, but saw no signs of Elven Hunters prowling the field or its perimeters. Work crews scurried about the larger warships, but mostly the airfield was empty.

"Come on," she said to her companion and moved quickly toward the two-man.

"That scow?" Coram demanded. "It doesn't look like it can get off the ground!"

She grinned at his dismay. "It's clearly done so many times before. I think it can manage a few more." She slapped him on his arm. "Let me do the bargaining."

A whip-thin Elf was seated nearby, studying an array of maps as the Dwarves came up to him. He looked up, clearly interested. "You want to rent her, maybe?" He gestured at the two-man. "How long?"

Seersha pretended to study the craft. "Is she capable? Does she handle well?"

The man made a face. "Well enough for you. Do you even know how to fly her?"

"I know a little."

"Good enough. A little is all she requires. A sound craft in spite of how she looks. Reliable. She's in her retirement years, but she knows the way."

"A week," Seersha said. "How much?"

"A hundred. Silver."

"Too much. Maybe fifty."

"Too little. How about a hundred?"

She gave him an annoyed look. "We've passed that point in the discussion. I can do seventy."

Abruptly, shouts broke out from across the field as a swarm of Home Guards appeared out of the trees. Seersha hesitated, and then hit the Elf so hard he was already unconscious when he struck the ground. Crace Coram scrambled aboard the two-man, and Seersha released the anchor ropes and followed him up. She unhooded the parse tubes, engaged the thrusters, and when the familiar sound of the diapson crystals heating up reached her ears, she grabbed the lifter levers and took the ship into the air with a series of lurches and jumps that sent her companion tumbling all the way to the back of the craft.

Picking himself up gingerly, Crace Coram made his way forward to sit behind her once more. "Very nice job of bargaining back there. That cost us much less than I thought it would."

They flew west through the Valley of Rhenn and out onto the upper Streleheim, casting anxious glances over their shoulders all the way. But no other craft appeared behind them. Possibly giving chase wasn't an immediate concern. Perhaps no one had orders about what to do if they fled the city. Any delay would help with their escape, so she accepted the lack of a pursuit as a gift and concentrated on what lay ahead.

"What are we doing?" her companion asked, leaning forward to be heard.

Good question. She thought about it for a moment. "We have a choice," she said to him, turning to catch his eye. "If we go to Paranor and I can get inside the Keep, I can read the scrye waters and might be able to determine where Aphenglow is. If we continue on, we can do what I said earlier and warn the Dwarves about the danger from the demons. Or we can do something else."

She waited. He said nothing for a moment. Then, "Seems as if we ought to find the sisters and warn them. We can't afford for anything to happen to them."

She gave him a quick nod of agreement. "Paranor it is, then."

They flew on through the remainder of the day, winging toward the sun, then beneath it as it passed overhead and finally beyond, as the light diminished and the night approached. By then they had reached the Dragon's Teeth and were close to their destination. Seersha still felt the grips of her fever, so she had taken

time to show Crace Coram how to work the two-man's controls—not only to give him a chance to try his hand at flying the
craft, but also to give herself an opportunity to rest and recover as
she could. He had taken control reluctantly, cautious and a bit
unsteady at first, but gradually gaining a sense of confidence.
They switched places several times more during their flight, often
enough so that she felt he could manage well enough at the helm
if the need arose. It gave her a chance to rest her eyes and body;
her fever had finally faded during their flight, chased by time and
the defenses of her body, and she was feeling much better.

When they arrived at Paranor, she took the two-man directly
over the top of the wall and close to the dark towers for a quick
look. But the Keep seemed to be abandoned still, unchanged
since Aphenglow had returned. Seersha maneuvered toward the
landing platform and set their vessel down.

They climbed out of the cockpit and stood amid the clustered
mix of wrecked and undamaged airships, taking a careful look
around. The sun had gone behind the trees west, and its light
was beginning to disappear. Shadows draped the stone and iron
of the Druid's Keep, and the cool of nightfall infused the deepening dark.

Seersha took a long moment to be certain that nothing living
was hiding in those shadows before satisfying herself that they
were alone.

"Stay with the two-man until I get back," she told Crace
Coram. "No one who isn't a Druid is allowed where I am going."

She left him behind looking irritable and went through the
rubble and debris and heaps of ashes littering the ramp, past the
wreckage of *Arrow* with its prow lodged in the collapsed
doorway, and into the Keep proper. She followed the hall for a
short distance to a stairway and then made her way upstairs. Two
flights up, she stepped through an opening to a second hallway

and followed it to the door that opened into the cold room, where she triggered a release of the protective locks.

Inside, the chill was bone-deep. Seersha shivered as she moved over to the elevated basin, stepped up onto the stone blocks that formed its base, and stood looking down at the broad, placid contents. Summoning the magic she had learned to command in the early days of her service to the order, she spread her hands and swept her open palms over the surface while not quite touching it, the motion stirring the waters to life. In the depths of the basin, the lines and shadings of the map of the Four Lands drawn on the stone brightened in a flaring of colors and sudden shimmers.

Then small flashes began to appear here and there across the face of the map. The most intense concentration was in the city of Arishaig, and it caught Seersha's attention immediately. The flashes were all blue, a sign of Elven magic, and she wondered right away if they were residue from use of the Elfstones. She could tell from the strength of the flashes that the magic was very recent and spread out all through certain sections of the sprawling city.

But what in the world would Aphen and Arling Elessedil be doing in Arishaig?

She scanned the remainder of the map as it shimmered and flashed within the waters of the scrye. There were strong indicators of the demon hordes assaulting the city. There were extraneous bits and pieces flashing here and there.

But nothing more noticeable than that.

She spent a few more moments studying the scrye. Then she wiped the images clean with sweeping motions of her palms, returning the basin to its former condition. Once finished, she left the room, locking the door behind her.

She stood for long moments in the empty hallway, mulling over what she had seen and what it meant for her plans. There was so much she didn't know and could only guess at. She wished she had the use of other tools with which to track her friends and their companions. She wished she had magic that would allow her to see beyond the horizons and into the hearts of those she worried for.

But she had none of this, only the skills and magic she had learned as a member of her order. Yet in her world, you worked with the tools at hand. These would have to do.

She pushed back strands of dark hair that had fallen over her rough features and stared off into space. She needed to decide what she was going to do. She had thought she already knew before she used the scrye, but now she wasn't so sure. The logical choice was to go into the Eastland and assist in the summoning of a Dwarf army to march to the aid of the Elves and the Southlanders, but something inside was tugging her another way, whispering that there were better, more important ways in which she could use her Druid skills.

She broke off the debate and returned down the hallway, descended the stairs, and went out the broken entry to the landing field where Crace Coram was pacing about restlessly, eyes scanning the tops of the walls that hemmed him in.

He turned at once at her appearance. "Can we go now? I don't mind telling you that all these walls make me feel like I'm locked in a cage. I don't know how you stand it here."

She nodded. Dwarves preferred the mountains and woodlands to fortress walls, felt more comfortable in open spaces than in confined ones. She felt the same way he did; it had taken her a long time to put aside her distaste and accept the presence of so much stone and iron shutting her in.

"You get used to it," she answered softly. Then she moved toward the two-man. "Come, we can go."

But once they were aboard their vessel, she found herself sitting in the pilot box undecided about what to do next.

"What's wrong?" her companion asked. He moved up beside her and bent close. "Not sure about where to go?"

She nodded. "I want to do something to help those people in Arishaig. I know I should go with you to muster an army from the Dwarf tribes to rally them to the fight, but ..." She trailed off. "I keep wanting to do something more immediately useful."

"You're a warrior, Seersha. A fighter." Crace Coram shrugged. "So you want to fight. You want to join the battle."

"That's it," she admitted.

He emitted an abrupt laugh, a hearty burst that made her smile. "Then do so! Fly to Arishaig and let's see if we can't help those trapped there."

She looked over her shoulder at him. "We?"

"You don't expect me to stay behind, do you? Miss out on a fight like this one?"

"What about warning the Dwarves?"

"Oh, come now. They don't need us to warn them. They keep watch on things just like everyone else. They'll already know what's taken place and have begun massing their fighters and making a decision about how best to use them. What can we add to that?"

She gave him a long hard look. "You're sure you want to come with me? You don't have to."

He laughed again, his huge arms reaching out to hug her. "Girl, I didn't have to come with you in the first place! I came because I wanted to. Nothing's changed about that. Fly the ship!"

She opened the parse tubes to the diapson crystals and powered up their vessel. She waited a moment for the levels to rise sufficiently and then engaged the thrusters.

"I'm glad you're coming with me," she said to him.

Moments later they were airborne over Paranor and flying south.

17

WITH GRIANNE OHMSFORD NOW ABOARD, the *Quickening* and its passengers were riding the back of a huge storm down out of the Klu Mountains and along the north–south corridor formed by the Charnals and the Lazareen. The storm had overtaken them shortly after they had lifted off from Stridegate and begun the long, slow journey back through the Northlands toward Callahorn. No more than gusting winds and distant clouds at first, the storm had quickly formed into a black wall of driving rains with intermittent hail. The temperature had dropped sharply, and the air grew so cold that it penetrated the heavy weather cloaks of the members of the airship's crew and began to form ice on the decks.

Mirai Leah was in the pilot box working the controls with Austrum standing at her shoulder, one spelling the other when weariness and cold threatened to affect performance. Neither had spoken a word since they had set out. They had barely glanced at each other. Farther back, the Rover crew was clustered along the aft railing with Skint, staring off into the darkness.

Railing Ohmsford was hunkered down against the front wall of the pilot box next to Challa Nand, tightly wrapped in his weather cloak and trying to find what little shelter he could by using the other's huge frame as a shield against the heavy winds and rain. He was thoroughly miserable, but his misery had more to do with the misfortune he had brought upon his friends and companions than with the storm. No matter how you looked at things, everything was his fault. His pigheadedness, his pride, his overconfidence, and his unwillingness to listen to anyone but himself—they had all contributed to his failure to realize that he was making a mistake.

Woostra, who had long since given up trying not to be sick or going below to hide his misery and suffer in private, was sitting with them. They were all looking forward to where a gray-robed specter crouched near the bow of the aircraft as motionless as stone.

Challa Nand bent close to the boy. "Stop thinking about it. It's over and done with. She's here now, and we have to live with it."

Railing shook his head. "What was I thinking? Why didn't I listen to the King of the Silver River? He warned me that she couldn't come back to what she had been. He warned me that things wouldn't work out as I wanted. But I just went ahead anyway. I wouldn't listen."

He shifted so he could look the Troll in the eye. "Worse, the Grimpond taunted me with what it knew was going to happen. It didn't spell it out, but very definitely hinted at it. It dared me to keep going. It mocked me. But I just ignored that, too. I thought I knew better than a shade. I knew I could do what I had set out to do, and nothing could stop me."

"It would have helped if you had confided in us a bit earlier," Woostra observed with more than a hint of sarcasm in his gruff voice. "Perhaps then we could have done something to help you."

The boy had just finished telling them everything moments earlier, all the little bits and pieces he had been keeping to himself, including his plans to save his brother by using Grianne Ohmsford reborn. He'd needed to tell someone besides Mirai, sick of dissembling, of keeping secrets. What point was there in secrecy now? It wasn't as if any of them were going to do anything she didn't want them to do. She'd made that plain enough even before they'd taken the airship aloft and begun their search.

Railing had been afraid she was going to kill one of them. She'd made it plain enough she wasn't above doing so.

"Who's to say you won't get what you want in the end?" The Troll was still watching him. "You've done what you intended. You've brought her back, and she's every bit as dangerous as she needs to be for what's required of her. What use would she be in helping your brother if she were kind and sweet and loving? You need her like this. Maybe the tree knew, and that's why it gave her back to you this way."

Maybe, Railing agreed silently. This thing, this *wraith* he had brought out of the past—how else to describe what had happened?—was not Grianne Ohmsford as she was when captured by the Straken Lord and nearly destroyed. This was Grianne Ohmsford as she had been while still under the influence of the Morgawr, controlled and manipulated by a being every bit as evil as Tael Riverine. The Ilse Witch—this was what she had been and how so many still remembered her.

This was who he was bearing back aboard *Quickening* to try to save his brother.

"If I thought destroying the Straken Lord would save Redden, I would feel a little better about all this," he said to Challa Nand. He exhaled sharply. "But there's no reason to believe for a moment that, even if she succeeds in killing Tael Riverine, she will help my brother. She would just as soon kill him, too. She doesn't care. *It* doesn't care. Not a monster like that!"

Woostra seized his arm. "You need to remember something. You took her away from the life she had chosen for herself. You are responsible for her being returned to us the way she is. So what are you going to do about it? Stand around feeling sorry for yourself or find a way to get her to do what's needed? Remember her history. She was a child deceived into believing the lies that drove her into becoming the Ilse Witch. She was feared and hated all her life by many, and nothing she did was ever enough to change that." The narrow face pushed close. "Don't call her a monster. If you think of her in those terms, you surrender yourself to your own worst fears. Remember her for what she was as the Ard Rhys of the Third Druid Order. Remember why you came to find her in the first place. Don't give up on hoping she can still help us."

Railing stared at him in surprise, impressed by both his words and his passion. It was an intense, fervent plea.

But he was not convinced. "I don't think she can do anything to help us. I don't think she can do anything but lead us to ruin."

In the pilot box directly behind them, Mirai caught snippets of this last exchange. She turned to Austrum, signaling her readiness to be relieved. As soon as his hands were on the controls, she left her station and went down on the deck to where Railing was sitting with Woostra and Challa Nand. She nodded in greeting to both, then reached down for Railing's hand and pulled him to his feet.

"Come over here."

She pulled him across the deck through a fresh onslaught of hail and wind and plopped him down in the lee of the mainmast. Then, heedless of those watching, she put her arms around him and kissed him.

"Just so you know who loves you," she said.

"I know who loves me," he replied.

"Good. Now don't say anything more. Just sit with me."

He did as she asked, although his unhappiness with himself remained undiminished, radiating off him like heat off coals. She let that be, waiting him out. She knew him well enough to appreciate that patience was important, that with Railing you had to allow his emotions to settle before you tried to use reason. He was hotheaded and impetuous, an impulsive risk taker, but strong in ways that others weren't, the kind of friend that would give his life for you. She had known both brothers all her life, but her feelings for them had taken markedly different directions. Even though they might be mirror images of each other, they were very different people, and what she felt for Redden was different from what she felt for Railing. For the former, the fire was sweet and comfortable. For the latter, it was hot and compelling. She could admit it to herself now, if not before. Before, such an admission would have risked disrupting the relationship the three of them shared; choosing one over the other would have caused a schism that they might not have been able to bridge.

But she had known from the first that it must happen one day. She had always thought she would choose Railing when the time came. It was not until Redden was lost to them both and Railing was in danger of becoming lost, as well—albeit in a different way—that she decided to act. Revealing how she felt in such a dramatic, explosive way was impulsive and perhaps even foolish; she had not thought it through beforehand, and could not at all be certain of the consequences. But it didn't matter. She needed him to be the way he had always been, not the way he had become since losing his brother. All of them did. He was the one—possibly the only one—who could save them.

So she had mocked him. She had lied to him about his brother and herself. She had spurred him to do something she had hoped he wanted to do even without realizing it. She had brought him back to himself by bringing him first to her.

But she could tell the worst wasn't over. He had stopped at the edge of the cliff and stepped back, but now he was in danger of stepping forward again, of giving way to the despair he felt because of what Grianne Ohmsford had become.

She couldn't permit that, couldn't accept it, and refused to stand for it.

"Listen to me," she said when sufficient time had passed. "You can't blame yourself for what's happened. There's no reason for it. We all agreed that seeking Grianne Ohmsford so she could come back and stand against the Straken Lord was the right thing to do. All of us agreed, Railing. You didn't force us. Yes, you kept things from us you shouldn't have, but we all suspected this. You realize that, don't you? We knew. We even talked about it. But that didn't prevent us from sticking by you. Because you were the one who could make a difference. Even without knowing how, we sensed it."

He nodded slowly, his eyes locked on hers. "But it might be a difference that will get us all killed. She's capable of that, you know. She's so deeply caught up in what's been done to her— what *I've* done to her—that she could turn on us in a second."

"I know that. The others know it, too. But we accepted that risk from the first. No one knew what she would be like if she came back. Not after a hundred years of being wedded to that

tree—as an aeriad, as whatever she was or is. We took the risk
that she could do what was needed. And she can, Railing. She
can! She can destroy the Straken Lord."

"We think she can, but we don't know. We don't even know if
she will try. It doesn't matter what she tells us. Look at her. She's
not even human anymore."

She grabbed him by the shoulders and pulled him so close
that his face was almost touching hers. She could see the rain
running down his forehead and cheeks. She could see the blush
from the cold reddening his skin.

"Whatever she is, you have to find a way to make her do what
is needed. No one else can do it but you. No one else can even
get close to her. She may hate you, but she talks to you and she
watches you. Have you seen how she looks at you? There's
something there, Railing."

He stared at her, voiceless, lost.

She released him and stood up. "I have to steer the ship so it
won't crash and burn. Maybe you should do what you have to
do, too."

Then she turned and walked away and did not look back.

Railing sat where he was for a while, thinking through what
Mirai had said to him, his mood alternating between acceptance
and rejection. He could see what she was attempting to do, how
she was reminding him none too subtly that he was the one who
had to find a way to make sure Grianne Ohmsford did what
they all knew was needed. It didn't matter how he felt about her
now that he had brought her back. It didn't even matter if he
felt guilty about it. The Ilse Witch was here and she wasn't going
away. What he couldn't do—what she was telling him she
wouldn't let him do—was to throw up his hands and retreat into
the mire of his despair over what he had wrought.

If nothing else, her words impressed on him anew that a large part of what he was struggling so hard to accomplish was not only to get Redden back from the Straken Lord but also to find a way to keep them all safe. He was the one who wielded the wishsong's magic. He was the one who carried the ring bestowed by the King of the Silver River. He was the one on whose shoulders rested the responsibility for keeping them alive.

And as Mirai had pointed out, he was the only one the Ilse Witch might heed.

The Witch had come with him, after all. Though she hated and despised what he had done to her, she had come nevertheless. She was a creature of pure malice, and she was eager to seek out and destroy any enemy, but particularly the Straken Lord if for no better reason than to eradicate the last traces of what he had done to her. Find the Straken Lord. Engage him in battle. Destroy him and reap both relief and satisfaction.

There was no consideration for Redden's fate, no interest in it at all. Saving him would be nothing more than a by-product of her efforts to get at Tael Riverine. Railing had tried several times to explain why she should feel otherwise, but the Ilse Witch cared nothing for the brothers and their suffering. The Ilse Witch spared not a single thought for the lives of mortal creatures, no matter their claims of family history shared with her. All of that was dead and gone to her. All of that belonged to someone else.

He climbed to his feet and, without pausing to think further on it, walked forward toward the bow where the Witch sat huddled in her gray robes in the pouring rain. She did not look up as he approached or glance back when he slowed, hesitant to come any closer without acknowledgment.

But then her hand lifted, and she beckoned to him, sensing his presence.

Unable to do anything else without appearing as frightened as he felt, he moved forward and sat down beside her.

"Don't get too close to me," she said out of the shadow of her cowl. "You don't want to breathe the air I exhale."

He looked down at his hands, rain dripping off them. "Are you alive now? Are you a living creature?"

Her laugh was harsh and bitter. "A fair question. I have asked it of myself. Am I? I breathe air. I move about. Is that enough?"

"You have thoughts and the ability to reason? You can see the truth of things when others speak to you?"

She turned her head slightly, part of her ruined face peering at him from out of the shadows. "My thoughts and my reasoning and my truths would burn the skin from your body should you study them too closely, Valeboy. They would burn you like acid."

He was silent for a long time. "I am sorry I had to bring you back," he said finally. "I did not know it would be this way."

"Yet here I am."

"My brother, your great-nephew, your own flesh and blood, is in the hands of the Straken Lord and will die if I do not free him. I did what I had to."

Her hands, gray and gnarled, clenched before her like great claws. "Even though, by freeing him, you doom me?"

"I didn't know that would happen."

"But you suspected. Do not deny it. You were warned. The King of the Silver River. The Grimpond. I heard them speak. Their words were carried to me by the wind, and their warnings were clear enough. I would not come back as I was, they said. You ignored those warnings. Self-indulgent, heedless, prideful boy, you ignored what you were told would happen."

Railing felt shame and anger burning in his chest. "I would do anything to save my brother. Even give up my own life."

The clenched hands disappeared back inside the sleeves of

the gray cloak. "You may get your chance to test that boast, for I care nothing for you or your brother. That is the stark truth of things. You brought me back to serve your own purposes, but I have no interest in them. I have my own purpose to serve. I have my own path to follow. Do you know what it is?"

He shook his head, words failing him.

"I am the Ilse Witch reborn. I must sate my rage and satisfy my bloodlust. I must rid myself of the memories of what I was as Mother Tanequil's child, an aeriad, a spirit of the air. All that is lost to me. I was at peace and free, and you took that from me. I had a life of tranquility and purpose, and you stole it. You took what I was and you gave me back what I now am. I can feel myself continue to change, to adapt. Do you know what that means?"

"That you can never go back? That you are fated to remain as you are?"

She was silent then for a long time without answering. Then he heard her sigh. "I found my way to what would comfort me when I became Mother Tanequil's creature. I left behind my human self with all its history of madness and violence and hatred. I shed my body and earthly connection and became a creature of the air, a spirit with no past and only a present. I found friendship and love and contentment in my sisters and in my freedom." She glared out at him from within her cowl's shadows. "And, no, I can never go back. And yes, I must remain as I am."

He stared out into the rain, feeling empty and despairing. "When this is over, I will go with you to speak to the tanequil and ask that she reconsider your dismissal. I will help you become again what you were before. I will admit what's happened is entirely my fault, and I was foolish to disrupt things. I will offer to take your place, if it will help."

She emitted a long peal of ragged laughter that ripped through the winds and rain. "Oh, you foolish boy! She knows all this, and she has made her choice, and there can never be a reckoning that would give me back what I lost."

One clawed hand reached out and seized his arm in a grip of iron. "Do you not yet see? I am beyond all that! I do not seek to go back to what I was no matter what happens. I feel that slip away with every passing second, and soon it will be gone entirely. I want something else, something much more satisfying."

"But maybe I can . . ."

"You don't understand," she snapped, yanking him closer. "You don't begin to understand. What has been done cannot be undone. You've brought me back as something other than I was because that was what Mother Tanequil saw that you needed. But there was no provision made for me. There was no consideration given to how I would endure and adapt to this thing I now am."

She turned full on him, and he saw the red fire in her eyes and felt the burning hate of her glare. "Now I am evolving still, and there is only one direction I can go—into such madness that there is no way back. Into an insanity that will make me much worse than the thing you have brought me to destroy. Oh, I will do what you wish, Valeboy. I will find the Straken Lord and do battle with him. I will see him vanquished. But what will happen then, do you think? What end will you have achieved?"

"My brother will . . ."

Her hiss cut him short and left him cringing from her. "Your brother? Your brother is nothing to me. Look beyond his worthless life and your own, as well. Look to the wider world and the future and then ask yourself again. What will you have achieved?"

Railing started to speak and then found he could not. The words were so terrible he could not speak them.

The Ilse Witch grinned, her teeth sharp and her face taut. "You know now, don't you? You see it clearly."

He couldn't help himself. He did see it.

"Ponder it, then. Consider it. Mull your choices and prepare yourself for what waits. In this new world of yours, young Ohmsford-who-would-save-them-all, what fate will you embrace?"

Ah, shades! He howled it in the silence of his mind. "There must be another way!"

"There might have been once, but you did not choose it. You chose this way, and now you must follow its thread to wherever it leads." She turned away from him, disappearing back into the shadows of her cowl. "Now get away from me and stay away."

What have I done?

He sat for a moment longer before rising and moving away, no longer able to stay in her presence. Of all the outcomes he had imagined, this one had never occurred to him. He had believed she would do what was needed to help the Four Lands because that was what she had done in life as the Ard Rhys of the Third Druid Order. He had been so sure she would set everything else aside so that she could save the world into which she had been born. She might not be happy about what he had done or eager to embrace his insistence on bringing her back from the life she had chosen for herself, but she would still do the right thing because that was what she had been trying to do ever since she had ceased to be the Ilse Witch.

He had never imagined she could come back as the very thing she had sought to escape. He had never imagined Mother Tanequil would return her as such.

Or that she would embrace this new identity and willingly become the very thing she hated. Or that she might have plans of her own that would be more terrible than the plans of Tael Riverine.

But she did, and they were.

He caught Mirai's eye where she stood behind Austrum in the pilot box and signaled for her to join him. She came down quickly, moving through the steady rain across the windswept deck to where he waited at the port rail.

"What is it?" she said on seeing his face. "What did she say?"

He leaned close. "It wasn't what she said, it was what she intimated. She is enraged at what has been done to her, but she is caught up in the persona she has been given and feels her former self being stolen away. She has become the Ilse Witch reborn, and she hasn't the strength or the means or even the will to change."

"But she will stand with us and fight the Straken Lord? Or does she refuse us completely?"

He closed his eyes, wiped the rain from his face, and looked at her anew. "She does not refuse us, but she does not ally with us, either. She cares nothing if we live or die. She will stand against Tael Riverine, and she says she will destroy him. But even that will not be enough for her."

"Then what?"

He gripped her shoulders. "She intends to take his place."

18

THE SECOND ATTACK ON ARISHAIG BY THE demon hordes was launched just before midnight on the same day as the first. It came against the south and west walls once again, but with fresh ferocity. The creatures swarmed out of the darkness bearing grappling hooks and scaling ladders and threw themselves against the stone and iron of the fortress with such determination that, for a few terrible moments, Keeton thought his soldiers would be overwhelmed. Setting fire to fresh oil in the ditches, forming tall walls of flame, failed to deter them. Even the presence of the warships attacking from overhead did little to slow their assault. They came at the walls in wave after wave, shrugging off arrows and spears and missiles fired from slings and launchers. They fell dying and their fellows simply climbed atop them, lifted a little closer to their goal atop the piles of bodies.

But Keeton had brought flash rips to the walls and mounted them at regular intervals. They were illegal everywhere, but there wasn't an army that didn't possess them. And since the

Federation had pioneered their manufacture, they had them stockpiled in secret caches throughout the city. Conventional weapons, however powerful, had not proven strong enough during the previous attack, and Keeton was not about to let legalities and Druid prohibitions stand in the way of saving his city and its people.

His decision was quickly vindicated by the results. When the flash rips fired on the attackers, dozens of the creatures simply vanished in ash and smoke and flame, disintegrating under the concentrated power of multiple diapson crystals. Strikes into the thickest clusters broke the momentum of the attack and sent it reeling away in spite of its vast numbers. Keeton thought maybe this would be enough to put an end to the attack for the night.

But the demons had other plans. After the oil fires burned themselves out and enough time had passed to persuade the defenders that the attack had been broken, the creatures returned. And this time they came from the air, borne in baskets carried by winged creatures that resembled giant bats and dropped onto the walls close by the flash rips and their crews. Hurtling themselves on both, the demonkind tore the men to shreds and disabled the weapons by smashing both the barrels and the swivel stands that were used to support and direct them. In a matter of minutes, all the weapons and mounts were destroyed and the creatures still alive had gone back over the walls and disappeared into the night.

Then the dragon reappeared, as black as its rider, little more than a shadow against the night, sweeping above the battlements, breathing flames on the defenders, and leaving everything dead in its wake. It happened so swiftly there was no time to use the few rail slings and fire launchers that remained intact or to bring to bear the weapons mounted on the warships that warded the corners of the fortress.

This time after the demonkind retreated, howling and screaming as they went, they did not come again right away, leaving the
defenders sitting in the darkness and carnage to wonder, through
the remainder of the night, when they would reappear next.

Keeton was angry and frustrated when Wint found him. "Tell
me how many we lost?"

His second shrugged. "Can't be sure. At least several hundred. Likely more. All the flash rips are destroyed. We have
more, but the mounts are another matter. We can fasten the rips
to the walls in some makeshift fashion, but we can't replace the
mounts."

"Because we didn't think to make more than a handful of
those—am I right? We manufactured all the weapons we could
ever need, but forgot about the importance of the mounts.
Shades!" Keeton looked away, glowering at nothing in particular.
"Do the best you can to find a way to secure a fresh supply of
the rips to the walls south and west. They know that's where
we're weakest now. That's where they'll keep attacking."

Wint disappeared without a word. Keeton stared out into the
dark for a few minutes longer, then went to speak with Sefita
Rayne. He found the Federation fleet commander standing
above the gates talking with several of her warship captains.
When she saw Keeton, she broke off the conversation and came
over to him. "I saw," she said.

He shook his head in disgust. "What can we do? What can *you*
do to help us with this?"

"Good question. Not much seems to help. I'll move the warships off the corners and place them just outside the walls where
they can better support the soldiers on the battlements. I'll take
them straight out at the first sign of an attack and try to disrupt
it before it reaches the city."

"But you'll have to watch for that dragon."

She nodded. "Our weapons aren't quick enough to track it; it's too agile for us. Then again, we might get lucky. Do you think the attack will come against the south and west walls again?"

"After the damage that's been done? I can't imagine they would bother attacking anywhere else. A bigger problem is the oil for the trenches outside the walls. We're running out."

She was silent a moment, considering. "Have you spoken with the Prime Minister about any of this?"

He exhaled sharply. "I haven't seen her."

"Then maybe it's time."

He nodded. "Past time."

He went down off the walls and into the city, making his way through the streets to the offices of the Coalition Council and the Prime Minister. He was admitted immediately and went straight to Edinja Orle's quarters, only to be told she wasn't there. No one had seen her since the previous night.

He left for her home after that, not eager to venture into that black den of rumors and strangeness but unable to do anything less if he wanted to find her. He reached it quickly enough and pounded on the door. A servant spoke to him through a slit in the door and told him her mistress wasn't there, either. She had been gone all day.

Keeton tried to think where else to look, but didn't know enough about Edinja even to make an educated guess. He considered speaking to members of the Coalition Council, but what would he say to them that would make a difference?

He went back to the walls, resigned to pursuing the matter in the morning. For now, he needed to sleep. He trudged through the darkened streets, plagued by the nagging feeling that events were overwhelming them and their chances were slipping away. This enemy seemed unstoppable, its size and the alien nature of its creatures beyond anything they had ever encountered. Traditional tactics weren't enough to stop them. In the end, they were going to break through and the city was going to be overrun, and all the weapons and warships in the world weren't going to be enough to prevent it.

Worse, he believed now that he wasn't the man for the job he had been given. He wasn't trained to command an entire army. He had never envisioned he would be the one made responsible for the defense of a city of thousands against an enemy no one had ever before encountered. He was a tactical commander of First Response, a small elite unit designed to execute surgical strikes and provide brief but intense defensive fire on larger enemy forces. He wasn't trained for what was happening now.

But then, who was?

All this was something more than anyone he knew was equipped to handle.

He reached his quarters and went to bed, exhausted and dismayed.

When he woke, the sun was just rising. He washed, dressed in fresh clothes, and went out to find Wint. His second was still sleeping, so he let him be. The city was quiet, the walls manned but unchallenged since the previous night. No further attacks had been launched. Peering out over the surrounding countryside, he found bodies and scorched earth, but not much else.

He asked after Sefita Rayne and was told she was sleeping but had asked to be woken if he needed her. He shook his head and said to let her be. As with Wint, there was no reason not to let her sleep. Even this small respite might be of some help. With no immediate sign of the enemy, he could assume the next attack would come with night's return.

Although he hadn't been able to correctly anticipate the

timing of anything the attackers had attempted so far, he reminded himself quickly.

He ate breakfast with some of his men, and then took his place on the wall to keep watch. He was feeling better rested than he had thought he would, and his mind was already hard at work turning over possibilities for improving their situation.

He was still struggling with that effort when drums began to boom from somewhere off to the west. They began all at once—a thunderous sound that broke the stillness of the morning with a steady pounding that reverberated all across the city. Keeton and those standing with him on the walls stood in silence and stared out across the flats leading off toward the ridgeline where the demons had first appeared two days ago.

Within minutes, Wint appeared at his elbow. "You should have woken me."

Keeton nodded. "I suppose."

They watched the ridgeline, waiting. The minutes slipped away, the drumming continued, but nothing else happened.

Then, abruptly, a long dark line of bodies surged over the crest of the ridge, trudging toward Arishaig's walls. They did not march or attempt to keep cadence, but simply moved in a huge wave that washed over the ridgeline and down onto the flats. Keeton peered north and south to measure the length of the line and could not find its ends. He waited for the wave to trickle off, but it continued to flow like a living thing—thousands of bodies of all shapes and sizes, churning and roiling toward the city and its defenders.

When the wave had gotten to within five hundred feet of the wall, it stopped. Keeton could just see the last of its stragglers as they came into view over the crest of the ridge. Were there even more beyond that? Keeton couldn't tell. Not that it mattered.

The numbers he could see were more than enough to engulf the city and its defenders and put an end to both.

"That's an awful lot for us to stop," Wint whispered.

Keeton nodded. "You must be reading my mind."

The attack force paused a few moments longer as the drums beat on, then it swung left as if becoming a single body and began to move clockwise around the walls in a slow, steady surge. It made no effort to come closer or to employ any weapons. It showed virtually no interest in the city at all. It simply began circling the walls, a huge silent snake winding about its prey.

Keeton backed away. "How many weapons and men do we have on the other walls?"

"Less than half of what we have west and south," his second answered. "What do you want me to do?"

In truth, Keeton didn't know. "Come with me."

He found Sefita Rayne where he had left her the previous night, standing on the battlements atop the west gate. She turned at his approach, brushing back her blue-streaked hair, a look of grim determination etched on her face.

"Can you signal the warships we have aloft to keep pace with them?" he asked quickly, indicating the enemy force.

"Already done," she answered, pointing skyward to the north. "I'm keeping a pair of vessels in reserve at the southwest corner in case this is another feint. The rest will track this new threat." She shook her head. "What are they up to?"

"Nothing good." Keeton watched the marchers turn the north corner and start east, the drums still beating in the distance. "We don't have enough defenders to hold all the walls."

"We don't have enough defenders to hold the city period if they come at us with all those bodies," she answered with a snort. "Even the warships won't be able to hold them off."

They stood together, watching the demon snake wrap itself around the city. "I can't march my soldiers around the walls like that," Keeton muttered. "It will wear them out if I do. They're worn down already as it is."

"Did you find Edinja?" Sefita asked.

He shook his head. "No one knows where she is."

"Then she's left."

Keeton stared at her. "She wouldn't do that. She wouldn't dare."

"That woman would dare anything," Wint said.

"Abandon us? Abandon the city?" Keeton shook his head. "It would be the end of her career as Prime Minister."

"I wouldn't want to bet on it."

Keeton fought down a sudden rush of anger. He turned to Wint. "Go see if there's been any word since last night. Go to the Council Buildings and to her home. Demand an answer. Insist she come to the west wall. Use my name."

Wint departed without comment.

Keeton waited with Sefita Rayne, watching the demonkind continue their march, listening to the insistent pounding of the drums. Odd, he thought, but they couldn't even see where those drums were positioned. It was as if the sound were coming out of the earth itself, as if the netherworld had opened up and released its dead.

Abruptly, a fresh horde of creatures appeared atop the ridge-line, cresting its heights and spilling over, thousands strong.

"I knew it," Sefita said.

Keeton watched in disbelief as this new threat gathered momentum and surged toward the west wall.

Farther south, but still within the Four Lands and outside the breach in the Forbidding, the shape-shifter Oriantha crouched beside Tesla Dart in the shelter of heavy woods and watched the attack on Arishaig quicken. They were only a quarter mile from the cage that held Redden Ohmsford prisoner, still looking for a way to set him free.

But doing anything more than she had already done had so far proven impossible. Too many guards encircled the cage. Too many of the demonkind prowled about, many of them the wolves that the Straken Lord kept as pets. It was necessary that something be done to lure all of them away before she could risk a second approach. For three days she had waited patiently, but no fresh opportunity had presented itself.

Until now.

A new attack on Arishaig had emptied out almost the entire camp, distributing virtually everyone between the hordes that had been circling the city in a slow march and those that had first hidden behind the ridgeline and then abruptly surged over its crest and attacked the city's west wall. Even those few that remained had moved onto the ridgeline to watch the impending destruction. No one was particularly worried about the boy in the cage. Who would even try to rescue him at this point?

Indeed, Oriantha thought. *Who?*

The city, she knew, would not survive what was coming. It would fall, and all those within would be slaughtered. There was nothing she could do to help them. But this was the chance she had been waiting for to help Redden Ohmsford, and she intended to take it.

She nudged Tesla Dart. "I'm going to try again."

The Ulk Bog gave her a despairing look, scrunching up her wrinkled face. "Bad idea. Still too dangerous. Still there will be guards."

"Still there will be ways," Oriantha replied softly.

She rose and began checking the supply of knives she had

strapped to her waist. She intended to go in swift and sudden, to
break the locks, haul the boy out of the cage, and kill anyone
who interfered. She would not bother with subtlety this time.
She had a new plan.

"Take Lada," Tesla offered.

Oriantha shook her head. "I don't need him. I know the way.
Better if he remains here with you. Once I have the boy, I will
come back."

"And do what? Go where? Tael Riverine will hunt us down!"

"He will try."

Tesla Dart shook her head. "The boy is not worth it."

"We've had this discussion. If you don't want to be part of
this, go back into the Forbidding."

Lada hissed at her, as if the idea were a personal affront. Tesla
Dart glanced down at the Chzyk. "Even Lada knows this is not
what we would ever do. Knows we want to be here. The
Forbidding is down. Our worlds are joined."

Now, *there* was a prospect that left Oriantha chilled to the
bone. She hoped it wasn't so because she had seen the size of the
army Tael Riverine commanded and judged it to be only a
fraction of the creatures that remained inside the demon prison.
The Races were doomed if the walls were not restored, but she
had no idea how that was supposed to happen.

Only that it must.

"I'm getting Redden Ohmsford back," she repeated. "Wait for
me or don't. It is up to you."

"You won't come back."

Oriantha left without another word, departing the trees for a
cluster of boulders about halfway between where they were
hidden and the center of the enemy camp. She moved swiftly,
not bothering to try to hide her coming. It was broad daylight;
there was no darkness to screen her approach. She had to rely on

the distraction provided by the battle for Arishaig. She had to rely on speed and surprise.

When she reached the boulders, she wormed her way into their center where she could not be seen and began to transform. She used her shape-shifting abilities to shed her human form and adopt a new look entirely. She turned herself into one of the Goblins she had seen patrolling the camp—just another familiar presence no one would question. It took her time and effort to achieve the look she wanted, but in the end she was as hunched and disjointed as those she had encountered on her first attempt at rescuing the boy. She could not see herself from outside her body, so she could not be certain she had gotten everything right. But she felt the way she wanted to feel, and the parts of herself she could see clearly looked as she had intended.

Without further deliberation, she set off.

She crossed the open space that separated her from the fringes of the enemy camp at a steady walk, assuming the loping gait and slope-shouldered stance of the Goblin she was pretending to be. She didn't try to hide her coming, intending to show she was a part of the camp and not an intruder. Only a single guard was positioned anywhere close, a creature she didn't recognize that glanced over without interest and went back to studying the landscape beyond. Oriantha reached the camp's perimeter without challenge and walked in.

Armed with confidence and steely determination, the shapeshifter moved steadily ahead, looking as if she had important business and a clear destination. This was true, of course, although not in the way anyone would suspect. She ignored those around her, exuding an air of importance that suggested they would do well to let her be. Her attitude and obvious indifference to others worked; those who watched her pass left her alone.

Within fifteen minutes, she was approaching the cage that held Redden Ohmsford imprisoned, already planning how she was going to free him.

There was nothing she could do about whatever alarms might be sounded if the magic that warded the cage was disturbed. That being the case, she intended to break the locks and take him out as quickly as she could before anyone realized what was happening. And for that to happen, she needed a distraction to cause those close enough to interfere to look somewhere else for the few moments she needed.

She slowed as she entered the clearing where the cage had been placed. Redden Ohmsford was slumped in the middle, apparently sleeping. Two Goblins were keeping a disinterested watch on their prisoner, and a pair of the huge wolves slept some twenty feet from the cage, curled up next to each other. A few other creatures could be seen off to one side, but everyone else had moved over to the bluff to watch the battle.

Oriantha walked through the clearing and passed on, seemingly without wasting a glance on anyone. Once out of sight, she quickly doubled back again. Moving to a place close by the cage, but just out of sight, she pulled a blowgun from her belt and a steel-tipped dart from her pouch, slid the dart into the barrel of the blowgun, took a deep breath, placed the end of the weapon to her lips, and stepped into view again.

She was ten feet from the closest of the sleeping wolves.

She sent the dart deep into its rear haunch and the wolf leapt up, roaring with pain and rage, and turned instantly on the other wolf. Taking advantage of the chaos, she came up behind the Goblin guards who were watching the wolves struggle, and used her knives to kill both with a single pass. Moving swiftly to the cage door, she broke the chain and tore the cage door off its hinges.

To her surprise, no alarm sounded. She leapt into the cage, snatched up the unconscious Redden Ohmsford, and bounded out again with the boy slung over one shoulder. The wolves were still tearing at each other, and the guards were all dead. The one or two others who had been present had fled toward the heights to give warning.

Grabbing a bloodied cloak from one of the dead guards, she wrapped it about Redden, tied off the ends so that only his legs were hanging out, and started back through the camp as if carrying a dead body. She angled off to the north where no one was in sight, trying not to hurry. There was still no alarm, and she couldn't decide what that meant. The magic that had been used to wrap the cage had been set in place for a purpose. It was more troubling to her not to know what that purpose was than to have to deal with it.

The boy was heavy and weighed her down. She knew she wouldn't be able to carry him all the way back. She needed him awake and on his feet if she was to get him to Tesla Dart. She was choosing ground on which her scent would be disguised by dozens of other tracks, but that wouldn't be enough. Eyes had seen her, and their owners would remember what she looked like.

She found a tent right at the edge of the camp and slipped inside. The tent was empty, and she quickly untied the ends of the blanket and rolled the boy out.

She noticed for the first time the strange metal band that was fastened around his neck. The conjure collar—Tesla had mentioned that he would be fitted with one. She reached into her tunic pocket, took out the key the Ulk Bog had given her on her first rescue attempt, slipped it into the lock, and twisted. The collar fell away.

"Redden!" she hissed, shaking him.

His eyes snapped open, widening as they saw the Goblin bending over him. He cringed, and squeezed his eyes closed again.

"It's me!" she hissed, realizing she was still in her Goblin disguise. "Open your eyes. Look at me!"

She shed her disguise, returning to her true form, her young face peering down at him, silver hair spilling over her forehead. His eyes opened slowly, and he blinked rapidly. "Oriantha?"

His fingers went automatically to his neck, searching for the conjure collar. Oriantha reached down to retrieve it and held it up for him to see. "You're free, Redden. But we're still in the demon camp and we have to get clear. Can you walk?"

He didn't seem to hear her. Tears filled his eyes and he began to cry. He broke down completely, and she reached out awkwardly and pulled him to her, cradling him as she would a small child. "It's all right," she said. "This is over now. You're free, and you're not going back. Hush, now."

It took precious minutes for him to compose himself, and while he did she was envisioning hordes of creatures scouring the camp for them. But she needed him to be mobile and composed if they were to make it back to Tesla Dart in one piece.

Without further discussion or delay, she pulled him to his feet and braced him by his shoulders so he was facing her. "Can you use your magic? Are you strong enough?"

He shook his head hesitantly. "I don't know. I don't know what I can do at this point." He looked down at himself. "I don't even know if I can move. Everything feels numb."

She sat him down again, took his hands and rubbed them between her own, first one and then the other, then spent several more precious minutes working on his feet and legs. "We're being hunted. They're out there looking for us right now. I don't know if I can defend us both. I need you to help me. Can you do

that? I'm sorry I have to ask this, but I don't have any choice. I
need you to be able to defend yourself."

He stared at her as if she were speaking another language, and
she slapped him hard across the face. "Can you do that?" she
snapped angrily.

His hand went to his face, and he nodded slowly, the light
coming back into his eyes. "I can do whatever I have to if it
means getting out of here."

She took his hands in her own and squeezed them. "Stay close
to me. Follow my lead. I won't leave you, I promise."

He nodded. "I'm not going back, no matter what."

"Then be strong, and you won't have to."

Still watching him, she shape-shifted back into her animal
form, all muscle and sinew and rippling power. Drawing him
after her, she moved to the tent opening, hesitated for a moment
to peer through the flaps and make certain no one was lying in
wait, then together they burst back outside.

19

REDDEN OHMSFORD WAS STILL STRUGGLING with the idea that he was free. One minute he was locked inside a cage surrounded by thousands of creatures out of the Forbidding, dragged along on an endless slog by a merciless demon intent on accomplishing something that defied explanation, and the next he was rescued. He had lost all perspective. He was starved and dehydrated and his body was aching and raw from being poked and prodded by the creatures that kept him prisoner. He had heard Oriantha's whispered words, saying that help was close, but he had half believed he must have dreamed them.

Now he was struggling with loss of physical strength and a psyche that was fragile and not altogether reliable. He kept drifting in and out of memories of the cage, of Tael Riverine's madness and cruelty, of the death of Khyber Elessedil, and of his time imprisoned at Kraal Reach. A pervading sense of hopelessness kept whispering over and over that this was only temporary, that it couldn't last, that his hopes were destined to turn to ashes faster than the setting of the day's sun.

But Oriantha was there to keep him grounded, and he took strength from her, changed back now into her sleek, muscular cat form as she led him out from the tent and into battle against their pursuers. There was a sense of indestructibility about her, an endurance that both defied all of the dangers that threatened and pushed back against the fears and doubts that plagued him. She had done for him what should have been impossible, and he would never forget it.

Oriantha was running the moment they went through the tent flaps—not so swiftly she outdistanced the boy, but fast enough to make him work at keeping up. Redden was still weak, and his legs would only allow him to move at a hobble. He was shaky, but he was also determined. The thought of going back to that cage was a nightmare he could only barely keep at bay. All of his concentration went into putting one foot in front of the other and staying upright in the process. He took his lead from her; wherever she went, he stayed close behind.

The pursuit was swifter in coming than he had expected. Growls and shrieks descended on them almost immediately, coming from behind and to the left. Oriantha seemed oblivious to them, moving ahead as if she didn't hear them. Redden tried to do the same, but felt himself cringing nevertheless. *Don't listen to it*, he told himself. *Just keep going. Just run.*

Then a body hurtled at them from between the tents, dark and swift and dangerous. Oriantha wheeled into it and left it lying in its own blood. Another creature appeared in front of them and she went right for it, putting it down so fast that Redden couldn't even be sure how she had managed it. He was aware that he was supposed to try to defend himself but, physically, such an act was impossible. He was debilitated to the point that a strong push might overthrow him.

What he had to rely on—if he could manage to bring it to life—was the magic of the wishsong.

Oriantha kept moving—a few steps one way, a few the other, always heading west, back toward where she said she'd left Tesla Dart. Shouts and cries pursued them, but the tents were thinning ahead and the way out onto the flats was open.

Then an ogre lumbered into view from one side, surrounded by demon-wolves. It carried a club studded with spikes and roared in challenge. The wolves, keeping pace, snarled in concert, and began fanning out to either side of their bigger companion.

Redden tried to summon the wishsong, his voice raw and dry and empty. He could feel the magic fizzle and spark, but there was no power behind it.

Oriantha crouched in response to this new threat, gathering herself as the ogre trudged toward her. She waited until it was close, then exploded into action, leaping onto the creature and running up its huge body to its head, driving claws and teeth into its eyes and face, leaving both in tatters. She was off it in seconds, but now the wolves were on her, bearing her down. She fought to throw them off, getting clear and breaking for safety, but they gave pursuit and brought her down again. The ogre was stumbling about close at hand, stamping at the earth in rage and pain, trying to find something to hurt. It caught one of the wolves by mistake and finished it. The others cringed away as Oriantha rolled close to the ogre's huge feet but somehow managed to keep out of reach. She was bleeding from a dozen lacerations, her sleek muscular body streaked with dirt and sweat.

Redden watched as one of the wolves noticed him for the first time and turned his way. It slouched forward, shaggy head lowered, muzzle drawn back to show rows of gleaming teeth.

Oriantha was too far away and there were four more wolves between him and her. Redden was on his own.

He again tried to summon the wishsong, and again he failed. The magic would not respond.

The wolf was crouching now, gathering itself, preparing to leap. Oriantha had thrown herself into the midst of the other wolves in an effort to break past them and reach him, but her effort was hopeless. Redden braced himself, fear racing through him, his nerves raw, his terror so strong it had eclipsed all sense of reason. He went down on one knee, fighting his panic, remembering his promise, his word, his determination ...

The ogre stumbled back into view right in front of him, cutting off the wolf, then turned toward him as if it could smell his fear. Its face was all bloodied and torn, and it roared in dull recognition of what it had found and might now act against. Great hands groped outward, reaching down.

Abruptly, Redden's voice exploded out of his throat, the wishsong a primal scream that gathered up the very air and turned it into a savage wind and changed particles of dust into deadly shards. Both tore into the ogre and the wolves, ripped them to shreds and threw them away.

Then Redden regained control of himself and stumbled forward, catching up with Oriantha. Her smooth feline face swung toward him momentarily, and there was satisfaction in her bright eyes. Teeth showed in an attempt at a smile, and the cat bolted ahead onto the open flats.

Redden stumbled after, trying not to look at what was left of the creatures he had just destroyed. He had that sick feeling again—the one he had experienced in the Fangs when he had fought back against and destroyed his Goblin attackers—as if something had been stolen from him by using the wishsong this way.

They raced onto the flats and crossed toward a series of low hills marked by clusters of boulders and deep ravines. He was stumbling badly, but forced himself to keep his feet and press on. He glanced back once for pursuit. He could see movement at the perimeter of the camp, but no organized effort was giving chase. Maybe they had given up, he thought. Maybe what he had done to the ogre and the demon-wolves had been enough to discourage them.

He looked away again quickly and tried not to think about anything but keeping up with Oriantha.

Then suddenly Lada appeared, scurrying out from the rocks to greet them, darting this way and that, his eyes bright as he chattered and jumped about. For reasons Redden couldn't explain, seeing the little Chzyk gave him such pleasure and generated such a strong feeling of hope.

"Lada," he whispered as the Chzyk leapt onto his boot and off again in the blink of an eye.

The little creature chattered in response and darted away again.

Ahead, Tesla Dart popped out from between the rocks, hopping from foot to foot as if impatient with the whole business and in no mood for anything even approaching delay.

"That took a long time!" she snapped at Oriantha.

There was something of an apologetic look reflected in her rough, whisker-fringed features as she shifted her eyes to Redden. "Well," she said, "it did."

She started to say something more, became completely flustered, and made a dismissive gesture instead.

"We should get out of sight," she said finally and turned away.

They hid in the rocks afterward while Oriantha, still in her animal form, licked her wounds with a long black tongue and

Tesla Dart sat with Redden, talking softly. Now and again, one or the other would glance over the tops of their shelter to see if there was any activity from the demon camp, but there was still no sign of pursuit.

"Did they hurt you?" the Ulk Bog asked the boy.

"Some."

"Nothing broken?"

"My pride. My confidence, a little."

"You were frightened?"

He nodded.

"Tael Riverine is very dangerous. You were lucky."

"More so than all the others that went with me."

"He wants Grianne Ohmsford. He wants his Queen. You would bring her to him, he thinks."

Redden stared. "Why would I do that? Even if I could, why?"

"You are her family. She would come to save you."

The boy almost laughed. "She's dead. A hundred years ago dead. If she weren't, she wouldn't come for me anyway. She doesn't even know who I am. What is Tael Riverine thinking?"

The Ulk Bog squinted at him. "Family is important. Especially to the Straken Lord, who has no family. He wants children. She will give them to him."

Redden shook his head. This argument was going nowhere. "He doesn't care about Grianne and children. He wants to conquer the Four Lands. He wants to make us all slaves."

Tesla Dart shrugged. "No one has ever escaped him. Just her. He thinks about nothing else. Everyone knows. He doesn't want to look weak. Having her bear his children will help."

"But he doesn't need to bother with any of that."

She gave him a look. "He needs what he doesn't have, what he lost when he lost her. He will never quit searching for her."

Oriantha had finished cleaning herself and had shape-shifted back to her old form. Pulling on the rest of her clothes and wrapping herself in her travel cloak, she took a quick look back at the enemy camp and said, "We have to be going. They'll be coming for us."

"Where do we go?" asked Tesla Dart.

They stared at one another for a moment. Until now, not much consideration had been given to the question.

"We should go to Arborlon," Redden declared. "That's where Railing and the others are likely to be. That's where we can be safe."

"We can be safe nowhere," Tesla Dart muttered.

But they set out anyway, Oriantha in the lead, the other two following. They were undecided about how to go, aware of the danger with the demon army so close at hand. Traveling directly north would take them through the Tirfing to Rover communities where they could find an airship offering passage to Arborlon. Without air travel, it would take them days or even weeks to get to their destination. But the terrain north required they pass just to the rear of the attacking army, threatening to expose them in a way none of them was willing to risk. So after a hurried conference, they decided that the safest choice was to go back the way they had come, west toward the rent in the Forbidding until they found an opening in the folded landscape that would allow them to move safely out of sight to the north.

Oriantha had already decided that the attack on Arishaig would keep the enemy locked up where it was for at least another few days, which should give them time enough to make their way to safety. Tesla Dart, on the other hand, was not so sure.

"The battle will end today," she announced. "The city will fall, the Straken Lord's army will go elsewhere. Tael Riverine will see it done."

"That city is heavily defended," the shape-shifter argued. "It won't be taken so easily."

"Today," the Ulk Bog repeated and refused to say more.

So even though there was a good deal of doubt about the Ulk Bog's prognostication, it generated a fresh sense of urgency, and the little company moved ahead quickly.

Even so, the three companions had progressed no more than an hour, traveling mostly back toward the Forbidding to find passage north, when Tesla Dart brought them up short.

"Wait," she cautioned, one hand raised. She sniffed at the air and listened intently for a long time. "We are tracked. Lada! *Ari'sho trush!*"

The Chzyk darted back in the direction from which they had come, even as the trio continued moving ahead. He was gone perhaps fifteen minutes before reappearing, racing across the barren landscape in a flash of dark movement, spines flaring out in warning. Tesla Dart dropped to one knee and bent close to the little creature as it charged up to her, and the two of them began chattering away in a mix of non-words and rough grunts.

The Ulk Bog rose swiftly, shaking her head. "This is bad. Tarwick hunts us with Goblins and wolves. The Straken Lord's Catcher can find anything he wishes. We will not escape if we try running. Another way is needed."

"An airship would give us a way," Redden declared.

"The only airships near are those fighting in Arishaig." Oriantha cocked an eyebrow. "You don't want to go back there, do you?"

There was a moment's silence. "Horses," the boy said.

"No horses out here, either. This isn't settled country. Not until we get to the Tirfing. We're a day from there."

"Too far!" Tesla Dart snapped.

"We can hide our trail," Redden said, though in truth he had no idea how they could do this.

But Tesla Dart clapped her hands. "No, we can do better! We can hide where they do not think!" She paused, looking from one to the other, excitement etched on her rough features. "We can go back inside the Forbidding!"

Redden stared. Surely, he had not heard correctly. "What did you say? Go back inside the Forbidding? I am not going back inside the Forbidding again. Ever!"

"Wait." Oriantha was suddenly interested. "How long would we have to stay?" she asked Tesla Dart.

The Ulk Bog grinned toothily at Redden. "You see? She knows what I do." Her bright eyes shifted to the girl. "We go quick, then out again. Lose Tarwick in land of Jarka Ruus, if he comes for us, get out again closer to place you want. See?"

"You mean we go back in long enough to travel to where we can find another way out and then leave again?" Redden demanded, flushed and suddenly terrified. "But what if we can't get out?"

"Lots of ways out! The wall crumbles many places. The magic is weakened. Can find ways for us, you see. Tarwick never catch us there. I know more than he does. Weka taught me. I can keep us safe."

It was a huge gamble, but the boy also saw why it made sense. There was reason to believe the pursuit might end at the entrance back into the Forbidding. Would anyone reenter while the Straken Lord's army was here? And Weka Dart had outfoxed the Straken Lord and his last Catcher in the time of Grianne Ohmsford. Maybe Tesla was similarly well informed.

But to go back into the Forbidding? Redden shivered, cold to his bones.

Oriantha moved around in front of him. "Let's do it. It has to be safer than trying to outrun pursuit out here. We're too far away from any help, and we have no one we can turn to. If we don't find an airship or horses, we'll be run down before the day is out."

"You realize what you're asking of me?" Redden snapped.

The girl leaned close. "No worse than what has been asked of you already." She paused. "I will stand by you to the end."

So we can both die together, Redden thought. But that was being small-minded and ungrateful. She was trying to reassure him. Clearly, she believed that this was their best chance.

He backed away from his anger and fear. She had not failed him so far. She had saved him when no one else could. She deserved his attention. And at this point, her judgment was admittedly better than his.

He took a deep breath and exhaled sharply, feeling all of the power that remained leaking out of him. "This nightmare is never going to end, is it?" he muttered. And without waiting for a reply, he started back toward the entrance into the Forbidding.

20

DEEP INSIDE ARISHAIG'S WALLS, HUDDLING in the shadows of the doorway to a shop that was closed and locked in the wake of the assault on the city, Arling Elessedil tried to decide what to do next. She had been running for two days, first from the crowds that swarmed the streets when the demon army appeared on the ridgeline and then from her own personal fears as she realized that the escape she had envisioned was now impossible. She had spent most of her time determining that this was so, running from one gate to the next to find all of them sealed and guarded, futilely tracking along the walls in search of other ways out, and finally stumbling exhausted through the streets in search of someone who might be able to help her. She hadn't stopped moving in all that time, desperate for help and terrified that Edinja might find her. What rest she'd gotten had been taken in brief snatches, all too quickly ended.

Now, about an hour before sunset on the second day, she had reached the limit of her endurance and could go no farther. She settled down on the doorstep and leaned back against the door in despair, crying silently.

Then she fell asleep.

When the hands shook her awake and the voices whispered her name, she could barely make herself respond.

"Arling!" she heard.

"It's all right. She's just sleeping."

She opened her eyes and found Aphen and Cymrian bending over her. She blinked hard several times, not quite able to believe they had found her—not even able to believe it was really them.

Then she reached quickly for Aphen, who took her in her arms and held her close.

"We've spent two days tracking you through the city," Cymrian said, "but you kept moving. We would use the Elfstones to find where you were, but when we'd go there you were gone. We couldn't manage to catch up with you. What were you doing?"

Arling shook her head. "Running. Trying to escape. Afraid I would be caught again." She exhaled sharply, gasping out her words. "How did you get here? I thought I would have to come looking for you in the Westland."

Aphen continued to hold her tightly, stroking her hair. "We caught up with those people who gave you over to the Federation. They told us what they had done. We were able to track you here using the Elfstones. Once inside the city, we began searching for you."

"We knew *where* you were at first," Cymrian interrupted. He crouched down next to the sisters. "But we couldn't find a way to get inside Edinja's house to free you. How did you get out?"

Arling managed a quick grin. "I escaped. I fooled Edinja into thinking I was hysterical and couldn't do anything. She had me locked in a bedroom, but when the serving woman came in to drug me again I hit her over the head and went out the door. Edinja was gone. I threw on a travel cloak and went right out the front door. No one stopped me. I've been running ever since, but I couldn't find a way out of the city."

Aphen and Cymrian exchanged a quick look, but Arling just continued on. "She took me into the cellars and showed me what she was doing to people down there. She changes them. She makes them into monsters, things that aren't human anymore. She wanted to scare me into helping her find you!"

Cymrian put his hand on Aphen's shoulder. "We need to get out of sight. Let's use this shop."

He broke the lock and the three of them moved out of the alley and inside, closing the door behind them. They were in a storeroom filled with boxes and racks of clothing. Cymrian set about finding something Arling could change into while Aphen kept holding her sister close, letting her continue with her story of what had happened to her while she was Edinja's prisoner.

"I thought at first I was a guest and she was taking care of me. I was told the airship that brought me was hers and the captain and crew had found no sign of either of you when they looked. I believed her. But then she started asking more questions and drugged me when I wouldn't answer so that I couldn't lie, and I had to tell her everything. Even about the Forbidding and the demons and the Ellcrys . . ."

She broke off, her face suddenly drained of color. "Aphen! I don't have the seed anymore!"

Aphen released her, holding her out at arm's length. "What do you mean? What happened to it?"

Arling was in tears. "I don't know! I was unconscious when those people found me and then aboard the ship, too. I didn't wake up until I was in Arishaig in Edinja's house, and when I searched it was gone!"

"Then Edinja has it," Cymrian declared.

"No, she doesn't," Arling said quickly. "She didn't know anything about it. When I told her about it after she gave me the drug, she kept trying to find out where it was, who might have taken it. It wasn't the captain and crew. She'd imprisoned them in the cellars, and she'd done things to the captain, turned him into a monster so that ..." She broke off. "We have to find it, Aphen!" she said frantically. "I have to get it back!"

"I can't find anything for her to wear in here," Cymrian announced from across the room. "Bring her into the shop. We can search there. We need to change, as well. Look at us. We look like we've been attacked by feral cats."

They moved out of the storeroom and into the front of the shop. The clothes on display were better organized and Cymrian quickly found garments they could change into. While Arling and Aphen did so, he moved to the windows and peered out.

"Quiet out there. No one about." He scanned up and down the street. "Everyone's gone into hiding." He shook his head. "I don't like their chances if they don't get out of here soon. Or ours."

"What do you mean?" Arling asked, lacing up her blouse and tightening the belt around her waist. She had wiped the tears and dirt away from her face and tied back her hair.

Cymrian looked at her. "We've watched the last two battles, and then we climbed up where we wouldn't be noticed and took a look over the battlements. There's an army of demonkind out there, obviously broken free of the Forbidding, and the Federation defenders aren't going to be enough to stop it. They've nearly broken through Arishaig's defenses twice."

"So we have to get out of the city," Aphen finished. "Escape and go back into the Westland and find the Ellcrys seed."

"But I'm not sure what happened to it!" Arling insisted.

"I am," Cymrian said. "The couple who found you and took you to the Federation warship took it. If you don't have it, and Edinja and her captain and crew don't have it, then who's left? They must have stolen it off you when they found you."

Aphen stared at him. "Are you sure about this?"

"Process of elimination. It's the only possibility. The man, in particular, seemed anxious to me, even before he found out Arling was your sister. He has it, all right."

Arling looked stricken. "But I don't know who he is. I don't know anything about the woman, either. How will we ever find them?"

"Before we worry about that, we have to get out of this city." Aphen put her hands on her sister's shoulders and looked into her eyes. "Arling, look at me. Let me see your eyes. Are you all right now? You look exhausted."

Cymrian had moved away from the windows and stepped behind a clothes rack to change, as well. "We'll start by finding Rushlin and see if he has any ideas. Rovers usually know one or two tricks for getting out of tight corners."

They found a better travel cloak for Arling, and together they moved toward the storeroom door, intent on going back out the way they had come in. They had just passed through the doorway when they saw a small, exquisitely beautiful woman with silver hair and dusky skin standing at the back door, blocking the way.

Arling gave a small cry and shrank back immediately.

"Why don't we talk about how I can help you leave all this behind," Edinja Orle said. "Isn't that what you want?"

*

Aphen's first impulse was to attack, but she resisted it when she saw the giant moor cat crouched off to one side. It was much too close for her to stop it from springing on them, which it would likely choose to do if she tried to attack Edinja.

"I'm not here to try to take Arling back," the sorceress said to them. "I'm just here to talk. Listen to me, and then you can go wherever you want. I won't try to stop you. In fact, I won't do anything to get in your way. But I can help you get to where you want to go, which ought to make what I have to say worthwhile."

Aphen could feel Cymrian tense next to her, so she reached out and took hold of his arm in warning. "How did you find us?" she asked Edinja.

"Cinla and I tracked you. We're very good at that sort of thing."

"You *let* Arling escape, didn't you?"

"I gave her the opportunity so that she could lead me to you and we could have this talk. I admit that in the beginning— weeks ago—I was looking for something entirely different from what I am looking for now. As Prime Minister of the Federation, I wanted to find a way to put pressure on the Elves to form an alliance. Or on the Druids, for that matter. But now that I know what is happening with the Forbidding, I've decided I need to pursue a different course of action entirely."

"You tried to kill us!" Cymrian snapped.

She shook her head. "I did not try to kill you. *Stoon* tried to kill you. I sent him to find you and bring you back to me so that I could discover what you were up to. He took it upon himself to do more."

"He had the use of your creatures, Edinja."

"Yes, my creatures. Thieves and murderers and men who lied to me; I made them into something better. I gave him three of them for protection. He's been terrified of Aphenglow ever since their encounter at Paranor. He insisted he needed them. How he used them was his own decision."

"Your man tried to kill us without your permission?" Cymrian pressed incredulously. "You expect us to believe that?"

She shrugged. "That's up to you. But I had no idea he decided to countermand my orders or that he managed to persuade the captain of my ship to be his ally. Killing you was easier than trying to bring you back alive. He just wanted you out of the way. Think about it. What would I gain by killing you? What would be the point? I have done nothing to pursue Drust Chazhul's plans for Paranor since his death. I have kept away from the Druid's Keep because it does not belong to me. It belongs to the Druids, and I respect that. So what would I achieve by inflicting any sort of harm on you?"

"I don't believe you," Cymrian declared, making a dismissive gesture.

"You could have known about the Ellcrys," Aphen said.

Edinja made a face. "Assuming for a moment I knew about Arling's purpose on your voyage, why would I want to interfere? Why would I want to take Arling prisoner when she is the only one who can save us? From the very beginning of my involvement, Aphenglow was the one I wanted to reach."

"So you sent assassins to Arborlon to try to kill me?" Aphen snapped.

"Assassins? I don't know anything about any assassins. I didn't send anyone to Arborlon. As for the Ellcrys, I didn't know anything about that until Arling was in my bedroom, recovering." She pointed at Arling. "Tell them. Do you think I knew anything about the Ellcrys before you told me?"

Arling hesitated. "No, I don't think you did."

"When I had you in my care, did I do anything to hurt you?"

"You drugged me."

"So that you would tell me the truth, which you weren't going to do otherwise, were you?"

"You could have just let me go."

"So that you could disappear and I would never know what happened? I couldn't allow that. I needed to keep you with me long enough to let you lead me to your sister. I admit I tricked you. I admit I used you. But only because I couldn't get the answers I needed otherwise. None of you were going to listen to me."

Aphenglow was beginning to see a modicum of reason in Edinja's arguments, which was troubling. Even worse, she was also beginning to hope that the sorceress was telling the truth so that she would help them find a way out of the city.

"You could have just asked me to come see you," she tried.

Edinja laughed. "Oh, and you would have come right over? After my predecessor tried to have Paranor seized and the Druid order disbanded? Why would you trust me? Why would you have anything at all to do with me?"

Aphen did not have an answer.

Edinja made a dismissive gesture. "None of that matters now, in any case. What matters is that the Forbidding is down and the demons are loose and most of them seem to be gathered right outside the gates of Arishaig. This is my city, and as Prime Minister it is my responsibility to protect it. All this has changed my thinking about what has to happen next. I need Arling to find the Ellcrys seedling and do what she must to put the demons back where they belong. So I want you to forget about everything you think you know about me or you think I am responsible for, and concentrate your efforts on saving us all."

The Elessedil sisters and Cymrian looked at each other doubtfully. "So you really intend to help us?" Aphen asked.

Edinja nodded. "I said I did, and I meant it. I will provide you with a fast airship—one that will get you past the dragon and the other flying things that are waiting out there. I will put you aboard and send you on your way because I am depending on you to save my people and this city. And because the Elves are also at risk. Everyone in the Four Lands faces extinction if we don't lock the demonkind back within the Forbidding."

"Do you intend to accompany us?" Cymrian asked suddenly.

Edinja laughed again. "I wondered when you would get around to asking that. In other circumstances, I would insist on it. But a Prime Minister of the Federation can't be seen abandoning her capital city when it's under attack. A Prime Minister is expected to stand or fall with her people."

"And you don't intend to send any of your creatures with us, do you?" Arling pressed.

"They would be of little use. I could give you a warship and a captain and crew, but that would just make you a more visible target. I think it best if just the three of you go. Don't you agree?"

Aphen nodded. "But what do *you* want in return for this? You, personally?"

"You don't think a promise that you will do what you can to save the entire world is enough for me?" Edinja snorted derisively. "All right. When this is over, maybe you might consider making a visit so we can talk face-to-face, perhaps find common ground. I am not Drust Chazhul. I am not seeking to destroy the Druid order or gain power over the other Races. I am looking for a way to build the sorts of bridges that Drust Chazhul could never have envisioned on the best day of his life. That will be satisfaction enough for me."

A momentary silence followed. "All right," Aphen agreed. "Show us the aircraft we will be flying, and we'll be on our way."

*

Aphenglow Elessedil did not for one solitary second believe that Edinja Orle was telling her the truth. At least, not all of it. Enough to convince the Elves that she had their best interests at heart, maybe, but not enough to give away her real plan, whatever it was. The problem was, she could not divine what was behind the sorceress's willingness to help them, and she could not afford to refuse that help when it was exactly what they needed. Too much was at stake not to accept the offer of an airship that would give them swift transportation back to the Westland where they could begin their search for the missing Ellcrys seed.

So with Arling and Cymrian in tow, she followed the Federation Prime Minister out of the shop and back through the city streets toward the grounds and buildings where the Coalition Council kept its quarters. Cinla disappeared shortly after they set out and did not reappear. They encountered only one blockade and a handful of soldiers on their way. The city streets were mostly empty.

"We bypass most of the barricades and soldiers going this way," Edinja declared at one point. "No sense involving them. They'll have questions, and I don't want to have to provide them with answers. This matter is between us."

In short order they reached the housing and administration buildings set aside for the needs of the members of the Coalition Council, but Edinja kept going. Down a side street and behind the official grounds, she led them into the cavernous interior of a warehouse-sized building where a pair of sleek Sprints sat side by side on a landing pad. They were big machines, each able to carry five or six, their design unfamiliar to either Aphen or Cymrian.

"This should convince you I am serious," she said. "These are prototypes. No one has them but myself and the military high command. They are a carefully guarded secret, and no one outside a handful of Southlanders has seen them. You will be the first. Have a look."

Cymrian gave the nearest vessel a quick once-over, walking around it, examining its parse tubes and hoods, radian draws, and light sheaths, which were folded up on deck and ready to be hoisted. Then he climbed into the pilot box and examined the control mechanisms. Finally, he roamed the gunwales studying the weapons attached to the railings on both sides.

"She's beautiful," he announced when he was done. "I have trouble believing you are prepared to give her to us."

"I'm not giving her to you; I am loaning her." Edinja's eyes were fixed on Aphenglow. "I want her back when this is over."

Aphen nodded. "Fair enough." She paused. "How long do you think the army can hold out against this attack?"

Edinja shrugged. "Maybe three more days."

"Have you sent for help?"

"The other cities need to look out for themselves."

"From the Borderlands, then?"

The Federation Prime Minister looked away. "You should get under way. It is possible the demons know the bearer of the Ellcrys seed is inside these walls. It might even explain the reason for their attacking us."

She walked away from them, her robes wrapped tightly around her small frame, her head up. She moved over to a wall where a huge wheel worked a series of pulleys. When she began turning the wheel, the roof slid open to reveal a sky filling rapidly with clouds.

"Climb aboard," Cymrian called down to the sisters. "Let's do what she says."

Aphen helped Arling aboard, and they settled themselves into deep cushioned seats set to one side of the open cockpit.

Restraining straps were provided, and they buckled themselves in. Cymrian took charge of the controls, powered up the aircraft, and engaged the thrusters.

Aphen glanced over one last time at Edinja Orle, but she was looking down and didn't seem to notice.

Seconds later they were airborne. Rising through the open roof into the deepening gray of the late-afternoon sky, they encountered the stink of burned oil and flesh borne on the wind. Then, abruptly, it began to rain, and Cymrian swung the nose of their craft west, pushed the thrusters forward, and left Arishaig behind.

Late afternoon found Keeton exhausted and discouraged. The battle for Arishaig had resumed shortly after the march around the walls by the Jarka Ruus, and it had not yet ceased. Nor did he think it would until they were all dead. He no longer doubted this was inevitable. The demonkind were too numerous and too powerful to be stopped by the city's defenders. He no longer believed there was any hope.

The beginning of the end had come earlier in the day. The massing of the demon hordes and their slow circling of the walls had been exactly what Keeton had suspected it might be—a feint to draw attention away from the real attack. The latter came shortly afterward, a fresh enemy army appearing abruptly from behind the ridgeline and launching a full frontal attack on the west wall and its already weakened gates. Both Keeton and Sefita had been ready for this, their soldiers on the ramparts and airmen aboard the warships armed and ready to respond. Unit commanders had been dispersed to their positions and orders to stand and hold issued to one and all. What else could they do, after all? The last of the oil was poured into the ditches and lit, the flash rips that had been mounted in a makeshift fashion atop the walls were brought quickly into play, and the vast armament of both waiting warships was turned broadside to repel the attack.

The effort had been successful. Although the creatures from the Forbidding pressed forward through flames and cannon fire and the launching of numerous steel-tipped missiles, the combined might of Federation military air and land forces had eventually thrown them back. It didn't happen right away and it didn't happen easily, but it did happen.

The problem was that this didn't put even a temporary end to things; it simply served as a prelude. Because now the demon army was positioned both east and west, and the moment the west force went into retreat, the east force attacked. This was the bigger of the two armies and the one to which the larger task had been appointed—to destroy the Federation landing platforms and their moored vessels.

Keeton, standing with the defenders on the west wall, didn't have a chance to assess its purpose firsthand and missed any chance to do so while there was still time. To those defending on the east it appeared this was just a further effort to break down the gates of the city. But it quickly became apparent that the thrust of the assault was not against the gates or even the east wall, but against the ramparts that protected the landing platforms at the southeast corner of the city. The hordes initially attacked the gates in waves, but quickly swerved off toward the platforms. Winged creatures returned in droves, dropping attackers that swarmed the defenses and quickly ignited whatever would burn. The warships were mostly aloft, but those that weren't went up in flames along with skiffs, flits, and dozens of others. Only the transports, housed within barns deep inside the city and still out of view, were spared.

Virtually every airship sitting out on the platforms was

destroyed, and the platforms themselves were so badly damaged they could not be used for landing without posing a danger to the ships and crews attempting to do so. The attack was swift and purposeful, and—once the intended result was accomplished—it broke off and retreated from sight.

That was when Keeton, consulting with Sefita Rayne and a handful of ground commanders, made the decision to begin evacuating the city. The Coalition Council was in disarray, its members scattered. Many had already left in private airships, fleeing for the safety of other cities. Many had simply gone to ground. No one seemed to be in charge. Edinja Orle was still missing, although there were rumors that she had flown to Wayford and Dechtera to seek additional support for the Federation's capital city. Whatever the case, members of the military were making all of the decisions by now, and Keeton was still their commander in chief.

The decision to evacuate was arrived at easily enough, however. With the transports still intact, there was no reason not to remove as many of the more vulnerable residents as possible, beginning with women and children and the sick and elderly. The city was in imminent danger of falling, and those trapped within were unlikely to survive what happened afterward. With warships available to act as escorts, saving those who could be saved was a choice that met with unanimous approval.

The loading of the carriers had begun at once, and transport had been under way ever since. The vessels would convey as many passengers as possible to one of the nearby cities and then return for more. Warships would act as escorts, and keep careful watch for airborne attackers—especially the dragon.

But now sunset was approaching, and the transports had been active all day. No further attacks of any sort had been made. What remained of the army had been divided by commands and dispersed to positions that would allow for at least limited defense of all four walls and a chance for overlap where it became needed. The warships not acting as escorts to the transports continued to patrol the air overhead, keeping watch against surprise attacks.

Not that Keeton believed there would be any. The next attack would come at nightfall, when the light was gone and the new moon rendered the landscape black and impenetrable, and there would be nothing surprising about it. It would include all of the remaining creatures, and they would sweep across the walls and into the city, and that would be the end of Arishaig.

"Wint!" he called, catching sight of his second as he neared the stations designated for loading the transports. Wint turned at the sound of his voice, and Keeton hurried over. "How many more do we have?"

The other looked as if he hadn't slept in days. "You don't want to know."

"Tell me anyway."

"Two. Both are in the process of loading. That's all we have left until the others come back. That won't happen before nightfall."

Keeton shook his head. "That's not soon enough."

Wint laughed. "You don't think so?" His laughter trailed off. "Nothing is soon enough, Captain. We've evacuated maybe half of the population. What we need is another day or two."

"Then we'll start using the warships as transports, too."

Wint stared. "If we do that, we can't hold the city!"

Keeton gave him a look of disbelief. "We've already lost the city! Haven't you noticed?" He made a dismissive gesture. "I hate this."

He glanced around as if the answer to his problems might be found in the growing darkness. "Could you form a command of

First Response and regular soldiers to act as a convoy, escorting those who still remain out through the north gates and into the hills?"

Wint shrugged. "Pretty dangerous, trying to do that. Women and children. Pitch-black. Creatures everywhere."

"At least they'll have a chance out there. They can get out through the evacuation tunnels. If we wait for the next attack, there's a chance they won't be noticed."

"I'll get on it." Wint paused. "You'll be coming with us?"

Keeton shook his head. "Someone has to stay behind."

"That would be you and me, I guess."

"I'd rather you went. The convoy will need a capable leader."

Wint shook his head no. "It will have to be someone else. Don't ask me again."

Keeton nodded. "Guess I knew you'd say that. Okay. Do what you have to and get back with me. Night is coming. They'll attack when it does."

He was turning away when Wint said, "Been a pleasure serving with you, Captain."

Keeton turned. Gave his second a broad smile. "Let's find a softer duty when this is over, you and me."

"You and me, Cap."

Keeton waved wordlessly over his shoulder and kept walking.

He spent a little time with Sefita Rayne, devising an exit strategy for when defending any part of the city was no longer possible, even though by now both knew that escape was reduced to a faint glimmer of hope. After that, he walked the walls, visiting with his Federation soldiers and their unit commanders, joking and laughing, teasing and cajoling, praising and reassuring, saying all the right things and speaking a few hard truths, trying to help them keep it together.

All the while, he watched the darkness deepen.

When the last of the sunset was a purple hue balanced on the edge of the western horizon and the darkness was just closing down, the last attack began.

It was a relief when it did.

21

IT WAS JUST APPROACHING MIDDAY WHEN SEERSHA and Crace Coram piloted their two-man out of the north and into the smoky ruins of Arishaig. The city was gone, the defenses breached, the gates forced, and the walls taken. The Druid and the Dwarf Chieftain could still hear the screams and cries of wounded and dying as the victors prowled the ruins in search of whatever caught their eye. Diapson-crystal-powered weapons still flashed here and there at regular intervals as the last of the survivors fought to keep their stalkers at bay. Black smoke coiled skyward in twisted columns and gave the cityscape the look of a volcano heating up for another explosion. Dark shapes darted through the rubble, and it was impossible to tell which army or persuasion they belonged to.

"We're too late," Crace Coram rumbled, the regret and dismay evident in the tremor of his deep voice.

Seersha nodded. "The Straken Lord's army must be huge for it to have done this. Arishaig was heavily defended, and the best Federation soldiers in the Four Lands were stationed here."

"Do you suppose anyone got out?"

She shook her head. "Not enough, I'd guess."

They were silent for a moment, looking down on the carnage, listening to its still-living voice rise up in a ragged plea. The destruction swept across the whole of the fallen city and well beyond. Thousands of dead lay heaped about the walls. Seersha searched for signs of airships, even small ones, but couldn't find any. They had either made it out already or been destroyed.

"Look there!" Crace Coram said suddenly, pointing north behind them.

She looked obediently. Beyond the immediate destruction, far in the distance west of where the Prekkendorran sprawled and the grasslands below the Tirfing divided in rugged folds, a dark mass seethed. She stared, not sure what she was seeing at first.

"The Straken Lord's army," her companion declared. "Already on the march. Not wasting a moment more on what's happened here. Why should they? They have a new destination."

She took a moment to orient herself. The Borderlands lay in that general direction. The great fortress city of Tyrsis. But the drift of the enemy march to the west suggested another destination entirely.

"History suggests the demons will want to be certain the key to their prison is destroyed once and for all." The Dwarf Chieftain shrugged. "Even a madman like Tael Riverine might be able to figure out the importance of that one."

She nodded in dismay.

The demon army was marching on Arborlon.

Far to the north, Aphenglow and her companions angled their Sprint toward the Tirfing to begin their search for the couple who had stolen the Ellcrys seed from Arling. It was a search that the Elven Druid expected to conclude quickly with the help of the Elfstones, but one that required some caution, as well. After all, none of them knew anything about the couple. Aphen and Cymrian had met them only briefly and Arling, unconscious at the time, remembered nothing at all. All this suggested that rushing in heedlessly, no matter the urgency, would be foolish. Recovery of the seed was too important to allow for mistakes at this point. With the Forbidding crumbling badly and the demons breaking free in force, protecting the seed was their foremost concern until it was back in Arling's hands.

It was a huge relief for all of them to have gotten clear of Arishaig. For hours after they fled the besieged city they found themselves glancing over their shoulders, unable to banish the images of the battle from their minds. Aphen could not stop thinking about what Edinja had said just before their departure—that perhaps the Straken Lord and his demons had found out that Arling was the bearer of the Ellcrys seed and would come after her. That would explain their decision to attack Arishaig instead of Arborlon.

She could already imagine what it would mean to the people of the Federation home city if the demons found a way to break through, and that, in turn, suggested Arborlon's fate was grim, should the enemy then come north to the Elven home city, which she thought likely. Destroying the Ellcrys utterly would permanently secure freedom for the creatures of the Forbidding, and the Straken Lord would actively seek this end. If he could track Arling, he would do so. Hundreds of years ago, the same effort had been made and had very nearly succeeded. It was only the desperate efforts of an Ohmsford boy and an Elessedil girl and a handful of companions that had prevented it from happening.

History was repeating itself, she thought darkly, and wondered anew about the Ohmsford twins and their allies.

"Why do you think she let us go?" Arling asked as the landscape sped by beneath them.

Neither of the other two had to ask who she was talking about. "She had nothing to gain by keeping us," Cymrian offered. He was slumped back in the rear of the cockpit, stretched out as best he could in the cramped space.

"She knows what's at stake," Aphen added, hands on the controls, eyes forward. "If we don't find and quicken the seed, the whole of the Four Lands will be overrun. Edinja would suffer the same fate as the rest of us."

Arling shook her head. "You didn't spend time with her like I did. You didn't see those creatures she keeps, locked away like animals. She wouldn't help us if she didn't have something else in mind."

"You mean something besides saving her own skin?" Cymrian said.

"She likes controlling things. And people. Yet she just gave us this ship and let us go. It doesn't feel right."

Aphen had to agree. It didn't. But she couldn't figure out either what Edinja had to gain by letting them go, or how she thought she could manage to gain it. They had escaped Arishaig, had possession of the Elfstones, were on their way to finding the missing Ellcrys seed, and had told Edinja nothing that would help her find them if for some reason she decided to come after them.

"She's a complicated person," she said quietly.

"She's a dangerous person," Cymrian declared with a snort. "She's probably behind the attacks you suffered in Arborlon. She's probably responsible for us being shot down by that Federation warship in the first place."

"She told me she had taken me and was keeping me to lure

you to Arishaig," Arling added. "She drugged me to make me tell her everything about what we were doing."

The other two said nothing for a moment. "But she didn't say why she was doing this?" Aphen's hands rested lightly on the controls as she turned around to look at her sister. "She didn't say what it was she was trying to accomplish?"

Arling looked miserable. "No."

"Maybe everything changed once she found out about the collapse of the Forbidding and saw the demonkind knocking on the gates of her city," Cymrian offered. "She didn't know about any of that before, and it might have made her change her plans. Not because she wanted to, but because she had to."

"Cymrian's right," Aphen agreed. "Nothing's the way it was a week ago. Even Edinja Orle would have to take a second look at what she was thinking to see if it still had relevance."

Arling nodded, but didn't say anything in response, and Aphen let the matter drop. She could tell her sister was not convinced, her doubts and fears of Edinja Orle deep-seated and troubling. Letting a little time pass was probably best. Arling had been through a lot—and unless Aphen was badly mistaken, the worst was still to come. Edinja was likely to turn out to be the least of her sister's problems.

They piloted the Sprint for several more hours through the darkening night. Close to the southern fringes of the Duln Forests, Aphen decided they should stop; none of them had slept for more than a few hours in days, and all were exhausted. They would moor their vessel for the night, take turns standing watch, and set out again at daybreak.

Arling curled up in the aft cushions of the cockpit and was asleep within seconds. Aphen sat with Cymrian in the bow, looking out at the night. The Sprint was anchored perhaps two dozen feet off the ground, and the landscape about them was grassy and flat and open for miles. The sky was clear this night, its dark bowl bright with stars in the absence of moonlight. The madness they had witnessed in Arishaig had begun to recede into the background.

"She's handling all this better than I would," Cymrian whispered, nodding toward Arling. "I don't know how."

"She's stronger than she looks."

"A lot is being asked of her."

Aphen didn't respond.

"What do you think is going to happen once we get the seed back and find the Bloodfire?"

"I don't know."

"She'll have to decide."

"I know."

"If there's even a decision left to be made."

"Stop talking about it."

"Because maybe there isn't."

She glared at him. "I'm aware of all this. I'm sure she's aware of it, too. It doesn't help to talk about it further. There's no point in speculating. We don't even know what's going to happen when we find the Bloodfire. We don't know how the quickening of the seed works."

Cymrian was quiet for a few moments, speculating. "I didn't think about that."

"Well, I did. I've thought about everything that could possibly happen and then some. I've thought about everything I might do to try to help Arling. Everything. But there's nothing to be done until we reach the moment of reckoning."

"I guess not." He went silent again, and this time he stayed silent. They sat together, shoulder-to-shoulder, looking back at the sleeping girl and thinking their separate thoughts.

"Remember when this all began?" she said finally. "You were

my protector against whoever was attacking me in Arborlon. That seems a lifetime ago. It doesn't even seem connected to what's happening now."

"Like the missing Elfstones. This started because of them, and now they don't have anything to do with anything."

She shook her head. "We don't even talk about them anymore. We don't even think about them. But hunting for them destroyed the Druid order. Hunting for them changed everything."

"It seemed the right thing to do at the time."

"It was a mistake."

He glanced over. "Hard to know that for sure. Events are connected—sometimes in ways we don't see. One thing leads to another, but the path isn't always recognizable. I don't think you can second-guess yourself."

"I can do anything I want. Especially second-guess myself."

"It's pointless, Aphen."

"I'm *feeling* pointless. Everything in my life is feeling pointless—in spite of what I'm trying to do for Arling and the Elves and the Druid order and everyone else in the Four Lands. Pointless and hopeless and overwhelming."

"You've done pretty well so far."

"Have I?"

"As well as you could. Anyway, that's the past, and what matters is the future. That's how life works, because it's short and precious and kind of doubtful."

She looked over at him. He met her gaze and held it. "You constantly surprise me," she said.

"You mean that in a good way?"

"I do."

"Then shall I continue to try to surprise you some more?"

"Like you did that first night in Arishaig?" She smiled, then leaned in and pressed her mouth against his, taking her time, making sure he understood what she was feeling. Then she broke the kiss, cocked an eyebrow, and grinned. "There. I feel much better. Now I'm going to sleep."

She rolled into her travel cloak, shifted on the Sprint's cushions until she was comfortable, and started to drift off. Her last memory before sleep took her was of his voice saying, "I feel pretty good, too."

They rose at dawn and flew throughout the day over the vast stretch of the Tirfing. By nightfall, they had just passed its northern fringes. Though they could have kept going through the night and made their destination by dawn, exhaustion claimed them shortly before midnight, so they once more made camp.

When Aphen finally brought out the blue Elfstones the following morning and summoned their magic, she no longer had to stop and think about what she was doing. By now she was familiar with the process and prepared for the magic's response. When the tingling began in her fingers and the heat washed through her body and out again in swift, insistent waves, she was neither frightened nor intimidated. She didn't even bother with closing her eyes when she conjured the image of what she wished the Elfstones to find for her.

She might have chosen to focus her efforts on the silver seed that was the object of their search, but she chose instead to find the two people who had taken it. Her memory of their faces was clear enough that she was able to visualize both easily, and she could tell from the magic's response that it recognized what it was she was looking for and knew where to find it.

Thus, she was carried out of her body and across the countryside, through woods and over grasslands, down roadways and paths to where the buildings of a tiny village were scattered in either singular isolation or tiny clumps all about a cluster of shabby businesses that included a stable and harness repair, a blacksmith, a mercantile and grocery store, two taverns, a tiny inn, and a meeting hall. Men and women moved through the shadows of trees canopied overhead, and horses stamped and nickered softly in their traces where they were hitched to posts.

There, right in the midst of it all, the man and the woman who had found Arling and taken her to the Federation walked beside their little wooden cart and donkey on their way up the road and out of town.

Aphen dismissed the magic and the images. "We have them," she announced, a grimness to her voice. "Let's get flying."

They flew on throughout the morning, then, somewhat past midday, set the airship down at the edge of a small clearing. Leaving it safely tucked into its leafy concealment, they set out on foot.

The afternoon was winding down by now, shadows lengthening as the gray day threatened to bring more than brief showers, dark thunderheads beginning to form to the west and move in their direction. They picked up their pace in response, walking more quickly, anxious to reach the shelter of the village before the worst of the storm caught up to them. Hoods lifted and the collars of their cloaks pulled tight, they bent their heads against the wind and rain and slogged on through the deepening dark like wraiths, as faceless and voiceless as the shadows through which they passed.

Aphen managed to keep them moving in the right direction, even after the road had disappeared in a muddy smear and they had to reach the village by following a cow path that wound upward through the surrounding hills and came down on the far side. She began searching for the cottage she had seen in her vision, the one the couple had been traveling toward. Sora, she remembered suddenly. That was the man's name. But she couldn't remember the woman's, only the sound of her voice— kind and filled with concern.

She darkened her heart against such feelings. These people had taken Arling and given her to the Federation. They had stolen the Ellcrys seed.

They were not entitled to any consideration.

They were perhaps a quarter mile outside the village when they came upon the cottage Aphen had been looking for. Leading the way, she entered the yard and walked up to the door. She was aware of how poorly constructed the house was, how shabby the few outbuildings. She looked for farm animals and saw several chickens and the donkey looking out the door of a small shed. She saw a tiny vegetable garden.

These people had very little. They were just barely getting by on foraging and whatever they could grow.

She felt her dislike softening.

She knocked on the door, and heard a voice call out to her. "Coming!" When the door opened, the woman with the kind voice was standing there. She was wearing an old dress and apron, and her hair was done up in a farm wife's bun.

"Oh!" she gasped in genuine shock. She took a step back and then caught sight of Arling peering at her over Aphen's shoulder. "Oh, my goodness, child—it's you! Are you all right?"

Arling nodded, smiling uncertainly.

"Thank goodness! I'm so sorry for what we did. We didn't know. Sora said you needed medical care and we didn't have any to offer. Not even here, in our village. No Healer, not even a midwife. But look at you! You seem fine. And your sister and her friend have brought you safely back. I'm so relieved." She glanced from face to face. "Come in, come in. I have hot tea on the stove."

They stepped inside, where the girls were ushered to seats at a tiny kitchen table. There were only three chairs, so Cymrian declined the offer of the third and said he would stand, moving off to warm himself in front of a small stone fireplace. The woman poured them each a mug of tea and then joined the girls at the table.

"Sora had business at the tavern, but he should be back soon." She seemed genuinely pleased that they were there. "He will be so surprised. How did you find us?"

Then she saw something in Aphen's face and hesitated. "What's the matter? Something's wrong, isn't it? That's why you've come. Something's wrong."

Aphen nodded. "My sister was carrying a silver stone when you found her. It was taken while she slept but before she was given over to the men on that Federation warship. Do you have that stone?"

The woman stared. "A stone? No. I never saw a stone. It was taken, you say . . ."

She trailed off abruptly, and right away Aphen could tell what had happened. "Your husband has it, doesn't he?" she said.

The woman was trembling. "He's a good man, really. But he thinks things should belong to him just because he's found them. He's been trying to sell something in the village for several days now. When he left today, he said he thought he had a buyer. I don't pay much attention to that sort of thing. Mostly, it never comes to anything, even when he thinks it will."

She shook her head, flushed and angry. "But stealing! I'm so sorry. I would have made him give it back if I had known."

She was crying freely now, her face streaked with tears.

Aphen and Arling exchanged a quick glance. Arling looked as if she might cry herself.

Not so Cymrian. "Where can we find him?" he asked.

*

The tavern was a single room with a bar, some stools, a few tables and chairs, and not much more. It didn't even have a fireplace. What heat there was emanated from a small wood-burning stove in one corner and from the bodies of the men clustered about the tables and pressed up against the bar. Tankards of ale were being passed around, and voices were loud and insistent.

But the voices died into mutterings and the eyes of the patrons shifted to the doorway when the Elessedil sisters and Cymrian entered. They were Elves in a community populated mostly by Southlanders who had drifted west to find a better life and only found more of the same. There was a Dwarf in one corner, bent over his drink. There were a handful of Rovers at another table. But no Elves.

A Borderman leaning against the bar a few feet away from her took one look at her black Druid robes, pushed away from the bar, and left without a word. Another, a hunter dressed in leather, followed him out.

At a table near the back of the room, Sora was seated with a pair of men. Another four stood just behind the two in what appeared to Aphen to be a protective circle. As she watched, Sora counted coins from a stack that had been shoved in front of him, taking his time, not even bothering to look up from his task when they entered and the noise level dropped.

But as Aphen and her companions started across the room, one of the men seated said something to Sora, who looked up, saw who was approaching, quickly produced the leather pouch in which the Ellcrys seed had been placed, and shoved it across the table to the man who had spoken. The man snatched up the pouch and tucked it into his jacket.

"There, now," Sora said, rather too loudly, "our business is concluded! I must be on my way. A pleasure seeing you."

He scooped the coins off the table and into his pockets and rose hurriedly, nearly tripping over his own feet as he tried to move away.

Cymrian was on top of him before he'd taken his second step, seizing him by his shoulders and shoving him back down into his chair. "Your business isn't quite finished," the Elven Hunter said, reaching down and extracting the hunting knife from Sora's wide leather belt and flinging it across the room.

"Don't move," Aphen said to the men seated at the table, her hand stretched out in warning. Her eyes lifted to take in the bunch clustered at the back of the table. "Don't any of you move."

She tried to keep Arling behind her, out of harm's way, but Arling had other ideas and pushed forward. "Where is the seed you stole from me?" she snapped at Sora. "While I was injured and unconscious, you took it. Where is it?"

The big man squirmed. "I was owed something for saving your life," he snapped. "You would have died without Aquinel and me!"

"You were owed much for saving me, but you had no right to steal what wasn't yours," Arling persisted. "Give me the seed!"

Sora's mouth tightened. "I can't. I sold it to this gentleman right here. He's the lawful owner now. You'll have to take it up with him."

He tried once again to get to his feet, and again Cymrian shoved him back down. "He is not the lawful owner if he bought stolen property," the Elven Hunter pointed out, eyes fixing on the man in question.

Arling's gaze, white-hot with anger, shifted to the man with the pouch. "Give it back to me."

The man was not intimidated. He was long and lean and had the look of someone who had not willingly given up much in his life. "What about my money? I paid for that silver orb. I'm owed."

Cymrian reached down and pulled the coins from Sora's pocket, casting them across the table. "There. We are even. Give back the seed."

The man looked down at the coins and shook his head. "I don't want the money. I want the seed. I bought it. It's mine."

"You have no right to it!" Arling shouted, her voice shrill enough to make Aphen flinch. "It was sold to you by someone who didn't own it! You have to give it back. You don't understand what's at stake!"

"Arling," Aphen said quietly, making a calming motion. "They don't need to know everything."

One of the men standing behind the pair seated at the table started to reach beneath his cloak. Aphen gestured, snapping her fingers as she did, and the man dropped to the floor, writhing in excruciating pain. The knife he had been reaching for clattered on the wooden floorboards.

The men at the table backed up, muttering and looking left and right at their fellows. They clearly anticipated doing something, but were undecided as to what that should be. Their leader kept watching Aphen, making no move to interfere. She didn't like the look on his face. He was enjoying this.

"Let's be fair about this," he said, not sounding as if he intended to be fair at all. "You." He pointed to Sora. "You sold me the orb for a fixed amount and I paid that amount. Isn't that so?"

Sora nodded reluctantly. "That's so."

"Did you steal it from them?"

"I . . . It sort of just dropped out of the girl's pocket while we was helping her. I actually saved it from being lost."

"So it's yours, after all. You see?" He smiled at Aphen. "Your claim is suspect. But if you want it back—orb, stone, seed, whatever—I'm willing to negotiate. Pay me four times what I gave up. Wait, five times. Then you can have it."

Aphen stepped forward, eyes fixed on the man. "Take out the pouch and set it on the table. Do it right now."

The man shook his head. "I don't take orders from anyone. Especially Elves. I don't care who you are or what sort of tricks you can do. A word from me, and you and your friends will be cut to—"

He never finished. Aphen's fingers made a curious twisting motion, and the man's words choked in his throat as he was lifted out of his chair by invisible hands and hauled across the tabletop. He thrashed momentarily, but could gain no purchase, and his efforts at calling for help failed. The men with him backed against the wall, then broke and fled toward the doors. Cymrian moved quickly to the second man seated across from Sora and put him down with a single blow to the temple. Sora tried to run yet again, but he was hemmed in on all sides by the Elves.

Shouts rose from the other patrons, but Arling wheeled on them and screamed at them to be silent. The force of her words was enough. The room went absolutely still.

Aphen flipped the man she had ensnared with her magic onto his back without touching him, her wrist twisting slightly to complete the task. Then she reached inside his robes as he flopped and thrashed like a fish out of water and took back the pouch with the Ellcrys seed.

She leaned close. "I ought to kill you and be done with it. You deserve no better. But men like you should live out their lives until the misery they cause to others comes back to find them— as it surely will in your case."

She cast him away as if he weighed nothing. He flew off the table and onto the floor, collapsing in a motionless heap.

Aphen and Arling were already moving toward the tavern door. Cymrian was a step behind, hauling Sora along by his collar, shoving him forward. A few angry mutterings rose from the tavern patrons, but no one tried to stop them.

Moments later they were outside, trudging down the road toward the end of the village. Rain sheeted down, soaking them through. No one spoke. Cymrian released his grip on Sora, but the latter made no attempt at running away again. He simply kept pace as if this were the only choice open to him.

"I'm finished here, you know that?" he said to Aphen without looking at her. "Finished and done. I can't go back. Not to those men. They'll blame me for this."

"You should have thought of that before you stole the seed," she snapped at him.

He went silent for a moment. "Aquinel didn't have anything to do with this, you know. It was all me. I took it when she wasn't looking. I just wanted to sell it and give her something nice, something more than what I've been able to for all these years she's stuck with me." He trailed off. "You just need to know. It wasn't her fault. She's a good woman."

Aphen wheeled on him and shoved him up against the side of a building. "Then take her and leave. Now. Pack a few things and go before they come for you. It will take them a day or so to muster the courage. Go somewhere far away, but get out of here!"

She reached in her cloak, brought out a handful of coins, and shoved them into his pocket. "Take these. Consider the matter of the seed settled. But don't forget what happened here. Don't try stealing from anyone again."

She pulled him away from the wall and pointed him down the road toward his cottage. "She's waiting. Look after her."

She stood watching as he stumbled down the road and

disappeared into the rain. She wondered if he would do what she had told him. She wondered if he would heed her advice about stealing.

She wondered if there was any hope for these people.

Then she grabbed Arling's arm and, with Cymrian trailing, started back down the road toward the waiting Sprint.

22

SEERSHA AND CRACE CORAM FLEW THEIR TWO-
man north through the remainder of the day, making
sure they kept well east of the Straken Lord's army.
Neither Dwarf had ever seen an army of this size, so massive and
sprawling that it seemed to have no beginning or end, blanketing
the countryside for as far as the eye could see. It let them better
understand why the Federation army in Arishaig had been
unable to defend the city. The Elves would be no more successful in trying to defend Arborlon.

"An evacuation is the only answer against a force of this size,"
the Dwarf Chieftain insisted within minutes of surveying the
onslaught below them.

"The Elves won't give up Arborlon," Seersha replied at once.
"They won't leave their home city. They won't abandon the
Ellcrys. They will stand and fight."

"Which is madness," her companion hissed in dismay.

"Maybe. But that's the way of it. And it's why I am setting you
down outside Tyrsis as soon as we sight her. I need you to get

word to the Border Legion. Let them know what's happened, if they don't know already. Tell them the Elves will need their support. Then fly on to the Dwarves and bring them, as well. Use the flatbeds for transport—as many as you can manage. No arguments from the other Chieftains. There's no time for it." She paused. "Can you do it, old dog?"

He scowled at her. "The 'old dog' will need three days to get reinforcements to Arborlon. Can *you* give me that?"

She grinned and nodded, and suddenly they were laughing. It was insanity, all of it hopeless, and there was nothing for it but to stare it down and laugh in its face. You did what you had to in a situation like this one. You did what your heart and your sense of right and wrong told you was needed.

They flew past the ocean of creatures serving the Straken Lord and continued north. It was close to midnight when she dropped him just west of the city of Tyrsis, the fortress settled high on the massive plateau overlooking the grasslands of the Streleheim. He would make the gates well before sunrise and do what he must to try to help her. She, in the meantime, would snatch a few precious hours of sleep, then go to the Elves and see if she could manage to open their eyes. Or, more particularly, the eyes of Phaedon Elessedil, who would most probably want her clapped in irons and locked away the moment he saw her.

But she was a Druid first and always, and a warrior to boot—a planner and a tactician. She would not give him the chance to do what he would like. She would find a way to turn his rage and obstinacy against him.

The hours were long and the tension high as she steered a course safely beyond the demonkind while keeping a sharp eye out for Elven craft, as well. But she reached the Valley of Rhenn by midafternoon and sailed through the shadow of its cliff-walled gap, giving a wave to the sentries—a sign of friendship that she hoped would be enough to keep them from trying to stop or engage her. Her hopes were realized when no aircraft moved to intercept her and no challenge was issued to stop her passing.

She moved on quickly from there to the outskirts of Arborlon, choosing to land at the Elven airfield where she believed she might be lucky enough to find a friendly face. In fact, she found several. A handful of the Elven Home Guards she had been training with were working on a skiff nearby when she landed and wandered over to see what had brought her back.

"I thought you might be missing me," she answered with a laugh. "Any warrants or postings out on me?"

She said it jokingly, tossing it off, watching them carefully for signs of uneasiness, but the Elves just shrugged.

"Who would bother with something like that?" one asked.

"Well, your new King wasn't exactly friendly toward me when we parted," she said.

"I wouldn't spend my time worrying about that," said another, pulling a face. "Our new King is too busy trying to find his backside with both hands to be bothered with the likes of Dwarves or Druids!"

"Unless he thought Dwarves might do a better job of finding it than he could, them being smaller in stature and all," said another.

They all howled with glee, and she let them do so. No point in making this into something it clearly wasn't. She laughed as if sharing the joke, and then casually asked, "Do you know where I can find Sian Aresh?"

They did better than that. One of them offered to find the Captain of the Home Guard and bring him to her. She almost agreed, but then decided it would be better if she found him herself. Sending word risked having Phaedon learn she was back in Arborlon, and she wasn't ready for that to happen just yet. So she excused herself amid a final barrage of insults and jokes and set off for the Home Guard barracks where she was told Aresh could be found.

She took the trouble to procure and don one of the green cloaks of the Home Guard, leaving her own distinctive black one behind. The less attention she drew to herself, the better. She was putting herself in enough danger as it was, even though it seemed no one was looking for her at this point. Perhaps it was enough that she had fled with Crace Coram, removing herself from the city and the Elven population. Even Phaedon couldn't seriously believe she had anything to do with the old King's death. Mostly, she imagined, he simply wanted the Druids out of the way while he went about the business of establishing himself as King.

She knew her way around the Home Guard barracks well enough by now to come into the building through the rear entry and make her way to Sian Aresh's office without being stopped. She stood just outside his door and listened to him speaking with another Elven Hunter, waited until the latter departed, and then stepped inside and closed the door behind her.

"Seersha," he said, looking up, clearly startled. "Have you lost your mind?"

"Probably," she answered. "Is the King still hunting for me?"

"The King has forgotten all about you. Is it your intention to remind him? What are you doing here?"

Quickly, she told him. The demon army had breached the walls of Arishaig, and the city was lost. The Federation army stationed there was broken and mostly destroyed, the population driven out, and the buildings in ruins. Now the attacking army—hundreds of thousands strong—was coming for Arborlon and the Elves, and seemingly without stopping for sleep. It marched north at a pace that would bring it to the mouth of the Valley of Rhenn in two more days.

"Do not rely on my word alone," she finished. "Send scouts to witness for themselves what I have just told you about the size of this threat. The Elves are in grave danger, Sian. The King must act."

He was on his feet. "The King will do what he wishes. That much has been made plain enough already. Even the presence of a demon army doesn't guarantee that he will do as he should. He lacks his father's good sense. He lacks . . . " He shook his head, as if unwilling to spend the time making a list. "Wait here while I dispatch the airships and men needed to confirm your report."

He went out the door and left her standing at his desk. She moved over to a high-backed wooden chair and sat while she waited for him to return. She was weary from all the travel and so little sleep, but there was nothing she could do about it just yet. Too much needed to be done first. She sat there thinking on it, going over again the plan she had hatched while flying back.

Aresh returned, closing the door once more and reseating himself. "We should have a report by tomorrow. Now, what of you?"

She shrugged. "I came back because there was nowhere else for me to go. I need to be where the fighting is if I'm to serve any useful purpose. I thought Aphen might have need of me, as well, when she returns. It's worth the risk."

"If you stay out of sight, the risk shouldn't be great."

"I can't do that. I want you to take me before the King and High Council. I want to speak to them about what's happening and what they need to do. What they must do. I've sent word to both the Border Legion and the Dwarves. I am hoping they will respond and send reinforcements to the Elves before the demon army reaches you."

"Not enough time for that," the other responded with a shrug. "Tomorrow morning? Even with airship transport, it will take them longer than that just to mobilize. But the bigger problem is the King. He doesn't want help from any quarter. I've already spoken to him about the danger of an attack. He ignores it. He believes the assault to be directed toward the Federation alone. He uses his time to consolidate his position; he worries that like his father he, too, might be assassinated. He sees enemies everywhere. He has rescinded Emperowen's order to mobilize and go to the aid of the Federation. He has decided to hunker down and wait this business out." The Elven captain shook his head.

"Why is he doing this?" Seersha asked in dismay. "How can he think the Elves are safe from what's happening? In any case, it points up the need for my report to the High Council. Perhaps they will find the backbone to act in spite of the King."

Aresh shook his head. "The King is not himself, and he was not working with much even before he ascended to the throne. He is distracted, and his decisions feel arbitrary. I have managed to mobilize the Home Guard and the Elven army under the pretext of securing Arborlon, but I have no orders to take any part of it out of the city. We sit on our hands, waiting on the King."

"Even knowing that the Ellcrys fails and the walls of the Forbidding are falling? Even knowing what Aphenglow and Arling have set out to do? Doesn't anyone see what lies ahead if they fail?"

The Captain of the Home Guard leaned back in his chair. "No one can quite believe the old King is dead. So they see Phaedon as an anchor, a fixed point with which they are familiar and to which they can turn—and not as a weight that will drag them down. They don't know him as you and I do. If Ellich were on the throne, it would be different. But Ellich is imprisoned."

Seersha gave it another moment's thought and then stood.

"Then let's do this another way. Arrange a private audience with the King. Do it any way you can manage, but do it quickly. Let me deal with Phaedon. I think I can find a way."

"What you can most probably do is find a way to get yourself locked up with Ellich. The King is not inclined to listen to anyone. He rules, but he is paranoid and in fear for his life. This is a dangerous business you undertake, Seersha."

But she insisted, and he finally agreed to do as she asked, though not without once more warning against it.

He went out again, and this time he was gone for the better part of an hour. While he was absent, she mulled over what lay ahead. The Elves would need to defend the entrance to the Valley of Rhenn. It was their only viable choice if they hoped to make a stand against an army of this size. A narrow opening could be defended and held for at least a few days, long enough perhaps for the combined forces of the Dwarves and Callahorn to reach them and attack the demons from the rear.

But still the demons would outnumber their combined forces. And even then, would the Straken Lord consider withdrawing?

She was bothered by the trajectory of the events that had occurred since the demons had broken out of the Forbidding. Why had the Straken Lord attacked Arishaig? The Elves were the real enemy and the Ellcrys the real danger. Of course, the Demons would have had to come out of the Forbidding where the wall was weakest and gave them access into the Four Lands. That might have brought them first to Arishaig, and they had simply taken advantage of it. But there was no doubting their ultimate goal—an attack on the Elves and the destruction of the Ellcrys.

She thought back to the last demon breakout, in the time of Eventine Elessedil. The Druid Histories of those years, compiled by Allanon, were familiar to her. Eventine Elessedil, a strong and competent King, had led an Elven army aided by Trolls, Dwarves, and the Border Legion of Callahorn, and even that had not been enough. Only a rebirth of the Ellcrys had saved the Four Lands— a rebuilding of the wall of the Forbidding so that the demonkind could be banished once again.

But this was a different world. The alliances of old were gone, and the possibility of the Forbidding being restored was far from certain.

She wondered suddenly of Railing Ohmsford and his companions and their quest to discover the fate of Grianne Ohmsford. Was it at all possible that anything would come of that? She had sent him away more to save his life than with any expectation that he would find a woman who by now would be well over a hundred years old.

But even so, she wondered.

Sian Aresh reappeared abruptly. "The King has agreed to a private audience. I told him I had someone who witnessed the fall of Arishaig firsthand and who could report on the size and movements of the demon army. I told him that what you have to say is for his ears alone. He does not yet know it is you."

She smiled. "Well done. My thanks, Sian. Will you come with me?"

He laughed. "Will I come with you? I have been *ordered* to come! What happens to you likely happens to me, as well."

She clapped him on the back. "Then I must make certain that we both stay safe."

They went out of the building and down through the streets of Arborlon to the palace. Home Guards met them at every turn once they were inside the boundaries of protected territory, but quickly gave way on seeing that it was Sian Aresh who escorted the green-cloaked lady Dwarf. If they recognized Seersha as a Druid, they gave no indication.

Once they were inside the palace, standing in a hallway that led to the reception chamber where Phaedon would receive them, Sian Aresh pulled her aside.

"Phaedon will attempt to have you locked up once he knows who you are," he whispered. "Try not to give him an excuse." He paused. "Whatever happens, I'll do my best to get you out if this goes wrong."

She fixed him with her good eye. "Phaedon will have troubles of his own before I'm done with him. Just be ready and don't interfere."

He gave her a doubtful look, but said nothing as he continued on, escorting her down the hall to the reception room doors.

Guards met them in force and closed about them as they entered the room. Phaedon sat in a chair at the far end of the room, smiling.

Seersha, mindful of protocol, bowed to the King in a clear show of deference. "High Lord," she greeted him.

He beckoned her forward, then put up his hand to stop her when she was still a safe distance away. "I knew it was you, you know. You were seen and word was brought. I find it curious that you would return after having gone to such lengths to flee in the first place. Does it occur to you that coming back might be a foolish decision?"

"High Lord," she answered, "I could do no less after seeing what has become of Arishaig and her people. I could do no less knowing that the enemy marches on Arborlon. All I ask is that you let me tell you what I have seen so that you can judge for yourself."

She paused. "But first, my condolences on the death of your father. I should have stayed long enough to say this in the first place, but time was of the essence when I left Arborlon for Arishaig, even though I was too late to be of any service to that city."

"Clever words, Seersha," he replied, brushing off her regrets as if they were meaningless. "Druids always know what to say in the moment it needs saying. You must practice such deceptions endlessly. My dear cousin Aphenglow is equally talented in her use of this skill. Too bad she isn't here now to lend you her support."

"And lend it to you, as well," she offered. "But we must make do with what we have at hand. May I speak? Do you wish me to do so in front of so many, or might it not be better if it were only one or two?"

He smiled knowingly. "I don't wish to be alone with you, no matter the import of the news you bring. I don't feel particularly safe with you, Lady Druid. Or with any of your kind. I will keep my guards close."

Nevertheless, save for two standing to either side of his chair, he sent the rest to the back of the room. "A wrong move on your part will see you dead before you can think to do anything about it," he warned. "Do you understand me?"

"Of course, High Lord," she said. "I know your feelings and am aware of your intent regarding the Druids. I don't come to please you. I come to help the Elven people. What you do about it is your own choice."

He studied her long moments as if debating whether to let matters proceed. "Sian Aresh," he said suddenly, his dark gaze shifting to the other. "Your own part in this charade will not be forgotten. Do not think I mistake what you have done here."

"High Lord," the Captain of the Home Guard replied, bowing slightly in acknowledgment.

Phaedon fixed him with eyes filled with malice and then signaled to Seersha. "Proceed."

In simple, straightforward terms, she described what she had witnessed at Arishaig—a city in ruins, walls breached, gates thrown open, buildings on fire, and thousands dead. Some, she said, must have escaped, but clearly not many. The army garrisoned there, one of the most powerful in all of the Federation, was destroyed. The demon army had surmounted all the defenses and weaponry brought to bear against it through sheer weight of numbers and unmatched savagery, and had prevailed.

Now that army marched north, spilling across the Tirfing as it came, hundreds of thousands of predatory creatures intent on continuing their destruction of the Four Lands and its people, making their way now toward Arborlon and the Elves.

"They will arrive at the Valley of Rhenn in two days' time if I have measured their speed of travel and their course correctly. If you wish to stop them before they reach Arborlon, that seems to be the place to do it." She paused. "I offer my services in defense of the city."

"Do you now?" Phaedon said, cocking an inquisitive eyebrow. "You make this offer for no other purpose than to help us? With nothing to gain but our undying gratitude? Such generosity sounds too good to refuse, and yet I must."

"Because you don't trust the Druids."

"Because I don't trust the Druids. Your information is appreciated, and I will take it under advisement. Of course, I will need to verify that what you have told me is accurate."

"I have already dispatched aircraft to do exactly that," Sian Aresh interrupted. "We should know by tomorrow."

"Yes, be that as it may. You, Captain, are relieved of your command and will step down when this meeting is over. I will speak with your scouts personally and decide what must be done. Other choices are available to us, and I need to consider them."

"I have summoned the Dwarves and the Border Legion to come to your aid," Seersha added, deciding abruptly to hold nothing back. "They should begin to arrive in the next three days."

The King turned scarlet. "Who gave you permission to speak in my name? Who told you to ask for their help—these outlanders and miscreants who have never been there for us? The Elves need no help from them! The Elves need no help from anyone!"

Out of the corner of her eye, she could see the Home Guards exchanging worried looks. They had heard her account of the number of attackers coming for them. They had heard her describe what had happened to Arishaig. Unlike their King, they were not so confident.

Phaedon was on his feet now, his eyes hard and his mouth set in an ugly, furious line. "I think I will lock you up with my uncle, Lady Druid!" he hissed at her. "You are no better than he is. You presume when it is not your place to do so. You insult me with your very presence!"

"High Lord," she said quickly. She gestured as if to emphasize what she was saying. "I would give you warning."

He stared at her. "You would threaten me?"

"Not I. I am not the one who threatens you. It is another."

"I care nothing for the threats of others!" he snapped. "Besides, you are lying. You would say anything to save yourself."

She looked away, shrugging. "As you wish."

"Wait!" he called out sharply, bringing her back around. "What warning would you give?"

She leaned toward him. "That you are in danger, High Lord."

He went still, unable for a moment to respond. Then, regaining his composure, he said, "From what?"

She shook her head. "What I would tell you is for your ears only. No other must hear. The danger is closer at hand than you realize."

She waited. Phaedon continued to stare at her, as if unable to make a decision on what to do. "May I approach?" she asked. She gestured to the guards clustered just behind her. "You are safe enough. But you should hear what I have to say."

She said it with such urgency that she knew he took the bait. He hesitated a moment longer, then he beckoned her forward.

"But watch yourself, Lady Druid. Be mindful of what will happen if this is a trick."

She advanced until she was standing right in front of him. She was shorter and wider and very much the stronger of the two. But he was taller, and his superior height gave him a sense of security it shouldn't have. In a less debilitated state of mind, he might have recognized this. But here he did not.

She slumped slightly at the shoulders to add to his confidence. "There are those who would replace you as King. One of them is in this very room."

His eyes went immediately to Sian Aresh. "Which one?"

"The one standing right in front of you," she whispered.

The fingers of her right hand snaked about his left wrist. Druid magic flooded through him, and he was paralyzed instantly. There was no apparent effort on her part, no indication that she was doing anything other than continuing to advise him. She used her body to block what was happening, still talking while the magic she had surreptitiously summoned flooded through him, working on him as she had intended, rendering him immobile but doing something much more insidious, as well.

"You are not much of a King, Phaedon, that you would risk your people's lives on a whim," she whispered calmly, her fingers like iron about his wrist. "Not much of a King that you would ignore help when it was offered. Not much of a man even, if you would let your pride and your fears dictate a course of action that would bring disaster to your entire Race."

His eyes were locked on hers, frozen in place like the rest of him. He could not manage even the smallest sound to summon help, caught up in the trap she had set for him. She kept talking as she waited for the magic to settle in and claim him completely, still pretending she was explaining something to him, engaged in a private conversation that no one else could hear.

When she felt him start to shake, she released his hands, waited a moment until she was sure he was infected, and then backed quickly away, looking over her shoulder at the Home Guards, a look of shock and concern mirrored on her face.

"Something's wrong!" she called out to them. "He's having a fit!"

Indeed, the Elven King was frothing at the mouth, weird sounds coming from somewhere deep inside him—not words exactly, but grunts and gasps and other indecipherable noises. His guards rushed to him, Sian Aresh with them, taking hold of him as he thrashed and convulsed.

Then, abruptly, he went limp, collapsing into unconsciousness in their arms. Aresh caught Seersha's eye; she met his gaze without revealing anything.

"Take the King to his sleeping chambers," the Captain of the Home Guard ordered, "and send for Healers to keep watch on him. Have them do what they can." He glanced at Seersha again, and this time she nodded slightly. "Don't leave him alone," he added.

The King was carried from the room, still unconscious but breathing and alive. Aresh waited until they were gone and he and Seersha were alone before beckoning for her to follow.

As they passed out into the hallway and moved toward the front doors of the palace, he whispered, "You did that to him, didn't you?"

She nodded. "Druids have a strict policy of not interfering in the affairs of the Races unless threatened. I deemed this a threat. Phaedon is dangerous, and he cannot be allowed to interfere with what we need to do. He will be incapacitated for a day or so. Longer, if I come back to him a second time, which I may very well decide to do if it is needed. But those two days will allow the Elven army time to move out of Arborlon and prepare to defend the valley." She looked over at him as they walked. "You have to do this, you know. You have to be the one."

"He removed me as Captain of the Home Guard," Sian Aresh pointed out. "Remember?"

"He was a man in the first stages of a fit that has laid him out like a baby," she answered. "Anyway, he said your position would be terminated after the meeting was over. That never really happened. You're still the leader your men will look to. You are the one they will follow."

"And you will stand with us?"

"As I promised. Until there's no longer anywhere for me to stand."

They went out the palace doors into the sunshine. "We don't have much of a chance, do we?" he said.

"Any chance is better than none."

"What we need is a miracle."

"What we need," she replied softly, "is for Aphen and Arling Elessedil to find the Bloodfire and come back to us."

23

AFTER DEPARTING THE VILLAGE HOME OF Sora and Aquinel, the Ellcrys seed recovered and their quest for the Bloodfire back under way, the Elessedil sisters and Cymrian reboarded their Sprint. With darkness already well advanced, they flew for a few more hours, then camped for the night on the edge of Drey Wood. And the following morning, they lifted away for the still-distant country of the Wilderun. They flew south through the remainder of the day past the last of Drey Wood and angled west over the Matted Breaks. Through the drifting clouds, they caught glimpses of the rock towers of the Pykon looming in the distance in solitary splendor. Dark and forbidding, they had seen centuries come and go, cities and governments rise and fall, and changes of all kinds in the world about them, and still they endured.

It was written in the Druid Histories that Amberle Elessedil had come this way centuries ago on a similar search, passing down through Drey Wood, the Matted Breaks, and the Pykon, as well. All who had come with her had been killed protecting her—all but the Valeman Wil Ohmsford. It made her think on Redden and Railing. She wondered if the latter had gone looking for his brother yet. She wondered if his brother was lost to him, as she feared Arling might be lost to her. She wondered, finally, if the twins—or even one of them—might in some way prove to be Arling's protector as their ancestor had proved to be Amberle's. She remembered that Allanon's shade had told Khyber Elessedil at the Hadeshorn that an Ohmsford must come with the Druids on their search for the Elfstones—that having one along would prove essential to their success. But there had been no success, and it made her think that perhaps no Ohmsford would stand as a protector of her sister and that everything would be different this time.

Farther on, they caught sight of the silver thread of the Mermidon winding through foothills north of the Rock Spur and followed the course of the river until it disappeared into the mountains themselves. They flew on after that across the broad, rugged span of the Rock Spur—a sprawling mass of jagged peaks and deep valleys into which the emerging sun barely penetrated. In spite of the morning's clouds, the midday sun was bright and welcoming as they passed beyond the mountains.

By early evening, they were entering the valley of the Wilderun just east of the town of Grimpen Ward. All three knew of Grimpen Ward's reputation, and none of them thought it a good idea to spend the night there. On the other hand, continuing on deeper into the Wilderun and attempting to locate the Bloodfire with darkness likely to fall long before they were finished was not an attractive option. So they decided to find a suitable place to camp for the night and then set out again at dawn to complete their search.

They landed in a clearing within the deep forests of the Wilderun, not far from the Rock Spur. The shadows cast by the huge old growth were already darkening the pale light that penetrated the canopy of branches—a clear signal that, when night approached, it would be on them quickly.

"I'm going to use the Elfstones," Aphenglow announced to the other two, once the three of them had climbed down from the airship. "We need to make certain we are on the right track before we go any farther. But I won't do it now; I'll wait until morning."

Neither Arling nor Cymrian said anything in response. They all understood that use of the magic might draw unwanted attention—a constant risk when the Elfstones were employed. But this place was as remote as any they were likely to find, far away from Arishaig and the other major Southland cities. They had to confirm both the exact location of the Bloodfire and the possibility of wards that might interfere with their efforts in reaching it. There had been nothing in the various histories they read that revealed either, but they couldn't rely on writings alone.

They unloaded gear and supplies for eating and sleeping, and Aphen set about building a fire. Cymrian said he wanted to have a look around to be certain they had chosen a safe enough spot, and then he moved off into the trees.

Arling began unrolling blankets and setting out food and drink. As she carried in wood for a fire, Aphen glanced repeatedly at her sister, wondering what she was thinking. On her third trip, she walked over and sat down next to her.

"How is my brave sister?" she asked.

Arling smiled. "Well enough. Better than I was before we got the Ellcrys seed back."

"We were lucky the task wasn't more difficult. Good thing we had the Elfstones to find it for us."

Arling didn't respond, but instead busied herself with

removing supplies from their containers. She had an unreadable look on her face, as if whatever she was thinking confused her. Aphen waited long minutes before speaking again.

"I wish we could take back everything that's happening and make it go away," she said finally.

Her sister nodded. "But we can't."

"We can keep trying."

Arling looked up at her and smiled. "You don't need to. I know what's going to happen."

Aphen felt a surge of panic. "I don't think you should—"

"Let's stop pretending, you and I," Arling interrupted. "If we find the Bloodfire and immerse the Ellcrys seed, the matter of what happens afterward is decided. There aren't any choices. There aren't any miracles that can change things. There never were. I think I knew it the moment the Ellcrys gave me her seed. She was so certain I was the one; it had to be me, she insisted. I kept telling her I wasn't right for this, that I couldn't do it. But she knew me better than I knew myself."

She paused. "When I was in Arishaig, down in the streets of the city, I was trying to escape, running anywhere I could think to run. But everyone else was doing the same thing. They were trying to escape, too. Not from Edinja, of course; from the demonkind attacking their city. But it was the same thing. Our fear of what was going to happen was the same. I could feel what they were feeling; I was sharing the rawness of it. But I knew something they didn't. I knew I could save us all, just by doing what I had been asked.

"Then later when we flew out of the city on our Sprint and I was looking down at the walls, I could see the Federation soldiers fighting and dying. I saw all those men and women struggling to survive against creatures that had no regard for them at all, and I pictured in my mind what that would look like if those people were my own—if it were Elves that were down there. I thought about what it would be like if it were Arborlon under siege rather than Arishaig."

She took a deep breath. "And it will be Arborlon if nothing is done, won't it, Aphen? Unless someone prevents it? Unless I prevent it because, really, there isn't anyone else, is there? We don't have time to find someone else; we don't even know where to begin to look unless one of the other Chosen volunteers to replace me. And that's not going to happen. None of it is going to happen."

Aphen stared at her, stunned. "You've decided to do what the Ellcrys wants? Everything?"

Arling nodded. "Because it's the right thing to do. Because I know how all those people in Arishaig felt, when they saw their own deaths coming. There were thousands of them, Aphen! And there will be millions more. I can't live with that. Not knowing I can do something about it. I don't care what the cost is anymore; I have to do whatever I can to put a stop to this. No more excuses. No more delays. No more false hopes. I'm the one."

"But you've been so determined not to ... to let this ... "

"I was wrong. I was selfish. I was thinking only of myself and not of anyone else." She brushed back her dark hair. "When the Ellcrys began telling me of her life, of how she had witnessed so much of the world's history, of how she had been there steadfast and determined, the sole barrier between the world of the demonkind and our own, I found myself admiring her. Even though I didn't want to do what she was asking—didn't want to be her—I understood the immense importance of what she was doing. Without her, the entire Four Lands would be in chaos. We would be at war constantly with the creatures she shut away—just as we were in the time of Faerie. She was the one who prevented that.

"So I began to change my mind. Gradually, perhaps without even realizing it, until all at once I saw that maybe I was wrong; maybe I would have to do this. At Arishaig, caught up in the middle of the fighting and the killing, running in fear amid all the others . . . I knew. I was certain. It took me until now to say this to you. But it needs saying before we reach the Bloodfire and I do what I must to save the Ellcrys from extinction."

Aphen was in tears. "Arling . . ."

"I can do it now, Aphen. I can become her. I can make myself . . ."

She was in tears now, too. Aphen reached out and pulled her close. She tried to find something to say that would express what she was feeling, but she couldn't find the words. Instead, she just closed her eyes and held her sister and let Arling hold her in return.

They were still locked in a tight embrace when Cymrian reappeared, coming out of the trees and walking toward them. He didn't say anything. He just walked past them and went over to the airship, climbed into the cockpit, and began working on something, giving them the time and space to be alone.

When Aphenglow finally broke the embrace she continued to grip her sister by her shoulders, their faces close, their eyes locked. She held her sister's gaze. "I will be with you every step of the way, Arling. I will be with you no matter what."

Her sister smiled. "I never thought you wouldn't."

They ate their dinner seated about the campfire, the sun going down and night's darkness sliding in to take its place. The skies were clear and bright with stars, and the forest about them was still. They spoke in low voices so as not to disturb the silence, speaking of small, unimportant things. There was no need to talk about what was going to happen on the morrow; what they needed now was to reaffirm the sense of closeness and confidence they had in each other. Talking made them feel better. It helped to chase back fears and doubts; it helped to instill in them a welcome sense of peace.

Yet still, Aphen dreamed of home and of strange images of the Ellcrys tree, its silver branches reaching for her, its scarlet leaves shimmering. She was trying to leave the gardens, to turn away from the tree, but she could not manage it. She struggled as the branches closed around her arms and then abruptly began to change into fingers and hands and arms. The tree became a girl, and the girl became Arlingfant, and she was begging Aphen to stay with her, to keep her company for all time—holding her fast, refusing to let her go, even after she panicked and screamed and was enclosed in an impenetrable black haze …

When she woke, she did not mention the dream to her sister. The day was cloudy and gray as they ate a small breakfast, and Aphen said little as they ate, thinking instead of what they were doing and what it would mean when they were done. She still hadn't given up hope that a way might be found to absolve Arling from responsibility for the rebirth of the Ellcrys, although by now she had come to see that her hopes were growing dim and Arling's chances small.

Impulsively, after they finished their meal and began to dispose of its leavings, she went over to her sister and hugged her close, saying softly in her ear, "I love you, little girl."

The first drops of rain were just beginning to fall as Aphen stood in the center of the clearing with the Elfstones nestled in her hand. She used the images of fire burning underground in rock surroundings and of an arm extending the Ellcrys seed toward the flames to trigger the magic's release. The response from the Stones was immediate. Sudden brightness surged through the cracks between her fingers with an unexpectedly sharp flaring of blue light—one that caused her makeshift image to shatter instantly and then vanish. In the dark emptiness left, the Elfstone magic formed into a tight line and raced southward through the heavy forests of the Wilderun, carrying Aphenglow with it. Curving through miles of ancient trees and vast patches of grasses and scrub, over fallen logs and broken branches, and across steams and ponds, it continued until it reached the edge of the Hollows and the spindled pinnacle of Spire's Reach.

Aphen had studied these landmarks on her maps after reading the Druid Histories that revealed the Wilderun as the source of the Bloodfire, so she recognized what she was looking at, even without yet knowing exactly where the magic was taking her.

Where it took her was down into the murky forested depths of the Hollows to the base of Spire's Reach. An opening in the rock revealed the entrance to a cave, and within that was a maze of tunnels, winding this way and that, crisscrossing and dead-ending all through the riven rock of the tower, until at last she found herself at a set of stairs surrounded not by cavern rock but by stone blocks shaped and set in place by mortal hands. The stairs descended hundreds of feet deeper into the earth, ending at a massive cavern opening. Huge columns braced the ceiling and stone benches, some whole, some broken, spread outward like ripples in a lake from a broad platform positioned at the exact center of the chamber.

Aphen thought the vision would end here, but it didn't. Instead, the blue light continued on across the room to a huge stone door that stood ajar, and beyond to yet another set of stairs leading farther down.

This time her downward journey ended much more quickly, and the light revealed a fresh passageway, leading to a second great cavern. This one was not constructed of stone blocks and columns, but carved out of the earth by nature and time, its walls and ceiling and floors ragged and broken and cracked. Sweeping across the floor of this chamber, the light illuminated a wall of huge boulders and shattered rock.

At its center, a portal formed of glass glistened in the magic's bright light, flat and perfectly centered on an opening.

Then the vision was gone.

Aphen took a moment to lower her hand and slip the Elfstones back into their pouch.

"I saw nothing of hidden dangers," Cymrian announced. His white hair glistened with rain, and his face was water-streaked. "Did you?"

She shook her head. "Which doesn't mean there aren't any."

"Why would anyone make a door out of glass in a cavern deep underground?" Arling wanted to know, looking from one to the other. "What would be the point?"

Aphen didn't know. "Perhaps this is another instance of us not recognizing what we're being shown. Like with the waterfall in the Fangs that turned out to be only a screen of light." She felt uneasy just talking about it, but hid her discomfort with a smile. "Shall we find out?"

They packed up their camp and climbed back aboard the Sprint. Moments later they lifted off, gained sufficient altitude to put them well above the trees, and began flying south into the mist and gloom of the Wilderun.

They set a course that took them toward the center of the valley, and after a few hours they caught sight of Spire's Reach. Its rock tower was at first no more than a vague outline in the curtains of brume, distant and indistinct. But within the hour, they had drawn near enough that they could make out its rugged features. By then the earlier drizzle had turned into a steady downpour and the day had become black and threatening. Fighting wind and rain, they huddled in the Sprint's narrow cockpit, their cloaks wrapped close about them, their shoulders hunched and heads lowered.

Aphen was piloting, hands moving swiftly over the controls in an effort to keep their flight smooth and steady. She was thinking it would be nice if she could stop being wet all the time, that it seemed as if she was never dry anymore when she was in the air, only cold and damp.

But it was what it was, and within the next half hour they had reached their destination, sweeping past the craggy heights of Spire's Reach and then swinging back again while searching the entire base of the pinnacle. It was Cymrian who saw what he believed to be the opening in the rock they were looking for while they were making their second pass, and on bringing the Sprint down for a closer look, Aphen was inclined to agree.

They landed not far away, setting down in a grassy flat at the base of the peak. They took a moment to prepare before disembarking. Cymrian added a few more weapons to his arsenal, Arling handed out waterskins, and then they set out to look for the entrance into the base of Spire's Reach.

They found it quickly, and it was immediately recognizable to Aphenglow as the opening the Elfstone magic had revealed. Cymrian had brought along a trio of smokeless torches he had found aboard the Sprint; he handed one to each of the sisters and kept the third.

"Let me take the lead," Aphen said. "That way I can make sure we are going in the right direction."

Aphen wasn't entirely sure that she remembered the right direction, but she pretended she did. Cymrian was back in his protector mode, if indeed he had ever left it, the best trained of the three in any case should they encounter trouble. But she had use of the Elfstones, and their magic would prove to be the more formidable weapon in almost any situation.

So they passed through the opening, leaving the rain and the forest behind, and found themselves in chilly darkness. Aphen led with Arling following her and Cymrian acting as rearguard. Their torches cast hazy, narrow beams into the gloom to reveal a rough-hewn entry chamber and a maze of tunnels leading away from it. After brushing the rain from their cloaks and giving Cymrian a moment to search for any sign of hidden traps and snares, Aphen chose the passageway she believed the Elfstones had revealed in their vision and the three companions set out.

They walked for a long time through the tunnels without reaching an end. Aphen was surprised to discover she remembered almost all the twists and turns she was meant to take. Only once was she required to employ the Elfstones to reassure herself she was making the right choice. The rest of the time her memory was good enough that using the Elfstones wasn't necessary.

Even so, she was carrying them in her hand now, ready to help Cymrian if matters suddenly turned dangerous. They had come so far and gone through so much that she was not about to let anything stop them now.

It was this determination that led her to reflect on the fact she was leading her sister to the very fate from which she had promised to save her. She could pretend otherwise, could say she was only doing what they had all agreed on and what Arling herself had decided, but the end result would be the same. When they reached the Bloodfire and the Ellcrys seed was immersed, Arling's future was as certain as the rising of the sun. She would become the Ellcrys and cease to be human.

And Aphenglow would have helped bring that about.

She sensed this was wrong—a twinge of recognition amid all the thoughts and deliberations on why it was both right and necessary. She sensed it even while telling herself she shouldn't.

It made her want to turn around and go back in spite of everything that insisted she do otherwise. It made her want to abandon reason and resignation and give in to the white-hot mix of emotions she was experiencing.

The guilt that tore at her deep inside.

The despair that filled her at the thought of losing Arling forever.

Turn back. Give up on all this.

They reached the opening to the stairway leading down into the earth, and with her emotions still roiling and her feet moving as if of their own accord, she started down. They heard no sounds other than the ones they were making as they walked. No one had spoken since they had set out. There was a disconnect among the three, as if they were strangers on a journey that could not be discussed and was being undertaken for reasons that were not entirely clear.

At one point, Aphen found herself in tears and was forced to wipe them away surreptitiously, to muffle the sobs that kept rising in her throat.

Their descent continued for a long time. They traversed hundreds of steps, perhaps thousands. She lost track of time. She only knew to keep going, to place one foot in front of the other and try not to think about what she was doing—the first an endless struggle, the second a hopeless task. She did it because she knew there was no other choice now and because she had lost the will to resist. Her fate was inescapable. She was her sister's guide and accomplice both; she would be the source of both her salvation and her undoing.

At the bottom of the steps was a passageway, and they followed it to a huge chamber constructed of stone blocks and supported by massive columns within which ancient benches spiraled out from the raised platform at the chamber's center.

The cavernous space smelled and tasted of stale, damp air. Large pieces of it lay in ruins. Together the Elves navigated its debris and crossed to the dais and from there to the massive stone door Aphen had described. It stood ajar, just as it had in her Elfstone vision, and they slipped through its opening to where a short set of additional steps descended to another passageway.

At the end of this new passageway was the second cavern, this one very different from the one they had just left—a rock chamber formed by nature's hand, carved out over endless amounts of time, rugged and damp with moisture. Huge stalactites hung from the ceiling in clusters, stone spears poised to impale should they fall. Chunks of broken stone lay scattered about the uneven floor, the leavings of earlier formations that had already given way and shattered.

The Elves glanced around, searching the gloom with the glow of their torches.

Then Cymrian called out and pointed, and all three focused their lights on a glass door set into the far wall between a pair of towering boulders, its smooth surface rising to where a rippling dampness higher up revealed a steady flow of water.

"That door isn't glass," the Elven Hunter said after a moment's study. "It isn't even a door. It's a sheet of water."

Aphen saw it, too. The supposed door was actually a thin, smooth screen of water that spilled from a trough in a curtain so still it barely shimmered at all.

"The Bloodfire is there," Arling said suddenly, pointing at the opening. She took a step away from the other two. "Beyond the waterfall, inside that opening. I can feel it now, tugging at me. It senses the presence of the Ellcrys seed."

She took another step away. "I have to go to it."

"Not without me," Aphen said at once, and started after her.

But her sister held up her hands. "No, Aphen, I have to go

alone. I have to do this by myself. I want you to wait for me here. You and Cymrian both."

Aphen started to object, but then saw the determination mirrored in her sister's eyes and thought better of it. *Of course she has to go alone. Of course she has to do this by herself. She understands the importance of finding the strength she needs to carry this through. She knows how hard it will be, and because she knows she will face it on her own terms and prove to herself that she is ready.*

"Aphen?" her sister whispered.

Cymrian was looking at her, waiting to see what he should do. "All right," she said finally. "We'll be waiting for you."

Arling turned, crossed the chamber to where the waterfall waited, ducked through its thin curtain without a backward glance, and was gone.

24

WHEN SHE WAS THROUGH THE THIN CURTAIN of water, Arlingfant paused a moment to brush the droplets from her hair and shoulders before continuing on down the short passageway that opened before her. At its end she found yet another cavern, although this one was much smaller than the other two and considerably warmer and drier.

It was also empty.

The floor of the chamber sloped upward before her, ascending gradually in a series of broad shelves that wrapped right and left of where she stood from wall to wall. She shone her smokeless torch into the gloom before her, but there was nothing to be seen higher up but more shelves and deeper darkness.

There was no sign at all of the Bloodfire.

But it was here. She could sense its presence, even without being able to explain why. It was calling to her soundlessly, continuing to tug her forward into the chamber.

So she began to make her way upward from shelf to shelf,

using her torch to light the way, searching carefully as she went. Even though she wasn't entirely conscious of what she was doing, she stretched out her right hand and her fingers groped at the air as if there were something of substance to which she might cling. She continued on until she was almost to the back wall of the chamber. She was far enough along that only two more levels of stone risers remained when she stopped on one that was much smaller and set at the exact center of the larger one beneath it.

Just to one side of the shelf was a large boulder.

Here, she said to herself. *The Bloodfire is here*.

She knew it instinctively. Acting on her certainty, she moved over to the boulder and touched it experimentally. When nothing happened, she placed both hands on the huge rock and put her weight behind the effort. To her surprise, it began to move, even as slight as she was and as massive as it was. It rolled smoothly out of its shallow seating and her momentum carried her after it so that now she was standing where the boulder had been.

Instantly the floor beneath her feet exploded into flames, and she was enveloped in a brilliant white fire that reached all the way to the ceiling. Frozen in place, shocked by the suddenness of it, she cringed in anticipation of the expected pain. But the fire did nothing to harm her. The flames exuded neither heat nor smoke; nor did they burn, but instead enfolded her in a blanket of warmth and comfort. The worries and the stresses of the days she had spent coming to this place faded away as if they had never been. Everything around her disappeared, and she was surrounded by an impenetrable brightness that first flared as white light and then slowly became crimson.

She was inside the Bloodfire.

How odd, she thought, *that I can stand in a pillar of fire and not be burned*. She glanced down at herself to be sure she was not mistaken, but her body was whole and her flesh undamaged.

What is happening to me?

She wondered again at the way in which she had been brought to this place, drawn to it by something larger than herself. She thought at first it must be the fire, but then she realized the fire had been summoned by her presence as the bearer of the Ellcrys seed and was no more than an impersonal magic that responded to her appearance. *She* was the source of the summons—the Chosen of the tree, the bearer of its seed, a young girl wrapped in cool flames.

She experienced a sudden revelation, a door opening back on her life that filled her with a terrible understanding.

There had never been any choice in this matter for her.

She had never been able to walk away from her fate.

Her life's story had been imprinted on her from the moment of her birth.

She was one of the Omarosian Chosen, an Elessedil carrying on the line so that the magic that kept the Forbidding whole and the demons imprisoned would not die out. She was the descendant of a girl who—desperate to atone for a tragic mistake—had given up her life so her people could be made safe. That was who and what she was. That was the life she had been given to live should the Ellcrys fail.

As it had failed. As it must have sensed, not so long ago, it would.

Unbidden and unafraid, she reached into her tunic pocket and closed her fingers about the Ellcrys seed. The smooth orb was warm against her skin, and she could feel it pulsate softly. She stared at the scarlet fire surrounding her, wondering what she was supposed to do next. Shouldn't something already be happening? Why wasn't the seed responding in some more dramatic way to the Bloodfire?

She wondered suddenly if she had misjudged things. Was

there something more to the ritual of immersion? Perhaps she lacked some piece of knowledge that was crucial to the process. Or perhaps the seed was failing to respond because she was not the one intended to produce it. Perhaps the Ellcrys had been mistaken after all. Perhaps the seed was not hers to bear beyond this point, as she had hoped all along. She was meant to bring it here, where it would be quickened, and then to return it to the tree so that the proper Chosen could be summoned and . . .

She trailed off abruptly, aware of what she was doing.

Denying herself. Equivocating. Looking to escape the responsibility she had been given.

None of which was right. She was the one. She knew it.

Ignoring the persistence of fears and doubts, hardening herself for whatever would happen next, she brought the Ellcrys seed all the way out of her pocket and held it forth, fully exposed. Instantly, the flames brightened around her and the seed blazed in their reflection. A feeling of connection between the seed and the fire bloomed within her, revealing that she was not wrong in coming here and that the Ellcrys had left nothing to chance. Tendrils began to weave and lace within her body, and images appeared before her eyes.

The images filled her with understanding and hope.

She dropped to her knees and brought the Ellcrys seed close against her breast.

And gave herself over to its power.

On the other side of the doorway to the Bloodfire chamber, Aphen sat with Cymrian on a large rock, eyes fixed on the thin sheet of water that separated her from her sister. It felt like hours had passed.

"She should be back by now."

Cymrian shook his head. "You can't know that. We have to be patient."

"I don't want to be patient."

"I don't blame you. You don't even want to be here. None of us does. This whole business is terrifying."

"Perhaps she isn't the right one. Perhaps someone else is. Perhaps there's been a mistake."

"Perhaps."

"But you don't think so."

"Arling doesn't think so. And that's what matters."

They went silent again, waiting. Aphen found her thoughts straying to other times—to when the girls were young and played together every day, when life was simpler and less threatening and the world was a better place. She couldn't help herself. She knew it was pointless to wish for something that was gone. It was pointless even to think about it. She was going to lose her sister and she would never get her back.

Arling would never see twenty. She would never take a lover. She would never bond and have children. She would never see even as much of life as Aphen had.

She would never return to her home. Aphen would have to be the one to tell their mother what had happened. Whatever that turned out to be.

"I don't feel as if this is enough to change what is happening with the demonkind. I don't sense that this will do what we think. Something is wrong, Cymrian."

The Elven Hunter nodded. "Everything is wrong. That's the problem. Nothing feels right."

"It shouldn't be like this."

He looked over at her. "I thought that once about you and me, back before you agreed to accept me as your protector. I loved you, and you didn't know it, and I couldn't bring myself to tell you. But I always believed that one day everything would change. Now, maybe, it has. Because we love each other and things feel right again. Do you see what I'm saying? Sometimes we just have to trust that time and fate will bring us back to where we are supposed to be. Sometimes patience and belief are all we have."

She stared at him. "I couldn't have done this without you. You have made all the difference. You kept me from falling apart."

"I think we did that for each other. I think maybe we always will."

She smiled. "I hope that, too." She paused. "But I don't know. I don't know about anything now."

They were silent again after that, eyes fixed once more on the waterfall entry, watching and listening. The minutes passed, and nothing happened. All around them, the gloom hovered like a specter's cloak spread wide. They had kept their diapson-powered torches turned on, but the slender beams did barely enough to illuminate a narrow span of the cavern's blackness and nothing to brighten the whole.

Somewhere behind them, back the way they had come, water was dripping in the stillness.

Abruptly, Aphen stirred. "I've waited long enough. I'm going in after her."

But it was Arlingfant Elessedil who came to her instead, emerging through the screen of water like a ghost, thin and wan in the gloom and damp, somehow less substantial than before—so diminished that it seemed as if the light from their hastily redirected torches shone right through her.

"Aphen?" she asked in a hoarse whisper.

Aphenglow was on her feet instantly, racing toward her sister until she had her firmly gripped in her arms and held close. She was shocked at the other's lightness. Arling seemed like a rag doll, her bones gone and her body emptied out. She hung on Aphen, clung to her like it was all she could do to remain upright.

Cymrian rushed over to help. "What's happened?" he demanded, lifting the girl into the cradle of his arms.

Arling's eyes found his. The formerly dark orbs were blood red and glistening. "The fire ..." she began, and then her eyes closed, and she was unconscious.

"Let's get her out of here," Aphen said at once.

Cymrian nodded and turned back the way they had come. "Wait," he said, stopping. "Where is the seed?"

But Aphen only shook her head and motioned him on. "Doesn't matter. She's done whatever she could. That's enough."

In truth, she didn't know if she could bear to find out where the seed had gone. It wasn't in her sister's open hands, but she was certain Arling had done whatever was required to quicken it.

Yet when they had reached the far side of the cavern and were about to enter the short passageway leading back into the chamber formed of stone blocks and columns, Aphen grabbed Cymrian's arm and brought him to a halt.

"Let me have a look at her," she said.

With the Elven Hunter kneeling and Arling resting in his arms, Aphen searched through her sister's clothing, checking pockets and even the folds of her tunic, trying to find the seed.

But it wasn't there.

She exchanged a worried glance with Cymrian. "She couldn't have lost it. Not after all this."

"She was in shock, disoriented," he reminded her.

"But she mentioned the Bloodfire just before she passed out. She was aware enough to do that much."

Cymrian shook his head. "Wake her. Ask her."

Aphen was loath to do this, but she couldn't continue on

without knowing. Too much was at stake. Using a healing magic with which she was intimately familiar, she brought her sister awake. Arling's eyes fluttered open, and her scarlet gaze slowly came into focus.

Aphen forced a reassuring smile. "Arling, where is the seed? Do you still have it?"

Her sister gave a small nod. "Safe inside." She lifted her hand and placed it over her heart. "She knew what was needed. She was right to tell me to come."

"Don't talk. I just needed to be sure. I was afraid you might have lost it."

"I lost other things. Not that." She rose to a sitting position. "Aphen, we have to go. We have to get back to Arborlon." Her voice was urgent. "Now, Aphen! We have to hurry! There's no time!"

She seemed to be getting stronger suddenly, her words carrying a certain force as she spoke them. Then, all at once, she was struggling to break free, trying to squirm out of Cymrian's arms and get back to her feet.

"No, Arling, don't!" Aphen cried out, trying to help Cymrian hold her down. "Stop it. You aren't ready!"

But Arlingfant Elessedil was more than ready. Stronger than both of them combined, she wrenched free of their hands, flushed and wild-eyed, a different person entirely. In seconds she was standing clear of them. "You don't know!" she screamed.

Aphen took a step back. Her sister seemed transformed. She didn't even look as if she recognized her. "Arling, it's me!"

Arling stared at her, then nodded. "I can walk by myself," she said.

Her companions exchanged a worried glance. "All right," Aphenglow agreed, holding up her hands in a placating gesture. "If that's what you want."

There was a tension between them that hadn't been there two minutes before, and it had resulted in a full-blown confrontation that Aphen didn't understand. Something had happened to Arling. She wasn't the same person. This new Arling was hard and determined in ways that the old had never been.

Aphen didn't know what to do.

They started down the passageway, moving through the darkness, following the beams of their smokeless torches, heading for the opening into the other cavern. They passed into it without another word being spoken, Cymrian in the lead again, Arling and Aphen right on his heels, almost side by side, the latter giving the former frequent sideways glances that were not returned. The stone columns rose all around them like giants frozen in place, sentinels against dangers long since forgotten, but perhaps right around the corner. The gloom absorbed the light cast by the torches so that it felt as if they were traversing a massive space in which walls had been cast down and darkness ran on forever.

They were almost to the far wall and could see its stone block surface behind soaring columns spread out before them in staggered rows when there was a flash of movement off to one side.

Cymrian wheeled toward it, and Aphen quickly moved to place herself in front of Arlingfant. But then she heard a sudden gasp, and she wheeled around to find her sister firmly clutched in the arms of Edinja Orle with a slender blade set just below Arling's chin.

Aphen, her sister mouthed silently.

Ahead, the moor cat Cinla materialized out of the darkness, long and sleek and dangerous as she advanced on Cymrian.

"Don't do anything foolish," Edinja said softly.

She emphasized her words by pressing the knife she held a little more tightly against the skin of Arling Elessedil's exposed throat.

"Why don't we take a few minutes to talk things over?" she said, and gave them a satisfied smile.

25

INSIDE THE FORBIDDING, THE LIGHT WAS HAZY and gray and the air tasted of metal and damp. Tesla Dart led Oriantha and Redden Ohmsford through the wilderness they had found upon returning to the land of the Jarka Ruus, skittering here and there as she went, constantly in motion. Fugitives from the Straken Lord's Catcher, Tarwick, and his minions, they were constantly looking over their shoulders for unwelcome pursuit. They had tried to disguise all evidence of their passing before coming back into the Forbidding, wading through creek waters and even traveling the trampled pathway left by the passing of Tael Riverine's massive army, hoping their few footprints would disappear amid the many. But they understood that Tarwick was Catcher for a reason, and that even these efforts might not be enough to fool him.

Still, it would be unexpected for them to return to a place they had struggled so hard to escape, so there was reason to believe Tarwick might confine his search to the Four Lands. He might not know of Tesla Dart's presence or suspect the help she would give the two outlanders with whom she traveled. Diverting their escape route from the obvious to the unlikely might throw him off sufficiently to allow them to complete a swift journey through the Forbidding and then to escape back into the Four Lands by means of another portal before their hunter knew what they were about.

It was a dangerous game they were playing, and Redden couldn't be certain how the odds were stacked. Because they had fled so suddenly and made the decision to come back into the Forbidding so abruptly, there had been no time to gather up water and food, and they had almost nothing of either. Nor did the boy think that Tesla Dart—for all her knowledge of her own country and its creatures—knew exactly where they could find another way back into the Four Lands. She acted as if she did; she even insisted that she did. But something about the way she phrased it suggested it wasn't as settled as she tried to make it sound. She might have confidence such an opening existed because the imprisoning wall was crumbling, but that didn't mean she had a road map of its location imprinted in her mind.

What she did have was Lada, and the presence of the odd little creature provided the boy with a small glimmer of hope. The Chzyk seemed capable of finding its way in any territory and under any conditions, racing all over the place at blinding speed, never seeming to tire, a lizard imbued with innate instincts. Even if Tesla Dart wasn't certain of the path they should take, he thought maybe Lada might be.

He thought, too, that something had better happen soon to resolve their situation. His strength was almost gone, and his state of mind was still precarious. He remained mired in memories of his imprisonment at Kraal Reach, of the sounds and stench and discomforts of the rolling cage that had brought him back into the Four Lands, imprisoned like some exotic creature. He still flinched at the thought of the abuse and taunts he had received from his captors and was still devastated by images of Khyber Elessedil's terrible death. And it felt to him as if his new-found freedom was an illusion that could fade as swiftly as a mirage. He had no faith in its solidity, no confidence in its permanence. He had a sense of impending collapse, as if everything might go back to the way it had been in a single instant.

He slogged on because he had no choice in the matter, but it was working at him, gnawing at his sanity and eroding his emotional and psychological balance. He could feel it happening and he had no defense against it.

The day wore on, and their journey across miles of barren emptiness continued. They were moving in a mostly northerly direction, trying to get to a hole in the wall of the Forbidding that would bring them out much farther north of where they had started and presumably closer to where Redden and Oriantha both thought they should be when they reentered the Four Lands.

When they finally stopped for a rest, Oriantha waited until Tesla Dart was chittering away with Lada before kneeling beside a dejected Redden.

"How are you holding up?" she asked quietly.

Redden shook his head, his wild red hair falling over his eyes. "Not well."

"Can you keep walking?"

"Probably. But I feel like I'm coming apart inside. I can't seem to stop it from happening."

She put her hands on his shoulders. "Remember what I said. I won't leave you, no matter what."

"I know that."

"I will stay with you, and I will find a way to get us both safely

back into the Four Lands and to Arborlon and to your brother. I
know these are only words, but they are a promise. You will not
be returned to Tael Riverine while I am still alive."

He was crying again, and he brushed at his tears angrily. "It
just feels like there's no end to any of this. I keep thinking about
all the others. All of the dead. I feel as if I'm being drawn to
them. I can feel their hands closing on me. I can't make myself
believe I won't end up like them."

"Listen to me," she said. Her lean, smooth face was so close to
his own, he could feel her breath on his cheek. "By the end of
this day, we will be outside the Forbidding and back in the Four
Lands. I will make Tesla Dart promise this. There won't be
another day inside this world. Then maybe you can start putting
what you're feeling right now behind you."

He nodded without looking at her. "I can't do anything before
then, I can tell you that much."

"Just concentrate on putting one foot in front of the other,"
she said. "Just stay with that for the rest of today. You'll be fine."

They set out again shortly afterward. They had finished the
little food and water Oriantha had brought with her from the
camp. Tesla Dart seemed to be able to go for long periods with
no food or water at all, and she said nothing of the supplies situation, insisting they press on.

"I want us out of here by nightfall," Oriantha insisted.

"I want us out of here forever!" the Ulk Bog snapped in reply.

It was midafternoon when they reached the rim of a crater-
shaped valley that dropped away in a huge, sweeping bowl, its
slopes rock-strewn and chopped apart by twisting defiles. The
valley floor stretched away for perhaps a mile, all of it riven with
jagged cracks and littered with boulders and clumps of thick
scrub. It was a stark, desolate landscape, an arena poorly carved
by ancient cataclysms and the passing of time, rough-hewn but

immediately reminiscent of the place where Redden had watched Khyber Elessedil do battle with Tael Riverine. When he made the connection, a deep shudder went all through him, and he wrenched his gaze away and concentrated on the ground in front of him.

"What is that?" Oriantha asked Tesla Dart.

The Ulk Bog glanced over and shook her head. "Kroat Abyss. Very bad. You don't go there. Dangerous things."

They kept walking, glancing over now and then to the valley. "Who was Kroat?" the shape-shifter pressed.

"Straken Lord, very early. One of first. Drilled down for place to keep the bad things collected."

"The bad things. What sort of bad things?"

"Elf magic, talismans and sorceries used against the Jarka Ruus in ancient wars. Locked away with us, these ones, when we were imprisoned. But no one knows their power, no one knows how to use, afraid to try." She gave them a sly look. "Weka touched them and no harm came to him, he told. But Straken Lords keep such for themselves, not let others come close. Weka not like others. Weka knows all the secrets of the lands, all the hiding places, all the treasure chambers and tombs and keeps. So he visits and looks."

She gestured at the valley. "Takes me there, once. Long ago. So long. I was still learning. Just a girl. Takes me down into darkness and shows me what is there. Things of the Old World. Of when Jarka Ruus were one with Faerie. Long since gone."

Redden, who had been only half listening before, suddenly realized what he was hearing. He stopped where he was. "What did you say?" he asked sharply. "Things of the Old World?"

The other two stopped and turned back to him. "No, Redden," Oriantha said in warning. She was already sensing what was coming.

"Were there pretty stones?" he asked, ignoring her. "Did Weka show you colored stones?"

"Some," said the Ulk Bog. "In a box, locked up. Pretty stones. Different colors."

"Were they in sets of three?" he pressed, moving over excitedly.

"Redden, stop it!" Oriantha snapped.

Tesla Dart glanced over at her, and then looked back at the boy. "Sets of three. Red. Green. Another two. Yellow, maybe?"

"Four sets, four colors? You saw these stones? They were down there?"

"Saw them like I see you. Took them out of the case and held them in my hands. Pretty in the light. Glittered and shined. But they were only stones, not magic. Nothing happened. I put them back."

"Shades!" Redden breathed, turning to Oriantha. "Do you believe it? We've found the missing Elfstones!" He held up his hands as she started to object, giddy with excitement. "No, listen to me. This is a miracle. We had the chance to find them all along; we just didn't know it. Tesla Dart knew where they were. She knew! But she didn't know we were looking for them because we didn't say anything about it. We just told her we were trying to find friends that had been carried off by a dragon. We didn't tell her why we were inside the Forbidding in the first place. We didn't say what we had really come looking for!"

"Redden, what difference does it make now? That search is ended!"

"Only because, until this moment, we had no place to look. We didn't know where to go. Only Khyber knew anything, and she took that knowledge with her when she died. But think about it! Tesla Dart knows this information, too. She can take us down there into that pit. We can still find the Elfstones and bring them back out again!"

Oriantha stared at him. "Listen to yourself. How many are dead already because they thought they could find the missing Stones? How many, Redden? Now you want to risk our lives, as well? You want to forget about getting out of here, about finding a way back to your brother? You want to go hunting for the Elfstones, too? You must be out of your mind!"

Redden stepped forward so that he was right in front of her.

"I need to do this. Do you understand me? I need to. I've watched everyone die—and most of them right in front of me. I watched Carrick die. I watched the Ard Rhys die at the hands of Tael Riverine. All of this happened because of the search for the Elfstones—I understand that. But if we now have a chance to find the Stones and bring them back into the Four Lands—to finally do what we set out to do—don't we have an obligation to try? It would provide some small vindication for what's been sacrificed. It would prove that those who are gone didn't die for nothing!"

Oriantha shook her head. "No. It was madness before, and it is madness now."

"But we've suffered so much! The Druids are mostly dead; the order is destroyed. Your mother is dead. My brother may be dead, too. The search was a disaster. If we could get possession of the Elfstones, at least we would have *something* to show for all that." He shook his head and stared at the ground. "I am not going back without trying. I can't. I won't ever be the same if I give up on this chance. I have to try to find a way back to who I was before all this began. Maybe I can do that if we recover the Stones."

Oriantha folded her arms. "The Elfstones have been the cause of everything bad that has happened. Why do you think it would be any different now? Insisting on this just gives you one more chance to kill yourself and take us with you. I risked my life to break you free of that cage. Was it all for this? To have you take up right where you left off and in the end die anyway?"

"But what if all that is behind us?" He wheeled on Tesla Dart. "Are you sure the Elfstones are still down there, in this underground storage chamber? Can we find a way down there like you did?"

She looked from him to Oriantha and back again, clearly uneasy. "Stairs take you down—a long way down. But the stones are there. No one touches Old World magic, not even Tael Riverine. We can do, can go, if you want."

"Does something guard the magic? Are there creatures watching over it? Is it dangerous down there?"

"Nothing guards. Nothing watches. It is a dead place with dead things from a dead world. Only the Straken Lord goes. And Weka, too, once upon a time. Now, you maybe."

"You see?" Redden turned back to Oriantha. "We can do this! If we bring back the Elfstones, it will mean we didn't fail entirely. You must see it. We can't let this chance pass! We have to take it. We have to at least have a look!"

She glared at him. "You were the one who claimed to be falling apart. You were the one who insisted we had to be out of the Forbidding by day's end. Remember?"

"But knowing the Elfstones are down there changes everything. Now we have a real purpose in being here, one that doesn't involve running and hiding and fighting to stay alive. We have a chance to bring back the most important magic in Elven lore."

"Bringing back the Elfstones won't bring back the Ard Rhys or my mother. It won't bring back any of them. The past is done. You understand that, don't you?"

Redden took a deep breath and exhaled sharply. He could feel this opportunity slipping away from him, and he couldn't stand the thought of it. Oriantha was determined not to go, and if she didn't she probably wouldn't let him go, either. She was too invested in saving him, had given up too much to bring him back to his family. He understood what that meant, and he knew he wouldn't fight her.

But if that happened, he would never recover from what he had gone through. He could sense it—and not just in an offhand way, but deep down inside where the pain never quite goes away. Doing this, giving it at least a chance, would help him heal. It would lend him the emotional strength that had been steadily eroding all during his imprisonment and systematic incapacitation.

He met Oriantha's hard stare squarely. "What if the Elfstones could be used to help us defend against the Straken Lord's invasion? What if one of those sets has the power to negate the size and numbers of his army—maybe even to destroy it? Would it be worth it then?"

"We don't know what the Stones can do, Redden."

"But if we had them in our possession, we might be able to find out. We would have four chances to find a magic that would make a difference. Isn't that worth the risk?"

She continued to stare at him, saying nothing.

"We just need someone with Elven blood to wield the Stones," he continued. "Even I would do! I'm more than half Elf. My mother's blood is Elven; my father had some small portion of Elven blood, as well. *I* could try to use them."

Oriantha sighed wearily. "You are determined, aren't you? Even given the probable danger. Even knowing that it might all come to nothing. Your stubbornness exceeds your fears and doubts and your need to escape this place." She shook her head. "Hard to believe."

He almost laughed. "No harder to believe than anything else that's happened. It's just another part of the madness we've been struggling with since we left Bakrabru. But this, maybe, will lead to something good. For me, it means finding a way to live what what's happened. It means putting an end to this whole business. I have to try."

She shook her head in despair. "You won't let go of this, will you?" She gave a deep sigh. "All right. Maybe there's something in what you say. We'll give it a try."

She held up one hand quickly as she saw the look of joy on his face. "But here are my terms. If something dangerous wards the treasure of the Old World and I decide we are overmatched, we come back out. If we fail to find the Elfstones quickly or are not able to free them from their chamber, we come out. Tesla Dart, how do we see anything once we're down there?"

"Torches," the Ulk Bog said. She looked at Redden. "I know how to go, the way down and out again. I can lead us. Let me watch for dangers, use Lada to help." She looked back at Oriantha. "Agreed?"

The shape-shifter nodded. "Agreed." She glanced over at the valley and its black pit, then over her shoulder, already looking for the pursuit she knew would be coming. "Against my better judgment."

They left the valley rim and started down a brush-covered slope that provided handholds as they went. Tesla Dart made the choice of approach, offering a dozen reasons why others wouldn't work, most having to do with hidden dangers involving poison and teeth. Oriantha didn't argue. It was bad enough that they were going at all, but once the decision had been made she was not about to start second-guessing. This was the Ulk Bog's country, and she knew it better than the outlanders. Oriantha decided the best use of her time was in keeping watch for danger.

Slipping and sliding down patches of loose rock and dry earth, grabbing one clump of brush and then reaching for the next, using outcroppings of rocks for footrests and handholds where the brush was sparse, the trio made a torturous descent into the valley. Daylight was fading quickly now, the already pale gray light darkening by the minute as the skies lost what little glow they offered and shadows spread in sweeping pools that soon covered everything. Visibility diminished to a point where Oriantha was left feeling adrift, but it seemed not to bother Tesla Dart at all. Lada had disappeared early on, skittering away at the beginning of things, a flash of color disappearing into the brush. Apparently, the Chzyk was out there somewhere, scouting the way forward, but Oriantha couldn't prove it.

She glanced often at Redden Ohmsford. The transformation was astonishing. From beaten-down and discouraged to reenergized and eager; it was as if he had been newly made. Before, he couldn't stand being inside the Forbidding and wanted only to get out again. Now he seemed to have lost his sense of despair and his fears, and his thoughts were dominated by what he saw as the very real possibility that he could find and carry away the treasure they initially had come searching for. Admittedly, it was an astonishing prospect. That, after all that had happened, they should actually lay hands on the missing Elfstones was beyond belief. In truth, all of them had long since forgotten or at least set aside the original purpose for their quest. No one had given thought to it since the destruction of the company and discovery that the demons were breaking free of the Forbidding. There had seemed no reason for doing anything else. Redden was right: They had lost their way and believed they had no real chance of finding it again.

Now this.

Fate worked in mysterious ways. Oriantha understood that much about life, and her own strange history convinced her that the future was unpredictable and the past often shrouded in confusion and mystery. But what was happening now, undertaking this effort to find what had seemed forever lost, surpassed everything she knew.

"Can you see anything?" Redden asked Tesla Dart, his voice a whisper.

"Can see everything," the answer came back. "Night eyes are Ulk Bog's friends. Nothing hides. We are safe."

Oriantha doubted that, but then she harbored so many doubts anyway that one more hardly mattered. It had been her plan for them to reenter the Forbidding and escape swiftly—not to veer off on an unexpected quest that she could not help thinking would be a failure. But no one's plans had worked out as intended since the moment they had set out from Bakrabru. Mostly, they had just muddled through, trying to do the best they could.

Minutes later they reached the floor of the valley and started across the shattered terrain toward the dark pit that would take them down inside the earth. She kept her eyes directed ahead, scanning for whatever waited.

But as the Ulk Bog had said, there was nothing to see.

26

HOW COULD THIS HAVE HAPPENED?

Aphen screamed the question in the silence of her mind, its echo reverberating as she fought to regain her composure. She had never trusted Edinja Orle, not even when the sorceress was helping them escape Arishaig. She had wondered then if Edinja had something to gain by giving them her airship and sending them on their way so willingly. Given what she knew, it seemed wrong to believe the other woman could change so abruptly from an enemy to a friend.

But there was no indication of an ulterior motive and seemingly no earthly way she could do them harm once they were away from her.

Now Aphen knew better.

"How did you find us?" she asked.

Edinja gave a small shrug. "I never lost you. Not as long as you kept your sister close, which I knew you would. She is fitted with my marker, a bit of magic buried beneath the skin of her neck, there in the hairline where it can't be seen. Had you searched her thoroughly, you would have found it. But I knew you wouldn't do anything like that where dearest Arling was concerned."

"You tracked us as soon as we left, didn't you?"

"Shortly after. I used the second Sprint. Arishaig was doomed by then. Even I knew that. There was no reason to stay once it became apparent. Besides, I had plans of my own that were more important than going down with the ship. I might be Prime Minister of the Federation, but I am not required to sacrifice myself when the cause is lost."

Aphen was thinking desperately of what she might do to turn the situation around. Edinja's knife was perilously close to ending Arling's life. A single swipe of that blade across her sister's throat, and there would be nothing anyone could do. In which case, the Ellcrys could not be renewed and none of them would be saved.

But Edinja must know this, too. Would she really kill Arling if they came at her? What was she trying to do?

Aphen glanced sideways at Cymrian. He seemed at ease, but she knew he was looking at a way to get at the sorceress. The difficulty with this lay not only in the danger to Arling but also in the closeness of Cinla, who was crouched down and ready to spring. He might try to reach Edinja, but the big cat would be on him before he completed his first step.

"Hold your light steady," Edinja said to Arling, tightening her hold on the girl. "Point it where I can see everything they are doing. No tricks. If you drop the light or try to switch it off, I will cut you."

Arling's features tightened. "You won't do anything to me. If you do, you doom us all. I have the quickened seed of the Ellcrys. I am the only one who can send the demons back to where they came from. You don't dare harm me."

Edinja's strange green eyes glistened. "I wouldn't be too sure of that. You don't even know what it is that I want yet. It would be better for you if you wait to hear me out before you risk your life in a foolish effort to escape."

"Stay still," Aphen said to her sister. "Let's hear what she has to say."

Arling—the new, hardened version of Arling, unpredictable and volatile—did not seem convinced, and for a moment Aphen thought she would abandon caution and do what she so clearly wanted to do. She would wheel back on Edinja, knife or no knife, and claw her eyes out.

"What is it you are trying to do?" Aphen asked quickly, hoping to forestall any reckless attempts of that sort. She continued to look into Arling's eyes, hoping her sister would remain calm.

"Are you ready to listen to what I have to say?" Edinja replied. "You might be surprised by what you will learn." She tilted her head sideways. "Move over there."

She wanted Aphen and Cymrian to shift away from where they stood between her and the passageway leading out. They hesitated only a moment, then moved over as directed. Edinja shuffled Arling several steps over until she stood where the way was clear.

"Now let's all be very quiet while I talk."

She forced Arling to sit on one of the stone benches while she stood over her, one hand gripping her hair, pulling back the girl's head, the other keeping the blade of the knife pressed up against her throat.

"My purpose in all this is simple, even though my methods have not always been successful. In the beginning, I wanted only to be Prime Minister. That meant getting rid of Drust Chazhul and Lehan Arodian. Stoon helped me with that. I assume from his failure to return with Arling that you put a stop to any further help he might give?"

"He was trying to kill us," Aphen said.

"Which he wasn't supposed to do, I should point out. He was supposed to bring you to me so we could talk. But he was terrified of you—ever since that confrontation at Paranor when you almost caught him. He couldn't seem to get past it. So he made his own decision about how to handle matters. It makes no difference now. Mostly, he did what he was supposed to do, so I have no complaints. His time with me was over in any case."

She shifted slightly, looking down at Arling. "Comfortable? Good." She smiled, and her gaze shifted back to Aphen. The knife never moved. "What I've wanted all along—even when I wasn't Prime Minister, but was planning to be—was to find a way to ally myself with the Druids. I am as much a believer in the importance of magic as those who make up the order. I have been exposed to magic all my life. Members of my family use magic. I use it. But it was clear that my chances for forming an alliance were nonexistent as long as the Druids and the Federation remained enemies, so I began looking for other ways.

"When Khyber Elessedil and the others set out for the Westland, I was curious as to why. I began trying to find out. Drust wanted to crush the order, and so he sent airships and an army to seize Paranor—all of which came to nothing. His spies in Arborlon, which were really my spies, could learn nothing useful. The Druids went out, but only one returned. I began seeking answers to this puzzle."

She pointed to Aphen. "You had those answers, but I couldn't find a way to get them out of you. I knew you wouldn't reveal them to me willingly. I needed to find a way to force you. That was the purpose of dispatching Stoon to intercept you. I didn't know where you were going, but once I had you in hand I would be able to find out. Stoon failed me, but through a stroke of luck Arling came under my control. I learned most of what I needed from her."

"You pretended friendship when you gave us the Sprint, but you tried to kill my sister in Arborlon weeks before that!" Arling snapped.

Edinja bent close to her. "Not kill her. Disable her. I wanted what she had found in the Elven histories. I knew she had found something, but I didn't know what. It was evident early on that it was important. I wanted whatever it was, but my servants failed me. Drust's creatures. He was the one who sent them, persuaded by Stoon on my orders. A mistake."

"How do you think to gain entrance into the Druid order at this point?" Aphen asked. "You've ruined any chance of that by coming after us."

"Have I?" Edinja shrugged. "It doesn't matter. There was never any real chance. I know that now. You would never have had me. None of you would have agreed to it. Things change, in any case, and they have done so here. I no longer care about an alliance with the Druids. The Fourth Druid Order is at an end. The Druids have become irrelevant."

Aphen realized with a start that she was right. All that remained of the order were Seersha and herself. The rest were either known dead or likely so—including Khyber Elessedil. The missing Elfstones, which might have made a difference, were lost. The Druids had failed in everything they had sought to accomplish.

"What is it you want, then?" she asked. "You've come after us for a purpose. What is it?"

"I want almost exactly what you want—to take Arling back to the Elves in Arborlon and let her do whatever she is meant to do with the Ellcrys seed."

Aphen and Cymrian stared. "Then why are we standing about?" the Elven Hunter snapped. "Why aren't we doing just that?"

Edinja cocked her head. "I said *almost*. *We* aren't doing this. *I* am. Alone."

It took Aphen only a moment to see what she meant. "Because you want to be the one who returns Arling and saves the Elves. You think that will elevate you to a position of power."

"I know it will. It will make me the single most powerful person in the Four Lands. How can it not? I will have saved the Elven nation by bringing back the one person who can restore their precious Ellcrys. I will be in a position to form an alliance not between the Druids and the Federation, but between the Federation and the Elves. I will be forgiven everything. Even leaving Arishaig to its fate as I did will no longer matter. I will be appointed Prime Minister of the Federation for life after this."

Aphen shook her head. "You won't be able to do any of this. My grandfather will never allow it. He will see the truth of things!"

"Oh, Aphen, you are such a child! Your grandfather is no longer King. His brother assassinated him while he slept. Phaedon is now King of the Elves."

Aphen stared, a cold dread flooding through her. "Ellich killed his brother? That would never happen! What have you done, Edinja?"

"What I needed to do. I've had a spy in your family circle for years. I have kept track of you—all of you—to learn what I could that might prove useful. My creature is clever and resourceful. Sometimes, it does favors for me. In this case, it eliminated someone who might stand in my way. Your grandfather was old. His life was almost over anyway. Now his son rules, and his worldview will be shaped by me because I will have access to him from the moment I return."

"Your creature," she repeated. "Who does it pretend to be? What disguise does it wear?"

Edinja laughed. "You don't need to know that. If you knew, you might be tempted to tell someone. Better that I leave you guessing."

"What does it matter?" Cymrian asked. "You intend to kill us and take Arling with you, don't you?"

The sorceress shook her head. "You still don't see. Yes, I intend to take Arling with me. I will return her to Arborlon and she will fulfill her destiny by doing what she has been given to do. But I don't need to kill you for that to happen. I just need you to remain behind until she has had sufficient time to serve her purpose." She shrugged. "Besides, if I kill you Arling will be much less likely to cooperate. And some cooperation will be necessary if she is to become the Ellcrys. Leaving you alive gives her hope for your future and hers."

"We'll follow you," the Elven Hunter said. "We'll expose you to everyone. We'll tell them the truth."

"And who will believe you? A disgraced member of the Home Guard? And an Elf girl who abandoned her people to become a member of the hated Druid order? What proof do you have to back up your claims? By the time you return, your uncle will be dead, too. There will be no one left to support your story about what you were doing here. Phaedon will never believe you. No one will."

She yanked Arling to her feet by her hair. "You should be satisfied with knowing that what you intended to bring about will still happen. You might not be the one who conveys your sister to Arborlon, but that shouldn't matter, should it? You've found the Bloodfire and allowed Arling to immerse the Ellcrys seed, to quicken it so that the Forbidding can be restored. That should be sufficient reward."

Dragging Arling with her, she began backing her toward the passageway leading out. "You've had your explanation. Or as much of it as you're entitled to. It's time for me to go. Don't try to follow. Delaying me might cost your people their chance at survival. And it might cause unintended harm to come to Arling. I know you, Aphen. You won't let that happen. Nor will you do anything to prevent the Ellcrys from being renewed. The fact that I'm leaving you alive should be enough to satisfy you. The rest is unfortunate, but necessary."

She was at the passageway entrance. "One last thing. You can't follow me, even if you try. I've disabled your Sprint. It won't fly. It will take you two days to walk out of here and reach even the smallest village."

She paused, a satisfied look on her beautiful face. "Cinla will remain behind long enough to make certain you stay where you are until I am clear of the tunnels. She can find her way out much quicker and more efficiently than either of you, so you won't be able to track her when she leaves. Don't think to use magic against her, Aphen. She will sense what you are about and tear you to pieces before you can complete even the smallest conjuring."

She gave the Elven girl a smile. "Have I forgotten anything?"

Arling's eyes were fixed on Aphen, and the rage reflected there was unmistakable.

Then Edinja backed her all the way into the tunnel's gloom, and they were gone.

In the silence that followed, Aphenglow and Cymrian stood frozen in place not six feet apart, staring into the luminous eyes of Cinla. The big moor cat had positioned herself directly between them and the passageway Edinja had disppeared down with Arling. There was no way forward.

"We can't let her do this," Aphen said to the Elven Hunter.

Cymrian did not respond. He was studying Cinla, his concentration so intense he didn't seem to hear Aphen. He took two steps away from her, widening the distance between them. His hands dropped to his sides casually, hovering just above a pair of blades strapped to his thighs.

Then, abruptly, the moor cat disappeared.

They could do that, Aphen knew. Cinla could melt away like mist and be there all the same, yet not visible. Cinla was simply responding to the threat she sensed from Cymrian, choosing to remove herself as an obvious target. If he wished to come at her, he would have to do so blindly.

"I need you to do something," he said to Aphen.

She shifted her gaze from the space the cat had occupied a moment earlier and back again to him. "What?"

"I need you to fake an attempt at escaping. A quick couple of steps should do it."

"That's a moor cat, Cymrian! And you can't even see it!"

"If it comes for you in response, it will have to reveal itself. Moor cats can only vanish like that when they are still."

She hissed at him, the sound born of rage and frustration. But he ignored her. "Can you do it?"

"It's you who can't do it!"

"Yes or no? We don't have time to argue."

She took a deep breath. "Yes."

"Summon your magic. Do what you can to help me."

She gave in to the obvious necessity of embracing this madness. This would never work, but she understood they needed to do something. Every second lost was precious, and she had no better plan.

She broke for the passage opening, two quick steps. Cinla reappeared several yards away from where she had disappeared, springing at Aphen. But Cymrian was quicker. Blades flashing in both hands, he launched himself across the space separating him from Cinla and threw himself atop her. The moor cat turned in response, claws slashing, jaws yawning wide. Cymrian's blades disappeared into her thick coat, buried to the hilt. Cinla screamed—a terrible sound that ratcheted through Aphen like an explosion. She was summoning the magic already, bringing it into her fingertips, desperate to help, but it seemed to take forever.

Cymrian had fresh blades in his hands as he lost his grip on the moor cat and rolled under it. There was blood on his clothing, much of it his own, and the moor cat was still tearing at him, teeth now fastened to his shoulder. But Cymrian ignored that. Both blades slammed upward into the moor cat's throat, plunging through the soft, exposed skin, sliding past the bones of her skull and penetrating her brain. Cinla's head jerked upward, her killing grip released.

Aphen's magic struck out at the big animal, hammering into the moor cat and throwing it away from Cymrian. Cinla was thrown backward and slammed into the cavern wall. The moor cat struggled up, the handles of Cymrian's knives sticking out of her body and jaws like blunt spikes as she lurched toward them. But the blades that had penetrated her brain had done too much damage. Her strength gone, she slumped in mid-stride and did not move again.

Cymrian was on his feet instantly, ragged and bleeding, his upper torso shredded. "Elfstones!" he gasped. "Show me the way!"

Forcing herself to ignore his terrible wounds, Aphen yanked out the Elfstones and summoned their magic. The instant their brilliant light angled down the passageway and up the stairs beyond, the Elven Hunter went racing off. Aphen followed, making certain the Elfstone magic continued to illuminate the path they needed to follow. She did not know how Cymrian managed to find the strength to run as fast as he did; she could not comprehend how he remained upright. By all rights, he should be dead.

She tightened her jaw at the image her words conjured. *Not that. Please, not that.*

She went after him with fresh resolve, knowing he would need her, wanting to be there for him, aware of what he was doing. Aphen had glimpsed that final look on her sister's face as she was being dragged from the cavern. Arling was not going to stand for what was being done to her. At some point, she was going to fight back. And she would do so before she was aboard Edinja's Sprint, where she had to know she would be trussed up and rendered helpless.

Cymrian was already out of sight ahead of her. Aphen was slowed by the effort it took to focus the magic of the Elfstones so that it lit a path through the blackness ahead of her. Without the magic to guide them, relying instead on torches and memory, it would take too long to catch up to Edinja and Arling.

What they would do when they actually found them again was another matter. But apparently Cymrian had already made up his mind.

She found the long flight of stairs and ascended them in frantic leaps and bounds until she reached the maze of tunnels. Bright splashes of Cymrian's blood dampened the rock surface beneath her feet as she ran. Her breathing was quick and labored, but she refused to slacken her pace. Every so often, she caught sight of the Elven Hunter ahead of her when the passageways straightened enough to reveal his progress. Each time he was a little farther away. She couldn't believe he could keep this up. The moor cat had torn him open front and back, and he was bleeding heavily. It didn't seem to matter. He wasn't slowing down.

He would reach Arling first, Aphen realized. He would have to be the one to save her.

Faster, she urged herself silently. Or maybe she was urging him. *Run faster!*

When Arling was forced out of Safehold's dark entrance and back into the deeper blackness of the tunnels, she was already preparing to break free. She couldn't expect help from Aphen and Cymrian—not realistically—so she would have to provide the help she needed herself. It was scary to think of trying to do much of anything with a knife at her throat and her hair clutched in Edinja's fist, but there was no other choice if she wanted to avoid being hauled off to Arborlon and sacrificed not for the good of the Elves and the other Races, but to serve Edinja's twisted purposes.

The distinction was clear in her mind. The end result might be the same, but the means and the intent were decidedly different. She didn't want for any of what was foreordained to transpire without Aphenglow beside her. She would need her sister's strength, and she was determined she would have it. What she would do when she reached Arborlon, she would do only on her own terms.

Edinja had gotten her the largest part of the way back to the opening into the Hollows when she gave a terrible scream—a sound that lay somewhere between rage and despair. For an instant she relaxed her grip on Arling, dropping to her knees as if stricken. Arling, seeing her chance, twisted free and fled through the tunnels toward freedom.

She was halfway across the clearing that separated the entrance to the tunnels beneath Spire's Reach from the surrounding woods when Edinja caught up to her. A tangling of her legs from an unseen force was her first indication of the other's presence, a magic spell used to bring her down. She collapsed helplessly, and then the sorceress was on top of her, dragging her back to her feet by her hair.

"They've killed her!" Edinja Orle screamed, the words an ear-splitting shriek that reverberated through the mist-shrouded air. "My Cinla!"

An instant later Cymrian burst through the opening into the caves and came for them. He did so at a dead run, no slowing, no equivocation. Blood was sheeted across the entire front of his tunic, and his white hair was wild and loose about his face. Edinja started to turn when she heard him, but hesitated just a fraction of a second. It was enough. Arling grabbed onto the other's knife arm, slammed the back of her head against her captor's exposed face, and wrenched free of the grip on her hair. Edinja screamed, broke the girl's hold on her arm, and slashed at her. A deep rent opened across Arling's chest, and blood turned her tunic crimson.

Then Edinja turned on Cymrian, both hands raised in a warding motion. Whatever magic she had invoked, it threw the Elven Hunter off his feet and sent him tumbling backward. But Arling flung herself on the sorceress once more, ignoring the pain of her wound and the sight of blood soaking through her tunic. She grappled with the witch, trying to pin her arms, to throw her to the ground. But even though Edinja was smaller than Arling, she was unexpectedly strong, and quickly broke her grip.

By now Cymrian had struggled back to his feet. He threw himself on Edinja, tearing her away from Arling and bearing her

to the ground. Arling heard the force of the impact as they col-
lided, saw Edinja's knife flash into view, and then Cymrian was
on top of her with his hands around her throat. She thrashed
wildly, trying to break free. But the knife had disappeared, and
her hands were empty. Her arms and legs flailed as she tried to
throw him off, but he was too strong. She attempted to summon
her magic, but her voice was choked off and her hands flapped
uselessly. Cymrian kept his grip on her throat and did not loosen
it until she went limp and her breathing was stilled.

But when she was dead, he slumped forward and rolled onto
his back, and Arling saw Edinja's knife buried in his chest.

Aphen burst into view, saw the blood from Arling's wound, and
rushed first toward her. But Arling, struggling to rise, motioned
frantically toward Cymrian, and after a quick glance Aphen
changed directions. By the time Arling had torn off the sleeves of
her tunic and used the folded cloth to stanch the flow of blood
from her knife cut, her sister was already at the Elven Hunter's
side, bending over him. Dragging herself closer, Arling could hear
them whispering.

"Hold on," her sister was urging. "Let me help you. I can use
healing magic. I can mend your wounds. I just need a little
time . . ."

His hand lifted to take hold of hers. "Just . . . remove the
knife."

She hesitated, but then fastened her hand about the handle of
the blade and pulled it free.

"Better. I don't want . . . to die with that sticking out of me."

His voice was strong in spite of his injuries. There was blood
everywhere. Where the knife had been extracted, it bubbled
from his chest.

"Arling?" he asked.

"Just superficial damage." Aphen glanced over, making sure, and Arling quickly nodded in reassurance. Aphen turned back. "I can't just sit here and do nothing!"

"Just stay with me. It won't ... be for very long."

She was crying freely. "You should have waited for me!"

"There wasn't time. Besides, the moor cat ... " He trailed off. "Things were ... already decided."

Aphen put her hands over her face, ignoring the blood that streaked them.

"Take Arling ... home," Cymrian said. "Don't let ... anything stop you. Arling is decided. She knows. Don't ... make her doubt herself. Help her ... stay strong."

Aphen nodded, her mouth a tight line. She took her bloodied hands away from her face and placed them over his.

"I wish I had more time ... "

"You know I love you," she interrupted.

His eyes steadied on hers. "I know."

"I should have said it more often. I should have done more for you."

"You did enough. Don't question it. Just remember ... "

He coughed, and blood sprayed from his mouth. Aphen bent down quickly and they whispered hurried words to each other that Arling couldn't hear. Aphen clutched at him as if to hold him back from what was coming. It wasn't enough. Seconds later, he sighed and went still.

When Aphen lifted away from him, she had a look on her face that Arling had never seen before.

It was a look of utter despair.

That night, as Aphen lay wrapped in her grief, unable to think or act, Arling asked her sister what she had said to Cymrian. The Elven Hunter's body lay wrapped in blankets and sheeting at the rear of the vessel's cockpit. Aphen had refused to leave him, even though he had asked her to, telling her not to waste time but to just go.

"He never thought of himself," she said. "Not once."

"He didn't love himself like he loved you." Arling waited a moment before asking again. "What did you say?"

Aphen looked down at her blood-streaked hands. She had done a poor job of cleaning them, but she didn't seem to care. "I told him I loved him enough that one day I would find him again. I would come for him wherever he was and we would be together." She paused, shaking her head. "Stupid words. Foolish promises. But I meant them."

"What did he say?" Arling pressed.

Her sister began to cry. "He said he would be waiting."

27

THEIR JOURNEY TO REACH THE HUGE PIT THAT occupied the center of the valley required Redden Ohmsford and his companions to proceed much more slowly than they wanted to. Huge cracks split the floor, some of them hidden by brush and rock until they were right on top of them. In daylight—or as much daylight as there ever was within the Forbidding—it would have been an acceptable risk. But with nightfall coming on and the already weakened light rapidly giving way to treacherous shadows, it became especially dangerous.

At the same time, none of them wanted to be caught out in the open after dark, where they would be exposed and vulnerable to predators.

If not for Tesla Dart, the boy and the shape-shifter would have been hopelessly handicapped by their unfamiliarity with the terrain and their inability to cover the distance demanded of them in time. But the Ulk Bog had no trouble finding her way even in the closing dark and kept them moving steadily across the valley floor toward their goal, urging them on with hisses and grunts and anxious movements of her head, all the while warning of unseen dangers and potential pitfalls. She scampered and darted as if possessed, a mirror image of the Chzyk Lada, who by now only appeared in flashes of muted color when coming back to speak with his mistress. The odd procession snaked its way across the blasted earth in short, choppy bursts and with constant shifts of direction, led mostly by the small lizard.

"It would help if we were Chzyks, too," Oriantha observed at one point.

It was almost completely dark when they reached the edge of the pit, the skies overcast with high clouds and low-hanging layers of mist, the air dry and murky within the vast cup of the valley's walls. On reaching their goal, Tesla brought them to a halt and pulled them close.

"Now we choose. Go down in dark or wait for light. Sleep until sun or use torch."

"Which do you think?" Oriantha asked.

The Ulk Bog scrunched up her feral face. "Dangerous in dark. Many steps, deep down. Then tunnel and cavern where magic kept. Hard to see with only torch." She shrugged. "But hard to see with only torch in daylight, too. Not so different. No sun in cavern."

"Helpful," Redden observed.

"So it doesn't matter?" Oriantha pressed.

Tesla Dart thought about it. "Doesn't."

"Then we should go now. The quicker we go down there, the sooner we get back out. Besides, it's dangerous everywhere in this country."

She glanced at Redden, who immediately nodded. He was anxious to know if there really was anything of use down in that pit. Waiting until morning would be maddening. "We should go now," he agreed.

So they moved ahead to the lip of the black hole, where they found a series of rough stairs leading down to a rock shelf some fifty feet below them. Beyond, the darkness was so thick and impenetrable there was nothing to be seen.

"Lada waits here," Tesla Dart announced. "Keeps watch for us."

Redden looked around doubtfully. "How will Lada find us if he needs to give warning?"

The Ulk Bog grinned, showing all her teeth. "Chzyks see in dark as well as in light. No difference for him."

So with the little creature scurrying off into the rocks, the three started down the broad steps to the shelf. Once there, Tesla moved over to a deep niche in the rock wall and produced torches. She lit the first using sparks from flint and stone, handing the other two to her companions after lighting them as well. Then she walked them over to the edge of the platform where a very narrow, uneven set of stone steps carved into the rock walls wound downward into the blackness.

Tesla Dart gave them a look, gestured at the steps, and shook her head admonishingly. "We go very slow. Steps very slick. Fall very long way if you slip."

The boy and the shape-shifter exchanged a brief glance. That was three uses of *very* in about a dozen words. They got the point. One mistake and you were dead.

They began their descent. Tesla Dart led the way, with Redden right behind and Oriantha bringing up the rear. They went slowly, just as the Ulk Bog had said they should, and it became apparent right away that haste on these stairs would be deadly. Twice in the first hundred steps the boy felt his feet skid and almost go out from under him. The chiseled-out stone was ridged and broken and dangerously uneven. Dampness coated the surface of the rock. There were no railings and no handholds should you start to fall. The steps themselves were less than two feet wide in most places and no more than three anywhere. Perversely, Redden found himself wondering what would happen if someone going down met someone coming up. He guessed that had probably never happened, but he couldn't help picturing the dilemma it would present.

They continued downward for what seemed an eternity. Redden lost track of how long, but he guessed it was over an hour. They traversed hundreds of steps, maybe thousands—a torturously slow process that challenged their concentration and balance every step of the way. Tesla Dart let them stop and rest at regular intervals, although not as often as the boy would have liked.

In truth, his imprisonment had eroded his powers of concentration along with his strength. Although a measure of emotional resilience had been restored with his freedom, and the level of his excitement at the thought of recovering the lost Elfstones fed additional adrenaline through his body, he was still not in the condition he had been before entering the Forbidding. Sheer force of will kept him upright and on the treacherous steps, but his agility and his concentration were weak. He kept his right shoulder pressed against the rock wall, rubbing along the roughened surface to reassure himself that he was still connected to something solid.

Ahead of him, Tesla Dart muttered and whistled soft incomprehensible sounds that apparently served a purpose, although he couldn't think what it was. Behind him, Oriantha was a soundless ghost, a presence no stronger than his own shadow. He had to force himself not to look around and make sure she was still there. He had to keep reminding himself of what she was and what that allowed her to do. But it was still unnerving.

The stairs ended in a tunnel that curved away from the pit and downward ever deeper into the earth. The cavern had the look of a passageway that had been hollowed out over a long period of time, its surfaces rugged but its broad circumference even and unchanging. It called to mind a giant wormhole tunneled through tons of rock, but Redden could not imagine the size of the creature that would have made it.

Farther on, at a juncture of tunnels and caverns that opened off a central chamber thick with stalactites and stalagmites, their stone tips jutting up and pointing down in vast clusters, they found another set of narrow stairs carved out of the rock and began another descent. The sense of depth was suffocating, and Redden had to fight not to give in to a growing panic. He felt imprisoned in the same way he had while in the hands of the Straken Lord, and the old feelings of hopelessness were threading their way through him with steady insistence.

Once he stopped altogether and leaned back against the wall, torch sagging in his hand, eyes closing against a sudden onslaught of fear.

"What is it?" Oriantha asked at once. She put her chiseled face right next to his and stared into his eyes. "Tell me."

"I'm feeling trapped in here."

He could barely speak the words. Everything was pressing down on him. The air had grown so cold, he was shivering.

Oriantha took off her cloak and wrapped it around him, fastening it securely. "Wear this. Stay fixed on what you are doing. Don't think about anything but that."

"You'll be cold," he said.

"The cold doesn't bother me." She turned him back around by the shoulders and faced him toward Tesla Dart, who was waiting several steps below. "Just keep walking."

Their descent ended when the tunnel flattened out and

continued on in a lateral direction, winding ahead through the
darkness. The air tasted of metal. Water dripped from the low
ceiling and collected in depressions in the rock floor; they had to
wade through pools that stretched from wall to wall. Redden did
what Oriantha had told him, focusing on what they had come to
do to avoid dwelling on his doubts and fears. He thought of the
Elfstones and of how they might look when he found them. He
thought of returning with them to the Four Lands and then at
last going home.

He thought of Railing. He wondered how his brother was. He
wondered, to his shame and horror, if he was still alive.

At last they arrived at a final chamber—another huge cavern
that opened onto a vast store of darkness. Tesla Dart brought
them to a halt and held up her torch. In the flicker of its light
something huge and still caught their attention, and all three
torches shifted at once.

It was a creature of some kind, massive and unmoving.

"A Graumth," the Ulk Bog advised. "Dead."

She moved them closer, taking them across the cavern floor to
their left to where a huge worm-like creature lay curled up
against one wall. Chains held it fast, but its unmoving bulk alone
was terrifying. Redden drew up short, but Tesla kept going.

"Are you sure it's dead?" he whispered.

She turned and nodded. "Many years dead. So long it
becomes hard."

"Hard?"

"Hard. Like rock. Empty shell."

Petrified. Preserved by nature's elements. "What's it doing
here?"

"Used to make tunnels. Rock eater burrows out space for
magic things. Long time ago. Very long."

"Where did this magic come from?" Oriantha asked.

"Comes when Jarka Ruus imprisoned. Comes with them when they are exiled, gathered up, put down here. Happens quick." She snapped her fingers. "Everyone, all at once."

Redden saw it then. When the first Ellcrys was created and the Forbidding went up, the exodus of the Darkling creatures didn't happen slowly. It happened instantly. Whatever they were doing, wherever they were found, those against whom the magic was directed were snatched up and carried away. It stood to reason that some of them would be in possession of magic when that happened. Aleia Omarosian's Darkling boy must have been one of them. He must have had the container with the Elfstones in hand when the Forbidding had imprisoned him.

He took a moment to think about the consequences of the Forbidding's creation. It would have been a swift, complete resolution of the war between the two factions—the implementation of a magic so powerful that any resistance was simply swept away. But it must have happened on a radical scale; entire species must have disappeared at once. There would have been no distinguishing between those creatures thought good or bad on an individual basis. No culling would have been involved; no objective measures would have been employed. It would have been decided on a species-by-species basis only, and those failing to measure up would have been extinguished. Aleia Omarosian's Darkling boy would have suffered such a fate, caught up in the cleansing because of what he was, no matter if his intentions were evil or simply misguided.

Redden was horrified, imagining what that must have been like. He had never thought of the imprisoning in those terms. For him, as for so many, it had been an event where good had triumphed over evil in a time when the consequences would have been unimaginable if things had gone the other way. But it was much more than that. It was a severing of species without regard to guilt or innocence, without determination of purpose or intent. Some were saved, some were not. Who had made that determination? Who had decided who would stay in his world and who would be locked away in this one?

Oriantha was looking at him. "Are you all right?"

He nodded. But he wasn't all right. Not by any measurable sense of the word.

"They stored magic for Faerie down here because they were afraid of it?" he asked, trying to shift his thinking away from any further consequences of the Forbidding's creation. "Is that what happened, all those years ago?"

Tesla Dart shrugged. "Magic not good. Belongs to those who put us here. Elves and such. Taken away by leaders and stored. No one wants it."

Because they couldn't make use of it. Because they lacked the ability to summon it. Because it was here by chance, and probably served as an unpleasant reminder of what had been done to them, so they stuck it away where it wouldn't be seen. Where it wouldn't offend by its mere presence. How would that have come about? What were things like in the beginning of the Forbidding, in its early days after everyone realized what had happened to them?

Anarchy. Chaos. Madness.

"Show us the Elfstones," Oriantha ordered the Ulk Bog.

Tesla Dart hissed at her, then turned and beckoned them across the chamber. Redden and the shape-shifter followed, staying well clear of the chained worm. Dead or not, they had no interest in getting any closer to it than they had to. Casting about in the darkness of the huge cavern with sweeps of their torches, they kept close watch for other creatures.

It took them only a few minutes to get beyond the dead Graumth to an alcove set into the far side of the chamber—a deep niche in which all manner of strange implements were revealed. There were globes of metal and glass, staves intricately carved of wood and fashioned with silver tips, books of all sizes and shapes, iron boxes, flags emblazoned with emblems unrecognizable to the trio, weapons of all sizes and shapes, intricately shaped pieces of jewelry, and even a cauldron. Silk cloaks and scarves draped boxes and shelves on which many of the artifacts rested. A fine coating of rock dust covered everything. Motes hung in the air, swirling in an invisible breeze coming from an unknown source.

Redden started forward, but Tesla Dart quickly put a hand out to stop him. "Traps," she said.

Motioning for both the boy and Oriantha to stay where they were, she walked to one side of the wall and did something to the rock. After that, she seemed to count off steps toward the center before passing into the niche. Once there, she moved to the other side of the niche to release a series of trip wires. Finally, she retrieved a small crate set close to the niche opening, carried it over to a box set next to them and slid back a panel at one end.

Instantly dozens of tiny snakes emerged from the niche's darkness, slithering quickly to reach the crate and crawl inside.

The Ulk Bog spent a few moments more checking the darker places in the storage space, running hands over the surface of the walls and floor before beckoning them inside.

"Safe now," she said. "Bad things put away. Traps disabled. You see?" She pointed to the crate with the small snakes. "Poison. One bite?" She made a choking motion. "Dead fast."

"You got all of them?" Oriantha said. "You didn't miss any?"

"All now, come here. Look."

Tesla Dart took them over to a collection of boxes, cloths draped casually over a few of them. She went behind the pile, reached down beneath a heavy cloak, and pulled out a metal box with an insignia stamped into it. The image was of crossed blades laid over a field of wheat with a bird that looked like a hawk circling overhead.

She handed it to Redden. "Stones inside. Pretty colors." She cocked her head. "What do they do?"

Redden took the box from her, holding it out so that he could study it. "I don't know. No one does."

He experienced an emotional tightening in his chest. The missing Elfstones, lost for all these centuries, were now in his hands. He couldn't quite believe it. Finding them was so far removed from anything he had imagined possible that he was afraid to look inside for fear it was all a mistake.

He glanced at Oriantha and shook his head. "I don't know if I can bear to open it."

She smiled encouragingly. "You can. Go ahead."

Still, he hesitated. This was what had brought the entire company into the Forbidding in the first place—what had led them to their destruction, what had swept most of them away and changed the lives of the rest forever. There had been no reason for weeks now to think that finding the Elfstones was any sort of possibility. In his own mind, the quest had been abandoned after the destruction of the Druid order.

Now here he was with the box that might contain the precious talismans in hand, and it was all he could do to make himself believe that it was real.

He knelt, balancing the metal box on one knee, and released the catch securing it. Slowly, he raised the lid and peered inside.

Soft black cloth layered the bottom of the box. Into it had been fashioned five molded depressions. Four contained sets of gemstones, each a different color—crimson, emerald, saffron, and white.

The last depression was empty.

Redden had never seen the blue Elfstones, but he knew instinctively they had come from the empty space, and these other stones were the ones that had been missing all these years. He stared down at them, studying the smooth facets and even, geometrical shapes. Save for their colors, all were exact duplicates. Even in the gloom and the swirl of rock dust, they glittered with brilliant insistence.

He looked up at Oriantha and Tesla Dart. "We've found them!"

Her companions crowded close, peering into the box, taking in the beauty of the gemstones. After a moment, Oriantha asked quietly, "Is that a piece of paper tucked underneath the edge of the cloth?"

She pointed to where something white poked out from the gathered velvet just above the nestled crimson stones. Redden bent close. She was right; something was there. He reached in and extracted a folded piece of paper, carefully opening it. There was writing, but he couldn't make out what it said. It was in a form he had never seen before. He guessed it might be as ancient as the stones themselves—a language lost in the passage of time, abandoned as the world changed. The things of Faerie had mostly been forgotten over the centuries because so much of the past had been lost.

Oriantha took a look as well, but shook her head. "I can't read it, either."

Redden started to put the paper back in the box, then changed his mind and slipped it into his pocket instead. He looked down at the Elfstones. "Should we see what they do?" he asked, suddenly eager to know.

"What do you mean?"

"Well, now that we've found them, shouldn't we discover

their powers? What if their magic could carry us back into the Four Lands with nothing more than a wish? Maybe it could let us fly? Don't you want to know?"

But Oriantha shook her head. "You need an Elf to test them, Redden. A full-blooded Elf, if you want to be sure. You know the history."

He did. Anyone other than a pureblood Elf risked injury or even death by attempting to make use of Elfstone magic. It was a part of the Ohmsford legacy, written down during the time of Wil Ohmsford, when he dared to use the seeking-Stones to save the life of Amberle Elessedil, the King's daughter, so she could become the new Ellcrys. He had chosen to ignore the danger posed to someone who was of mixed Elven–human blood. As a result, his body had been altered by the power of the magic, generating within him the seeds for the birth of the wishsong—a magic he had passed down to his children, Brin and Jair Ohmsford, and which had subsequently been discovered in other Ohmsford descendants ever since, including most recently Redden and Railing.

"We should go," Tesla Dart said to them. She was looking about now, hopping from foot to foot. "Past time. Still dangerous here."

Redden looked up from the box, realizing he had lost all track of time while he was admiring his find. He closed the lid and secured the catch. "Do we go back out tonight or wait for morning?"

"Not wait," the Ulk Bog answered at once. She looked suddenly skittish, uneasy. "Takes time to climb back up. Morning light is close by then."

They started back across the chamber and were almost to the passageway that had brought them in when a flash of movement appeared in the gloom and Lada shot into view. Tesla Dart bent down to greet the Chzyk, and the two chattered back and forth for brief moments before the Ulk Bog sprang up again.

"Tarwick comes! Has tracked us!" Her face was taut. "Comes down into this place. Traps us here!"

There was real fear in her dark eyes. "He brings Furies!"

28

NO ONE PANICKED, THOUGH THERE WAS AMPLE reason to do so. Furies were monsters, catlike beings that hunted in packs and lacked any semblance of rational behavior. It was said they could not be controlled, but it appeared that someone had found a way. If Furies were included among Tarwick's hunters, they had to be doing his bidding, and the Catcher would not hesitate to use them.

Redden was so cold inside that it seemed the temperature in the cavern must have fallen below freezing. He could not imagine what they were going to do. They were deep underground with the way out blocked and their pursuers coming for them. They lacked any reasonable chance of escaping or even of defending themselves. The wishsong remained an uncertain protection, although Redden would use it as best he could. Oriantha was quick and strong in her animal form, but she alone would not be enough. Tesla Dart had no discernible defenses at all.

"Is there another way out?" he asked the Ulk Bog.

She shook her head. "No way. Only how we come in. We must fight our way free."

"Can we hide?" Oriantha asked. "Another tunnel? Another cavern where they won't find us? Can we slip past them somehow?"

Tesla Dart's wizened face knotted. "One way down, one way up." She hesitated. "Maybe I can say you are prisoners of me. Maybe say I found you here."

Oriantha shook her head. "We're not letting them take us. I promised Redden, and I meant it. We break free or we die."

Redden nodded, not caring for the odds, but knowing he could never go back into a cage. Another imprisonment and he would lose what was left of his already damaged mind. He could feel what it would be like already, just thinking of it. Nothing would save him if they got hold of him again.

He was still clutching the box with the Elfstones as he turned around and looked back across the cavern at the niche with the collected implements of magic brought over from Faerie. "Do you think there might be something there?" he asked the shape-shifter.

Oriantha sprinted back across the chamber and began searching. Tesla Dart had not reset any of the traps or released the serpents anew, so there was no danger of anything harming her while she did so. The Ulk Bog followed, looking decidedly forlorn.

Redden watched them for long moments, standing close to the mouth of the passage, desperately trying to keep himself together. His emotional stability was already dangerously thin, his sense of self reduced to a small hard kernel of doubt. Being trapped like this was the worst fate he could imagine, the one thing he hadn't wanted to happen. Oriantha had recognized the danger when she had urged him not to go looking for the missing Elfstones.

He should have listened.

But he had been determined to come here, to search out the Elfstones, to find them and bring them back. Diverting from their original plan posed a terrible risk, and in hindsight he knew he should not have insisted on it. This would not end well for either of his companions. Oriantha would almost certainly fight until she was killed. She would never be taken alive. Tesla Dart might choose death, as well.

It gave him pause. Was he strong enough to follow them? Was his determination enough to keep him from being imprisoned anew?

Still watching his companions as they rooted through the ancient treasures in the niche across the cavern, he opened the box containing the Elfstones and glanced down at them.

Was there a way to make use of them? Even without knowing what they did, even without knowing what it would mean to summon their magic, should he try anyway? Should he risk releasing their power, whatever form it might take, against the creatures coming for them? Even knowing the magic was dangerous to use since his Elven blood was so thin?

Or should he rely on the magic of the wishsong—a magic he had employed once already against his pursuers. Would it be powerful enough? Could he even manage to summon it again?

There were no answers to be found. The risk was clear, whichever way he went. But he had to do something. Neither of the others had the power he possessed, regardless of which path he chose. Their lives were in his hands.

He stared across the blackness of the cavern at the bobbing torchlight of his companions, conflicted. If he guessed wrong, if he made a mistake in his choice of magic, they were finished. In all probability, he would only get one chance. He watched Lada skitter past him, disappearing into the black hole of the tunnel behind him. He had only a short time to wait before the little creature was back again, chittering wildly.

He knew at once that their hunters were close.

Barely conscious of what he was doing—almost as if his fingers were acting on their own—he reached inside the metal box and extracted a single set of Elfstones. He knew instinctively which ones he wanted and where within the velvet cushioning they lay. Then he closed the lid, tucked the box under his arm, and moved back across the room to join his friends.

The search had yielded little. There were weapons available, but they were ancient and clearly meant to be used as talismans. And there was nothing to reveal what sort of magic any of them possessed and no way of knowing how to summon that magic.

"When they come," Tesla Dart announced suddenly, "I will throw the box with the serpents at them."

Oriantha said nothing. She moved away from them and began to shape-shift into her animal self, stretching out and turning sleek and powerful, abandoning her human form in favor of something faster and stronger and more dangerous. She had made her choice in this matter, as Redden had known she would. She would make no concessions to her hunters.

Tesla Dart started scurrying about, finding additional torches at the entrance to the niche that she lit with fire from the torch she carried. Then she began placing them about the cavern at regular intervals, trying to make it easier for them to see what was coming, hoping to give them some small advantage.

She took the last two brands, dashed all the way across the

chamber, and jammed them into the rocks on either side of the tunnel opening before rushing back again.

Sounds from within the tunnel's blackness grew audible. Their time was almost up. Redden summoned the magic of the wishsong, emitting a soft hum to begin the process, bringing the heat of it out of his core to be balanced invisibly within his chest, ready for use when it was needed.

Oriantha was completely changed by now. On all fours, she slunk into the shadows and disappeared. She would choose her own place to make her final stand. She would face what was coming on her own terms.

Across the chamber, shadows emerged from the tunnel and started toward them. They were just a handful at first, then a dozen, and then many more. At least thirty or forty by Redden's quick count, too many for them to withstand. Too many for them to escape. They crossed the chamber and hovered in the shadows just beyond the light, vague forms that emitted a strange hissing; that grunted and growled; that gave high, keening moans. Eyes glittered from out of the dark here and there, but never for more than a moment, always shifting away again.

Tarwick appeared suddenly before them, his scarecrow form materializing out of the gloom. His lean feral features were bladed and planed by the deep shadows, and his eyes glittered as they fixed on his prey. All around him, his hunters pressed forward eagerly—Goblins with demon-wolves on leashes, Furies with their terrifying cat faces, and creatures that had no name Redden could determine.

There were so many, he thought in despair.

Tarwick began speaking, and the language he used was unknown to the boy. But Tesla Dart understood. "Says we put down weapons. Says we are his prisoners."

Now the Furies were mewling and hissing, and the demon-wolves were snapping at the air. If they all came at once, Redden knew it was the end—even with the power of the wishsong to aid them.

"What does Tesla say to Tarwick?" the Ulk Bog whispered back at him.

She was deferring to him, which he found oddly ridiculous. As if he knew what to do. As if he were leader of their little group. He did not answer, but instead concentrated on bringing the magic of the wishsong closer. He took deep breaths and centered himself inside, where the fear and doubt fought to claim him. Words whispered in his head, repeating themselves over and over.

We will fight them. We will stand until we fall. We will never go back into the cages.

Almost without thinking about it, he stepped backward into a pool of shadow and knelt, setting the metal case on the cavern floor. When he rose again, his fingers were closed so tightly about the crimson Elfstones he could feel the edges cutting into his palm.

What sort of power did they possess?

He was remembering those times he had linked the magic of the wishsong to another form of power—to when Railing and he had flown the Sprints through the Shredder and again when he had used the wishsong to enhance the power of the fire launchers aboard the *Quickening*.

But he remembered, too, when he had tried to escape the Straken Lord's camp, been confronted by a giant that could crush him with a single blow, and almost failed in his efforts to summon the wishsong's power.

He remembered what he had felt in those crucial moments, and how he had responded. He remembered how good it was to be free again and how desperate he was to remain so.

"Move back," he said to Tesla Dart. "Behind me."

She stared at him in surprise, but then did as she was told. "What are you doing?" she hissed at him.

He ignored her. He didn't know what he was doing. Not specifically. But he knew what he wanted to happen, and that was enough.

Tarwick was watching him suspiciously and the creatures that served the Catcher were beginning to edge forward, no longer content to stand and wait. The volume of their cries was increasing, and the gnarled bodies were edging closer, pressing them backward toward the niche.

"I will get serpents and throw!" Tesla Dart insisted.

"Stay where you are," Redden said.

He was gathering himself, trying to make certain that what he did next would achieve the result he sought—or at least something close. He was seeking a way to shape it into something formidable through the use of his magic, through strength of heart, mind, and body.

With so little of each to call upon, he must be certain he found enough of each if they were to survive.

Something dark flashed through a wash of torchlight to the left of where he stood, and Oriantha tore into a clutch of attackers. Redden's arm rose instantly, extending like a weapon, and his voice filled the cavern with a roar that sounded like a mountain coming down.

At the next instant, red light blossomed from his clutched fingers, turned to fire, and exploded into their attackers. Two forms of magic at once, one feeding the other, wishsong and Elfstone magic blended into a firestorm of light and sound. He felt them tear out of him, generated not just from throat and hand, but from everything he was, as well. A strange, terrible wrenching shook him to the soles of his feet, and he could tell that something unpleasant was happening.

But the result he had been seeking was achieved. Red light surrounded and absorbed the creatures of the Straken Lord. Tarwick and his minions were snatched up like toys, wrapped in unbreakable chains of magic. Shuddering and thrashing, they were encased in red fire.

It happened quickly, a wrenching away of substance—of flesh and blood and bone. Through a miasma of pain and shock, his body shuddering from what the combined magic of wishsong and Elfstones was doing to him, Redden Ohmsford watched it unfold. Some essential part of him was disappearing, disintegrating with the power he was releasing. Another almost physical form of disintegration was taking place among the demonkind. Bodies lurched and shook and convulsed as if jerked by invisible strings. The sounds the stricken creatures made were terrible to hear, and the boy knew he would never be able to forget them. Screams and howls and shrieks; they were burned forever into his memory. His own sounds were equally terrifying, for what was emanating from them seemed to be coming from him, as well.

He was going to die. He knew he was. By ending their lives, he was ending his own.

But it was worth the price. It was worth any price.

Then his voice and his strength gave out. The light and the sound collapsed, and the magic faded. Redden sagged to his knees, drained of strength and in shock, but still alive. In the flickering of torchlight he saw the predators that would have torn them apart reduced to heaps of ash and scraps of clothing. There was nothing left of any of them.

Tesla Dart bent close, bracing his shoulders, speaking to him. He couldn't hear what she was saying and stared at her blankly. Oriantha reappeared out of the darkness, having escaped the fate of the Straken Lord's creatures. He had hoped to keep her safe, but he hadn't been sure he could make that happen. He hadn't been sure of anything.

He found himself crying at the sight of her, whole and unharmed. She was changing back into her human form even as she approached, her strange eyes fixing on him, reflecting her disbelief and awe.

"Had to try," he gasped as she knelt before him.

He opened his hand, and the Elfstones glittered through the darkness like drops of blood.

She supported him with an arm wrapped about his waist when they set out again, leaving the cavern and its dead behind. Little was said as they departed; even the normally gregarious Tesla Dart had gone silent. Lada, who must have gone into hiding at some point, scurried out to meet them at the tunnel entrance before rushing ahead once more to scout the way.

"You shouldn't have taken such a chance," Oriantha whispered.

"I knew it would work," he whispered back.

And he had, he realized now. He had known. But he had not reckoned entirely on the consequences. A feeling of having been dismantled and then reassembled in a different way still reverberated through him, refusing to pass. The magic of the Elfstones had done something inside him; he could feel it but not define it. At some unspecified point in the future, he would know. He did not particularly look forward to that moment, but there was nothing he could do about it now.

Up from the darkness they trudged, wending their way through caverns and tunnels, climbing the endless succession of steps to the platform where they had started, emerging once more into a daylight gray and murky beneath overcast skies. The Forbidding, rediscovered. They crawled out of the pit like burrowing animals into the light, blinking in confusion, making a hurried search for additional enemies, but none were in evidence. Apparently all those who had come after them had gone into the pit.

Oriantha lowered Redden to the ground, bracing him with her hands on his shoulders. "Can you walk on your own from here?"

He nodded. Speech had pretty much deserted him, and he wasn't rushing to retrieve it. The whipsaw feeling from using two forms of magic in combination still roiled inside, leaving him sick and disoriented. He didn't want to talk. He didn't even want to think.

"Let's be off," Oriantha said, taking note of his reticence. Instead of pressing him, she simply walked him toward the stairs that led upward to the pit's ragged lip. "I want to be out of this place and back in the Four Lands before another sunset."

She was carrying the metal box containing all of the Elfstones save the crimson ones Redden had used earlier, which he had shoved deep into his pocket afterward. The shape-shifter must have seen him do this but had said nothing about returning them to the box. Apparently, she had decided that there was no hurry. Or perhaps she had thought it better just to let the matter be.

Redden shuffled ahead once they reached the valley floor, eyes lowered to the path, watching for crevasses and drops, not wanting to fall into a bottomless pit after just climbing out of one. He clutched at himself as he walked, and the feeling of his own arms about his midsection seemed to help him manage the tumult inside. Walking was easier, too, if he kept his eyes downcast instead of trying to look beyond the next few steps. Peering up at the sky was impossible.

Ahead, while Lada chattered back and forth with Tesla Dart, the valley floor gave way to its walls and the air warmed.

Unable to help himself, he began crying anew.

Staying close by, Oriantha monitored his progress but kept her distance and made no effort to speak to him.

When they had climbed out of the valley and moved farther away from the pit, his crying stopped. It was all right now, he told himself. It was enough that they were all still alive.

But even as he said it, he knew it wasn't true.

29

THE ARMY OF THE STRAKEN LORD ARRIVED shortly after sunrise on the fourth day after setting out on its lengthy journey from the ruins of Arishaig. The Elves could see it coming from miles away as it slowly materialized out of the morning haze that spread across the broad sweep of the plains all the way south to the horizon. Because the Jarka Ruus were of varying sizes and shapes and did not march in formation or with any particular regard for order, but instead simply lurched forward in the manner of a massive herd in migration, it appeared to those watching as if the earth was undulating.

The first of them reached the pass through the skies, winged creatures flying ahead to announce the coming of the others. Predatory birds the size of small horses, giant bats leaking poison from their talons, and Harpies with bird bodies and witch faces, all hove into view and began to circle the defenders, crying out in shrieks and screeches, great black shapes swooping low enough that their faces could be clearly seen.

The Elves were entrenched at the mouth of the pass leading into the Valley of Rhenn—the only way through to Arborlon from the east for an army the size of the Straken Lord's. Sian Aresh had mobilized the defenders within hours after Seersha had disabled Phaedon Elessedil, temporarily taking control of the defense of the city and its people and restoring some semblance of purpose and order. Holding the Rhenn was critical to the city's survival, but Sian Aresh had determined early on that the most defensible positions were the passes at either end of the valley rather than the valley itself. Once that was decided, it became much easier to choose the nature of the defenses that would be employed. Building traps and snares or digging concealed pits or setting trip wires felt pointless against an enemy of this magnitude. The battle would be fought on the run, with shifting formations and quick attacks and retreats. Entrenchments beyond the passes themselves would likely fail to contain the creatures of the Forbidding, who were of multiple shapes and possessed of varied skills and abilities. Bolt-holes and concealments would be useful, but building barriers across the mouth of the pass at the eastern end of the valley to slow a massed attack, and erecting a barricade across the even narrower west pass, would be a more practical use of the time available.

In the end, their defenses ran all the way from the east pass, where the bulk of the Elven army had been gathered to defend against the initial assault, and down through the valley itself to the second pass, in which the opening through a pair of huge rock pillars had been closed off by a massive barricade. An army attempting to reach the city from this direction would have to breach the obstacles of the first pass, run a gauntlet of defenders entrenched behind concealments on the slopes of the valley walls, and then breach the barricade stretched across the even more forbidding and inaccessible second pass.

The backbone of the Elven defense, of course, was a fleet of warships several dozen strong, all manned and equipped for battle and waiting to engage. Except for flits passing overhead in reconnaissance, the balance of the airfleet was grounded just behind the second pass in an airfield set close to the valley proper. When the battle came, the warships would have the best chance of turning the tide by attacking from the relative safety of the skies.

Over the years, a number of attempts had been made to take the valley, but all had failed. No one could imagine it would be different now, not with the added strength of the warships and their weapons.

But then, no one would have thought that Arishaig could be taken, either.

The Straken Lord's winged scouts, sweeping down through the valley in quick bursts, seemingly heedless of the missiles whizzing past them as they went, took full measure of the Elven defenders and their defenses. They flew as if oblivious to the flits that darted at them, easily avoiding their efforts to bring them down. They defecated on the defensive positions as they passed—a taunting that brought howls of rage and dismay from those hidden in the brush and trees and rocks.

"Can you put a stop to that?" Sian Aresh snapped at Seersha from within their concealment near the head of the pass.

The Druid shook her head. "I could, but that's what they are hoping for. They want to know if you have the use of magic. If you have anyone standing with you who has the same powers Khyber Elessedil did." She gave him a look. "It would be best if we let him wonder for a while."

Eventually, the flying creatures lost interest and flew away. Not one had even been injured.

The day dragged on after that in a desultory, anticipatory slog, tension heightening steadily as the enemy army drew closer, as it widened and deepened like a tidal wave and increasingly assumed definition. It was one thing to be brave in the face of something nebulous and distant. It was another entirely to maintain that position when you could see the sorts of things that were coming for you—creatures with twisted limbs and crooked backs, teeth and claws that could rend you in a single swipe, and faces so gnarled and misshapen they resembled your worst nightmares fully realized.

It took the army all day to reach the mouth of the pass, and there they massed, widening out to either side of the mountain walls north and south for miles, and eastward until their end could not be seen. Dust filled the air and drifted over the Elves, clogging their breathing and obscuring their vision. The stench of enemy bodies spread in a sickening wave and left some defenders gagging and retching. There seemed to be no leaders, only beasts herded to this place like animals, brought to a halt and unable to do more than mill about.

Sunset was almost upon the Elves—their tempers frayed to the point of breaking—when the dragon flew out of the encroaching dusk. It came in a rush, its huge plated body rust and crimson beneath layers of shadow, its wings spread wide as it glided on the wind. Astride its neck, armored head-to-foot, was a creature no Elf had ever seen before. It was as black as moonless night, heavily muscled and ridged with spikes that poked through gaps in the armor that had been cut apart to afford them space and then chained back together with links. A huge scepter was clasped in one hand, its jagged head glowing a wicked green.

The Straken Lord raised his arms as he passed over the dark swell of his army, and a million throats roared out his name. He might have been the sum of all things from the greeting he was

given, and he acknowledged it as if it were his due. He let the
dragon take him past his army and into the mouth of the pass,
still high enough that no missile could reach him and big enough
that no flit dared approach. He was showing himself to his
intended victims—a clear indication he would be the last thing
they ever saw in this life.

Just before wheeling away and flying back into the night,
bearing its black rider with it, the dragon opened its huge maw
and exhaled sudden gouts of fire.

"I don't like that," Sian Aresh observed.

"No wonder Arishaig was at risk," Seersha replied.

"This changes my thinking about the value of our airships.
That dragon is much more maneuverable than anything we
have. Do you think there are any more?"

Seersha shook her head. "I'm sure we'll find out."

They waited patiently to see if there would be any others, but
the Straken Lord did not return, and the creatures of his army
began to settle down on the open flats, curling up in the manner
of animals and dropping off to sleep. If there were guards or a
sentry line, the Druid couldn't find them. No precautions
seemed to have been taken against a surprise attack. For a
moment, Seersha considered the advisability of mounting one—
of not waiting for the inevitable, but of striking first. She almost
said something to Aresh.

But there were a million creatures out there—many times the
number of Elves that might be thrown against them—and in the
end she abandoned the idea. Better they hold their ground and
let the enemy come to them.

Especially the dragon. No point in going hunting for something like that.

Seersha and Sian Aresh moved over to a promontory on the
left cliff wall at the entrance to the valley, just apart from the

guards assigned to protect them. The two were now joined by common cause and shared events. Together they had conspired to set aside Phaedon Elessedil as King, rendering him helpless enough that he was now kept under constant watch. He still couldn't talk, couldn't make himself understood, and was wrapped in a cloak of apparent madness that had everyone speculating about what had happened to him. Only Seersha and Aresh knew for certain, and neither was saying anything. It was sufficient that he could no longer interfere. He would remain in his present condition for at least another day, by Seersha's reckoning, and by then the battle would be joined and its course likely decided. That was the best they could hope for.

"They will wait for the moon to rise and attack then," the Captain of the Home Guard said quietly.

"I don't think so," Seersha said in response. "They will wait for dawn. The sun will be at their backs and in our faces. The Straken Lord knows something of tactics. That was clear at Arishaig."

"We have a bet then. In my view, he won't have the patience to wait until morning. He will act before then."

Seersha shook her head in disagreement. "He sees himself as invincible. He chose to attack the Federation first because he believed it to be the strongest force he would face. He's been scouting the Four Lands since the Forbidding started to crumble, sending out spies through gaps in the wall. This is a sustained invasion, and he intends to see it through. We were told this was his intention unless . . ."

She trailed off. There was no point in talking about Tael Riverine's demand for the return of Grianne Ohmsford. Not unless it actually happened, which seemed unlikely. She found herself wondering if Railing and his companions had discovered the fate of the former Ard Rhys or if the search had fallen apart by now. She had never really believed it would come to anything, but she had never entirely discounted it, either. It was a time of strange happenings, and nothing was so impossible that it could be discounted out of hand.

Aresh waited for her to finish and, when she didn't, said, "I don't know how we can hold out against so many."

"We can't without help. But the Dwarves will come. Crace Coram will bring them. And maybe the Border Legion will join us."

The Captain of the Home Guard nodded. "I cannot believe it has come to this."

"Nor I."

"I wish we had time to ferret out whoever killed the King. Because it certainly wasn't Ellich."

Seersha nodded. "More likely his son."

They were silent for a time, scanning the darkening horizon, peering down the slopes of the cliffs to where Elven Hunters with torches were lighting watch fires that had been built earlier. Pockets of brightness blazed eastward across the length of the cliffs on either side of the pass, providing a shadowy view of the sleeping enemy army and of any creatures that might try to approach under cover of darkness. The fires would burn all night, their wood replenished as it turned to ash, the sentries on duty guarding against surprise attacks.

"What do you think has happened to Aphenglow and her sister?" Sian Aresh asked after a time.

Seersha shrugged. In the firelight, her dark tattoos reflected the brightness of the flames. "It will take them as long as it takes, but Aphen won't fail."

"If she finds what she's looking for. Or if something doesn't interfere with her search."

The Druid gave him a look. "She won't let anything interfere. She'll find a way back to us."

Aresh shook his head. "She's really our only chance. And Arlingfant, of course. The only chance for the whole of the Four Lands."

"Then we have to give them the time they need. You and me and all those gathered in this valley." Seersha stepped away. "I think I will try to get some sleep."

"And me. At least until they attack. I still think it will be tonight."

The scarred face wrinkled with her smile. "Then we have a bet."

She went off to find a place to bed down. Aresh remained where he was, wrapping himself in his blanket, sitting upright and bracing himself in a depression on the hillside where he could look out over the enemy hordes.

Both did the best they could to fall asleep, but neither had much success.

Seersha won the bet. The Straken Lord did not attack during the night. He attacked at dawn.

It was a clear, bright day, and the sun rose in a brilliant yellow glow out of the eastern skies, the light blinding the defenders on the slopes of the Valley of Rhenn, exactly as the Straken Lord must have hoped. By then the entire demonkind army was awake and organized, restless to the point of making feints against the defenses—quick rushes at the entrance to the pass that seemed less well defended.

But it quickly became apparent to Seersha that Tael Riverine had other plans. Separating his army under cover of darkness into a series of commands, he had positioned them all across the vast sweep of the Streleheim, north and south for as far as the eye could see. When Elven flits flew out to have a closer look, bands of Harpies brought two of them down and the rest quickly turned around. Thus, when the attack finally came, it caught the unsuspecting Elves by surprise in more ways than one.

Instead of a head-on assault against the entrance to the pass, the enemy came at them from the flanks. Led by their lighter, more agile climbers, they scaled the forested slopes in simultaneous strikes intended to break through and get behind the defenders massed at the pass. Attacking not in large groups but in small clusters, they used the rocks and trees for cover as they swept up the cliffs in record time, barely slowing as they came, swarming over the front ranks of the Elven defensive positions and killing everyone not quick enough to fall back.

It was a variation on the tactics the Straken Lord had used at Arishaig, and it was equally successful here. In minutes, the wings of the Elven army had collapsed and gone into retreat, and the Jarka Ruus were atop the rim of the Valley of Rhenn on both sides of the eastern pass.

Sian Aresh acted quickly to counter this advantage, sending warships from the fleet to drive off the attackers. His orders were clear: Use fire launchers to burn them out of whatever concealments they tried to find and chase them back down the slopes to the plains. And don't let up until the rim of the valley is retaken.

A trio of warships moved into position on either side of the valley and launched a sustained attack. Because the Elves did not have the use of flash rips—having adhered to the rules established by Grianne Ohmsford following the end of the war on the Prekkendorran—fire launchers were the strongest weapon they possessed.

It quickly seemed as if that would be enough. The demonkind

resisted only briefly before falling back—a steady, if grudging, retreat that required the warships to remain in place and continue to fire on them as the Elven Hunters driven back earlier slowly began to reclaim lost ground.

But at this juncture, the main body of the Straken Lord's army attacked the pass. Armored giants and thousands of Goblins swarmed through the staggered clusters of obstacles created to slow them as if they weren't even there. Dozens died or were injured in the effort, but the rest kept coming. The Elves met them just inside the pass, solid walls of spearmen crouched behind shields while Elven longbows rained arrows from perches higher up. For a time, it seemed the defensive lines would hold. But the enemy forces were too strong, their numbers too great, and eventually the lines began to sag.

At that point, Sian Aresh sent another two warships to buttress their efforts, the great ships-of-the-line sliding down the length of the valley and settling in to either side of the enemy, which had pushed the defenders all the way out of the pass. Using rail slings and fire launchers, the airships struck back at the demonkind, shattering the front ranks of their assault and forcing the rest back into the shelter of the pass.

The battle was joined, attackers and defenders locked in combat within the east pass and atop the valley rims to either side, when the dragon reappeared.

It swept down out of nowhere, swift and agile, eluding the charges fired from hastily redirected weapons aboard the airships facing the pass, snaking back around behind them. Sitting astride the great beast, the armored black form of the Straken Lord howled in glee.

Seconds later, fire exploded from the dragon's widespread maw and sent the light sheaths, masts, and decking of both airships up in flames.

Seersha couldn't save them. She was already running back across the rim of the bluff, having sighted the dragon moments earlier and knowing at once what it intended. But she wasn't fast enough. She got there just after the ships went crashing earthward, decks and light sheaths afire. The Elves who were still able to do so were sliding down or leaping over the sides before they were consumed. Without pausing to consider whether it was wise or reasonable or even sane to do so, she attacked. Sweeping aside her black robes, she extended her tattooed arms, assumed her battle stance, and sent lines of magic hammering into the huge beast. Because it wasn't looking at her, it wasn't prepared. Confident that the worst of its enemies had been disabled, it was hovering in midair, waiting for the ships defending the flanks of the Elven army along the valley rim to turn toward it.

But Seersha got to it first, and her blows knocked it sideways with such force that the Straken Lord almost lost his seat, and for a moment it appeared that the dragon would go down. It staggered wildly in mid-flight, its wings beating frantically to keep it aloft as it swung about to track the source of this unexpected assault. It spotted the Druid, the residue of her magic rising like steam into the air, and, banking sharply to avoid another strike, it began to climb skyward to mount a counterattack. Everyone surrounding Seersha had gone to ground, leaving her alone and exposed atop the valley rim. Even Sian Aresh had dropped away, although she hadn't seen him go. But that was the way she preferred it. No one could help her now, in any case. She would have to face what was coming alone.

She didn't have long to wait. Screaming in fury, the dragon dropped toward her like a stone, banking sharply left and right to confuse her. She struck out at it anyway but her strikes went wide each time, and then the dragon was on her. It tore into the earth as it tried to crush her, claws extended, ripping out great gouts of earth and rock as the Straken Lord urged it on.

But Seersha was already gone. Using magic, she slipped the attack like a ghost, momentarily disappearing until she was suddenly twenty feet away. The dragon swung about, but she had its measure now and her magic slammed into it once more, singeing its scaly body, burning away whole sections of armor.

Then the Straken Lord's scepter came down, pointed toward her, and something hard and brutal caught hold of her, picked her up, and almost threw her off the clifftop. She only just managed to save herself by clutching at clumps of scrub grass as she was tumbling over the edge.

Seersha had lost all perspective. She was in full battle mode as she leapt back to her feet, her warrior blood and training fueling her response. She lashed out at the Straken Lord, nearly unseating him a second time. But the dragon was using its fire again, and she was forced to throw herself out of the way as the bluff around her went up in flames. The dragon lifted off, still breathing fire, trying to finish her. She fought back frantically, her magic shielding her, dispersing the flames. The dragon banked away, momentarily breaking off the attack, though its fire continued to fill a sky gone dark with smoke and ash.

She waited until it came back around, crouched low to the ground to make herself as small as she could manage, and hardened herself against what she knew the Straken Lord would do to her with that scepter if she carried out her plan.

She hesitated to be certain of her target as the dragon swung toward her, then lashed out with every particle of magic she could muster and struck the beast right in its closest eye.

The dragon roared in pain and fury, whipping its head from side to side in agony, the eye gone, blood streaming down its face. In the same instant, while all of her concentration was focused on the dragon, the magic of the Straken Lord's scepter slammed into her, caught her up, and threw her away like a rag doll. It felt as if every bone in her body had been broken. A small portion of her magic had been diverted to protect her from the expected attack, but she knew at once it had not been enough.

She thought she was dead then. She lay where she was, her strength gone, her magic exhausted, fighting to get to her feet and unable to do so. But to her astonishment, no further attack came. The dragon was bucking and thrashing through the roiling smoke, unable to do anything to ease its pain, the loss of its eye so damaging that it could not, for the moment, manage to think of anything else. Though the Straken Lord fought hard to bring the beast under control, the dragon refused to respond.

In the end, Tael Riverine was forced to let the creature fly him back out into the relative safety of the Streleheim so that it could deal with its injury.

Seersha had just enough time to watch it disappear, then Elven Hunters were gathering all around and pulling her to safety.

30

THE BATTLE BETWEEN THE ELVES AND THE
Jarka Ruus raged on through the remainder of the
morning. The armies surged up and down the slopes of
the cliffs that warded the Rhenn, and back and forth through its
eastern pass. At times, it seemed the attackers had gained the
advantage they needed to force their way inside the valley, but
each time the Elves fought back with such ferocity and determination that the advantage quickly disappeared. Though the creatures
from the Forbidding fought on with a furious intensity, it was
clear they were adversely impacted by the failure of the Straken
Lord and his dragon to return to the battle and lacked the means
to counter the damage inflicted by the Elven warships, which
were now safely in control of the skies. While they were able to
maintain overwhelming numbers on the ground and, under different circumstances, would likely have overrun the Elven defensive
positions and claimed both the east pass and the valley before the
day was out, they had no real means of protecting themselves
from—or fighting back against—their adversary's airships.

Even so, the damage to the Elven troops was severe enough that Sian Aresh was forced to bring additional reserves forward from the western pass to buttress those fighting in the east. Seersha, too damaged to return to the battle herself, saw some of this from the care station at the western end of the valley as Elven Healers worked to bind her cracked ribs and stop the blood flow from multiple wounds. Salves were applied to ease the pain and provide the beginnings of a healing for her burns. Because she lacked Aphenglow's skills in this area, she gave herself over to her caregivers and their experience. Oral medications were provided as soon as it was determined where the interior damage had been done, and soon after she became drowsy and fell asleep.

When she woke, she was lying in a bed inside a plain, nondescript room with several other injured, and she could hear the sound of raindrops spattering against the windows from outside. She lay where she was for a time, working hard to come awake, still groggy and weak and trying to determine what had happened to her after the battle with the Straken Lord. Eventually, she regained enough presence of mind to realize she was back in Arborlon and must have been brought there at some point following field treatment for her injuries.

Once she felt ready enough, she forced herself into a sitting position and then out of bed and onto her feet. She hurt everywhere, and the effort would have been too much for a less determined person. But she could not abide not knowing how things stood, and so she gritted her teeth against her agony and weakness, dressed herself in the singed and bloodied clothes that had been removed and placed on a chair, strapped on the weapons that lay on the floor next to them, and stumbled from the room into the corridor beyond.

She was somewhat strengthened by a self-administered

infusion of Druid magic meant to deaden pain and accelerate healing—a basic tool of any Druid, though not one she was especially proficient with. But it lent a certain steadiness as she moved down the corridor, taking her time, peering into rooms filled with injured men and women who had been brought back from the battle, treated, and then bedded down under care from Healers and their assistants. She paused a few times to take in the numbers and watch the efforts of the caregivers before continuing on. No one tried to stop her. No one paid her any attention at all. Everyone was too busy with the needs of other patients to worry about one who was upright and wandering about in a functional condition.

Eventually she reached an area at the front of the building where a handful of Elven Hunters engaged in transporting the injured back from the Valley of Rhenn were taking a short break before heading out again. Normally, there wouldn't have been time for this effort in the midst of a battle, and it made her wonder anew what had happened in the valley since she had been returned to Arborlon.

She approached a grizzled veteran she recognized from the training field who was standing by the doorway and peering out into the rain. The day—or what was left of it—was dark and gloomy, and the rainfall on the other side of the walls a steady downpour.

The Elf glanced at her and immediately straightened. "What are you doing? You shouldn't be up. In fact, you should be dead."

"I'm hard to kill," she answered.

"So it appears. But would you mind not testing that theory? I'm one of those unfortunates who had to haul you back here. You were not in such good condition."

She nodded. "Thanks for your efforts. Can you tell me how things stand out there?"

He shrugged. "The fighting's stopped for the moment, and both sides are pretty much right where they were at dawn. We almost lost the pass a few times, but the warships got the best of those things trying to force their way into the valley. Ugly stuff."

"I imagine so. Did the dragon come back?"

"Not that I saw. You did some real damage. I don't know that it can return now."

She nodded. Would the Jarka Ruus attack again after dark? All this rain would make it hard to sustain watch fires, and there would be no moon or stars to provide light otherwise. It would be a perfect opportunity.

"I need to get back to the valley," she said. "Can you find me a flit?"

"And risk the captain finding out I helped a madwoman kill herself? Not hardly. Besides, nothing is flying in this stuff. We have to wait for it to clear. All of us, I might add, which includes you. Get back in bed. Sleep some more."

"I'm all slept out," she said, glancing around.

"Then pretend. Captain said to take good care of you when he sent you back here. He said we're going to need you healthy enough to come back strong by morning. Maybe sooner."

She took a deep breath and exhaled. "All right. Come wake me if there's any news. If *anything* happens. A night attack, especially."

He nodded and looked away, studying the rainfall, not saying any more. He wouldn't do a single thing to wake her unless the enemy was right outside the door, she thought. He probably had orders from Aresh to that effect. Maybe all of them did. She turned away and, ignoring the old veteran's suggestion about going back to bed, went back down the hallway to a side door and slipped out into the rain.

From there, she slogged her way over to the Home Guard

barracks and tried to find Aresh. She didn't expect she would, but wanted to try. She was told he was back from the valley, but had gone over to the palace to see how Phaedon Elessedil was doing. Apparently, both the King and Ellich Elessedil were being kept there—a concession to their status as members of the royal family—until further disposition could be made regarding their respective situations.

She paused to decide whether she was wasting her time wandering about like this and should just go back to bed as the old veteran had advised. Then she shrugged off the idea, departed the barracks, and headed down the roadway for the palace, head bent and shoulders hunched against the rain. In the storm and darkness, no one was about. With good reason, she thought. Even wearing a cloak for protection, she was soon soaked through. Her body was beginning to ache and her wounds to throb in spite of the bandages and salves. She shouldn't be out like this, but she couldn't make herself go back and lie around in a sickbed doing nothing. If she couldn't get back to the valley, she could at least walk over to the palace and have a conversation with Aresh.

When she reached her destination, she was met by Home Guards who recognized her and took her inside. She was told that Aresh was in the building visiting the prisoners, but that she must remain where she was until he returned. She knew neither of them personally, and so her efforts at persuading them to make an exception were ignored. They did take her into a private room so she could change out of her drenched clothes and into a set of ill-fitting spares scrounged from a trunk, remarking on her damaged condition and mentioning they had heard all about her battle with the dragon. They told her she was an inspiration and added they were sorry they couldn't do more to grant her request.

She smiled and said she understood.

Ten minutes later, dressed in dry clothes and in possession of an all-weather cloak, she walked past them down the hallway and into the depths of the building. Neither guard cast even a single look in her direction.

Druid magic had its advantages.

She had no clear idea where she was going, and she ended up wandering about for a time until she found a guard who had befriended her on the practice field standing watch at a closed door.

"No one is allowed back here without permission," he said, blocking her way. "Do you have a pass?"

"No," she answered. "I was sent to find Sian Aresh to give him a message from the Elven defensive front in the valley. I need to see him."

He considered a moment. "I heard about the dragon. That was good work." Then he shrugged. "I don't see why you shouldn't be allowed to speak to the captain. He's with the King, in his bedroom. Down the hall, around the corner left, then first left again. Big, double doors. Another guard on duty." He gestured to the closed door behind him. "Ellich is in here." He shook his head in disgust. "A good man, Ellich. I do my duty, but I don't mind telling you I think this whole business is a travesty. He would never harm his brother. Everyone knows that. There's something wrong here."

"Agreed," Seersha said. She bent close, lowering her voice. "Someone else is to blame for Emperowen's murder. Any clue as to who it might be?"

The guard shook his head, lips tightening into a frown. "None. But I wouldn't have, would I? I'm just a soldier serving out my time in the Elven Home Guard. I don't know these people well enough to be able to guess at either the names or the number of their enemies."

She nodded. "Well, things will get sorted out. So Aresh is down the hall in the King's room?"

"Left here just ten, fifteen minutes ago. He was in here with Ellich before that. And Jera. She's an odd one. She's not been to see her husband once until today. Then shows up, visits until Aresh comes, and then insists on seeing her nephew. They argued about it. I could hear them through the door. Finally, he gives in."

Seersha stared. "She wanted to see Phaedon?"

"She said she did. Aresh didn't like it, though."

Seersha went still. "Give me those directions again."

She left without seeming to be in a rush, but once she was out of sight she picked up her pace until she was almost running. She didn't know what was troubling her exactly. Perhaps it was the idea of Jera visiting her nephew. Perhaps it was hearing that Jera had not come to visit Ellich until tonight. Especially that. It did not sound at all like the woman Aphenglow had described on repeated occasions—a wife whose entire life had been built around caring for her husband.

She reached the next corner and came around it in a rush. She saw the double doors immediately, but there was no guard on duty. She slowed, quieting her approach, her instincts telling her she should be cautious until she knew the lay of the land. She couldn't imagine what might be happening, but she didn't like what she was thinking.

She came up to the doors and stopped in front of them, listening. She could hear voices, low and indistinct. Or maybe it was only one voice. There was crying, too. A kind of low sobbing that had hints of despair and exhaustion. She listened for Sian Aresh, but didn't hear him.

She almost knocked. But in the end she simply opened the door and stepped inside.

Next to the bed, a single smokeless lamp burned on a night-stand. In the faint splash of illumination it cast, she could see everything.

Sian Aresh and the Elven guard lay sprawled on the bedroom floor, lifeless eyes staring. There was blood pooling all around them, metallic and pungent. Phaedon Elessedil had been released from his restraints and was sitting on the side of the bed in his bedclothes. He was holding a knife in his lap, bending over and staring down at it, mumbling and sobbing. There was blood both on his clothes and on the knife.

Jera was sitting next to Phaedon, her arms around him. She was speaking to him in a low voice, and she seemed to be trying to comfort him.

She looked up instantly as Seersha appeared and put a finger to her lips. Seersha stood in front of the open door, staring in shock. "What's happened here?"

Jera gave her a stern look. "Close the door. Don't say anything more."

The Elven woman continued to whisper to Phaedon, her voice low and compelling, her hands on his shoulders, bracing him as he sobbed and whimpered. The King seemed to be completely undone. There was no hint of the old Phaedon, the one Aphen had famously described as cold enough to freeze fire.

Seersha took a few steps toward them and stopped, trying to make sense of what she was seeing. The shadows of the dark room felt as if they were filled with secrets, and all of them hidden from her.

Phaedon went suddenly quiet, leaning into Jera, his face buried in her shoulder.

Jera looked up at Seersha. "He killed them both. Somehow he got free of his restraints and got hold of this knife. When Sian and I entered the room, he attacked immediately. Sian was killed at once. When the guard heard the sounds of fighting and came running, Phaedon killed him, too."

She stroked Phaedon's head, smoothing his dark hair. "He didn't do anything to me. He doesn't seem to want to. He keeps calling me 'Mother' and telling me he's sorry. I don't think he even knows what he's done."

"He was supposed to be secured to the bed," Seersha insisted in disbelief. "We told everyone he was a danger to himself and others. How did he get loose?"

Jera shook her head. "I don't know." She gave Phaedon a quick hug and rose. "I'll leave him to you. I have to tell the other guards what's happened. Ellich, too. Perhaps they'll free him now."

Seersha nodded blankly, looking down at the bloodied form of Sian Aresh. She couldn't quite make sense of it. Jera's explanation seemed plausible enough, but there was still something wrong. Maybe it was the knife, still in Phaedon's hands. Maybe it was the tenderness Jera was showing Phaedon—a kindness that felt out of place.

The shock must be causing her to react like this, she told herself as Jera walked past her toward the door.

Then her eyes shifted back to Phaedon, still sitting on the bed, staring into space, and she noticed that the knife was gone.

An instant later she felt a sharp blow to her back followed by a wrenching pain, and she collapsed to the bedroom floor. It was as if all her strings had been cut, and she could no longer make anything work. She lay in a red haze of anguish and fury, watching as Jera Elessedil stood looking down at her, bloodied knife in hand, and she realized what had happened.

"You killed them," she managed to gasp.

Suddenly Jera didn't look like Jera anymore, but like something not even human. Her features were losing shape and twisting into something feral. It lasted just a minute, and then she was back to herself again.

"You're not dying fast enough," she hissed.

She lunged for Seersha, who barely managed to catch hold of her wrists and stop the knife's downward descent. Jera shrieked and thrashed in her grip, and for a moment Seersha, her strength all but gone, was certain she was finished.

But Jera was too eager, and her wild efforts caused her to lose her footing and tumble to the floor, the knife skittering away. Seersha saw her chance—one so small it offered no real hope, but she embraced it anyway. In an instant she was on top of Jera, her wounds forgotten, her weakness thrust aside, her body flooded with the Druid magic that had always sustained her. Everything happened all at once, and even making the effort to regain control of her injured body was done on faith.

A warrior to the last, she refused to give in to the damage and the pain, refused to admit she couldn't do what she needed to survive. Refused to admit she was finished.

She bore down on Jera Elessedil with every last ounce of strength she could find, hammered her head into the floor, then jammed a forearm across her neck and pressed down.

The cry that broke from Jera's mouth was terrifying and inhuman. Instantly, the creature that had surfaced earlier—the creature Seersha now realized had been disguised as Jera—reappeared in bits and pieces. Clothing ripped and split apart. Skin fell away. Jera Elessedil began to fade, and something muscular and lithe emerged in her place, something covered head-to-foot in earth-colored hair and possessed of sharp claws and teeth—a being like nothing Seersha had ever seen before. She knew this was what had killed not only Aresh and the guard but also the old King. It was the spy who had tried to steal the diary from Aphenglow and leave her injured or dead.

All this came to the Druid in seconds, and that was all the time she was given. The creature hiding within Jera's skin had emerged, and she did not have the strength to fend it off. It was enormously strong, and Seersha knew it would be free in seconds and that would be the end.

She cried out for help, then flung her arms about the creature's neck in a vise-like grip that crushed its windpipe. The beast thrashed and writhed once more, and this time its claws ripped into the Druid, tearing at her exposed back. She summoned her magic anew and tried to create a protective covering for her body. But mostly she used it to infuse her arms with renewed strength so that she could apply crushing force as she tightened her hold about the creature's neck.

They rolled and twisted about the floor of the bedroom, bumping into the bodies of the dead and covering themselves with blood. Atop the bed, Phaedon Elessedil was screaming, backed up against the headboard, trying to curl himself into an invisible ball.

When the door finally burst open and Elven Home Guards poured through and managed to pry Seersha free, they found that the creature she was locked onto was already dead.

Blankets were brought in which to wrap her, and voices called out to her as they picked her up.

"Hold on. We're getting you help."

"There! Her legs! Keep them steady."

"She's been stabbed in the back, too. Look at the wound!"

"Seersha, can you hear me?"

She was drifting now, far out on the ocean, borne by the waves in a rocking motion that left her warm and sleepy.

"Seersha! Don't go to sleep!"

On the bed, Phaedon was weeping. For himself, she imagined.

"Seersha! Listen to me!"

Listening.

Drifting.

Don't go.

31

VERY LATE THAT SAME RAIN-DRENCHED NIGHT, having spent three days coming down out of the Charnals and crossing the Streleheim west, the *Quickening* at last reached the forests of the Elven Westland. It was never anyone's intention that they make the journey so quickly, but the witch wraith they carried aboard insisted. With little hesitation and in a voice that permitted no argument, she demanded they sail on with no stops. Sleeping and eating would be allowed, but there would be no anchoring the vessel until they had reached their destination.

She was a chilling presence—ragged gray robes and haggard, ruined features, a ghostly creature whether crouching near the forward mast, which had become her favorite haunt, or sliding through the gloom and mist to some position farther astern. Men moved away at her approach, and no one other than Railing bothered to speak to her. Even he had given up after their last conversation, having learned all he cared to about her intentions. There was an inhuman aura to her that matched the story behind her time in thrall to the tanequil. To those around her, it felt as if she had evolved into something no longer even slightly human but more akin to the demonkind they were taking her to face.

Railing thought he understood what Mother Tanequil had decided to do for them. Or to him, when you came right down to it, for he was the one who had brought Grianne Ohmsford back. When he had come to the tanequil's island, crossing the bridge to the song of the aeriads, he had found Grianne a spirit of the air and had hoped she might be set free to aid them. But what had happened instead was that the part of her still in mortal form, the flesh and blood and bone parts that were kept imprisoned in Mother Tanequil's tangled roots down within the earth, was what had been released. Because it wasn't Grianne Ohmsford, the Ard Rhys of the Third Druid Order, that would defeat Tael Riverine. It was Grianne Ohmsford, the Ilse Witch— a monster that could stand up to another monster and find a way to prevail.

What he had not reckoned on and was still uncertain about was what sort of price they were all going to pay for having brought this to pass. There was not even a hint of an intention on her part to do anything that would help him regain his brother or free the Four Lands from the Jarka Ruus. There was no empathy for the fate of the Races. There was only a driving need to confront an enemy that had haunted her for more than a century in her memories and dreams, and to eradicate any trace of him.

Railing couldn't know if she possessed the abilities and skills to bring this about, even though she seemed certain enough. But he did not doubt that she intended to try, or that they were along for the ride and completely superfluous to her ultimate goals. Whatever happened if she prevailed and the Straken Lord was defeated would in no way benefit them.

Which meant that, when all was said and done, he was going to have to find a way to return her to where he had found her.

As they sailed across the Streleheim and down along the eastern edge of the Westland forests toward the Valley of Rhenn, he wondered anew at her immediate plans. She had quit letting them dictate their course once they were out of the Charnals. Responding to something she alone understood, she had given them explicit directions on where they were to go. When Austrum had questioned her—the one such question anyone had dared to ask—she had responded by lifting him off his feet with one withered arm and carrying him to the railing. She had held him over the side as if she intended to drop him, and it was only when Railing shouted at her to stop—telling her that Austrum was their navigator and the captain of their vessel—that she relented, bringing him back on board and tossing him aside as if he were not worth the effort.

So they did her bidding and marked time and tried to keep from losing hope. The atmosphere aboard the ship was tense and despairing. Even Challa Nand, usually so bluff and open, kept to himself and spoke only in short, abrupt sentences when forced to speak at all. No one knew where the ship was going, but they were all reasonably certain it had to do with finding Tael Riverine. Although from the force and insistence of her commands, Railing had the unshakable feeling that Grianne already knew where he was.

Now dawn was less than an hour away, and he was beginning to believe they were flying to Arborlon. What he didn't know was why they would be going there. If she intended to confront Tael Riverine, wouldn't she be flying them into the Forbidding, assuming she could determine a way to pass through its protective wall? That was what he would do.

But then he saw the other possibility, and it turned him to ice. What if the Straken Lord and his creatures had already broken free and set upon Arborlon and its Elves? Wasn't that what had happened before in the time of Wil Ohmsford? Wasn't that the logical course of action where the one sure way to destroy the Forbidding was to destroy the Ellcrys? Aphenglow and Arling-fant had set out in search of the Bloodfire to quicken the Ellcrys seed, but what if they had failed? What if the demons were inside the Four Lands for good?

All of which made him wonder about Redden's fate. If the Straken Lord had come into the Four Lands, what had he done with Redden? Perhaps his brother had been brought along, although he couldn't think of a reason for this. But leaving him behind made no sense, either.

"You seem more distraught than usual," Mirai observed, coming up beside him. "Which is saying something."

"I have good reason," he answered.

Quickly, he explained his fear about what might have happened and why they were heading where he believed they clearly were.

Mirai nodded. "All possible. But we can't do anything about it either way. Not with her watching everything we do." She gestured toward the Ilse Witch, a ragged shape in the predawn gloom. "We have to wait and see."

He followed her gaze. Whatever happened, it was his fault for finding and bringing Grianne Ohmsford back, his obsession with believing she was their only real hope.

"She hates us," he said.

"She hates everyone and everything." Mirai moved over to stand in front of him, blocking his view of the witch. "But regret and guilt are a waste of time. You did what you thought you had to. That's over and done with. We just have to keep our heads once we get to where we're going, because not much of what might happen is likely to turn out the way we hoped."

"I have to find a way to get rid of her," he said quietly.

Mirai shook her head slowly. "Stop thinking like that. Don't take on anything more, Railing. Let this play out however it needs to. But step back from it now. Promise me."

He kissed her instead, not caring who saw. He was past the point of having to pretend. To his surprise, she didn't pull away or cut the kiss short. She kissed him back and held him to her.

By sunrise, they had reached the Valley of Rhenn and were confronted with the terrible truth about how things stood.

In the dark of the night, Redden Ohmsford and his companions, footsore and weary, stumbled through another of the familiar shimmerings that marked a hole in the wall of the Forbidding and found themselves back in the Four Lands, not far from where Drey Wood opened onto the Tirfing. The skies were dark and clouded over, the lands drenched by a recent rain. Redden and Oriantha stood where they were for long moments trying to get their bearings, while Tesla Dart frantically searched for Lada. She scurried left and right, calling his name, whistling and cooing. But the Chzyk had not come through with them.

Finally, the Ulk Bog gave up and wandered back over, her face a mask of sadness. "No Lada. He leaves me. Perhaps he decides this world is not his. I am alone now."

"Alone with us," Oriantha pointed out impatiently. "Which is not quite the same thing as alone altogether."

Tesla Dart nodded, still looking forlorn. "You are friends," she acknowledged, managing to sound doubtful.

"You can go back if you want," the shape-shifter pointed out. "You've done enough. You don't owe us anything more."

The other shook her head. "Stay with you. If you promise you keep me. Not leave me behind."

Redden didn't hear. He was busy surveying what appeared to be a landscape of crop fields dotted with farm buildings. Or at least that was what he could make out in the diminished light. He could not see the horizon in any direction, and even though there were a few lights shining from the windows of the farmhouses, their glow was dim.

"Where are we?" he muttered.

Oriantha moved to stand close. "The Sarandanon, if I'm guessing right."

He looked at her. "How can you tell?"

"I can't, really, for sure. But we were already in the Westland when we reentered the Forbidding. Then we turned north. We traveled a long way, Redden. I think we would be standing in forests if we were anywhere else in the Westland but the valley."

"Do you know which way to go from here to reach Arborlon?"

She cast about for a moment, almost like her animal self would have, head lifted into the soft wind, sniffing the air, tasting it. "That way," she said at last, pointing.

He had no reason to argue with her since he had no idea himself which way to go. He assumed she could tell things from reading the air currents in a way he could not. Since she had been right about most things during their time together, he simply nodded in agreement.

"Speak words to me!" Tesla Dart shouted abruptly as the other two started to turn away. "Not leave me!"

Both Redden and Oriantha stared at the Ulk Bog. "What are you talking about?" Oriantha asked irritably.

"Not do to me what Straken Queen did to Weka. Promises she will take him, then doesn't. Breaks her word. Weka is abandoned and hunted by Straken Lord. Frightened and alone! Has only me, a little girl, to be with. She does this! She leaves him. Weka tells me!"

"Grianne Ohmsford?" Oriantha was having trouble understanding. "Is that who you are talking about?"

"I know the story," Redden interrupted. "Grianne was helped by Weka, so she said she would take him with her when she left. But she couldn't. Penderrin came for her, but the magic he used would only let him take her back with him, not Weka. So she had to leave the Ulk Bog behind. But it wasn't her fault, Tesla. It wasn't what she wanted. Penderrin told my father this. She regretted it deeply, but there was nothing she could do."

The Ulk Bog looked unconvinced. "Hate her for this! Weka never forgot. Betrayed by her! You could do this, too. To me!"

"We already took you out of the Forbidding, didn't we?" Oriantha snapped. "What more are we supposed to do? We brought you with us and we'll keep you with us. We know you helped us like Weka helped Grianne, but we are not like her."

But Tesla shook her head, her jaw set, her eyes fixed on them. "Speak the words. Promise."

Oriantha looked angry, but Redden quickly stepped forward, setting down the box with the Elfstones, and held out his hands, motioning for the Ulk Bog to take them in her own. She did, watching him closely, her grizzled face scrunched up. "I promise we won't leave you," the boy said. "We will keep you with us, no matter what."

Tesla Dart stared at him for long seconds, then she nodded slowly. "I believe. You don't lie."

Redden kept holding the Ulk Bog's gnarled hands. "Tesla, if you felt like this about Grianne, why were you waiting for her all these years? Why were Lada and the other Chzyks keeping watch when we came through the Forbidding?"

"I tell them to." She looked sullen once more. "I stay to watch."

"But why? Why would you do that?"

Tesla Dart's face darkened further. "Because."

"Why, Tesla?" he pressed.

Tears appeared unexpectedly at the corners of the Ulk Bog's dark eyes. "She must say she is sorry! She must tell me so. She must say why she leave Weka behind." She hissed furiously. "If she doesn't, I kill her. Kill her for him!"

There was such fury in her voice that Redden was left speechless. Oriantha, standing to one side, shook her head and turned away.

They set out walking across the broad fields and grasslands, heading in the direction Oriantha had indicated earlier. Redden was still trying to absorb the impact of the Ulk Bog's scorching condemnation of Grianne. He wanted to ask her more, wanted to know how Weka had found her, how long they were together, if she really was his niece, and what had become of him.

But he sensed there was nothing to be gained from this, and after a time he stopped thinking about it and began searching for signs that would tell him they were going the right way. Maybe Oriantha didn't need such signs, but Redden would have preferred to find one or two if only to give him peace of mind about what they were doing.

Because a little reassurance at this point was something he could sorely use.

His recovery from his ordeal as the Straken Lord's prisoner continued to be slow. He was emotionally stronger since putting an end to Tarwick and his hunters. After all, he had escaped being captured and returned to the Straken Lord. He had found and gained possession of the missing Elfstones—something no one else had been able to do. He was free of the Forbidding once more and on his way to Arborlon and a reunion with Railing. He had reason to feel good about all of this.

On the other hand, another encounter with the Straken Lord was not out of the question. Even the thought of it caused a shiver to run up his spine, his memories of his previous imprisonment and the prospect of a repeat experience a nightmare.

Nor was he recovered physically. If anything, he was feeling worse than ever. He was keeping it to himself, but something very troubling had happened to him when he had combined the magic of the crimson Elfstones and the wishsong to destroy the Catcher and his minions. His body had been left hollowed out and his strength diminished in a way that suggested he had suffered at least a part of the fate of the creatures he had emptied of their lives. He knew enough of the ways of magic to understand there was always a price exacted for its use. The more powerful and destructive the magic, the higher the cost.

The crimson Elfstones might have stolen away the mortal substance of their victims, but it felt as if they had stolen some of the same from him, as well.

Still, there was nothing to be done about it. He had saved their lives, and so there could be no regrets now about how he had accomplished it. Nor was there any point in worrying about healing himself until he found Railing again. All he could do was keep going and remember what was at stake.

He clutched the box with the Elfstones to his chest, aware of the irony implicit in doing so. Even though their magic had damaged him, he held on to that box as if he would never let it go. Only the crimson stones were elsewhere, still shoved down inside his pants pocket. He had thought many times to return them to their designated space, but each time he started to do so he changed his mind.

Because beneath his fear of what it meant to use them again was another fear, one that was even more overpowering.

If he did not have them, he could not protect himself or his companions. If he did not have them, they could still all be killed. Or they could be imprisoned, as he had been before. They could be caged and left to die. He would never see his brother or his mother or Mirai or any of his friends again.

He could hardly bear even to think on it.

They walked for hours through the gloom and emptiness, searching for a town or a village where they might find an airship. Walking was too slow and wearing. They were already close to exhaustion. Redden in particular, but even Tesla Dart, who never seemed to tire, was showing signs of weariness. She no longer darted ahead or scurried about like a bug. She mostly stayed next to her companions, her wizened face taut, her eyes searching everywhere at once. In part, Redden thought, it was the effect of the land—an unfamiliar place to which she was not yet accustomed. She was more cautious, less certain of herself, more inclined to hang back and stay watchful.

Oriantha set the pace, the Ulk Bog matched it, and the boy did the best he could to keep up, even when what he wanted most was to sleep.

When they finally stopped to rest, sometime much deeper into the night—the blackness still vast and complete and the countryside still a vague and shadowy place all about them—he felt like he might never be able to rise again.

"You look terrible," Oriantha noted, bending close to study his face.

He shook his head. "I'm fine. Just tired."

"You might be tired, but you are not fine. Something is wrong.

It's using the Elfstones like you did, isn't it? That did something to you."

He nodded, not trusting himself to speak. Tesla Dart moved over as well, looking interested.

"You used them when you shouldn't have," the shape-shifter declared, not accusatorily, but in sympathy. "Only an Elf is supposed to use them, and you are not an Elf. You are of mixed blood, and the magic doesn't work for you like it would for a full-blooded Elf. Am I right?"

"I suppose so. But it's not as if anything can be done about it now. It's over and done with."

"But it hurts?" Tesla asked.

He shook his head. "I don't feel right, but I think it will pass. I just have to give it time."

"Meanwhile," Oriantha said, "give me that."

She took the case with the Elfstones out of his hands before he could think to tighten his grip. "Hey!" he protested.

"I can carry them as easily as you. There is no immediate need for them. You need to conserve your strength. Let me keep the box for now. You can have it back again in Arborlon."

He started to object and then decided against it. What was the point? She was right to think that relieving him of the box would help.

"We should start walking again," Oriantha said abruptly, rising.

They set out once more, Oriantha taking the lead and carrying the case with the Elfstones, Tesla Dart close behind her, and Redden trailing. He thought Oriantha was right, and the effects of using the Elfstone magic were not a consequence of using it with the wishsong, but rather using it at all. He knew from his family's history that only Elves could use Elven magic safely.

History repeating itself, he thought. Lessons learned long ago so often needed to be learned all over again in the present. It might be true here, and he might be the student who was being taught.

But he did not dwell on it, putting the matter aside and thinking instead of Railing and home, of Mirai and Sarys, of better days behind and more ahead. This would be ended soon, the Straken Lord defeated and sent back into the Forbidding, and his old life restored. Things would return to how they had been.

Just so long as he didn't think about those who had died inside the Forbidding.

Or forget that the Druid order was decimated.

Or assume that Railing would be waiting for him, safe and whole.

Oriantha came to a stop, peering ahead. "There are lights less than a mile off. A cluster of them. Maybe we've found the help we need."

And she picked up the pace.

32

RAILING OHMSFORD HOODED THE PARSE TUBES sufficiently to slow the *Quickening* to a crawl as they came out of the darkness into the first light of the new day just north of the entrance to the Valley of Rhenn. Below and as far south as they could see, hordes of creatures were massed across the open grasslands, pressing toward the pass that led into the valley. The size of the Straken Lord's army seemed limitless—a vast sprawling migration that darkened the plains like a tidal wave threatening to inundate the entire Westland.

Everyone aboard—save Railing and Mirai standing in the pilot box, and the Ilse Witch crouched by the foremast—gathered at the ship's railing and stared down at the invading army, trying to make sense of what they were seeing. Austrum and his Rovers, Skint, Challa Nand, and even Woostra—but no one was saying anything. There were no words for something like this.

Mirai, standing close to Railing, whispered, "Shades! How can there be so many?"

He didn't know. Those hundreds of creatures he had fought

against in the Fangs seemed like a mere handful compared with the seething maelstrom roiling below them. What chance did the Elves have of turning back so large a force?

For that matter, what chance did Grianne Ohmsford have, Ilse Witch or not? She was still only one, and they were millions.

"Railing, look!" Mirai said suddenly.

To the east, still far distant, a fleet of airships was approaching. Railing snatched the spyglass from its rack and trained it on the newcomers. There were a handful of fighting vessels, but mostly hundreds of skiffs pulling flatbeds crammed with soldiers.

"Dwarves," he told Mirai. "Come to aid the Elves. But there aren't nearly enough of them—and they're mostly foot soldiers, not fliers. If they land those barges, they will be destroyed before they can even get off the ground again."

"I'd guess they can see that for themselves. But what else can they do? They've come all this way; you don't expect them to turn around and go back again, do you?"

He didn't know what he expected. A miracle, he supposed. Dwarves or no, the army of the Straken Lord was too massive to be stopped. The Elves might hold the passes through the Valley of Rhenn for a while, but in the end they would fall and Arborlon and the entire Westland would fall with them.

The creatures below were milling about but not yet advancing, just growling and shrieking, making aggressive gestures and sudden rushes that ended after only a few yards. They were working themselves up, readying for the coming battle. Railing brought the spyglass up again and swept the rim of the mountain walls warding the valley. He saw Elven Hunters everywhere, but no sign of Seersha or Crace Coram. He wondered if perhaps they were responsible for the Dwarves' appearance and were aboard the skiffs, but that didn't seem right.

"What are we going to do?" Mirai demanded. "We can't just watch this happen. We have to do something!"

As she said it, a handful of winged creatures—Harpies and huge vampire bats—lifted off the ground and came at them. They were agile and swift as they closed on the *Quickening*. The men at the railing backed away, realizing the danger. Weapons appeared. A couple of the Rovers rushed to the rail slings and swung them about protectively.

But before the winged attackers could reach the airship, the witch wraith rose from her crouch and walked to the railing, ragged clothing flying in the wind, dark visage gone almost black. For just a second it seemed to Railing, watching from the pilot box, as if she weren't there at all. As if all that inhabited the inside of her tattered clothing was a shadow.

The Harpies and bats must have seen something of it, too, and they didn't like it one bit. As if formed of a single creature, they broke off their attack and swung away abruptly, gathering speed as they went.

The witch wraith turned to him. "Fly to the mouth of the pass!"

He did so without hesitating. Whatever was going to happen now was not something he cared to interfere with. They were here at the witch's behest; she must have known she would find the Straken Lord's army attacking the Westland or she wouldn't have bothered. How she had known he had no idea. But now that they were here, it stood to reason that she intended to face her nemesis—perhaps to do what she had been asked, or perhaps to do something else altogether.

The witch stood where she was, staring down at the army beneath them as they neared the pass. She didn't speak or move; she gave no indication of what she was thinking. They might have been invisible for all the interest she evidenced. Railing thought it better that way. The less attention she paid to them, the better.

They were closing on the pass when the dragon flew out of the east.

Redden and his companions reached Arborlon before dawn, flying in from the Elven Hunter outpost they had stumbled on several hours earlier, aboard an ancient transport they had persuaded the garrison to put at their disposal. It wasn't so much what they were asking as the force with which they asked it. Redden in particular had invoked both Aphenglow and her grandfather as friends and protectors. Mention of the latter immediately led to the revelation that the old King was dead, assassinated by his brother, and that the city was preparing for war. But the Hunters agreed it was a good idea that the strange trio proceed to their destination so they could give their report to someone who might act on it—especially after the young girl had begun to cry uncontrollably.

Oriantha, it turned out, could shape-shift in more than one way when the need was present.

But when they arrived in Arborlon, they found the city in chaos, with rumors of another attack on the royal family, this time on the King's son; of several others killed in the attack, including the Captain of the Home Guard, Sian Aresh; and of a demon army massed at the passes east in the Valley of Rhenn where a terrible battle had been fought the previous day and was expected to continue at sunrise.

The tension and fear they encountered were palpable, and there was a strong sense of panic setting in. It was impossible to get an accurate story from anyone, especially since Tesla's appearance seemed to scare them away. Not able to find anyone they knew personally or to learn what was happening from those they didn't, they decided to fly to the site of the pending battle, reasoning that wherever there was fighting they were likely to find one or more of their friends.

So Redden and Oriantha boarded their transport once more, hauling a decidedly uncertain and fearful Ulk Bog with them, and flew out toward the Rhenn as the sky ahead slowly began to lighten.

"Did you hear the woman who claimed there was a Druid involved in last night's attack?" Redden asked Oriantha over the rush of the wind in the open cockpit.

"I heard there was and that she might have been killed. I also heard it was only Aresh. I heard lots of things. Did you learn anything useful?"

Redden shook his head. "What are we going to do once we get to the passes?"

Oriantha shrugged. "Look around?"

She was weighing her options, he imagined. His own were troubling. If Railing wasn't in the Rhenn, did he join in the fighting anyway to help the Elves? Or did he continue looking for his brother? Where were Seersha and Crace Coram while all this was happening? Where were Skint and the Rovers? Oriantha knew no one except Coram, who had been part of their group when she had left him at the portal leading out of the Forbidding but of whom she had heard nothing since.

Still, someone had to know something about what had become of the other members of the expedition.

They flew on, their uneasiness increasing the closer they got to their destination. All Redden could think about was what waited there—Tael Riverine and the entire demon army. He could not stop imagining what it would feel like to be back in their hands—a very real possibility if he were forced into a fight against them. His insides recoiled at the prospect, and if it hadn't

been for his even more pressing fears about his brother, he
would have turned around on the spot.

I don't have to be a part of this fight, he kept telling himself. *I
don't have to do anything I don't want to. I just need to find Railing.
I just need to make sure my brother is safe.*

But he knew this wasn't so. He was an irrevocable part of
what was happening and had been from the moment he had left
in search of the missing Elfstones. He was even more committed
now that he had found the Stones and knew they might make a
difference in any struggle with the Jarka Ruus. He could tell
himself anything he wanted, but the path his feet were set upon
would take him in only one direction.

At one point, Tesla Dart wormed her way forward and
pressed up against him. "You don't forget your promise to me?"
she asked, bending close.

He glanced over at her worried face. "I will keep my promise,"
he said.

He would try to keep all his promises, he thought, even the
ones he had made to himself and was afraid he could not face.

Time passed. The sun crested the horizon, a blazing light
shining out on a bright clear day. Ahead, the passes loomed dark
and shadowy in the lee of the Rhenn's forested walls.

They flew straight across the near pass and continued on
toward the far. No one tried to stop them; apparently, no one
thought it worth the effort since they were flying such a harmless,
decrepit vessel. There was no battle yet, it seemed. There were no
sounds of it or activity atop the valley rim. If anything, it was
unusually quiet.

"What's happening?" Redden asked over his shoulder, but
Oriantha only shook her head and moved closer to where he sat,
peering ahead with him to see what waited.

They had just reached the opening through the second pass

when they heard a thunderous roar rise from the creatures massed without.

The witch wraith half turned toward the monstrous dragon when it appeared, facing it with no indication of concern.

"Take me down," she called over her shoulder to Railing. "Land at the mouth of the pass. Not inside. Out in front, where all those gathered can see."

Railing did as she ordered. He banked the *Quickening* a quarter turn and began dropping it earthward. His heart was racing, anticipating what was going to happen next. Clearly, the witch intended to let the Straken Lord know she was there. What more she would do remained to be seen.

Challa Nand moved away from the rail where he had been watching the army of the Jarka Ruus and stepped closer to the pilot box.

"Once we are down and she leaves to do what she thinks she must, we are getting off this vessel," he said quietly. He glanced in her direction, but her attention was fixed on the dragon. "We'll make a run for the pass and get inside, where the Elves can offer us protection. We don't wait. We don't hesitate. We don't stop."

Railing glanced at Mirai, and they both nodded. Challa Nand nodded back and moved away.

As the *Quickening* descended, Railing hunched his shoulders against a sudden chill and took a surprised look around. Something odd was happening. The temperature, until now warm and pleasant, had suddenly gone as cold as deepest winter. There was no reason for it, no apparent cause, but the change was unmistakable. He glanced over at Mirai and saw that she was tightening her cloak about her shoulders.

On the decks of the sailing vessel, frost was forming.

They landed directly in front of the pass leading into the Valley of Rhenn, placing themselves between the Elven defenders and the Jarka Ruus. He could feel a million eyes watching, all fixed on the airship, but no one came toward it. By now the Quickening was coated with frost from bow to stern, from its decks to the tips of its masts, turned as white as a ghost ship.

The Ilse Witch had changed, too. She had gone from a tattered gray shade to a ghostly white.

Then, abruptly, she began to move. She seemed to float across the main deck to the rail. Before her, the gate leading off the ship unlatched of its own accord, and she passed through the opening without slowing. She was twenty feet off the ground, but she stood in midair and then slowly descended to the plains below. She did not speak to Railing and the others. She did not even look at them.

"Railing!" Mirai hissed, shock reflected in her voice as she pointed.

The witch, having reached the ground, was walking directly toward the army of the Straken Lord. As she did so, she left foot-prints coated with frost in the grass.

Challa Nand wasted no time. With Austrum beside him, he anchored the ship and threw out the rope ladder. Hurrying from one crewmember to the next, he ordered them off the ship. The Rovers went first, then Woostra, then Skint; finally the Troll lifted Mirai bodily from the pilot box and beckoned Railing after them. Down the ladder they all went, trying to move silently, casting anxious glances at the spectral figure still moving away from them and at the skies where the dragon continued to circle.

On the ground, Railing turned toward the valley pass. Austrum and the other Rovers were already rushing for safety.

Skint and Woostra were only a few yards behind. Challa Nand tried to take Mirai's arm, but she shrugged him off, making it clear that she could manage on her own. Railing, a few steps back, saw the big man glance at the Highland girl, shake his head in surprise, and hurry on.

That was when the boy turned back, unable to resist the urge to know what would happen.

A short distance away, just beyond the *Quickening*, Grianne Ohmsford's grim reincarnation was confronting the hordes from the Forbidding. The creatures were massed before her, thousands strong, all of them staring with wonder and uneasiness at this strange being, their eyes shifting back and forth from her to the Elves to the dragon circling overhead. Their growls and snarls and hisses were muted almost to silence. Some had moved back warily.

The witch wraith was not moving at all.

Railing could hear the calls of his companions, urging him to get away. But he stayed where he was. His mind was made up. He would see for himself what he had brought about by trying to bring back Grianne Ohmsford. He would not run and hide.

Seconds later Mirai was at his elbow. "Get out of here," he said.

She dismissed the suggestion with a shake of her head. "Don't be ridiculous. What's she doing?"

Stubborn to the end, he thought. "Waiting, I think."

So it seemed. With foreknowledge of what was fated to happen, perhaps. He could feel it in his bones.

In moments the Straken Lord descended astride his dragon. The great beast seemed even larger from this new perspective, coming down like a mountainside and landing with an impact that shook the ground and reverberated across the grasslands. Its face was ruined on one side, its eye gone and the pit ragged and raw. Steam leaked from its nostrils and maw, huffing out with each breath—an indication of the intensity of the fire that burned in its inner furnace.

But it was the Straken Lord that riveted Railing Ohmsford. The boy had never seen anything like him. He was huge, even when compared with the Trolls with whom he had spent time on their quest for the missing Elfstones. As black as coal, with spikes sticking out all over his powerful body, he had the look of something conjured in a nightmare and brought to life. He was holding a huge black scepter, and his eyes were fixed on the witch wraith.

Railing could hear the calls of his companions, frantic now, warning both Mirai and himself to run, but he paid them no attention. Instead, he moved forward, skirting the hull of the airship so that he had a clear view of both the dragon and the witch. He watched as Tael Riverine slid down the dragon's scaly hide to a carefully lifted foreleg that waited to lower him to the ground and advanced on the witch.

"I sense your presence!" he roared. "My Queen-to-be, my promised gift! Where are you?"

"I stand before you, Tael Riverine," the ghost-white witch replied, her voice ringing out.

The Straken Lord stopped where he was, staring. "Do not lie to me, crone. Reveal her!"

"No one lies to you. No one trifles with your foolish dreams. This is what you wished for. Now you have your wish. What will you do with me?"

"You are not her! What sort of game is this? I feel her to be close! You hide her somewhere!"

The anger he was experiencing was evident in his voice, raw and edged with bitterness. He was advancing again, drawing nearer to her. Railing thought that if she spoke again with words that displeased him, he would use his iron staff to smash her into the earth.

But the witch seemed unperturbed, still standing in place, calmly watching him draw near.

"Long ago, you took me prisoner and collared me like an animal," she hissed at him. "You tried to discover the extent of my powers. You tried to make me your Queen so that I would bear your children. You failed. I escaped. I returned to my own world and found a place in it where I could forget you and your dark plans. But even though decades have passed and things you cannot begin to comprehend have changed, you still cling to your foolish dream. You still think to make me yours."

She gestured expansively, arms flinging wide, particles of frost and ice flying into the air about her like a miniature storm. "Well, Tael Riverine, here I am. Don't you want me?"

"You are not Grianne Ohmsford!" The other screamed it as if it were a personal affront planned to thwart his purposes and deprive him of his due.

Behind him, the dragon stamped the earth and breathed fire onto the grasslands, setting patches of vegetation aflame. The Jarka Ruus surged backward in response, stumbling over one another in an effort to remain safely clear. Smoke from the dragon fire rolled across the plains in black clouds.

"Well, in that you are both right and wrong," replied the witch. "I am here and I am not here. The truth is beyond you, and my patience with this business is at an end. Since you do not wish for me after all, I can admit that I want nothing of you, either. But one of us must give way and I think it must be you. What I want matters most."

Was he seeing things, Railing wondered, or was the witch wraith growing larger? "We should go," Mirai whispered in his ear, taking hold of his arm and pulling on it.

"You beg for your life, do you?" Tael Riverine stood rock-still not six yards away from her.

The witch laughed. "I *beg* for nothing. What I need, I will take. And what I will take is your place as ruler of the Jarka Ruus."

For a long few seconds, the Straken Lord stared at the apparition, attempting in vain to take her measure. In the vast sweep of the plains, where even an army of hundreds of thousands could not manage to fill the emptiness, Tael Riverine might have recognized the danger. But the demon's life had been long and hard and filled with other dangers, and his pride convinced him that this was just one more.

"It is you, isn't it?" he said at last. He bent forward to peer closely at her. "You've become a hag, a gathering of cloth and smoke, a bit of nothing. You are Grianne, but changed into this ... thing. Once, I would have made you my Queen. Now you are not worthy."

They faced each other in silence, and it seemed to Railing that each was waiting on a response from the other. He couldn't have said which of them was the true aggressor and which the intended victim at this point. Perhaps they were both looking to discover this, both deciding what more was to be done.

But it was Tael Riverine who attacked, leaping at the witch with his iron staff raised, swinging for her head. He was quick for such a big man, much quicker than Railing would have thought possible, and for just an instant the boy thought she had simply disintegrated under the blow. But then he realized she wasn't even there anymore. Instead, she had appeared off to one side.

He struck at her a second time, now using the magic of the scepter, fire lancing from its intricately shaped iron head, burning through the witch and turning her to ash and smoke, but again she wasn't there. When the fire diminished and the smoke cleared, the witch was standing off to the other side, her white, ragged form untouched.

The Straken Lord nodded to himself and went into a crouch. "If you refuse to let me come to you, Grianne-that-once-was, then why don't you come to me?"

His spines lifted off his back and down the sides of his arms and legs, and he gestured for the witch to approach. Railing felt Mirai pulling on him, urging him to back away. He shook his head. He was not ready to go. He was not willing to miss any of this.

In front of them, not thirty yards away, the witch wraith was moving. It was a slight shifting of position, one that caused the Straken Lord to go still in expectation. Railing had no idea what she was doing. She had avoided Tael Riverine's attacks twice now, seeming to be one place while actually in another. But she hadn't fought back. She hadn't shown any intention of doing so.

Until now.

Casually, with a movement so languid and relaxed it appeared to offer no threat at all, she advanced on him.

It seemed suicidal. She was making no move to attack and was doing nothing to defend herself. She had assumed a submissive posture, hunched a bit, head down. It was as if she were conceding his dominance and had decided there was no point in prolonging the inevitable.

The Straken Lord's hand dropped to his side, and when it lifted again he was holding a conjure collar. He meant to bind her to him by means of complete and deliberate subjugation. Apparently he had abandoned his plan to disable or kill her and was now seeking domination, perhaps to demonstrate his superiority to his followers or perhaps to reaffirm it to Grianne Ohmsford, whatever incarnation she had assumed.

When she was within several yards of him, the witch wraith dropped to her knees and began to crawl forward, a penitent ghost begging for mercy. Railing knew all the stories of her imprisonment by Tael Riverine and her fierce hatred of him and could not believe what he was seeing.

"What is she doing?" Mirai gasped.

Railing had no idea, but he felt the last of his hope slipping away as the witch continued to crawl to her doom.

When she was right in front of the Straken Lord, she lifted herself onto her haunches, head still lowered in a posture of subjection. The Straken Lord bent down, holding out the conjure collar to fasten it around her neck.

"Perhaps you are her," Tael Riverine mused, surprise and disgust reflected in his voice.

But an instant later she had snatched the collar from his hands and snapped it around his own neck. He jerked backward in shock and dismay, but it was too late. Railing and Mirai, who were the closest, barely saw the movement of her hands; her quickness and strength left them blinking in disbelief.

The witch rose and stood with her face so near to his, it seemed she might offer him a kiss. "Am I close enough now?" she asked. She laughed softly. "You will do nothing without my permission, Tael Riverine. Do you understand? You belong to me now, as I once belonged to you."

He struggled anyway, thrashing to reach her. But the collar reacted instantly and the Straken Lord cried out in anguish, dropping to his knees.

She stood over him a moment as his body convulsed and his face twisted, and then she reached down for his scepter, retrieving it from where it had fallen. She studied it a moment, as if considering its use. Then she turned toward the Jarka Ruus, scepter in hand, and held it overhead for all to see.

A babble of murmurs and hisses filled the momentary silence as the creatures of Tael Riverine's army gave voice to what they were feeling. Uncertainty and fear turned to amazement and the beginnings of a shift in loyalty. The Straken Lord had ruled through strength; that was the law of the Forbidding. But now someone stronger had subdued him with almost no effort at all.

Abruptly, Railing Ohmsford remembered something Crace Coram had said many weeks ago, after Seersha had rebuked him for calling Grianne Ohmsford the Ilse Witch.

"That's who she still is somewhere deep down inside. Maybe that's who you want to find if you expect her to stand up to the Straken Lord."

The murmurs and hisses grew to a steady roar.

With that, the witch turned back toward the pain-racked Straken Lord and struck him with the butt of the scepter. Tael Riverine collapsed, dazed from the blow. Recognizing his peril, he fought anew to break free of the conjure collar, struggling violently against the witch wraith's magic, his entire body quaking and shuddering. But even the howls that rose from his throat came out as little more than subdued gasps.

The witch wraith stood over him, raised his steel-tipped scepter over her head, and brought it down with a lunge. The steel tip penetrated Tael Riverine's black armor and then his body, driven all the way through and into the ground. The scream the Straken Lord emitted was blood chilling, but reached new heights when the witch pulled the shaft free and then drove it through him once more.

He fought only a few seconds longer and then lay still on the blood-soaked grass.

Another roar rose from the Jarka Ruus. The roar was of satisfaction, of recognition that an old order had passed and a new one had risen. Strength had prevailed over weakness, and once again there was a new leader.

Railing was rooted in place, unable to look away even though Mirai was yanking on his arm and shouting in his ear. "Turn around!" she screamed.

Finally, he did so, and for a moment he could not catch his breath.

His brother was standing right in front of him.

33

EDINJA'S CONFISCATED SPRINT WAS ALMOST TO Arborlon, the roofs of the city's buildings coming into view through the treetops, when a sickening realization of what was about to happen struck Aphenglow with dismaying suddenness. Her time with Arlingfant was almost over. She was about to lose her sister forever.

Since her breakdown over Cymrian's death, Aphen had traveled all day and all night trying to make up for her lapse, flying straight through from the Wilderun with brief stops for food and drink and occasional snatches of sleep when she could no longer keep her eyes open anymore. She had found it necessary to change out the diapson crystals that powered their craft only once, even with the thrusters opened all the way. And aware of the dangers posed by the Straken Lord's army to the east, she had kept them well clear of the Tirfing and the Streleheim, coming up west of the Matted Brakes and Drey Wood to cross the Rill Song just below the Sarandanon in order to reach the Elven home city safely.

Still, it was a grueling journey, with no one but herself to depend on. Arling had slept most of the way. Weakened by her wounds and all she had been through while bearing the Ellcrys seed to the Bloodfire, she had barely spoken since their departure. For the past several hours, she had been asleep in the seat just behind Aphen, bent forward in her harness with her head resting against her sister's back. Aphen had tried hard not to disturb her, wanting to leave her as she was, to feel Arling pressing up against her. There was an undeniable comfort in keeping her close for the time that remained to them.

The loss of Cymrian had stripped Aphen of strength and courage both, undermined her sense of hope, and left her emotionally drained. She had never thought she would lose the Elven Hunter, her companion through so much. She had only just come to understand how much he meant to her, and now—in what seemed the blink of an eye—he was gone. She could still picture him alive and well, his wild white hair blowing, his striking blue eyes fixed on her, the angles and planes of his strong face shaped by the sunlight, just his presence a powerful reassurance.

All of it was more compelling than it had ever been with Bombax, and yet her relationship with Cymrian had been so abbreviated, ending so abruptly. She had cried for him until it felt as if there were no tears left. His death had dominated her thoughts from the moment she had begun flying Arling back to Arborlon, which was why now, as they approached the Elven city, she found herself confronted for the first time with the inescapable knowledge that the worst wasn't over.

Arling, possessed of the Bloodfire-quickened seed of the Ellcrys, was about to be taken from her. And she would be left with a future in which the two people she loved the most would have no part.

It was all she could do to keep her hands steady on the

Sprint's controls. A part of her thought simply to turn the ship around and fly another way—even as she knew this could never happen. Even aware of how impossible such a thing was.

She was suddenly awash in despair. The unfairness of what was happening was inescapable. She had gone through so much, endured so many losses and disappointments, seen so many companions die, and found so many bitter truths along the way that she could not face her situation with anything resembling grace. She should be stronger; she should be so for herself and her sister both. But all she wanted to do was to scream out the rage and hurt she was feeling.

Which was selfish, and she knew it. But even knowing she should be thinking of Arling was not enough to leaven the pity she felt for herself.

Farther ahead, visible now through the darkness, the new day was beginning to brighten the eastern sky. Were they in time? Was the old tree gone by now and the Forbidding collapsed completely? She knew that the demonkind army would be on the move again; Arishaig would have fallen and its citizens would have been destroyed or driven out. Some would survive, but many would not. That was the fate that awaited Arborlon and the Elves, too, and she had no way of knowing how much time remained before it found them.

All too soon, she thought.

Bile rose in her throat, and she forced it down. She banked the Sprint toward the treetops and in the general direction of the Gardens of Life. Her hands moved mechanically even as her brain shut down and fresh tears filled her eyes.

"Little girl," she called over her shoulder to Arling. She felt her sister lift her head. "We're almost there."

At first, there was no response. Then, clear and steady, came Arling's voice. "I'm ready, Aphen."

The words broke Aphenglow's heart, but she managed to keep it from showing. "Do you have the seed ready?"

In truth, she had not seen it since Arling had emerged from the cavern that contained the Bloodfire. She still didn't have the faintest idea what was to be done with the seed once they were on the ground and in the presence of the Ellcrys. There had been no explanation in any of the tomes she had studied or recitations she had uncovered. Arling had not said one word about what she knew. She had barely referred to her most precious possession. There was a black hole in Aphen's understanding of what was to happen next, and she felt a wrenching need to know.

"What will you do when we land?" she asked her sister.

A long silence. "Go to her."

The tree. "You will give her the seed?" Aphen pressed.

"In a manner of speaking."

"But you do have it? You brought it out from the cavern, didn't you? You can pass the seed on?"

"Aphen," Arling whispered, leaning forward again, her lips close to her sister's ear. "There will be no passing. The Ellcrys seed is inside me. The Bloodfire put it there. It is a part of me now."

Aphen squeezed her eyes shut, knowing at once what that meant. Tears leaked from her eyes, but she managed to cry silently, keeping her body still. "I will be there with you all the way," she whispered back.

Arling's voice grew softer still. "I would like that."

They descended into Arborlon, Aphen reading the terrain, seeking their destination. She found the gardens easily enough— a part of the Carolan Heights, far west at the edge of the city overlooking the Rill Song. She chose a place where the bluff was grassy and open and landed the Sprint on its billowing softness, using wind and sails to ease her into place before cutting power to the parse tubes and locking down the thrusters.

Elven Hunters placed on sentry duty swarmed the craft, but when they saw the sisters emerge, clinging to each other as if a strong wind might blow them apart, they didn't seem to know what to do. They stared at the Elessedil women and at one another as they waited to discover what was happening.

"Stand away, please," Aphen demanded, determined to care for Arling by herself. "Go back to your watch."

She helped Arling cross the Carolan to the Gardens of Life, pointing them toward a gap in the bordering hedgerow that sheltered against the strong west winds. Once inside, they made their way through the flower beds and bushes to where the Ellcrys stood on a rise near the gardens' center. The gardens were shadowed, the new day coming awake with the sunrise, and Aphen let Arling set her own pace. Her sister was unsteady on her feet; the unexpected strength she had found after emerging from the Bloodfire cavern had faded.

At one point, she stumbled and nearly fell. Aphen only just managed to catch her. "You will stay close to me, won't you?" Arling asked, lifting her face momentarily, her strange red eyes blinking rapidly.

"All the way," Aphen whispered back, repeating her earlier promise. "Do you need to rest?"

Arling's trademark smile was quick and rueful. "Lots of time for that later, Aphen."

When they reached the gardens, they found the other Chosen gathered, but it was hard to tell for certain if they had just arrived or had perhaps been there all night. They ringed the tree, preparing for the morning greeting. It was clear they had done what they could, but none of their efforts seemed to have been even the least bit effective. The Ellcrys was a skeleton by now, a shadow of what she had been. Emaciated, withered, her bark turned crusty and her scarlet leaves black, she was in the final stages of her life. In the retreating darkness, lit only by the first rays of the rising sun, she seemed diminished to the point of nonexistence.

Freershan and the others saw the sisters approach and, after a moment of shock, leapt to their feet and came running. They gathered around, all talking at once, trying to find out where Arling had been and what had happened to her. But Arling said nothing. She didn't even look at them, her head lowered and her scarlet eyes closed.

"She can't speak with you now," Aphen said quickly, realizing her sister lacked the strength and perhaps the desire to communicate with others. "Please move back. Let us go ahead alone. We are here to help the tree."

She badly wanted to ask about her grandfather, about the city and its danger, about a dozen other concerns that crowded to the forefront of her mind. But she knew that any discussions would only slow them further. And in point of fact, what difference did it make? All that mattered now was restoring the tree.

Rebuilding the Forbidding and hastening Arling toward the end of her human life.

The words burned in her mind like live coals, but she endured them, facing the truth about what she was doing. There was no point in turning away. That would be disrespectful and cowardly, and a clear attempt to repudiate her sister's decision.

The Chosen fell away, and she moved Arling ahead again, advancing on the skeletal form of the Ellcrys. The sun was cresting the horizon, its brilliant light splashing across the sky, penetrating the shadows and layering the tree in golden streaks. But the effect simply revealed even more of her damage.

When they reached the base of the rise, Arling stopped. "I must go alone from here, Aphen."

"I can help you a little farther ..." Aphen started to say, but stopped when she felt Arling's fingers dig into her arm.

"No. You must wait here." Her sister's head lifted, and the scarlet orbs of her eyes stared out from her stricken face. "I love you, Aphen. I always will, wherever I am, whatever happens to me."

Aphen tried to speak and couldn't. Instead, she wrapped her arms about Arling and held her close.

Her sister was crying now. "I wish we had more time. I wanted so much to be with you in Paranor. To be Druids together, you and I. I wanted nothing more than to be like you."

"No." Aphen shook her head, still holding her sister tight. "You were always better than me. Always."

"Tell Mother, Aphen. Try to be there for her when she finds out. Be kind to her, no matter ..."

She trailed off uncertainly. "I will," Aphen promised.

They held on, unable to let go, unwilling to break the connection. Seconds slipped by, and Aphenglow felt the hurt of what was about to happen so badly it was physically painful. Even without knowing the details, even as uncertain as she was about what she would witness, she could hardly bear it.

"Come see me often?" Arling whispered, making it a question.

"Yes," Aphen answered, and broke down completely, crying openly.

Arling hugged her once more and then pushed her away. She stumbled up the rise, a frail figure in the growing light of the sunrise, making her uncertain way toward the Ellcrys. Aphen watched helplessly, longing to go after her sister. But she did as she was told and remained where Arling had left her, watching and waiting.

At the crest of the rise, Arling paused for a moment, staring at the desiccated tree. Then she moved closer, reaching out her hand and touching the blackened trunk. The Ellcrys shivered, more dead leaves falling away, more bark sloughing off. But it seemed to Aphen the tree was responding, recognizing who Arling was and what it meant to have her there.

Arling held her ground for a long moment, then moved close to the Ellcrys and wrapped her arms around her, leaning in.

A second later, the tree disintegrated completely, turning into a fine dust that showered down on Arling until she was completely covered.

Arling stood where she was for another few seconds, becoming a gray ghost, before lifting her arms skyward and uttering a long, mournful cry.

Then she began to change.

On the blood-soaked plains fronting the entrance to the Valley of Rhenn, the brothers Ohmsford stood face-to-face. It was, for Railing, the culmination of everything he had hoped to accomplish since the onset of his long, disappointing search for Grianne Ohmsford, begun all those weeks ago. Finding and returning his brother had been the driving force behind his efforts, and he had never stopped believing—even in his darkest, most despairing moments—that he would make that happen. But to have it come to pass so abruptly, with no warning whatsoever, was shocking.

His brother managed a crooked grin. "Thought you'd seen the last of me, didn't you?"

Even given the cacophony rising from the Jarka Ruus as they celebrated their new leader's victory, Redden's words were clear. The sound of his voice broke the spell that had frozen Railing in place, and he flung his arms about his brother, hugging him so hard he had to let go almost immediately and step back for fear he might be injuring him. For Redden Ohmsford was but a shadow of his former self, with haunted eyes and a troubled look on his face. His face and arms were battered and bruised, his body was emaciated, and he was hunched over as if bearing an unseen weight. The strength he had exhibited when they had parted was gone entirely, and what remained was a poorly sketched representation.

Railing kept his hands on his brother's shoulders, refusing to break contact. "I thought *I* would be the one to find *you*."

Redden looked down, tears in his eyes. "I couldn't wait any longer for that to happen. So here I am."

He had flown with Oriantha and Tesla Dart from Arborlon to the Valley of Rhenn, Redden explained, arriving just as the battle between the Straken Lord and the witch wraith was reaching its conclusion. Still at the controls of the transport, he was trying to decide where to land when he caught sight of the combatants and the dragon where they occupied the open ground between the Jarka Ruus and the Elves. An instant later he noticed two figures standing close by and recognized his brother and Mirai. With no hesitation at all, even when Oriantha began screaming in his ear to turn around, he piloted his ancient vessel over the cliffs warding the entrance to the pass and down onto the flats. Neither Railing nor Mirai had noticed him land, their eyes directed toward the epic struggle between the demon and the wraith.

He was on the ground and out of the pilot box before the diapson crystals had cooled. He caught a glimpse of Tesla Dart's horrified face and Oriantha's catlike leap over the ship's side as she came in pursuit while he raced across the trampled ground to reach his brother, but he never slowed.

"I found them, Railing," he shouted now over the din of the

demonkind's wild, mindless cries, suddenly remembering. "I found the missing Elfstones!"

Railing stared. "How did you manage that? How did you even get back here? I thought you were trapped inside the Forbidding!"

Redden glanced over his shoulder as Oriantha came pounding up behind him, her face a mask of fury. "How could you be so stupid? There's an entire army right in front of you! Are you trying to kill yourself? Get out of here!"

"Look!" Redden persisted, ignoring her, motioning her closer. "She has them. Oriantha does. Except for one set. Show the Stones to Railing."

But the shape-shifter's hands were empty. "I gave them to Tesla Dart to hold while I came after you." She pointed over his shoulder. "And forget what I just said about getting out of here. It's too late to run."

They looked toward the Jarka Ruus. The witch wraith was approaching. The crystalline white frost that had covered her earlier was gone, and she was once again a slight figure dressed in ragged gray and bent against the morning light as if it hurt to be exposed to it. She showed no interest in what was left of the Straken Lord as she passed his remains, and no concern for the dragon crouched at her back.

Instead, her eyes were on Railing and his brother.

"Get behind me," Railing told Mirai and gently eased her back.

"What's this about?" Redden asked, stepping up to take her place.

Railing didn't know where to start. "I tried to bring back Grianne Ohmsford to help us against the Straken Lord. But she returned like this, and now she's killed him and has taken his place as leader of the Jarka Ruus."

Redden looked confused, as if he was hearing the words but not understanding their meaning. Railing had already turned away to face the witch. There was no time for anything now but finding a way to send her back to where she had come from, and he hadn't the faintest idea how to do that.

"You've found your brother without my help!" the witch wraith called out to him, slowing while still twenty feet away. Her body seemed to shift and change inside her robes, as if she were not entirely solid.

"You have to go back," Railing replied. "You have to return to Mother Tanequil. I will go with you."

"Will you now?" she said. She pointed to the multitudes assembled behind her—a casual gesture. "What do you think they will say to that?" She seemed genuinely interested. "They might not like the idea!"

"It doesn't matter. You can do whatever you want! You've freed them from Tael Riverine. They won't challenge you now."

She came closer, and he could hear Mirai hissing at him in warning. "We have to go! Now!"

But Railing only moved ahead a few more steps, bringing him within ten feet of the witch. He was scared out of his wits by the prospect of what this creature could do to them—what she might at any moment choose to do. But he was still hoping he could reason with her.

"What will you do with me once we've returned to Mother Tanequil?" she wanted to know.

"Whatever I must to get you back to what you were. I promise."

"What are you talking about?" Redden hissed, still at his elbow.

There was a long silence as the witch considered. "I think maybe you would try to do as you say," she said finally. "The problem is that I don't want you to. I don't want to go back to being what I was. All I want is what awaits me here." She gestured behind her to the dragon and the Jarka Ruus. "I want what they want."

Railing felt his heart sink. In the dual life of Grianne Ohmsford, the part that was the Ilse Witch had won and the part that was the Ard Rhys had lost. She no longer felt the urge to go back to being an aeriad. She no longer wanted that life, the one he had dragged her away from in order to bring her here.

It was his fault, he knew. All his.

"So you see the problem," she continued, "because you won't let that happen, and neither will your brother. Will you?"

"We're your family!" Railing reminded her frantically.

Within the shadows of the cloak's cowl, her head gave a small shake. "No, boy, you are not. I have no family."

The Ilse Witch struck out at Railing without warning and without preamble—a fiery strike exploding from a withered limb that she thrust out from her gray robes like a snake. But Redden was quicker. Sensing what was about to happen, acting on his instincts, he flung himself at Railing an instant before the fire was expelled and sent them both tumbling to the ground. Rolling clear of his brother, Railing responded by using the wishsong to fling dagger-sharp particles of rock at the ragged figure before them. The pieces tore into her, shredding her coverings, riddling her through and through.

But still she stood upright, seemingly unaffected, conjuring a torrential gust of wind that picked up both Redden and Railing and threw them backward into Mirai, sending all three crashing to the ground. Redden was stunned, but Railing, quickly rising to a guarded crouch, tried a fresh tactic, using his wishsong to damage her senses, clogging her mouth and nose with dirt, hammering at her ears with shrieking sounds and blinding her with the sun's own brightness. He went after her relentlessly, holding nothing back, striking out at her with everything he had because he knew he was unlikely to get a second chance.

For a moment, it looked like he might succeed. Grianne went stumbling away, trying to fend off the unexpected attack. Unable to clear her vision or her hearing, she began choking and gasping. Railing pressed his advantage, using the wishsong to summon roots that wrapped themselves about her like shackles and pulled her down.

But she fought back against what was being done to her. An explosion of light ripped through the air and ended with a concussive boom like thunder following a lightning strike. Railing was flattened instantly, his magic dispersed and his consciousness gone. He lay sprawled on the earth, steam rising from his inert form.

Oriantha attacked the moment Railing went down, coming at the witch from her blind side, moving so fast she was little more than a blur. But the witch saw her anyway, caught her in midair, and threw her away like a scrap of paper. The shape-shifter landed in a heap and didn't move again.

Mirai was kneeling over Railing as the witch turned on her. "Why don't you join him?" Grianne asked almost gently, arms extending. "You love him, don't you? So why don't you die, too?"

The Highland girl reached for Railing and tried to pull him away, but he was too heavy, so she grabbed on to him and shielded him protectively. "Get away!" she screamed.

It would have been the end of all of them if not for Redden. Still shaken from the blow the witch had given him, he struggled to his feet, clutching the red Elfstones. He ignored the dark flicker of recognition, warning him of what he was about to risk—of the danger and the likely cost. The threat from the witch was immediate and he had no time to think, only to act.

Combining both forms of magic in the same way he had when facing Tarwick and his hunters in the underground caverns of the Kroat Abyss, he struck out. A brilliant stream of red fire burst from his clenched hands and washed over the witch until she was encapsulated. She fought to break the magic's casing, but it was thick and strong and refused to be dispelled. Redden could feel her efforts in his own body, the ripples of her power washing back through the stream of scarlet light in wild reverberations. But he held fast, even when he felt the dissipation begin. It was similar to what he had felt when he had drained the Catcher and his creatures down in the Kroat Abyss, yet different because the witch was a singular being. Ever so slowly, the essence of the witch began to drain from her ragged form, siphoned away by the magic of the Elfstones. Some of it was drawn into the Stones themselves and into their user. Redden gasped as the first painful sparks of the magic's detritus reached him and began to fill his body. Shards of the witch's shattered emotions and broken power washed through him, slashing like sharpened metal. He felt everything she did, all of her terrible rage and madness and despair, every savage and damaging belief and compromise she had embraced in becoming the Ilse Witch reborn.

For a moment, it seemed to him that it would be too much. But in desperation, he tightened his hold on his fears and reinforced his determination. The power of his Elfstone magic surged, and within the haze he felt from the rawness of the pain assailing him, he heard the witch wraith howl in anguish. She twisted and writhed in an effort to break free, trying to use her own magic to stop what was happening to her.

Redden remained steadfast, bleeding her, but an overpowering sensation of loss and emptiness filtered through him, a feeling of unwelcome invasion filling the void. Though he refused to ease back on the power of the crimson Stones, his mind was losing traction. The fury and power of the witch's substance was filling him up and replacing his sense of identity and self. He tried to grasp something that would hold him in place, but the void was smooth and empty, and he felt himself sliding away.

In the Gardens of Life, Arlingfant Elessedil's alteration had begun. Aphenglow watched with both horror and amazement as her sister's slender body began to bend and stretch, arms and body taking on a silvery cast. Limbs sprouted and grew long and crooked, arching out in all directions. Her legs merged and sprouted roots that worked their way deep into the earth. Layers of bark covered her skin, and scarlet leaves replaced her hair.

Her face disappeared last, and Aphen could see from her expression that she was feeling no pain or discomfort but instead a kind of euphoria that transcended her fears and doubts, bringing her to her fate unafraid and accepting.

When it was done, a new Ellcrys stood in place of the old at the crest of the rise, perfectly formed and unblemished, its silver bark and crimson leaves shining with sunlight and fluttering slightly in a suddenly fresh morning breeze.

Aphenglow rose and walked up the rise to the Ellcrys reborn, placing her hands on the bark of the trunk and running them slowly across the smooth surface.

"Arling, I'm here," she whispered, her words graced with hope.

*

Railing Ohmsford was conscious again. Shaking off the dizzying effects of the blow he had been struck, he pushed himself back to his feet. Mirai was screaming at him, her voice frantic.

He saw his brother then. He just stood there staring at nothing, his body stilled, his outstretched arm wrapped in crimson light. The witch was on her knees but trying to stagger back to her feet, apparently recovering from whatever damage the Elfstones had done to her. In moments, she would be after them.

"Run!" he yelled at Redden, grabbing him by the arm and turning him around.

But Redden didn't hear him. He didn't seem even to notice him. He was staring at nothing, completely oblivious to what was happening around him, his face blank and his eyes fixed. The way he held himself let his brother and Mirai know instantly that he couldn't make himself move. He appeared to be somewhere else entirely, unaware of what was happening. Whatever was wrong with him, it was deep and abiding.

Railing glanced down to where his brother's right hand was curled into a fist, still holding the crimson Elfstones.

"He used them on the witch," Mirai exclaimed. "In combination with the wishsong!"

Oriantha stumbled over to them, bloodied and streaked with dirt, but clear-eyed and apparently not seriously damaged. Together the three took Redden by his arms and hastened him back toward the Elven defenses, away from the thrashing, screaming masses of the Jarka Ruus. Already Elves were running from the mouth of the pass to reach them. Railing thought he saw Challa Nand, his huge figure distinctive among the smaller forms of the Elves. He saw Skint, too.

Then he caught sight of someone else, a wiry creature with elongated arms and legs standing much closer than any of the others. The creature had both arms wrapped about a metal box, clutching it against its chest.

"Who is that?" Mirai asked before he could get the question out.

"Tesla Dart," Oriantha said. They were practically dragging Redden. "An Ulk Bog from the Forbidding. She helped us get free."

Behind them, a roar went up from the enemy army, and Railing glanced over his shoulder to see the dragon lifting away. The enraged Jarka Ruus, freed of its presence, had recovered sufficiently to mount an attack and were swarming across the plains after them. The witch was upright, as well, and joining in the hunt.

Railing and his companions tried to flee more quickly, but Redden's movements remained wooden and uncoordinated. He was still not responding to them. *He's catatonic*, Railing realized. *He's been rendered incapable of speech, movement, sight—of even knowing what is happening around him. He can't do anything to help himself.*

Impatient and desperate, Oriantha moved in front of Redden and hoisted him onto her back. "I'll carry him. Hurry!"

Railing glanced over his shoulder once more. The creatures from the Forbidding were gaining on them. Even with Oriantha shouldering his brother's weight, they would not be able to reach the pass and the protection of the Elves in time.

"Get him into the airship!" he shouted.

They turned toward the transport and the crooked figure of Tesla Dart, who was screaming at them unintelligibly and jumping up and down while holding the metal box.

"Wait!" snapped Oriantha suddenly. "What's happening?"

She stopped where she was and began searching the sky. A hush had settled over the plains, sweeping eastward from out of the mountains warding the Rhenn and across the Streleheim and Tirfing onward into the rest of the Four Lands. It was as if every sound had been muffled and the whole of the world rendered silent. Railing, Mirai, and Oriantha all started talking at once, but their words could not be heard. Tesla Dart was still leaping about and shouting wildly, but they could not hear her either. It was as if they were all screaming into a massive void. Even the Straken Lord's army, slowed now in its charge across the plains by what they sensed was happening, had lost its collective voice.

Then a wind rose from out of nowhere, coming from all directions, filling the silence with an enormous howl. Railing clutched Mirai against him, and they dropped to their knees. Oriantha lowered Redden's inert form and crouched over him protectively. The wind was still gathering force, becoming a violent, dangerous presence—a whirlwind that turned the air dark and hazy, blew away the clouds, and shut out the sky.

Seconds later the Jarka Ruus were pulled skyward, disappearing moments after their feet left the ground. One by one, they went into the ether. They ran wildly in all directions to escape what was happening, but there was no place to go and no time left.

Railing realized at once what was taking place. He turned to Mirai and screamed it into the silence, but she couldn't hear him. He watched as the dragon was caught up and carried away. He watched ogres and Furies and Goblins disappear. He witnessed the sudden vanishing of thousands of the creatures of the Straken Lord's army.

Even the witch wraith was not immune. Her choice to replace Tael Riverine as the Straken Lord and become one of the creatures of the Forbidding had doomed her, as well. She was snatched up and carried off into the blackness, screaming in fury and despair.

Near the end of the terrible culling, he caught sight of Tesla Dart futilely trying to reach them. But then she, too, was caught up, still holding on to the metal box. Oriantha leapt up, abandoning Redden to run after the Ulk Bog, but she couldn't reach her in time. Tesla Dart disappeared with a thrashing of arms and legs, still crying out, still fighting against what was happening, taking the Elfstones with her.

34

I T WAS DIFFICULT EVEN FOR THOSE CLOSE TO HIM
to guess how Redden Ohmsford would have reacted if he
had known the missing Elfstones were lost once again. He
had suffered terribly during his time trapped within the
Forbidding. He had watched his companions die one after
another, become a prisoner of the Straken Lord at Kraal Reach,
and been hauled back into the Four Lands as Tael Riverine's pet.
That he had gone once more into the Forbidding and thereby
found the object of their initial search was a stunning triumph,
and it had released him from a darkness of the mind that had
threatened to undo him completely. It seemed as if he might be
on the road to recovery, free of the past and of the madness that
had been steadily overtaking him.

But all that was rendered moot by what the combined
magic of the Elfstones and wishsong had done to him during
his battle with the witch wraith. He did not emerge from his
catatonia, but remained locked away in a place that no one,
not even his brother, could reach. Three days after the

conclusion of the terrible struggle against the Jarka Ruus and in spite of the efforts of Elven Healers and the long, quiet pleadings of Railing and Mirai, he remained unchanged. He sat or stood as placed and did not move. He stared into the distance. He never spoke. He neither ate nor slept. He had to be cared for as the smallest baby would, unable to fend for himself. This was the price he had paid for saving them all in those final moments before Arling Elessedil transformed into the Ellcrys, restoring the Forbidding and returning its inhabitants to their prison.

He would have felt badly about Tesla Dart's fate, Oriantha said more than once to Railing. Worse about that, she suspected, than about the loss of the Elfstones. He would have hated that he had broken his promise to the Ulk Bog to keep her with them in the Four Lands, even though there had been no chance of doing so once the Forbidding was restored. But it was impossible to know for sure what his response would have been. It was just what she believed.

Railing knew how *he* felt about the loss of the metal box and its Elfstones, however. He was glad they were gone. He was devastated by what had happened to his brother, and while he could not escape his own guilt about those events, he found reason to transfer a substantial portion of it to the talismans. After all, it was the search for the Stones that had triggered everything that followed. It was their magic that had brought about Redden's current condition. They were the source of the power that had damaged him so badly, he might never recover.

He knew this decisively, convinced himself it was so, and then reluctantly admitted he was lying. The truth was so much worse. *He* was the one who was responsible for what had happened to his brother. If he hadn't been so set on bringing back Grianne Ohmsford. If he hadn't been so convinced she was the answer to their problems, if his courage had been stronger, he would have undertaken Redden's rescue by himself.

Then, perhaps, things would have worked out differently.

Or at least they wouldn't have worked out as they had.

He told all this to Mirai, but she brushed his concerns aside. Regret was useless, she declared. There was no way of knowing what would have happened if he had gone after Redden himself. Besides, the past never changed, and dwelling on it was pointless.

He knew she was right. He told her so, and he promised to let it alone, but he couldn't. No one was as close to Redden as he was. Everything that happened to one always had a direct impact on the other, and the more so because they were twins. They were inseparable parts of a whole, united in a way other siblings could never be. Having Redden locked down as he was, gone somewhere inside his head, was like becoming lost himself.

They waited three days before setting out for Patch Run, and during that time Railing kept close watch on his brother, hoping against hope that he might show some sign of improvement. But nothing changed, and in the end he resolved to take Redden home as he was and confront his mother with the truth.

Some of the others from the expedition had already left. Challa Nand had departed almost immediately, the first to head out.

"Enough of this madness," he had announced to the boy. "I don't belong with you. Give me the wilderness and the mountains and no more searches for dead people who ought to stay dead. You did what you could, but some of it was ill advised."

He'd paused then, perhaps deciding he had gone too far, and added, "Take good care of your brother. Don't give up hope."

Skint was a little kinder. "You couldn't have known she would come back as she did. If your plans had fallen into place as you wanted them to, she would have returned as the Ard Rhys and done what you wished. Don't waste time blaming yourself for something that was never your fault in the first place. You showed real courage more than once, Railing Ohmsford. I'm proud to have known you."

Crace Coram and Woostra stayed on, ostensibly for different reasons, but neither had much to say to Railing or Mirai. Even Aphenglow stayed away, but they understood why she might, given the loss of her sister and the destruction of the Druid order, and they didn't blame her for being otherwise occupied.

Yet on the day of their departure, she came to them and took Railing aside. "We've both lost someone we loved," she said, "but that doesn't have to be the end of it. We are luckier than most. We still have them close. Don't be so sure your brother doesn't hear you or realize you are there when you speak to him. Your brother might be in hiding, but he might also be trying to find his way back. Help him do that. Be there for him when he returns."

Railing nodded, almost in tears.

"I wish I could have done more to speed him on his journey back to you, but for now at least it appears he is beyond anywhere my healing skills can reach. But I will come to you and try again soon, if you will let me."

"I would like that very much," he said.

"Then we have an agreement."

He smiled, hesitated. "I forgot to give you this until now, but I think you should have it. Oriantha gave it to me. Redden found it in the case where the Elfstones were hidden. He tucked it away in his pocket, and she remembered it was there when she helped bring him in from the battlefield."

He reached into his own pocket and brought out a folded slip of paper. "I tried reading it, but it is written in a language I don't

understand. Oriantha says you might be able to translate it." He
handed it to her. "If you can do so, will you remember to tell me
what it says?"

"Of course," she replied. "When I come to see Redden, I will
bring the note with me."

"I'm sorry about Arling," he said suddenly, looking down at his
feet.

Aphenglow glanced at the note and slipped it into her pocket.
"Thank you for saying so." Then she stepped forward and hugged
him. "You've been very brave, Railing. You and Redden both.
What Allanon's shade said to Khyber Elessedil proved to be true.
We couldn't have succeeded without your help."

She said that even though she wasn't much older than he was,
and her involvement hadn't been any less crucial. He shook his
head. "It doesn't feel that way."

She smiled. "Give it time."

Aphenglow sat with Seersha in her bedroom in the healing
center—something she had been doing every day since her
return to Arborlon. The Dwarf had drifted in and out of consciousness for the better part of a week, and there were times
when it appeared she might not recover. But Seersha was strong
of heart and body, and even the grievous wounds that Edinja
Orle's creature had inflicted on her were not enough to end her
life.

By now, a week had passed since the Ohmsford twins and
Mirai had departed for home. Ellich Elessedil had been crowned
King, and a much-needed stability had been restored to the
Elven people. Phaedon was under care in a healing center, and it
had become increasingly clear he might remain there for the rest
of his days. His breakdown during the struggle between Seersha
and the changeling seemed to have permanently unhinged him.

Nothing the Elven Healers had done had helped him improve. The High Council had not needed to debate the question of succession once it was determined that Phaedon was not capable of ruling. Ellich, now absolved of any guilt concerning his brother's death, was named King by rule of law and right of succession.

"I've made a decision," Aphen declared. "I'm not coming back to Paranor. I'm staying here."

"So you can be close to Arling," Seersha said.

Aphen nodded. "She gave up everything for me—for all of us. Now I have to give something back."

"In spite of what you know the Chosen will do for her?"

"They can't talk with her the way I can. Besides, I have to find a way to reconcile with Mother."

"Have you spoken with her since Arling's transformation?"

Aphen nodded. "Several times."

"Does she respond to you?"

"Not yet. But she will, eventually. It will help if I stay close."

"Because that is what she has always wanted you to do. I see."

Aphen nodded. "I'm sorry."

Seersha studied her friend out of her one good eye. Her face was crisscrossed with slash wounds and bandages, but her gaze was steady. "I will miss you. It will be lonely being the only Druid left in the order."

"Oriantha will come, if you will have her. She's already asked if we would take her. Her mother intended that for her, and if she wants it, why not? She would be a good companion for you, and a good addition to the order. Besides, others will come to join, as well. It won't always be you."

Seersha pursed her lips. "I think you are making a mistake. You don't belong here. You belong in Paranor. Can I tell you why?"

"You can tell me anything."

"You are the best of us, Aphen. You were always meant to be the Ard Rhys after Khyber. She wanted it that way. I know. I'm not the right choice. I lack the necessary balance. I don't have the necessary skills. Mostly, I'm a fighter, a weapons master. I'm not a diplomat. I don't have the patience. I would match my use of magic against anyone or anything in combat, but it takes more than that to be the Ard Rhys."

She paused. "If you stay here, good intentions notwithstanding, you will be wasting your life. You will try to find a way to make your mother love you again, but that's a small victory even if it happens. And while talking with Arling will make you feel better about yourself, it isn't what she wanted for you. If she were still your sister and not the Ellcrys, you wouldn't think twice about coming back to Paranor. And you would bring her with you the moment she finished her term as a Chosen. You've already told me this is what she wanted. It was what you wanted, too. It can't happen for her, but that doesn't mean you should abandon your place in the order. It doesn't excuse you from carrying out your obligation to see it continue. Arling would want that, and you know it. She would tell you to go back. Come to Arborlon to see her when you can, but don't make that your legacy."

The words were blunt and hurtful, though Aphen couldn't say exactly why. But she was used to Seersha speaking her mind, and she knew that what her friend was saying wasn't meant as a reprimand.

"I've thought about all that," she replied, though in fact she hadn't thought about it in those exact terms. "I just think staying here is the best choice."

Seersha gave a small smile. "Will you think about it some more?" she asked. "Can we talk about it another time?"

Aphenglow smiled back. "I don't see why not."

They visited for a while longer, and then Seersha grew tired and fell asleep. Aphen watched over her for several long minutes, thinking of what she had said. Sound advice from a good friend, but not the advice she wanted. She rose and left the room, closing the door quietly behind her.

Outside the healing center she stood blinking in the bright afternoon sunlight, deciding what to do next. She chose to go to Ellich, hoping he might find time to speak with her. She was troubled by what Seersha had said, suddenly uncertain about her decision to stay in Arborlon. She thought she knew what her uncle would tell her, but she wanted to hear him say it. If he reaffirmed what he had been telling her for months about coming home, she might find it easier to dismiss Seersha's arguments.

She found Ellich ready and willing to speak with her, which was something of a relief. Although he was elbows-deep in his newly minted role as King—a role she still believed should have gone to him in the first place—he put everything aside immediately and walked out into the palace gardens to speak privately with her.

"I'm still coming to terms with things," he told her. "Very much the same as I suspect you are. Discovering the truth about Jera was heartbreaking. I won't ever know for certain how long that creature was playing at being my wife. I won't ever know how long she had been dead. It's very difficult to believe, any of it."

"We were all deceived, Ellich. It was cruel and evil; it took someone like Edinja to conceive of such a plan."

"It cost us both people we loved. It cost me the ability to trust my own senses."

She looked at him carefully, noting how worn and haggard he looked and the haunted glint in his eyes. He would never be the same, she knew. He would rule the Elves wisely, but he would not again be as strong a man in himself.

She pushed back against her sadness. "I need to ask you something about my own life, if you will consider listening. I have a difficult choice to make."

What he advised was pretty much what she had expected. She belonged in Arborlon with the Elves. She needed to be close to her mother and to her people. Her time with the Druids was over. The order was decimated in any case, all of its members dead save for Seersha and herself, and there was no firm guarantee that Seersha would recover. It was a grim thing to say, but he believed Aphenglow should be realistic about how matters stood.

When he had finished, he told her again how sorry he was about both Arling and Cymrian. She knew what he was feeling. With Jera and his brother gone, he was left with Aphen and her mother as his only family, and quite naturally he wanted to keep both with him. He was uncertain, at this point, how he would do as King, and it would help to have Aphen, in particular, there to advise him.

In fact, he confided, he had been thinking of asking her to consider becoming a member of the High Council.

She left him more convinced than ever that staying in Arborlon was the right thing to do. But when she returned to her cottage—the one that once had seemed so welcoming and safe, filled with Arling's presence and the warmth and closeness the sisters had shared during the year she had been researching the Elven histories—she encountered an oppressive emptiness and silence, and wondered how she would ever manage to fill it again.

She was just about to fix herself something to eat when there was a knock on the door. When she opened it, Woostra was standing there.

"Seersha told me you don't intend to come back to Paranor,"

the scribe announced without preamble. He was nervous and fidgety, and his white hair was a wild tangle. "I wanted to hear it from you."

"Come in," she said, stepping back. "We can discuss it."

They sat at the little table where she and Arling had discussed things so often in the past. It was the first time she had spoken to Woostra alone since her return, and it felt immediately uncomfortable.

Perhaps he sensed it, too. "I want you to know I am sorry about Arling. Even if it was necessary, even if there was no choice, it is still a terrible tragedy. I wish it hadn't happened."

"Thank you for saying that."

He nodded curtly. "That said, if you are thinking of leaving Paranor and the Druid order, you are making a terrible mistake." His face was stern. "Have you thought this through?"

"I think so."

"Then you must realize you are betraying every vow and breaking every promise you made when you joined the order. You were never meant to take those promises and vows lightly, and I don't think you did when you took them. Now you seem to have decided otherwise, in spite of the fact that your sister did for your people exactly the same as she would expect you to do. She sacrificed herself for the greater good. Is it possible you don't understand that this is what's being asked of you?"

"I don't know that anything is being asked of me. I'm doing what I believe to be the right thing."

His mouth tightened into a knot. "Right for you, perhaps, but not for everyone else. It is certainly not the path Arlingfant would have followed. It is not the path Khyber Elessedil would have taken. It is the path of least resistance, and a nod to the self-pity you are feeling and the effort you are making to avoid having to deal with a much harder reality than you've had to face up to before."

"Which is?" she said.

"That, without you, the order will fail and the Druids will vanish. Perhaps not forever, but long enough that everything that's been accomplished since the time of Walker Boh will be lost. You think I exaggerate. You think I am an old fool, rambling on about the good old days. But I'm talking about the future, Aphenglow. The future the Druids can either help to shape or leave to its own miserable fate. Khyber chose the former; she gave her life to that effort. She would have expected you to do the same—even though your sister is gone, even though your life is in upheaval, and even though it may prove to be difficult and perhaps even costly beyond any price you've paid up until now."

"You make it sound so inviting," she snapped, suddenly irritated.

"I'm making it sound like the truth. It isn't up to me to persuade you that Druids in the future will have an easy time of it or that things will improve now that the Forbidding is restored and those creatures are locked away again. None of that is up to me. You should be making these arguments yourself. But you're not, so I have to say what I think."

He rose. "Now I've done so, and I'll leave. If it's to be Seersha and myself, then that will have to do. Maybe the shape-shifter daughter of Pleysia will come along. She seems to know what I'm talking about."

He walked to the door, opened it, and stopped, looking back at her. "But it won't be the same without you. Nothing will. You think on it. You remember what the others gave up for the order. Do the right thing."

Then he was gone.

*

Afterward, she made her dinner and ate it alone in the privacy of the cottage she had once shared with Arling. Although her sister was gone, her ghost remained, a silent watchful presence that inhabited every room and every memory. Aphen almost couldn't bear it, but then told herself she must learn to, that it would never change, never get better. Nor did she think she wanted it to. Arling belonged here more than she did. Missing her sister was a fact of life. She must learn to get used to it. Even a ghost could offer a small bit of company.

When she was finished with her meal and had cleaned up after herself, Aphen sat down to translate the note Railing Ohmsford had given her several days earlier. She had not felt pressured to do so before now, but Woostra's visit and the ghostly presence of her sister had generated a need to do something more than sit staring out at the darkness.

She began slowly, but the language was familiar, a rather crude variation on the same ancient Elfish used by Aleia Omarosian in her diary, and soon she was working her way through it quickly. The note was written by Aleia's Darkling boy, and Aphen had no doubt that she had taught him the language he had used to compose the note while they trysted all those centuries ago.

She wrote out the words carefully, read them through once swiftly to affirm she had them right, and then read them a second time more slowly.

She was crying within seconds.

My Dearest Little Elf, Aleia:

I can only hope you do not hate me too badly, but I will never know for certain. By the time this letter is read, you and I both will be long dead. I did not intend for matters to end this way. I risked too much by taking all of the Elfstones but the seeking blue and hoping you would use them to come to me. But events conspired against us, and now we will never be reunited.

Know that I love you and will always love you. I took the Elfstones because I could tell I would lose you otherwise, and must find a way to bring you to me. I intended nothing more than that you find me; I never gave a single thought to using the Elfstone magic against you or your people. I was desperate to hold on to you and took what risk I deemed necessary to do so. But my transgressions were discovered, the Elfstones were taken from me, and I was imprisoned. I was disgraced and declared a traitor. No one would listen to my explanation; no one would heed my pleas. When you came searching for me, I was locked away and magically concealed from you and from the blue Elfstones' power. My people had magic also, you will remember, and they used it.

Still, I thought to escape and come to you. I sought a way to make that happen. But all of my efforts failed.

When a new form of magic swept up all of my people and their allies and many other creatures and exiled us to another world, I knew there was no longer any hope. At first, we did not know what had happened. It seemed as though we were still in our former world, but the landscape had been ruined and the air and water were fouled. Everything was dark and hazy and bleak. Thousands of us died. I was released finally, for those in power saw no particular reason to keep me locked away.

I was old by then, after all, and no longer a threat to anyone.

The Elfstones had lost their importance. Efforts had been made to make use of them, but an Elven magic can be summoned only by Elves. The Stones had become nothing more than a reminder of how powerless we were and how shamefully we had been treated. Along with other magic and other talismans we had come to possess, they were locked away and mostly forgotten.

But through the kindness of a friend I have gained access to them. When this note is finished, I will place it in the case where the Elfstones remain and hope that someday your people will find it. I have no reason to think that will ever happen, but I must do what I can. I do not want to be thought of as a thief and a liar. I do not want the record I am sure has been written of my treachery to be the final word on what I did. Or of what you meant to me.

You must believe you were everything to me and will remain so until the day I die. There will never be another. If I could have one day back in my life, I would choose a day I could spend with you. Nothing would be sweeter. Nothing would mean more.

And so I leave you, faithful to the end, lost in another world.

Your one true love, Charis.

Aphenglow Elessedil put down the note and wiped away her tears.

"See what love brings you, Arling?" she whispered.

But at least now she knew the entirety of the story of Aleia Omarosian and her Darkling boy, Charis.

She wondered with whom she would share it.

35

WEEKS PASSED. RAILING HAD BEEN BACK home for almost three months, his memories of the past starting to lose their sharp edges and grow less painful. Mirai was living with him at his home, embraced by his mother in a way he still was not. Sarys had come to accept Redden's condition, and had even told Railing it wasn't his fault. She had forgiven him, she said, for his part in what had happened. But she looked and acted differently in his presence, and he couldn't tell if it was because of perceived failures in his character or a fear of losing him as she had lost Redden.

Whichever it was, it hurt him enough that he could not manage to put aside either his sense of guilt and failure or his deep, abiding sadness. He could only press on, helping with Redden's care and trying his best not to disappoint his mother further.

Having Mirai living with them helped. His mother had always loved her, and this didn't seem to change with the

Highland girl's complicity in hiding what the twins were up to. Mirai was partnered with him, and they would be married, when Redden was better. But for now they let things be as they concentrated on looking after Redden and waiting for his condition to change.

But Redden refused to wake up. He was deep in his catatonia, unimproved since the battle with the witch wraith at the Valley of Rhenn. Nothing any of them said or did seemed to get through to him. Wherever he had gone inside himself, it was far distant from the real world and he remained unreachable. Sarys cried less over him with the passing of every new day, but still she cried. Railing saw it and hated it. Mostly, he hated that he was seen as the cause.

"She doesn't feel like that," Mirai argued when they were in bed together at night, whispering in the dark. "You have to let her grieve and not make it personal. No one could have done more than you did to try to save him."

But her words didn't help. Nothing did. In spite of everything she said, in spite of patience and faith, Railing could feel his brother slip a little farther away with the passing of every day. He couldn't sense any possibility of Redden getting well again.

He was sitting alone with his brother at the edge of the woods behind their home on a gray summer day months later, talking to him and staring off into the trees by turns. He wasn't saying anything particularly important or looking for his brother to respond, even though that was always at the back of his mind. He was just passing time while Mirai and his mother prepared dinner inside. Redden sat slack-faced and as still as stone, just as he always did. They kept him alive by hand-feeding him and seeing to his personal needs, and Railing hated all of it. It was undignified and it was demeaning. This was his brother, his twin, and it felt like it was happening to him. Redden never got sick and he never wanted for anything, but he also never seemed much more than a stuffed toy.

He bit his lip as the thought slipped into his mind like a snake. It felt like a betrayal of how much he loved his brother.

One hand drifted down to his pocket and the ring given him by the King of the Silver River. He carried it all the time, even though he had sworn off magic and had not used the wishsong once since his return. This forsaking, at least, was something his mother appreciated. He carried the ring mostly because it reminded him of the warning the King of the Silver River had given about what might happen if he persisted in his search for Grianne Ohmsford. It was his own private form of punishment—and one that he felt he deserved. He wasn't sure what else he should do with the talisman even if he quit carrying it. Should he cast it away or give it to the Druids as he had the crimson Elfstones, as they were now being called? Aphenglow might like to have it, as well, for the new Druid order. Maybe he would give it to her on her next visit from Paranor. She was overdue for taking a fresh stab at using her Druid magic to heal Redden. Her other attempts had failed, but she had insisted she would not give up.

He brought the ring out and studied it for what must have been the thousandth time, and as he did so something occurred to him—something so preposterous that for a moment he just sat there staring. The ring had been given to help him find his way out of the darkest places, to show him how to work his way clear when he was lost. Each thread was a link in a chain that would lead to a safe haven.

But what if . . . ?

He stopped himself mid-thought, afraid to go farther. Then he relented.

What if it could help me find my brother?

He had used it only twice during the search for Grianne, and in retrospect those usages didn't seem particularly important. Now he found himself wondering if it might have a further use, one he had somehow failed to consider until this moment. Go to your brother, the King of the Silver River had urged. Save him yourself. Could the Faerie creature have given the ring to him for that very reason? Could he have foreseen the future?

The possibility was so wild it left him breathless. He stared at Redden, his mind racing. "Are you in there?" he whispered to his brother. "Are you waiting for me to come find you?"

No reaction. But, then, there wouldn't be, would there?

He slipped on the ring, and then took a deep breath and gently extracted one of the malleable threads. He was terrified he would fail. He was even more terrified he wouldn't, but that his effort to bring back his brother would end the same way as his effort to bring back Grianne. He couldn't bear the thought of that happening. But he couldn't let this chance slip away, either.

He placed one end of the thread between the fingers of Redden's right hand to hold it in place. Then he took the other end in his own. He didn't know exactly how this might work; he was operating solely on instinct. He sat very close to his brother, their faces only inches apart, and looked into his eyes. *I'm here, Redden. I'm right next to you. Don't be afraid. Don't hide. Come back to me.*

He waited for a response from his brother. There was none. He experienced a sinking feeling in the pit of his stomach.

Then the thread disappeared.

He waited, hopeful once more. But nothing happened save that now the thread was invisible.

He reached over and took Redden's hands in his own. *Redden, please!*

He felt a tugging in his mind from the thread, just as he had at Stridegate, insistent and forceful. He went inside himself, trying to find something more, a further response, a signal that Redden was reaching out for him. The tugging continued, with sudden, sporadic jerks.

He closed his eyes. *Redden*.

But there was nothing else. And after a few minutes, even the tugging ended.

He sat back, releasing his brother's hands and placing them back in his lap. He would not give up, he thought. He would use the ring again another day. He would keep trying. He would pull out another thread and repeat the process. He would pull out threads until none remained.

He kept what he was doing to himself. It was his experiment, and he didn't want to raise anyone's hopes on so slim a possibility that something good might come of it.

Days passed. One by one, he pulled out the threads and used them to try to reach his brother. One by one, they disappeared. But Redden never responded.

When he was down to the last three and the gemstone they wound about, he put the ring aside, telling himself it was better to give it some time. Then he went back to sitting and talking with his brother.

Summer passed into fall. The days shortened, but were filled with softer light and the changing of the colors of the leaves on the trees, green giving way to gold and yellow, orange and red.

Then one day, solely on impulse, he decided to try once again. He sat alone near the woods in back of their home, close to his brother, facing him, and he pulled out one of the three remaining threads. He placed one end between Redden's fingers and the other between his own. The thread disappeared, the tugging ensued, and he waited.

Nothing happened.

For the first time, he began to think nothing ever would. He stood and looked off into the trees, wishing things could be different, even if just a little.

"How long have I been asleep?" he heard Redden ask suddenly. He wheeled back in shock. His brother was looking at him, blinking his eyes. "It must have been a while."

Railing couldn't make himself move, afraid if he did it would turn out this wasn't happening. "A long while," he said.

Redden nodded and stretched his arms, yawning. "Can you tell me what happened? I can't seem to remember anything. Is everybody safe?"

Breaking free of his paralysis, Railing knelt in front of his brother and embraced him, holding him as if he would never let go. There were tears in his eyes, and it felt as if his heart was breaking. But there was joy, too.

"Yes, Redden," he whispered. "Everybody is safe."